Longing

a novel

Pushpinder Sadana

Top Duck Productions

Longing

First Edition

ISBN: 979-8-9863306-0-0

Published By Top Duck Productions
Long Beach, CA
www.TopDuckProductions.com

Cover Design by Izzy Rushdy

Disclaimer

This novel is a work of fiction. Although some of the characters are inspired by historical figures, most are the author's imaginary creations; furthermore, locations and events, although based on actual places and historical events, are fictional. Apart from historical figures, events and locations, any resemblances between the novel and actual people--living or dead--their circumstances and location are coincidental.

This book contains mature subject matter and themes which may not be suitable for all ages.

Dedication

This book is dedicated to all women who have suffered and who have also achieved remarkable things.

Acknowledgments

In writing a first novel, I am thankful to many people who have encouraged me along this journey and offered their time and assistance. Peter Werrenrath and Alice Rushdy worked step-by-step in the publishing process. They motivated and had faith in me in writing the story. I am grateful to our writing group for their valuable feedback. Additionally, the California Writers Club in Long Beach offered guidance and information. Lastly, I am deeply appreciative of my family who urged me to complete the story and supported my work throughout these interesting months of writing, re-writing and sharing.

Cast of Characters

Mona – A tenacious woman who makes a success against all odds
Ramesh – Mona's husband
Karan – Mona's first love
Amar – Mona's uncle
Binny – Mona's younger sister
Vijay – A family friend who treats Mona as his younger sister
Rebecca – Vijay's wife
Usha – Mona's mother
Krishna – Mona's father
Sarla Devi – Mona's grandmother
Teresa – Ramesh's girlfriend
Dan – Mayor of Ocean Beach
Aviva – Dan's ex-girl friend
Dora – Dan's mother
Janet – Dan's assistant

Prologue
1959
Kanpur

The weather was pleasant, and evenings were cool. Mona was sitting on a chair, in the front verandah of the bungalow and watched people move around, putting their last arrangements in place for the wedding procession. The bungalow was decorated with garlands of marigolds and lights were strung throughout the garden. Mona had dressed early for the wedding. Her orange frock with gold embroidery on the hem and sleeves gave a bright glow to her dark skin.

Mona met Vijay for the first time at his wedding. She was twelve years old then, in 1959.
She was born in Kanpur City, 1947, the year India got independence from the British rule. Although the new constitution had given freedom and equal rights to all women, the cultural and social pressures of society continued to keep women down.

Vijay, the groom, came out of the bungalow and stood in the verandah. He was getting ready for his Hindu wedding with Rebecca. He looked at Mona from a distance. To avoid his gaze, Mona lowered her face and pretended to be looking for something on the grass.

He came and sat down next to her, "I don't know you, what's your name?"

She looked at him with her eyes fluttering and lips pursed.

"My name is Mona. When I go to America, everybody

will come to know I am the daughter of Mr. Krishna," she said.

"Oh, you are Krishna Uncle's daughter. How come I have not seen you before? My dad and your dad live in the same building," Vijay said.

"Because you do not live in Kanpur City. You live in America," Mona said.

Vijay found Mona very sharp, "When are you going to America?"

"When I grow up, I will go to America for higher studies."

"What made you think you would go to America for higher studies?"

"Don't you know, my dad went to London for higher studies. I will go to America," she replied.

"That is great, and what higher studies do you want to do in America?" he asked.

"I am good at mathematics. You know, I am sitting here for one hour, I can tell you, how many people are working, how many are just shouting, and how many are sitting and doing nothing," Mona said confidently.

Vijay was surprised at her observation and confidence. This young girl spoke of such definite plans for her future.

"You are intelligent. You are pretty too, with beautiful curly hair and big eyes," Vijay said.

Mona had dark skin, a little fat and had gained no height over the last year. The compliment from Vijay, a handsome man liked by all women, made her eyes sparkle. She raised her head and gave him a coy look. It was the first time somebody said sweet things about her. Her face turned red. She could not move, as if she were glued to the chair.

"You know your dad and my dad are childhood friends. We are like family. I am like your elder brother," said

Vijay.

"I know," replied Mona.

Before Vijay could say another word, Amar Uncle, her father's younger brother and friend of Vijay, walked in. "Vijay! Groom! There you are. Everybody is looking for you. And what are you doing here, flirting with my niece?" said Amar.

"My, little dark cat, give Uncle a little popi." Amar held Mona's face in his hands and pecked her on both cheeks. Mona squirmed away from his touch.

"So, Mona, go for your dreams and go to America to do your Ph.D.," Vijay said.

Mona, at the age of twelve, decided that one day she would marry a man like Vijay - handsome, intelligent, and witty. Vijay was always smiling and cracking jokes with ladies. He could make any gathering a happy party.

Chapter 1
Holi Festival
1965
Kanpur

Spring came early in 1965. The festival of Holi represents the end of winter and the beginning of spring, the celebration of good harvest, and delight in the multitude of spring colors. Holi marks the triumph of good over evil and the legend of Lord Krishna's flirtation with Gopis. An occasion of mirth and joy, all people from different castes, creeds, and religions mingle together. They throw powdered flour of bright colors on each other, splash buckets of water, eat together, and forget their differences. The Holi festival brings a hope of a new beginning, and a renewal of the spirit of life.

Young men throw red, green, orange, and blue powder on women, which signifies passion and desire. Women reciprocate with the same zeal. Bawdy songs and jokes are part of the fun. People run after each other to smear colors and try to steal a kiss or an embrace. All ignored as innocent play, men act aggressive and women, equally dashing, pretend to be meek and bashful.

Mona was eighteen now. Watching the Holi celebrations, her new feelings were forcing her to join the festival and dream of playing Holi with her friends. Everywhere flowers were blossoming, and roses spread their sweet fragrance around the city.

Mona and her family lived in Kanpur. Her father Krishna had bought an apartment a few years before his retirement. The whole family, her mother Usha, father Krishna, her grandmother Sarla Devi, and her younger sister Binny had moved into their new residence two months earlier. Her mother had brought all her rose pots from their old home in Nasik. Every morning Mona would get up early, to inhale the fresh smell of roses. Rahul Uncle, Vijay's father who lived upstairs, had planted jasmine in the yard. At night, the soothing smell of jasmine radiated throughout the whole building compound.

This year at the Holi festival her mother Usha, her sister Binny and her grandmother Sarla Devi were in Delhi with her father Krishna. Mona could not accompany her family to Delhi; she was appearing for her high school exams and had to stay in Kanpur alone, as the papers for the tests leaked out and the Examinations Board had postponed the tests for one month, until the new test papers were ready. Mona was planning to join her family in Delhi and spend her vacation there, but now she was stuck for another month in Kanpur with time for her studies. Her dreams were at stake: Pass exams with the best scores, go to a university, then earn her master's, and onwards to the Ph. D., in the US, where she hoped to marry a good man, someone like Vijay. She would work hard and enjoy a good life in America and send money back to her parents to live comfortably.

Vijay had come back to Kanpur for the Holi festival with his American wife Rebecca. Early that morning Amar Uncle arrived from the famous Khajuraho Temples, where he was posted as a tourist officer. Amar came to meet his friend Vijay to enjoy the Holi festival together. Amar was staying at Mona's place, and the next day, in the early morning, he was going back.

Holi celebrations were in full swing. Neighborhood families gathered in the compound of the building, in a mirthful and merry mood, throwing colored water on each other.

Bhang was flowing among the elders, and teens were stealing sips here and there. Gestures of flirtation in dance, songs and in talk were all around.

Vijay and his friend Amar, with their eyes bloodshot after drinking glasses of bhang, were having the time of their lives. Vijay and his wife Rebecca were the main hosts of the gathering, and their many friends would arrive from neighboring places. Vijay would greet everyone, with his hands full of dry colored powder, looking for the prettiest woman in the group and jokingly smearing her face.

Rebecca did not mind having a few glasses of bhang. She was having fun too. For her, anything in India was fascinating. She would stealthily go behind Vijay and pour a full bucket of colored water over him. She would hold Vijay from the back and tell Amar to paint Vijay with red and green colors. Amar was equally intoxicated, enjoying all the festivities. The women had wet saris and blouses clinging to their bodies and their satin skin shining against assorted colors. Men of every age with their mouths churning beetle nuts, full of tobacco, would await their chance to meet a beautiful woman.

Mona was watching from her bedroom window. She wanted to join them, but her tests were not yet over. She preferred to concentrate more on her studies. Mona hated when her face and clothes were smeared with colors. She nervously walked from one bedroom to another and knew that her body felt agitated. She did not know what was happening.

Mona peeped out from her bedroom window again.

Vijay was trying to hug a pretty lady and after he held her tight like a bird of prey, he told Amar to smear her face with colors. Mona thought, *How disgusting*. Mona did not remember how long she was engrossed in her thoughts, standing in the shadows. She sensed the strong smell of tobacco. Someone was breathing on her back. Before she could turn, Amar Uncle grabbed her from the back and tried to smear her face and neck with colors.

"Happy Holi," Amar Uncle shouted.

"Uncle, no colors please, you know I do not like Holi. It will dirty my face," Mona pleaded.

"I will put a small touch of dry colors. See, no watercolors," he said.

"No, no please," she said.

"Fine, I will call all my friends from downstairs," he threatened.

"You promise you will not call anybody."

"I promise."

"All right let me turn around; you can put color, a small dot on my forehead, only one spot. Don't smear my face," she said.

She turned and put her face close to her Uncle; he gently smeared a pinch of red color on her forehead and rest of the color on her cheeks.

"Happy Holi. You look beautiful with red color on your cheeks," he said.

"This is cheating. Please, Uncle, let me go. I have to prepare for my tests," Mona said.

"Don't worry about your tests. You always are tops in the class. Let me put colors on you. I promise I will not call anybody from downstairs," he said with dry colors in his hand.

He put more color on her face, smearing the front of her

neck, caressing her face with his fingers. She tried to move away from him. His grip was tight, and he pressed her closer to him.

"If you give me popi, I promise, I will not call anyone upstairs." Amar was drunk with bhang, unsteady on his legs and his eyes half closed, "It is Holi. Enjoy. I promise I will not call anybody." He clutched her more firmly.

He kissed both her cheeks and then he planted his lips on her lips. She looked at his bloodshot eyes. He was her Uncle, she was confused. He kissed her again passionately.

"Oh God," she said and tried to get free from him.

He pushed her on the bed.

"Uncle, I have to study! Uncle, what you are doing?" she said loudly.

Outside in the compound, all were celebrating Holi. No one could hear her shrieks. Her sari pulled open, Amar climbed on top of her. She saw his nakedness but closed her eyes to block out the pain of his assault. How long he violated her, she did not know. Her vision turned blurry. Colors of red, yellow, blue streaked through.

He went out. She could not comprehend how her father's younger brother could do this to her. She lay frozen in her bed.

She got up, after a while, and she saw her sari and her bed sheet both were soiled. She went to the bathroom and washed the soiled sheet and all her clothes. She cleaned herself thoroughly, put on a new sari and lay down on the bed. She was still shaking and lay there past evening.

The house was dark. She had not put the lights on. She tried to understand what had happened earlier. Then, she heard someone opening the entrance door.

She quickly jumped up and picked up the kitchen knife and stood in a corner.

Amar returned. He opened the door and entered the house. In both of his hands were big bags full of cooked food from a restaurant.

"What is this, Mona Beti? You have not put the lights on in the house?" He came near her.

He was drunk. The foul smell of liquor was coming from his mouth.

"Stay where you are, don't call me daughter, and don't even dare to come near me," she said angrily.

He put the bags on the table and took few steps towards her.

"Stay where you are. I will kill you or I will kill myself." She pointed the kitchen knife towards him.

"Easy, easy, I brought fresh cooked food for you and packets of different sweets. See." He came near her and started unloading food from the bags.

Mona looked at the bags. As soon as her attention was diverted, he grabbed her and pulled the knife away from her.

She started sobbing. She did not know what to do. He picked her up and took her into her bedroom and all night he assaulted her. He left the house before daybreak.

Chapter 2
Helpless
1965
Kanpur

Mona awoke late in the morning. Her body ached. She dragged herself with great difficulty to eat something in the kitchen. Again, her clothes and bed sheet were soiled. That day the smell of roses penetrated her nose, but the smell was stale. All her dreams and joy in her life were robbed by Uncle.

She cleaned herself, all the clothes and sheets thoroughly. She put the kitchen and her bedroom in order and lay down curled in her bed. She was still dazed. Her body was torn, the pain was still there. How could she face her father and her mother? Her confidence and her ambitions to go abroad vanished.

She got up from the bed. The bruises on her body stung with pain. There was no one to talk to or assist with what she was going through. She thanked God her family was in Delhi, so they could not see her shame. She decided to see Dr. Renu Kapur. Her clinic was in her bungalow, where she lived in Arya Nagar.

Dr. Kapur was their family physician and a close friend of her mother. She had converted part of her bungalow into a clinic, and the clinic was close to Mona's apartment. Mona believed she could trust her mother's friend. Dr. Kapur was a gentle and loving lady who liked Mona very much. She helped Usha deliver both of her daughters, Mona and Binny.

Seeing Mona in her clinic suddenly, caught the doctor by surprise. "How are you, Mona? I have not seen you since your mother went to Delhi. Why are you walking that way, limping?" Dr. Kapur asked.

"Aunty, I want to talk with you privately," Mona said.

Dr. Kapur looked at her and Mona looked back with tears in her eyes. She got up from her chair and took Mona inside her bungalow, closing the door behind them.

"What's the matter?" Dr. Kapur asked.

"Aunty, what to tell you, my whole life is ruined. I lost my respect, and my honor. I was raped by Amar Uncle," Mona said.

"What?" Dr. Kapur said.

Mona told her what had happened.

"Oh my God, oh my God, I can't believe my ears. We all like and trust Amar. My ears are not ready to believe that Amar would do such a hateful thing." She was shocked and angry.

She held Mona in her arms and said, "I want to call your mother."

"No, Aunty, not my mother. I came to see you because I trust you. I do not want anyone else to know. My mother will tell my father and my grandmother, and how I will face them? The whole family will be ruined," Mona said quickly.

"This is a serious matter. Your mother should know. You need someone from family with you. I will tell her not to mention it to anybody, even your father," Dr. Kapur explained.

"Aunty, you don't know my mother. She treats Amar as her son. She will die with shame and grief," Mona said.

"But, Mona Beti, someone has to know and help you in this situation," she said.

"That is why, Aunty, I have come to you. You were

there at my birth, and you were the first one to make me cry, and for last eighteen years you have been my doctor. Who could be a better person than you to help me?"

Dr. Kapur was quiet. "Please lie down on my bed and stretch out so I can examine you," she said. After checking Mona thoroughly, the doctor gave her a glass of water and two blue pills to swallow.

"That wretched man has treated you very callously. I wish I could hang him. Take these medicines, they will make you calm." She assured Mona she would be fine.

"You take these pills with water, stay calm, and don't get up. Lay down here and take rest for some time. Let me close up my clinic and think this over," Dr. Kapur replied.

Half an hour later Mona was sitting up in bed. The doctor entered the bedroom.

"Did you lie down and rest?" Dr. Kapur asked.

"Aunty, you want me to be calm, but I want to kill him. I want you to come with me to the police station. Let us go to police station now," Mona said clenching her fists.

"On the one hand, you are telling me not to tell your mother, but on the other hand you want me to go with you to the police station, now," Dr. Kapur said.

"I want to see that dirty man is punished. I am eighteen. I can file a police report," Mona said, holding the bed tightly.

"Let us talk," the doctor said with a serious tone. "I know you are strong, and you are not afraid to fight this world. We can easily go to the police but think about the repercussions of your actions before we act."

"I don't have to think. That filthy Uncle raped me, and you want me to look into repercussions," Mona said.

"Listen carefully. When you go to the police, within one hour the whole town will know Krishna's daughter was raped. I have been a doctor for the last thirty years and I have gone through several rape cases. Have you ever thought about how the police will treat you? There are not many women police officers in the town, and male police officers would put you in an isolated room. They will ask you low, dirty questions, and you don't know what they could do to you in isolation," Dr. Kapur continued.

"You will be sent to a government hospital next. There doctors will strip you naked to examine and move their fingers in all your orifices. Do you want to go through this kind of humiliation? This is 1965, but our customs and thinking are centuries old. Our society is not ready yet to accept a soiled woman."

"You are saying that no one will help me?" Mona looked at her with pain and helplessness.

"Some might. But most will look down at you. Everyone will say it was your fault. Nobody will respect you or your family. Around the world, virginity is regarded as a high value commodity. All men think, once a woman is tainted that she can be soiled again," Dr. Kapur said.

"What are you saying that I am finished? That I am not a dignified person? You are saying to forget and pardon his crime?" Mona said.

"A woman never loses her dignity, and I do not want you to forget what happened to you. I will never pardon him, and I don't want him to get away with this heinous crime, but I also know you are vulnerable," Dr. Kapur said.

"What do you mean by vulnerable?" Mona said.

"Do you know what type of questions lawyers will ask you in the court? Those nasty questions will lay bare every inch of your body and they will repeat those questions in unusual ways. They will force you to recant your statement repeatedly, until you regret it all and think it was your fault.

The newspapers will publish the juicy deliberations of the court every day. You come from an orthodox family. The whole community will disown you. Who will marry you or your younger sister? No relative will come forward to help you. With stigma of rape on your family, your community will shun you," Dr. Kapur added.

"But I want to fight," Mona said.

"If you want to fight in court, you have to be a strong person. You will have to prove in court that he raped you, but you have no evidence," Dr. Kapur said.

"What do mean I have no evidence?" Mona said loudly.

"You told me, all the soiled clothes, soiled bed sheets and your body, you washed thoroughly," Dr. Kapur said.

"I felt dirty, looking at the clothes and bed sheets. What did you expect? I should have left all the filth on my body?" Mona interrupted.

"I know. But lawyers need evidence and you washed it all away. The decision is yours and I will always support you. Remember, at this moment, only we know what has happened. My first job is to calm you down and bring you out of the trauma you are going through. I can treat the scars on your body. At the time of your marriage, I promise, I can make you virgin. I have done this for several innocent raped women. But your mental scar of rape will remain all your life and you will have to live with it somehow."

Mona's heart burned with revenge. She was in a fix. If she hushed the matter and let the criminal go free, that would be injustice to her, and if she reports the crime to the police, all her family could be dragged into court. The consequences could last forever. After some thought, Mona decided to keep the rape secret. Only Dr. Kapur knew the truth.

Over the next few weeks, she remained numb and

detached with everybody. She felt intense fear and had frightful dreams of her assault. She was bitter and had low self-esteem and confidence in herself. She would avoid being touched and she would go to the bathroom repeatedly to bathe and clean herself. Mona looked and acted like a normal person, but on the inside, she was angry and defensive. One month later she went to see the doctor for a follow-up visit.

"Tell me, why do men behave like this?" Mona asked.

"The blame lies with our society, where men have not truly accepted women as equal. Lot of ignorance fills the mind of men. They do not know how to treat their sisters and daughters. In our society from birth, sons are pampered and treated better than daughters. I have seen mothers feed their sons first and the daughters are fed with leftovers. It will take centuries for these old perceptions and inequalities to go. And remember the biggest perpetrators are often those you trust most," Dr. Kapur emphasized.

Chapter 3
College Days
1965-1969
Kanpur

Mona's family came back from their trip to Delhi. She did not relate what happened to her. She worked hard for her tests and passed her high school exams with honors. She was awarded the gold medal and free tuition to study in college. Krishna invited friends and the neighbors to his home to celebrate Mona's success.

Kanpur was hot and sticky in the summer of 1965. The sky was covered with dark clouds, but no sign of rain appeared. The warm air was blowing; anything one touched was hot. Everyone was waiting for the monsoon to blast through the clouds at any moment.

Three months had gone by since Mona was raped. She physically recovered, but her mental scar was still there. She still had bad dreams and never understood how her father's younger brother could rape her.

Vijay had come to drop his family in Kanpur for the summer holidays. Mona's father had invited Vijay, Rebecca and their two children, Anand and Sugund, to celebrate Mona coming on top in the university. Krishna always looked up to Vijay for his advice regarding Mona's studies and her career. Her father had always had full trust in Vijay.

"Uncle Krishna, Mona is like my younger sister, said Vijay. "I can guide her, but I cannot tell her what she should do. She is young and she needs to learn from her mistakes. Time is changing nowadays. Children like to be independent and choose their own destiny." Vijay paused. "Mona has always known what she wanted. She will achieve, no matter what."

In the fall of 1965, Mona joined Christ Church College at Kanpur for undergraduate studies. The college was famous for liberal arts and commerce studies. She had a desire to be an economist, and it would take the first four years of college to complete the undergraduate degree. Then for the next two years, she would do her master's, and following that, study for another five years to complete her Ph. D. Mona was back on track to plan out her life.

In college, Mona was popular and voted Miss Christ Church College. A born competitor, she always came first in all activities. She became president of the debating society and the editor of the college newspaper. Mona, a very vocal person, always fought against the inequality of the caste system.

College life gave her confidence and independence. She and her friends rode on their bicycles and go to the exclusive sites near the military cantonment on the riverbanks of the Ganges. Standing at the banks, they watched buffalos crossing the river. Moving in a row like a caravan, diagonal to the flow of the river, the herder held the tail of the last buffalo to cross with them.

She and her friends had picnics under the big banyan tree at the banks. They had poetry contests, sang movie songs, and walked along the riverbank. Girls tugged their saris higher, showing a partial view of their legs and a thin silver anklet over the feet. Boys threw glances at smooth legs shining with turmeric rub. Everyone had a dream to become a doctor, engineer, or a lawyer. How free they all felt. Nobody knew where their future was. Mona's only worry was her father's comments about marriage after graduation and how it could impact her plan for higher studies.

One day Mona returned from college to find her grandmother Sarla Devi in a huffy mood. "What happened, Dadi Ma? You seem to be upset?"

"What to tell you, Mona Beti. The Ram Temple at the grand bazaar has refused to allow women to enter the temple. Can you imagine? It is the twentieth century, and our country is independent for the last twenty years. Our constitution says all people are equal. Still the nerve of the high priest! He will not allow a woman to step inside the temple," Sarla Devi said.

"That is disgusting. What you are going to do, Dadi Ma?" asked Mona.

"I am going to do a peaceful protest in front of the temple, and until they agree, I will continue to sit, and protest in front of the temple," said Sarla Devi.

"I am with you, Dadi Ma," Mona said.

Mona took part with her grandmother in Satyagraha. Her grandmother, a follower of Gandhi, never believed in inequality of men and women. Mona, young and enthusiastic at the age of nineteen, was at the forefront of the protest. For three days Mona and her grandmother sat at the entrance of the temple. Watching their actions, Mona's young friends from college joined them at the temple. By the third day, the whole city joined in protest. The temple authority had no choice. They reluctantly accepted the demand and let women pray inside the temple. Mona became a celebrity among her friends in college. She was always in the frontline for any cause about equality and freedom.

"Beti, you are my hero," Sarla Devi said "You brought all your college students to join the Satyagraha and proved to the world, there is no color, caste, or creed. All are equal."

Mona bowed her head in silent pride in front of her grandmother. She knew she was changing.

Mona was growing up, and her cheeks were bursting red, giving a glow over her dark skin, which looked golden in the sun. Her big eyes dazzled, and her succulent lips sparked burning desire in young men in the college. She did not let any man come near her. It was difficult for her to control her desire. Sometimes when she was alone in the house, Mona removed her top and look at her firm, pointed breasts in the mirror.

She lightly touched her nipples and thought, *"How hard they are."* The blood rushed into her nipples, and she started sweating. The unbearable pain of her breasts frightened her. She ran to the bathroom, soaking her face with water and chanting hymns in praise of Lord, until her body heat calmed down.

She was saddened when she remembered her rape. Amar came often to meet the family. Mona avoided her Uncle whenever he was in town, and she got silently but bitterly enraged seeing him.

Vijay Bhai, whenever he was on his company's business at Kanpur, came to see Mona's family. He was fun to talk with, like an elder brother, a friend, a mentor and ready to give her good guidance. She could talk with him for hours.

Mona turned twenty. She and her mother Usha became closer to each other. Her father Krishna remained posted in Delhi, and he was seldom with his family. Each time he came to Kanpur, she could hear her parents discuss getting her the right boy for marriage.

Their apartment was considered a model home for the neighbors. Mother and daughter worked together and decorated the apartment. She spent the best times in her life with her mother. They attended birthdays, weddings, and other social gatherings. Whenever the mother and daughter went to see a movie, they returned home full of excitement and analyzed the movie step by step. Her mother was a great fan of one of the movie stars, Rajinder Kumar. He was her mother's heart throb. Mona accompanied her mother to see the same movie three to four times in the theater.

Mona finished her undergraduate studies in 1969. The unsettled battle between her and her parents for marriage started again. Her father desperately wanted her to get married. According to her father, twenty-two was the right age for a girl to get married, but Mona countered his plan with the reality of family finances.

"Dad, do you realize, we do not have a penny in the house? Who will marry the daughter of a pauper?" Mona said.

Mona's father Krishna was an engineer and worked all his life in an administrative job at a government department. After his retirement, he decided to start an ancillary factory in Kanpur for making spare parts for the automobile industry. He put his entire provident fund and cashed half of his pension to start the factory.

He had no firsthand experience how to run a factory, however. He bought refurbished machines made in the United States, thinking they would be high quality. The refurbished machines would run for a few months and soon after would break down. He borrowed money from Usha's brothers and ordered spare parts for the machines. The machines ran for a while and then broke down again. He borrowed more money from Usha's brothers, and the machines failed to perform. The borrowing from Usha's brothers went on for some time, until they refused to give more money to Krishna.

The relations between Usha's brothers and Krishna

became strained, and the families were not on speaking terms. That did not deter Krishna, hoping that the factory one day soon would start making profits. Krishna borrowed money from loan sharks and poured more money into the factory.

The factory did not do well, and the money borrowed from loan sharks added up over time. Her father was buried in debts. For the last four years, Mona made some extra money by tutoring local children at home. The family was running the house with the money Mona earned and her father's meager pension.

Krishna was optimistic of finding a suitable engineer or doctor as Mona's bridegroom, but. Usha knew they had not a penny in the bank to entice a good match. Most families of prospective grooms expected a dowry and cash from the bride's family. All grooms had a price tag, and the professional grooms were expensive. Mona's relatives knew her father had no cash, and no relative was able to help them. Usha's two rich brothers would not come near them, treating them as if they were strangers. Mona faced another cultural barrier: Mona accepted that her complexion was dark. She was an attractive woman, tall, five feet, seven inches, thin waist, rounded hips, and very sharp sculpted features. Her breasts hugged her blouse, and her long black curly hair swirled behind her when she walked. Men craned their necks as she passed by. She belonged to a high-caste, insular community. Other girls in her community were fair-skinned, short, and chubby with big noses. She never understood how, although she was born into the same community, she did not have a light complexion. In the marriage game, a prospective groom preferred not only a large dowry but a fair-skinned bride.

With great difficulty Mona was able to afford her education, through scholarships and tutoring junior students.

She graduated at the top of her class and received the gold medal and substantial scholarship money to do her master's. However, the family's financial condition worsened. Mona felt that she had no choice, so she opted to take a job and postpone higher studies for a year.

"I want you to get married and you want to work," Krishna said.

"Dad, you know we don't have any money. Mom is running the house on a bare bones budget, and we must pay for Binny's education. And on top of that, grandma is getting old, she needs money for medicine. I want to do my master's, but we will see how our financial condition will be after one year."

Usha supported Mona in her argument. "Mona is right. Let her work for a year, and we see the situation after that, " Usha said.

Mona took a job in an accounting firm and a year later, in 1970, when the family's financial situation was better, she joined Christ Church College and began her master's studies in economics.

Chapter 4
Professor Karan Swarup
1972
Kanpur

Mona worked hard for her master's degree. She did not stop tutoring in the evenings. Her master's degree was a two-year course and at the end of the last term, she had to write a thesis.

They say love is spontaneous when it happens. One day she was coming out of the library when she bumped into someone. Mona said 'sorry' and he said 'sorry' and they smiled at each other. This is when Mona knew her life changed when she met Professor Karan.

Both walked away in opposite directions, then stopped and turned their head towards the other, smiling at each other again. In a split second all their senses exploded in an electric thrill.

That afternoon Professor Karan came to teach in Mona's class. He looked around and said hello to each student. His eyes lingered on Mona, and she kept looking back at him. He smiled at her. Mona was enchanted and smiled back. Mona looked down, and that was when their stars aligned.The next day Mona saw Professor Karan in the library again, standing near the information desk. Mona casually walked inside and asked for a book which she knew was not in the library. The information desk clerk told her that the book was not available. She tried to walk out, casting stealthy glances towards him. Professor Karan quickly called her, "Excuse me, Miss Mona, the book you are enquiring about, I have a copy. If you like, I can lend it to you for few days," he said very softly.

She whispered 'Yes.'

That was the start of a new friendship.

Karan was a handsome young man in his late twenties. His light eyes and tanned face brought girl students in class to clamor around him. His knowledge of world economics was exceptional, and he charmed his students into learning.

Mona used her beguiling eyes to gaze at the professor, and he always reciprocated with a smile that pierced her heart. He became her ultimate idol, and her idol fancy turned into passion. Sometimes she could not sleep in the night and would sit near the window dreaming about Karan.

They became more than good friends. Mona was undecided on the topic for her thesis. Professor Karan was an authority on international economics and banking.

"Dr. Karan, advise me. On what topic should I choose for my thesis?" asked Mona.

"Miss Mona, India is a vast country; you can choose any topic you like."

"How about 'International Economics and Banking.'"

"Why this topic? Give me your reasons," Professor Karan made a serious face.

"First, India is a developing country. To develop its industrial base, the country will need a lot of international loans and a strong economic base. And the second reason is, because, because ... my mentor is very handsome, intelligent, and I like him."

They looked seriously at each other and suddenly they burst out laughing.

They started spending more time together. He was an

inspiration for her thesis and a genius. She would listen to him for hours, and his charming smile would leave her spellbound. Their friendship turned into a deep commitment, and they soon fell in love. They would sneak out on their bicycles to the banks of the River Ganges, hide under the big banyan tree, and talk for hours. Mona would not let him come closer to her or touch her. If Karan tried to take her hand in his, she would gently move her hand away.

"Karan, no, if anyone saw us, we will be in trouble."

He respected her reluctance. Gradually they learned about each other's families. She wanted to know everything about him.

Karan spoke freely. "My father belongs to old Delhi. He joined the Army Medical Corp at the European front during the Second World War as a medical doctor. Later he was transferred to the Burma front. There he met my mother, who was also a doctor. They fell in love and one month after they met, they got married. I was born during the War. After the War, they moved to Dehra Dun. They still have their clinic in that city. I visit them once a month; it is a day's journey from Kanpur. I studied at Doon School, later at London School of Economics and then my Ph.D. at Harvard. What about you?"

"Wow, what an illustrious career. Well, I come from a family of lawyers. My father's grandfather was a lawyer, my grandfather was a lawyer, but my father broke the tradition, and he became an engineer. He worked in the Military Engineering Department all his life. After his retirement, he started a factory, but it is not doing well. We have no money. With his meager pension we continue. I studied at a convent and later at Christ Church College. At present I am doing my master's in economics under the famous professor Dr. Karan Swarup, and later I will go to the United States, to do my Ph. D. at Columbia University," Mona said smilingly.

"And?" Karan said with a mischievous look.

"And, what?" Mona said with serious face.

"You have always been at the top in every activity at the University, and you have ten gold medals stashed in your metal trunk," Karan said sweetly.

They were sitting under the banyan tree. Karan suddenly got up and then kneeled on the ground in front of her. "Mona, will you marry me?"

Mona was baffled. Her eyes were wet, and for a minute she did not know what to say.

"Karan, I am serious. We have no money to pay for the dowry or pay any cash."

"Mona, I come from a family where we never ask for the dowry or cash. My family will give you full respect when you walk into our house. But there will be one condition?"

Mona gave Karan a quizzical look, "What?"

"When you come to see mom and dad at Dehra Dun, bring a small packet of ladoos made from Tirpathi's Sweet Shop. My mom and I love them! They are sweet, and those ladoos melt in your mouth," Karan said teasingly.

"Don't worry; I can bring lots of those. And what about your dad?" Mona said.

"He does not like sweets," Karan said.

They hid nothing from each other, about their life, about their parents. But she could not bring herself to tell him the tragic incident of her rape.

Karan lived alone and rented a two-bedroom flat in a posh locality of Pandu Nagar. The first time Mona visited his place, she was nervous and frightened. She was curious to see how he lived. They placed their bicycles in the courtyard.

He stood at the door. "Welcome, Princess, to my humble abode," Karan said.

"Thank you, Prince. This royal mansion is very

impressive." She entered through the doorway.

The flat was newly built. The courtyard had big floor tiles in a pattern and a high wall surrounding the flat. He occupied the first floor. The place was neat and clean. It had one big living room, the kitchen in the corner and two bedrooms facing each other. To her surprise, the large living room had no place to sit. All free space was laden with piles of books stacked one on top of the other. Name any topic and the book was there.

"My Prince, you are an avid reader. I guessed right that day in the library when I asked for a book I knew you would have. You have hundreds!"

Karan chuckled at her flirty confession. "What will Princess have hot tea or water? I don't drink Pepsi."

"Hot tea," Mona said.

Karan prepared an excellent masala chai. On the way home he had bought freshly made samosas at a shop in Arya Nagar.

She went from one room to another, but she did not see any picture of his family. Mona asked, "Why have you not put any pictures of your family on the wall?"

"I have some, but I did not get any chance to take them out of my suitcase, and I am not sure on which wall I should put them," Karan replied.

"You have pictures, show me. Come on, show me," Mona said excitedly.

"They are in one of the suitcases. Next time when you visit, I will show you," Karan replied.

"Please show me now," Mona requested eagerly.

"Alright," Karan went to the bedroom and brought out an envelope of pictures.

He handed her the pictures. "Here are my dad and mom, just after their marriage." His parents dressed in military uniforms.

"Oh wow, your mom is very pretty. She has lovely features, and your dad looks very handsome in his military uniform. And this one?" Mona held up an old sepia picture of a gentleman in formal pose,

"Grandfather. My father's father. High court."

"I did not know your grand-dad was a high court judge," Mona said looking at the picture.

"My mom is still very pretty, and my father is as handsome as ever. My dad's entire family is of high achievers. My dad's father retired as high court judge, and my dad retired as an army general. I hope I will someday live up to their example," he said.

"Yes, definitely you will, my Prince," she said with conviction and put her hands on his shoulders.

She visited his place often, and she would enter his place as if it were hers. Piece by piece, she helped him choose furniture for his living room. She persuaded Karan to buy bookshelves and arranged all his books according to their topics. Every visit she would find books scattered around his place, but she would always pick them up and put them back where they belonged. Both were in love and decided to get engaged in the next three months.

During Mona's visits, spicy masala chai would raise their desire. Karan with great restraint could kiss her hands. She would immediately push him off. Sometimes, she would push her chest forward and let him gaze at her protruding breasts. She would not let him touch them and immediately she would move away.

Mona was afraid that his touch would make her remember her assault. Her Uncle's face would continue to haunt her. Karan was confused why Mona stiffened at his touch.

One day they were alone at his place. He was desperate to kiss her and could not control himself. He wanted to take her in his arms. Whenever he tried to come close, she would make an excuse and slip away from him. He grabbed her in his arms and tried to put his mouth over her lips.

She did not expect a sudden grabbing, and she pushed him aside. He was shocked at what had happened. Why had Mona pushed him?

"What is the matter, Mona? Whenever I try to come near, you move away. Whenever I try to kiss, you turn your face. We are getting engaged in three months. We will be living together. Don't you like me?"

Mona was frightened and regretted her action. "I am sorry. I did not mean to behave like that. I am ashamed and scared,"

"You are ashamed and scared of what? Don't you love me?"

"I do, I do. I want to tell you something, please."

She started crying.

Mona could not hold herself back anymore and told him the whole story about how she was raped, except she changed the story a little. On Holi Day, an unknown man knocked at her door and when she opened the door, he forcibly entered the apartment and raped her. She intentionally did not mention her Uncle's name.

Karan listened to her story. He was disgusted and angry at what had happened to her. He held her in his arms tightly and after few minutes of silence he said, "It is all right. Do not be scared. It was not your mistake. We are educated people. It does not matter what happened in the past. It was not your fault. I love you," Karan said.

He was not happy that she did not lodge a complaint at the police station. Still, Karan's assurances helped to take away Mona's fears of her horrid past. She began to feel more comfortable.

The next time Mona kissed Karan, she was ready with her protruding lips and open arms. She had her first romantic kiss, their lips joined, and their eyes closed oblivious to the world. Her first kiss was the kiss of a lifetime. She trembled and almost fainted. They were afraid of their uncontrollable urges. They were nervous, soaking with perspiration and frightened of their own passion.

One day she asked him, "You have proposed to me, but have you ever thought about how it will work?"

"What do you mean, how it will work? It is simple, I will come riding on a horse, your parents will receive my family and there will be a wedding ceremony and after that you will come to our home. We will celebrate our conjugal night and you will be permanently mine," he said.

"It is not going to be easy, on our wedding night. My Prince will have to give me a lot of promises."

"I will be very gentle and agree to whatever you ask, Princess." He kissed her cheeks.

"I am worried that we may face a problem."

"What could be a problem? I do not anticipate any. Your thesis is almost complete. We both are in love, and I promise to take care of you all my life. If you are hesitant to ask your parent's permission, then let me ask them for your hand."

"No, I will tell my mom. I love you, my Prince; I don't want to lose you." She was frightened.

"Neither I, my Princess, want to lose you," he said.

Karan was the most eligible unmarried man in the town, sought by families for their daughters. Mona's family liked him. She told her mother her intention of marrying Karan. Krishna met him and gave his approval as the suitable boy for Mona. Her grandmother also approved of Karan.

Her thesis was now complete, and Mona's plans were moving in a successful direction. Everyone in the family was happy that she found a highly educated, eligible young man . Her grandmother boasted to all her friends of his academic qualifications. Most of her family members met him and approved of him. He was accepted into their family.

The family hosted a small betrothal ceremony, but the big engagement function where all the clan was invited, was not planned yet. Mona was twenty-five in 1971, and finally, she was going to be engaged.

Her father was out of town. In the next few days, he was coming to Kanpur to finalize the date of the engagement function. They had invited the whole community to the ceremony. One day she asked her mom, "Mom, what is love, and when does it happen?"

Usha was watching her daughter's awareness and growing pains of youth coming into age. Her mom replied, "Love is when you forget to eat your dinner."

"Mom, come on, please. Tell me what love is," she asked again.

"Love is a feeling when your body and soul want to be in unison with another soul."

Mona thought for a moment about Karan, "That means when I am in love, and I want my body to unite with another body, which is love."

"No, that is your passion, not love. It is one-sided, and it could be infatuation. When both the souls are ready to unite as one, then it is love."

"Mom, how do you know you are in love?"

Usha looked at her daughter with affection and said, "When you are in love, something inside you becomes alive. You feel the presence of someone that makes your heart beat faster. Every inch of your body is in agitation. With that happiness, enticement, and desire, you experience a beautiful feeling."

"Mom, you and dad did not meet each other before marriage. How did you fall in love?"

"Love happens in strange ways. Nowadays, children meet each other, fall in love and then they marry. In our time, people marry first and fall in love after. We were married, and we had no expectations of each other. On the first night we talked until morning, and it took a few days before we felt comfortable with each other. When we accepted what we are, and not what we should be, it was easy to consummate our marriage. We built our love in a gradual process."

Mona took a minute and mustered courage to ask her mom, "Mom, how were you able to consummate your marriage?"

Her mother chuckled, "We both were novices. It took us some time to learn everything." Her mother took few breaths, "You are asking too many questions. I know this much. Even today, when your father touches me, the flame of love and desire arises."

Mona had her own fears. She asked Karan again. "We are going to be engaged in the next few weeks; have you ever thought there could be any problem?"

"What could be a problem?" Karan replied.

"I don't know the reason. I am frightened," Mona said.

"I don't know why you fear. Time has changed, India is independent, and you come from a well-educated, modern family. Your grandmother is a follower of Mahatma Gandhi and for her caste and creed does not matter, though we both belong to the same caste. She is a revolutionary. Don't you remember how fiery your grandmother was when women were not admitted in the temple?" Karan replied.

"But....", before Mona could say more, he put his finger on her lips. "We are educated, belong to the same caste, and we can make our own decision. We are in love, and I promise to take care of you all my life."

"I am nervous," Mona was frowning.

"Please don't, my Princess," he said with confidence.

Chapter 5
Thunder
1972
Kanpur

Mona thought she knew about Karan's family past, and was alarmed when her mother and grandmother suddenly had quiet conversations behind closed doors.

Then, all hell broke loose.

Sarla Devi knew that Karan's father was of their same caste. The true shock came when one of the older ladies from the neighborhood told Sarla Devi the whole story of Karan's family history. Mona's family was dumbstruck.

Karan's great-grandfather Madho Ram came from a Dalit family, the lowest of all castes and commonly known as "untouchables." Madho Ram used to work at the bungalow of Gora Sahib, a British Commissioner of Kanpur City. At the time, Madho Ram had a fourteen-year-old daughter, Janaki. Janaki was wild, a tall and skinny girl. A rustic beauty, she walked tall wearing tattered clothes which revealed her developing body.

Gora Sahib was forty years old and not married. The young lass caught his eye, and he quickly took fancy to her. A year later, Janaki bore him a daughter, and they named the child Sophie. Gora Sahib took great interest in his daughter Sophie's education. Eventually, Sophie became a doctor. During the Second World War, Sophie joined the Army at the Burma Front. There she met Karan's father, a military doctor, and they married. Sophie gave birth to Karan during the war. After retirement from the Army, Karan's parents settled in Dehra Dun City.

For Mona's orthodox family, the problem of untouchability was insurmountable. Coming from a Dalit heritage proved to be a fatal blow. Karan's mother, distinguished, a doctor, was still, after all, a Dalit. All Mona's plans for marrying Karan were quashed, and the invitations for the engagement were cancelled. Mona was heartbroken and did not know what to do.

Amar Uncle was posted in Bombay. He had come specifically for the engagement. After listening to the story, he shouted, "Oh my God, a Shit Picker's great grandchild? Never, never!"

One of Mona's relatives called Karan a child of a Dalit family. Another relative cursed him with choice abuses and said they could not believe their ears that Mona wanted to marry him.

Mona took her mother aside and asked, "Mother, what is this nonsense that he belonged to the lowest caste? His father and grandfather and great-grandfather, all his family, are of our caste. Karan is of our caste, in spite of the heritage. He loves me, and I love him! He gave me full confidence to face the world, and you want me to discard him because some ancestors were low caste? What is going on?"

"Mona, lower your voice. Listen, at this moment, things are out of my hands. Grandma loves you most in the family, and she is the only person who can help you now. Her words will be final," Mona's mother said in quiet tone.

Mona had always been the favorite of her grandmother. Mona knew Sarla Devi hated the British, often calling them Frungees who ruined India. Mona often heard her grandmother's opinion: "The British Raj encouraged the caste system and the myth of color in which fair skin is superior to dark skin. They killed fifty million people in Bengal by starving them. They divided the country. More than a hundred million people had to leave their homes due to partition of India after Independence. There were Hindu and Muslim riots. Nobody knew how many millions died in bloodshed. This all happened because of the Frungees."

Mona did not know how to convince her grandmother to accept Karan. Her grandmother was considered a role model in society, a disciple of Gandhi, an icon of a new female awakening and equality of all people.

Mona sat down with her grandmother Sarla Devi. All her relatives gathered close to listen.

"Grandma, please give me a single reason. Why can't I marry Professor Karan?" Mona asked.

Amar interjected, "The reason is because he is a Dalit."

"I am not asking you. I am asking my grandmother. And if Karan is from a Dalit family, so what? Gandhiji never believed in untouchability," Mona said.

All elders raised their eyes; Mona's father spoke gently, "Mona, we all gathered here to explain the reason behind not marrying him. You should respect your elders."

"I am sorry, to all of you. But you must understand, Karan is a highly educated man, and he won international awards in economics. There are universities in the world, which want him to teach in their college, and many international banks want him to join their organization. He has never done any menial jobs. His father and mother retired as surgeons from the army, and his father's father was a famous high court judge."

"You forget, Mona," said Amar. "Karan's grandmother, this Janaki, was Dalit and the mistress of a Gora Sahib, a Frungee. And you know we hate Frungees. I cannot dream that my niece would marry into that kind of family."

Mona ignored him. She turned to Sarla Devi.

"Grandma, why don't you speak up? You are against untouchability, and you do not believe in the caste system. Why don't you tell them they are wrong?"

As the head of the family, Sarla Devi's words were going to be final. She remained silent for a while. Then she spoke, "Mona Beti, I am speechless. I am ashamed of myself. Living on idealism is not reality. The reality hit me today. I have one more granddaughter to think about after you. Once I let you marry Karan, no one will marry our Binny. You know that our community is orthodox. We may pretend India is independent, but we are still in shackles. We are the victims of false beliefs and narrow thinking. Our old-fashioned society will leave us behind. No one will invite us to community functions or enter our home. We would be disowned by our community. I don't have the courage to face that consequence."

Amar had a smirk on his face.

Over the next few days, Mona's pained cries, protests, and refusing food did not move her family. She pleaded Karan's college degrees, his prestigious job, his good nature, and his intelligence. All were of no value for her family. Her family was not ready to listen to her reasoning because they feared the wrath of their community.

After the engagement was broken, Karan decided to leave Kanpur. He had accepted an offer at the World Bank in Paris. For the last time, Mona and Karan met secretly at Mona's friend's house.

Mona put her arms around Karan and started crying, "I cannot live without you. I will commit suicide."

"Shu, shu, don't talk like that. It makes me nervous. Mona, you are a strong girl, and I do not like the tears dropping from your eyes. Your whole life is in front of you," Karan said.

"How will I live without you?" Mona asked.

"I know you can because you are a survivor. You will face the world bravely. Here, take this handkerchief and wipe your tears," Karan said.

"We are adults. Why can't we elope and get married in court? You can take me with you," Mona pleaded.

"It would have been possible if no one knew of our love. Now it is too late. The whole community knows we were getting engaged. Your old classmate and friend secretly arranged for our meeting, and if we elope, the community will not spare her," Karan said.

"Then what should I do?" Mona asked.

"You are a brave girl. Think only of the happy times we spent together, the walks on the banks of the Ganges River and afternoons where we sat under the shade of the banyan tree. My heart knows we will meet again," Karan said.

Karan left the room and mused. *We Indians are hypocrites. Brahmins, Dalits, and other high and low caste Indians - rich and poor - when we go abroad, we mingle together despite caste. To survive, anyone will clean bathrooms and toilets, scrub the floors, vacuum carpets, and take garbage to the dumpster. During struggles, all forget their caste. But the same people would never socialize with each other, back in India.*

Karan left India in 1972 and never returned to Kanpur City.

Chapter 6
Restlessness
1972
Kanpur

Mona had completed her Master's in Economics. She was only twenty-five, but her restless soul was giving her trouble. Karan had left Kanpur, and her heart was broken. She would sit in her mother's room and sulk.

She was angry with her family, her clan and with the community, where the stigma of caste ruined her life. Mona decided she would never tolerate injustice and she would show everyone she was an independent, emancipated woman.

India had been independent for twenty-five years. Mona realized the mental and cultural barriers were still there. A Brahmin had to marry a Brahmin, a Dhobi had to marry a Dhobi and a Dalit had to marry another Dalit. That was the main unspoken rule of Indian society. Her mother Usha came to console her.

"Mom, no one took my side. Where in the Holy Scriptures is it written that one cannot marry out of the caste? In our history many kings married low caste women. In Mahabharata, King Santanu, father of Bhishma, married a fisherman's daughter. If a man marries a low caste woman, it is fine. But a woman wants to marry someone from different caste, all men raise their eyebrows. These are man-made rules. I am going to fight against this system for the rest of my life."

Usha said, "Our society has run with man-made rules

for thousands of years. To escape these rules of the caste system is new to everyone. You should have been born a hundred years later; perhaps by that time India may become a casteless society."

Usha was worried about Mona, and she did not want Mona to fall into a depression. She thought, to divert Mona's attention, the best way was to look for a job.

"Mona, what is the use of remaining sad all the time? What has happened is bad. You cannot bring Karan back, " Usha counseled. "You have finished your master's. Why don't you apply for a decent job and show the world you are a fighter. You wanted to study abroad; what happened to that ambition?"

"Mom, you know we have no money, dad cannot pay for my education abroad, and I don't feel like sending the job applications."

"Why don't you feel like sending the applications? You know your family condition. I have done my Master's in English Literature; I can write your applications," Usha said with a force.

"Alright mom, I will apply to companies that have advertised for accounting jobs," Mona said.

Mona was looking for a job at a good firm in all corners of the country. But if she received any replies, they were rejections. It was of no avail. She discovered that the vacancies were filled through friendly recommendations.

Vijay Bhai was in town to visit his parents in Kanpur. He always came to see Mona's family. Vijay and Mona were on the terrace with Vijay's children Anand, six years old, and Sugund, four years, playing blocks and pushing toy cars around. Mona and Vijay were leaning against the terrace wall, looking at the River Ganges. It was a cool evening. The sun was going down, hiding behind tall trees, and the shadows of trees were covering the building.

"Look at the thin River Ganges, winding. It looks like a snake," Mona said.

"Farmers are waiting for the monsoon, and rains are not due 'til July. The river water level has dropped. If we did not get enough rain like last year, there will be shortage of water everywhere," Vijay replied.

Vijay found Mona strangely silent and tried to bring on more conversation. After a while he asked, "You have completed your master's. What are your plans for the future?"

"I don't know," she replied.

"What, you don't know?"

"Yes, I don't know."

"Don't tell me that! You always look ahead, and you always chalk out your plans for the future," Vijay said.

"I have sent applications to many companies," Mona said.

He looked at her, and Mona gave him a beautiful sad smile.

"Did you get a positive response from any company?"

"Not yet, and I do not care which city I go, Delhi, Bombay or Calcutta. Someday, I still have my one dream to be on the top of the ladder," Mona replied.

He thought of her ambition. "But your dad would like you to get married."

"Marriage, Marriage! Vijay Bhai, after the clan ruined my life, who will marry me? I do not care if my parents get me married, or they throw me into the Ganges. You know my dad does not have a penny to run our house. Who will marry me without a dowry? I don't know why they mention the topic of marriage," Mona said.

Vijay had heard the disastrous story of her engagement. He was disgusted how mercilessly his clan had treated Mona and her family. He was modern but he, too, was still afraid of the wrath of the clan.

Vijay felt sorry for Mona and her family. He had decided to migrate to America permanently in the next three months. He was in midst of winding down his household items and office arrangements. During his last visit with Mona and her family, he tried to be positive. "Let me know if I could be of any help to bring you to America. I can explore some universities for their Ph.D. program in economics," Vijay said.

"Is that a promise?" asked Mona.

"Yes, it is a promise," Vijay said.

Chapter 7
Training
1972
Kanpur

Mona continued looking for jobs and sending applications for any openings. There were no letters of interest, only rejection. She was disappointed and picked fights with her family for silly reasons because she was depressed.

A few days later, Self-Insurance Company advertised for management trainees in their accounts department. The company was headquartered in Bombay. Vijay had some friends in senior executive positions in Self-Insurance Company. He wanted to help Mona, so he took an employment application from his friend, and mailed it to Mona at Kanpur. He wrote a note, 'Mona, complete this application and send it back to me, at your earliest convenience.'

Mona was surprised to receive the application. She quickly filled the papers and mailed the application back to Vijay. Mona was called for an interview in New Delhi.

Mona's first interview was easy. The company told Mona to come back for a second interview, and it was tough. They asked her for a third and final interview with the Board of Directors. After the final interview, she was told the Board would let her know soon. Mona went back to Kanpur and anxiously awaited their decision. Two weeks later, she received the letter that she was selected for the job of Accounts Executive Branch Manager. Mona was jubilant.

The Board of Directors were impressed in the interview, and they were strongly in favor of hiring her. The main reason for delaying the decision was that the company had never hired a woman at the management level.

There was a one-month managerial training in Bombay. Her hotel, salary, and all other expenses were paid by the company during the training. The salary included fifteen hundred rupees per month, and a ten percent provident fund, merit bonus, house and travelling allowances. She never dreamt she would get so much money at the start of her career, and to top it all, there was a company-paid pension. She was as happy as a lark. She could finally support her family and stop tutoring children.

The company planned for her stay during training in Bombay at the Hotel Marina Palace but gave her the choice if she preferred to have her own accommodation. The company would pay her an additional one hundred rupees daily for her expenses.

Dadi Ma said, looking at Mona, "If you don't stay in the company's hotel, and stay at Amar's place, you can save an extra three thousand rupees in a month. It is a lot of money. You can throw away all your tattered saris and buy new saris and buy new clothing for your mother and Binny also."

"But, grandmother," started Mona. "I would think the hotel would be better."

Mona's father did not know anybody in Bombay other than his brother Amar who was transferred there on a promotion a few months back. He was living in a studio apartment near his work. Mona's training center was walking distance from Amar's apartment.

Her grandmother had just returned from Bombay after staying with Amar for a month.

"The building is behind the training center, within walking distance. His studio apartment is big. A large room, a nice kitchen and a big size bathroom. On one side of the room, he has a long sofa, and the opposite side has a divan big enough for two people to sleep," said Sarla Devi.

Mona was excited about her job and the salary. She had planned to buy lot of things in Bombay for her parents, sister Binny, and for the home. The thought of staying with Amar put her in panic. Her mind was full of fear, *He may again do……* She would tremble even hearing his name. She vehemently objected to the arrangement.

"Dadi Ma, staying in one room, it would be crowded. We will be stepping on each other's toes," Mona said tactfully.

"Beti, Bombay is expensive and due to lack of space, lot of families sleep in one room, and they all sleep on the floor. You sleep in one corner on the sofa, and Amar can sleep on the divan."

"Dadi Ma, you don't understand, I need my privacy."

"You think you need privacy. In our time, the whole family slept in one room. I agree the times have changed: everybody needs privacy. But you are safer to stay with Amar Uncle, than to stay alone in an unknown city. You are visiting Bombay for the first time. There are lots of wolves in the big city," Sarla Devi said.

Mona bit her tongue. She could not say to Dadi Ma that her son was the biggest wolf.

"No, Dadi Ma, I won't stay there."

"Stop lamenting. You are lucky to get this job, and look how much money you would save," Sarla Devi said.

Sarla Devi called Amar, and it was settled. Mona would stay with him. Mona could not reveal to her family why she did not want to stay at Amar Uncle's place. She was overruled, earlier when her engagement was broken with Karan, and she was overruled this time again. She had no strength left to fight back.

Mona scored one promise from the family: that her mother would go with her and stay for a week and see that Mona was well settled.

Before Mona departed for Bombay, she went to see Dadi Ma in her room. Sarla Devi said, "Mona Beti, you are my favorite, and you are the toughest one in our family. You had a wonderful childhood when your father had a job and lot of money. You suffered utmost poverty when your father lost all his money in that useless factory. This job opportunity will not come again easily, and it gives you a chance to bring back your family to a comfortable livelihood. Remember, Binny and your family depend on you. No sacrifice is too big for the family. Your family always comes first."

Chapter 8
Mona In Bombay
1972
Bombay

The train reached Bombay Central Train Station late. Amar was waiting at the station, and he looked irritated. Usha waved to him from the train window, and he waved back.

"Namaste, Bhabhi, you must be tired after twenty-four hours' journey in the train," Amar said with folded hands.

"How are you, Mona?" He looked at Mona.

Both nodded. Mona was surprised that he did not show any emotions or happiness to see her, nor had he tried to embrace or touch her. He was a changed man.

Amar loaded the luggage in the taxi, and they reached his building. The elevator man brought their suitcases and left them in front of Amar's apartment door. Amar opened the door and tried to take both suitcases into the apartment.

"Let me carry one of the suitcases," Mona said taking one suitcase from his hand. Their hands touched. Mona felt a cold shiver in her body.

Amar's apartment was on the sixth floor. It was a spacious studio with few pieces of furniture, two large windows and a small balcony facing the sea.

Usha said, "Big room and large windows! How far is the sea from here?"

"The sea is only a quarter mile from the building, and you can see the ocean from the balcony. Mona's training center is behind this building." Amar pointed his finger towards the training center. "You can keep your suitcases in this corner," Amar replied.

He put their luggage in the corner.

"The divan is big enough for two people to sleep on it. You both sleep on the divan, and I will sleep on the sofa. You must be tired from the journey. Take rest, and then you can take a bath. I have put soap, towels, and toothpaste in the bathroom. I must run a few errands. I will be back in two hours." Amar left the apartment.

Mona was tired. She laid her head on the pillow and went to sleep instantly. She awoke after two hours and took a shower. The dust of the journey had turned her hair brown. She was used to taking a bath with one bucket of water. A shower was very tempting. She got dressed and walked on the balcony to put her wet clothes to dry. She was feeling fresh after her bath, and in a trance from being in Bombay. Amar was making tea in the kitchen.

Her mother was already dressed, and she was looking down from the balcony, watching the bustle of people on the street.

The sun was going down. The golden reflection on Mona's face was giving it a shining glow. Usha thought, *How pretty Mona has become. It's a pity she could not marry Karan.*

Amar came to the balcony with tea.

"Are you ready? I will take you to eat near the sea tonight, where the finest vegetarian food is served, and tomorrow I will take you to the Elephanta Caves," Amar said.

The restaurant was close to where Amar was living. Usha and Mona were impressed to see the spread of the vegetarian dishes at the restaurant. After a rich meal, they felt a little bloated.

They walked for a brief time, near the beach. Amar

walked slowly, with his hands clasped behind his back.

"Today is a full moon and high tide. Let me take you to a special spot. It will be fun to stand there and feel the fast, cool breeze from the sea. A place where you feel the end of earth, and the sea all around you. You will love it. The spot is called Nariman Point."

They hailed a taxi, and all got in for a short drive through crowded streets.

The taxi stopped one block away from Nariman Point.

"We will walk from here," Amar said.

The path was dark and crowded with people. To keep pace with the strong wind, Mona had to hold her mother's arm. They stood at the tip of a stone paved road. The sea air was swift and cool. Mona could not stand still. The strong air current could sweep Mona's feet from the ground. Mona and Usha held tight to each other and shrieked like children.

They walked back where taxi dropped them. At the corner, they sat down facing the sea. The breeze was not that swift anymore. They sat there silently. Mona's head was on her mom's shoulder.

"Let's go for a cup of coffee at Uberoi Hotel," Amar said.

"Coffee at night? We won't be able to sleep after that," Usha said.

"Don't worry, you both will be fine. Let us go," Amar said.

Mona and her mom both were a little hesitant. It was their first visit to Bombay. They had never entered a giant coffee shop before. Amar was with them, and he was very assuring. Mona was dazzled to see the ambience in the coffee shop. All sat down and ordered coffee and pastries. They stayed there for a long time. Mona was chirpy and not frightened. It was eleven at night before they were back in the apartment.

"When you get up in the morning, watch the sunrise over the calm and quiet ocean from the balcony," Amar said.

The next day, their trip to Elephanta Caves was enjoyable. The temples were on an island a few miles away from Bombay, so they had to travel by boat to reach the island. They were impressed by second century rock-cut temples with carvings of the legends of Lord Shiva.

Amar remained silent with his eyes closed, throughout the boat ride. No one could fathom his thoughts. Mona's mom was thinking of how Sarla Devi was managing Binny. Mona's ears were resounding with the words of Dadi Ma, *Mona, your job and saving your family are most important. No sacrifice is too big for the family. Your family comes first.*

On Monday morning, Mona walked to the training center for her management indoctrination. She dressed neatly in a sari, and men were in suits and ties. As the day grew hot and sultry, men put their ties and jackets aside and attended the lectures in a relaxed manner. Mona, an ambitious person, sat in the very first row.

Chapter 9
Frightened
1972
Bombay

The time passed quickly. Mona did not know how to explain to her mother that she did not trust her Uncle. She was miserable that her mother was leaving for Kanpur after one week.

"Why do you feel frightened? You are a grown-up girl. You will be staying with your Uncle, safe," Usha said.

Amar gave no glances, no sly look, not the slightest touch. He kept his distance. He would start his morning with his Yoga exercises. After his bath, he would do puja for more than an hour and insist on making a vegetarian breakfast. He gave no hint of his being non-vegetarian or a drinker of alcohol. He was pious and helpful, a God-fearing man. In the evening he would help Usha in cooking dinner and setting the table.

Usha was packing her suitcase. Amar was not in the apartment.

Mona was nervous, "Mom, please stay with me for some more time. I feel frightened and lonely," Mona said with tears in her eyes.

"You must understand, you have a sister, the wild Binny. I can't leave her alone, without a watchful eye," Usha said.

Mona was heartbroken, and her mind was full of fear.

Usha left by train early evening, and Amar took Mona to another famous vegetarian restaurant for a dinner. After reaching home, he told Mona to sleep on the divan as he was comfortable sleeping on the sofa. Amar stepped onto the balcony, closing the door of the balcony to meditate for one hour.

Mona changed her sari, brushed her teeth, washed her face, opened her braids, and combed her hair. She put her head on the pillow and dozed off, but she heard the noise of the balcony door creaking open. Quickly, Mona covered every inch of her body with the bed sheet. She turned her back towards door and shut her eyes.

Amar came and lay behind her, trying to turn her around. She was scared and jabbed him with her elbow.

"Oh my God, you hit me hard," Amar groaned with pain.

"What are you doing? Why do not you leave me alone? Tomorrow, I will take the first train and go back to Kanpur." She was scared.

"Yes, go back. Do you want to live in poverty? What will you tell your poor parents and your unmarried sister?" hissed Amar. "Everyone in the community knows about your affair with a Dalit. You got a job, in one of the top insurance companies in the country. Going back Kanpur, one day after your mother left, everyone will blame you and not me. Just keep quiet; this will be between you and me. No one will ever know," Amar said in a low, threatening voice.

"You want me to remain silent, but what if I get pregnant?" she said.

"Don't worry; I had an accident when I was young. Doctors told me I cannot have children, and that was the reason my wife left me," Amar said.

He had complete control over her, and Mona was

defenseless. Her body gave in. Mentally she could never accept his advances. Every night Amar forced Mona to have sex.

Chapter 10
Taste
1972
Bombay

A forceful and dominant Amar took two boiled eggs every day at breakfast. He tried to persuade Mona to take eggs as nourishment, but Mona was a staunch vegetarian.

"You must take one egg a day. You look pale, you need nourishment," Amar said.

"Not in this life. I am a vegetarian. As long I live, I will not. What answer would I give to God?" Mona replied.

"God will ask you, have you taken eggs and you will say no. He will send you back on earth immediately to taste a few eggs before you could be admitted back," Amar said.

"Please don't joke about my religion, it hurts my feelings."

"You see, these eggs are vegetarian. They have no life."

"What do you mean, they have no life?"

"These eggs have no life; I mean the eggs are not fertilized by a rooster. Hens lay eggs without the help of rooster."

Mona looked at her plate.

"Taste it a little and if you don't like it, you can spit it out."

He scraped a small portion of egg from the shell on the spoon and added a little salt and pepper. He thrust the spoon in her mouth. She was perplexed. Tears were in her eyes as if she had committed a sin. Her lips were tightly closed around the spoon, and he gently removed the spoon, forcing her to eat.

"Stop, Uncle. I am eating the egg!" Mona made face to please him but felt as if he had thrust poison into her throat.

Mona began to like the taste of eggs and started with one egg a day, and later she was taking two. She would order two eggs and tomato omelet in a restaurant, along with her vegetarian food. Amar would order meat dishes. Soon after, Amar forced Mona to sip beer, and occasionally, a small peg of scotch filled with Pepsi. Later, Amar insisted that Mona try meat dishes, and Mona became a non-vegetarian who drank alcohol. She started walking briskly and with confidence.

She had never used any makeup in her life. After looking at glamour magazines, she started using nail polish, a touch of lipstick and face cream. Her mother always used Hazeltine face cream every morning, and the bottle's label promised '*It whitens your skin.* 'Mona started using it as well. Though it did not whiten her face, it did give her a bright dewy look.

Chapter 11
Trip To The Resort
1972
Bombay

Mona's completed her training, finishing her exams in second place, and prepared herself for a return to Kanpur. Before scattering for their assignments, all trainees had a chance to go sightseeing in Bombay. To celebrate her success, Amar took Mona to a holiday resort close to Bombay. The tourist department had a cottage there for visitors from abroad.

The cottage was small, with two beautiful bedrooms, a comfortable living room and a cozy fireplace. The facility had a cook, a security guard, and a gardener. They reached the resort in the afternoon.

In the evening, the cook set the table on the verandah and brought two empty glasses and a bottle of scotch, ice, and Pepsi. Amar poured scotch in his glass and asked Mona if she would drink a little. Without waiting, Amar poured scotch and Pepsi into her glass. "A small drink may put your mind at ease, and you will be in a good mood tonight."

"That is all you think of me, an object of pleasure," Mona interrupted. She had become bold. "You are having sex with me every night."

"No, I didn't mean that. A drink will relax you. Have a few sips."

"Have you realized, you corrupted me? I drink scotch, I

eat meat, and I put on makeup and use lipstick? And you have taken my body. You ruined my life," Mona said.

She took her glass and gulped down the scotch. The cook brought kababs and cheese snacks. Mona and Amar both remained silent.

"From a timid person I made you a strong, independent woman," said Amar. "Take some kababs, you love cheese pakoras. I know you are not in a good mood. I have no idea of what I should do." He waited a moment. "Mona, be reasonable."

"Oh ho, you mean to say I am unreasonable. Since when has rape started to be reasonable?" Mona said loudly, ate one full kabob, and gulped down the scotch whisky from Amar's glass. "Mentally, I never agreed to have sex with you because you are my Uncle. Physically I let you have me. You know why?" Mona said loudly.

"Why?" Amar asked.

"My family comes first. I do not want them to get hurt. If I must sacrifice myself, I do not care."

"Please talk softly. I do not want the cook to hear anything and spread it around to others."

"You are worried what your coworkers would say, but you are not worried at all what will happen to me!" Mona shouted in anger.

"I am worried about you, but I am confident that you will survive. You are a survivor and a fighter, and you will fight it out. Years later, you will think of this as a passing phase of your life. You know, in one month my life has changed. I had one of the loveliest times with you. I will cherish the memory of these thirty days all my life. What do you say? Do not look at me with accusing eyes. It happened, and I have no solution."

"You...." Mona could not complete the rest of the

sentence. This was the second time someone had told her she is a survivor.

"I feel very sorry you are hurt," Amar said.

"You said I am hurt. What are you going to do about it? What will happen to me, who will marry me?" Mona said with tears in her eyes.

"Why you say, who will marry you? There will be thousands of people who will be lucky to hold your hand. Marriage is not only based on physical intimacy, but also an emotional commitment," Amar said.

"What about the emotional damage? Do you have any idea that when I am alone, I panic? In the night, I wake up as if someone is molesting me," Mona said.

"You are right. Emotionally I cannot do anything; I have never loved anybody except myself. You are exceptional, and you came out of the blue. You altered my thinking. As I said before, you are a fighter and survivor. In one month, you and I both have changed. We both cannot take back what has happened. I will be leaving Bombay soon and this time I am likely to be posted abroad, France, Germany, or America, and I may not come back. You will forget about me in the next few months. I am ready to help you in whatever way you want."

Mona remained quiet and then said, "You can't bring back my dreams."

Amar looked at Mona, "If I asked you to marry me, what would you say?"

"What, have you gone berserk? You want to marry me, your brother's daughter?" Mona was amazed.

"Why? In many communities around the world, it is acceptable!"

"Are you crazy? This is not acceptable by our community. This would be a scandal. If you ever utter a word to my mother or father, they will kill you. Grandma will hang you, upside down. If anybody came to know, my family will have to leave the town. No one will ever marry my sister. You were the first one to put roadblocks for my marriage to Karan, and now you want to bring more destruction to our family." Mona's tears flowed.

Amar was disappointed. He was emotionally getting too close to her.

They came back from the resort Saturday evening. Mona was leaving for Kanpur the next day at noon. She was hurt. She cried the whole night.

Mona was composed in the taxi but once her luggage was put in the railway compartment, she was weeping again. Amar got down from the train compartment to avoid curious passengers and people at the platform. He stood in front of the rail car window. The train started moving, and he waited there motionless. He could not see Mona.

Chapter 12
Back To The Old World
1972
Kanpur

Mona reached Kanpur City after twenty-four hours on a train. The city had not changed in four weeks, but everyone noticed changes in Mona. She was a different woman. No one had a clue. It was impossible for her family to imagine she had been sleeping with Amar Uncle.

Mona had learned a lot in Bombay, going from a small-town girl to a cosmopolitan woman. Amar changed her tastes and opened her mind to a big horizon. She could look at the world with maturity and practicality. Her job training gave her the confidence to make her own decisions. Meeting her colleagues, listening to them and voicing her own opinion set her mind free.

After returning home, Mona could feel the conflict between modern and old ways of thinking. What she had learned in Bombay, she had to unlearn to fit in with the conservative society of Kanpur. Her confidence was shaken when she found that no man was ready to listen to her opinion. She had to remain silent in front of men. She gave up makeup altogether. The stern eyes of seniors and her grandmother objected. "Only married women can wear makeup." The family curtailed her brisk walk and smart talk.

Mona focused on her new job. She took charge of Binny from grandmother. Binny had failed twice in her college exams. Krishna and Usha would leave early in the morning to go to the factory and return late in the evening. Mona came to know that Binny, instead of going to college, would roam around in the city with her friends.

"Dadi Ma, did Binny go to college today?" Mona said, after coming home from the office.

"Yes, today she left early. She said she has to prepare for a test and that she would come home late," Sarla Devi said.

"Somebody saw her at the movie theater," Mona said.

"Oh my God, what should I do with that girl?"

"Dadi Ma, you will not be able to control Binny. From today onwards, I will take care of Binny," Mona said.

"But Mona Beti...,"Sarla Devi said.

"No Dadi Ma, let me manage her, and I will not listen to any of Binny's excuses."

Mona's verdict created a big commotion in the family. Sarla Devi resented Mona for taking away her responsibility.

Mona was back to her old, routine life. Winter or summer, the city was dark and full of smog, but she seemed insulated against the filth around her. Sometimes she was very frustrated and liked to be left alone. Her mother Usha had the suspicion that something had shaken Mona. She was no longer her little baby. Mona had matured in one month, but Usha could not fathom why Mona was sad and melancholy.

"Mona, let us see a film this Sunday. My favorite actor is in this movie," Usha said.

"Mom, you go with Binny. I don't feel like going."

"Leave Binny; she has to finish her homework."

Usha realized she had neglected her favorite daughter since she had returned from Bombay. It was an ideal time to bond with her again. Mona and Usha gradually became close friends again. Mona started keeping company with her mother and helping her in cooking and with home chores. They hid no secrets from each other. But Mona could never tell her mother any part of her rape, or of the weeks in Bombay when she slept with Amar every night.

Chapter 13
Promise
1972
Kanpur

One month later, Vijay Bhai came to say farewell before leaving for America. Everyone was talking about life there, how to get there and how he could help them.

Sarla Devi said, "Mona had become a memsahib after coming back from Bombay. The best thing for her is to go to America. Vijay, find a suitable boy for her there, and the boy should be from the same caste."

"Of course, Grandma, I promise," Vijay replied.

Vijay looked at Mona, "Tell me, Mona, if I invite you to come to America, would you come?"

Mona gave a despairing smile and nodded, "Yes. Wasn't that your promise long ago? " Mona was twenty-five and the year was 1972.

Vijay Bhai and his distant cousin Ramesh left India to go to America around the same time in 1972. Vijay got his old job back, in New York. He and his family moved to a three-story house in Flushing, New York.

Vijay's cousin, Ramesh, was leaving India for the first time. After getting his green card, he moved to Cleveland, Ohio, where his aunt lived. Vijay and Ramesh were in touch with each other after reaching America.

Mona was living in Kanpur like a dead soul. She was restless and fed up, and led a restrictive life. She longed for

Karan, his strong arms holding her and assuring her. He had given her a first kiss which opened her soul.

She longed to go to America and do her Ph.D. at Columbia University and fulfill her dream.

Chapter 14
Ramesh's First Time In America
1972
Cleveland

Ramesh reached America in 1972. Sitting on the plane with his eyes closed, he had big dreams. He imagined that jobs would be waiting for him at the airport. He would buy a new car in the next few months, an apartment in a year and after couple of years, he would go back to India to marry a beautiful girl.

He flew to Cleveland, where his father's younger sister lived. Ramesh's Aunt Ashi and her husband Ratan were in their late thirties, and they had two young children, aged ten and twelve. Both husband and wife were doctors and had emigrated to America years earlier.

Ratan and Ashi were working as interns in the hospital. Being interns, they were paid little and had expensive school loans to pay back. They both had irregular schedules. . Sometimes Ratan worked continuously in the hospital for three days and sometimes Ashi also had to work irregular shifts in the hospital as well.

They were living in a two-bedroom apartment because they could not afford a bigger place. Aunt Ashi accommodated Ramesh with the understanding that Ramesh would find a job and move to his own place in a couple of weeks.

Ramesh was an easygoing person, and working hard

was not one of his strengths. He was optimistic but did no planning before coming to America. He had no clue how life in America functioned. At every opportunity, his aunt suggested that Ramesh find a job.

"Ramesh, did you get any reply from the applications you sent?" Ashi asked.

"No, Ashi Aunty, no company has replied."

"Why don't you look for a job in a restaurant or a grocery store? At least you will earn some pocket money!"

"Aunt Ashi, how can you even think I will accept a job in a restaurant? An engineer and a son of a civil surgeon, making food in a coffee shop and cleaning the toilets? No, don't ask me again," Ramesh said.

"Before we both got admission in the medical college, my husband and I worked in a grocery store."

"Aunty, you did it, but I won't. No way."

Aunt Ashi was not happy that Ramesh was staying with them for longer than she thought. The apartment was small and cramped. Ramesh did not like sleeping in the children's bedroom. All five of them had to share one bathroom. In India, Ramesh had a separate, spacious room and attached bathroom. He could sing, dance whatever he liked to do in his own bathroom. Ramesh was repelled at sharing a bathroom with other people.

Ramesh remained unemployed, which frustrated him. He stopped visiting the offices, factories, and employment agencies in search of a job. He would call a few companies on the phone and spend the rest of his time sitting in front of the television and watching soap operas. As the days passed, he was losing confidence and getting afraid of venturing into the New World. His aunt continued to push him to go out and get any job.

Six months had gone by, and he did not know what to

do. He was gaining weight quickly, and his hair was looking shaggy. He had no money, and he could not go back to India.

"Ramesh, why don't you try to work in a restaurant?" his aunt suggested again.

"Aunt Ashi, I spent four years studying engineering, and I did well. I had a job at a manager level in India. How do you expect me to work in a restaurant making hamburgers?" Ramesh said. Being an engineer, he could not reconcile the idea of someone as educated as him washing dishes.

His cousins would not talk with him. Small discussions would end up in hot arguments among everyone in the house. Nobody was speaking to each other. Finally Ashi gave him an ultimatum: to get out of the apartment, job, or no job. Her own marriage was in jeopardy.

Ramesh called Vijay, and Vijay suggested he come to New York and stay with his family. Ramesh borrowed two hundred dollars from his Aunt, knowing he could never step back in her home.

Chapter 15
Ramesh Settles In
1973
New York

Ramesh flew to New York, and at La Guardia Airport Vijay picked him up. Vijay let Ramesh stay in his basement. Winter rains in New York subsided, but it was very cold, and the streets were covered with muddy water filled with partially melted snow.

Later that week, after Ramesh became settled in, Vijay took him out for a walk.

"Tell me, Ramesh! What is the problem preventing you from getting a job?"

"Oh, my dear friend, I do not know what is happening. I can't get a job as an engineer, even for a meager salary of eight thousand dollars a year."

"Do you know how this country works?"

"Of course, I know."

"OK, tell me," Vijay asked.

"Well," Ramesh started thinking.

"Have you worked in this country before?" Vijay asked.

"No," Ramesh said.

"Have you studied in this country?"

"No."

"Did you do any sort of training in this country?"

"No."

"Look here! You do not know how the system works in this country. You do not know where the C or D trains go. You do not know what is uptown or downtown. You may speak excellent English, but you do not know the lingo of the local people. In fact, you know nothing about this country."

"Then, what should I do?"

"You have two choices: number one, buy an air ticket and return to India and I will pay for the ticket. The second choice is to redefine your aim of coming to this country. You may have to start at the bottom, and work in a restaurant or clean toilets. We all started at the bottom." Vijay looked at him.

Ramesh looked down and stared at his muddy shoes.

"If you do not like the second alternative, go back to India. I am giving you three days to decide. I do not want to spoil the relationship between your family and ours. If you decide you want to make your life here, you are welcome! I will let you stay in the basement. You will pay rent when you start earning."

Ramesh decided to stay in America, and he started looking for a job in a grocery store to sustain his living.

Chapter 16
Ramesh's First Job
1973
New York

Ramesh took a job soon after, at a small supermarket to restock grocery items. He was paid one dollar and fifty-nine cents an hour. The job began in the late afternoon, and it was simple. He would make the list of which groceries were depleted on the shelves and replenish them.

In the morning he would wear a tie and suit, carry his resume in a small briefcase and set off in search of a job. One day he saw a help wanted sign for an engineer outside a factory. Ramesh went inside and gave his resume to the receptionist. She took the resume inside the factory and told Ramesh to wait for an interview.

A man in ordinary jeans and a plaid shirt came out and took him inside his office. They shook hands.

"Your name is Ramesh. I see you have good qualifications. How long have you been in this country?" the man in the jeans and shirt asked.

"Eight months," Ramesh replied.

"Do you have any plastic manufacturing experience?"

"No, but I can do any kind of job," said Ramesh.

"You are sure you can work in a factory?"

"Yes, Sir."

The man took a deep breath. "Don't call me Sir! Call me Sam."

Ramesh remained quiet.

"Alright, go inside and fill out some paperwork. You will start working this afternoon and will be paid 145 dollars a week."

Ramesh looked at him. He could not comprehend that the man was asking him to start work immediately.

"Do you want the job or not? Go inside and start working," Sam repeated.

Ramesh could hardly believe his good fortune. He forgot about his responsibilities at the grocery store job until later that day. He promised himself he would call to resign the next morning but failed to follow through.

For Ramesh to get a job and start working immediately was a shocking surprise. Back home he had to wait many days for a job offer. He never had this type of interview before. He removed his tie and jacket and walked with Sam into the factory. Ramesh was nervous when he came to know the man in jeans was the boss of the company. Sam spoke few words, and he knew all his employees by their first names. He was alert and knew exactly what was happening inside the factory.

Inside the plant Ramesh was introduced to the shop supervisor John, who was helpful, and he showed Ramesh diverse types of machines to make plastic parts.

Ramesh looked around. Many of the factory workers were women from different countries. They were young, strong, and tall.

He asked his supervisor John, "What I am supposed to do?"

"Just follow me, and you will learn what you have to do," John said.

Ramesh followed his supervisor around the factory all day. Ramesh was an adaptive learner. Every day he learned something new. John had fifty years of experience and had a thorough knowledge of plastic forming. No one could challenge him on quality of the product. He was a good-natured person and never rebuked any worker. All the men employees respected him and were awed by his expertise. Ramesh could see it was difficult to discipline the women workers. They would pretend to complain about shop conditions or overtime requirements, but they always followed John's directions. The jobs got done well, with quality, on time and on budget.

Ramesh had never worked on a shop floor, especially with people from different countries. After finishing his engineering degree, he had worked in a design office.

Discipline and bringing propriety among the workers were no simple tasks. Ramesh found he lacked supervisory skills. Men workers never liked him. They were very apprehensive of him. Whenever he asked them any question, their reply was always curt and aggressive. Young women workers would love to talk and gossip with him because he was a good-looking man.

Two young, attractive women from Puerto Rico, in their early twenties, were famous for their pranks in the factory. Both were interested to know more about Ramesh, but he was very shy and could not keep conversation going with them. The two young women found that he was the best target to play pranks on. One of the women would quietly sneak behind him and stand still. The other woman would face him in the front and touch him. Ramesh would step back, and the woman in the front would touch him again. Ramesh again stepped back, and his back hit the chest of the woman behind him. He froze.

The girl standing behind him squeaked, "OOO."

Ramesh said nervously, "I am sorry" and looked for help from his supervisor. John did not bother to look his way because he was standing far away. Ramesh was embarrassed and saw all the women laughing, while the men had frowns on their faces. The next day, it happened again. The women in the factory were having great fun at Ramesh's expense.

After a couple of days both women stopped teasing him, and they tried to be friendly. One of the women invited him to go with her to a movie. She was handsome, with dark curly hair and a well-endowed chest. It was something he never learned in India, where men were supposed to ask women out. Women inviting men was out of the question. He dreamt of chasing fair girls from high society. Working-class girls in the factory, although beautiful, were dark and not in his dreams. He was class conscious, and he thought they were not up to his mark. It was difficult for him to understand and accept the concept of a classless society.

Ramesh asked Vijay for advice. Vijay enjoyed Ramesh's daily adventures and treated his stories as entertainment. After hearing about the movie invitation, Vijay was in fits of laughter.

"How the times have changed. I have never been invited out by any woman. You are lucky."

"But you are a married man. How could you be invited by any woman?" Ramesh said.

"Shu, shu, don't talk loudly. Rebecca can hear from the kitchen. Don't talk about me and keep the conversation about your encounters quiet," Vijay said.

Vijay looked at Ramesh, "Here you are, a thirty-year-old virgin who wants to enjoy every moment of life. So far, you have never slept with any woman and don't have guts to do so."

Ramesh protested, "You know it is difficult to sleep with a girl in India. No high-class woman would let you touch her, unless you promise her marriage."

"We are not talking about India, where you meet a woman to get married," said Vijay. "You are in America, and this is an open-minded society. Those girls like to talk to you, but it does not mean they want to marry you. New York is a melting pot for people coming from different countries. They are as lonely as you are. They would like to meet other people to talk, to learn more about a person. You told me earlier both the girls are college graduates from Puerto Rico, and they could not find an office job, so they opted to work in a factory. If you think their invitation means going to a woman's apartment, tossing off your clothes, and making love to her? That is only in the movies. Don't you even dream of that, or you will land yourself in big trouble," Vijay said.

Ten days later the owner Sam told Ramesh that John would be out for three weeks due to a medical problem, and Ramesh had to take care of production in John's absence. Ramesh was scared and worried, he was new on the job, and he was learning. He did not yet have a firm grasp on his responsibilities.

The first day of John's absence was a disaster. In the morning, the compressor lines were not working because somebody had shut the valves down. Two of the molding machines broke, and very few workers were willing to follow his instructions. The women teased him, and the men hated him.

Those three weeks were like a nightmare where nothing went smoothly. Workers did not produce as planned, and nobody paid attention to him. The major surprise was the women in the factory who had laughed at him but now helped him. They often protected Ramesh from getting into trouble with the men. But their efforts were not enough.

After three weeks, John finally returned. Ramesh had a meeting with Sam in the afternoon and the outcome was obvious. Ramesh was fired with gentle and encouraging words, plus given one extra week's salary.

"Ramesh you are a very nice person, but you can't manage the staff," Sam said.

That was the custom of getting fired from a job – to be nice and kick the person out the door. Ramesh felt sorry for himself. He knew he was an adaptive learner. He found design faults in toys, he could do small repairs on machines, he was a good engineer, but he could not manage employees. And the women seemed to manage him.

He realized that to survive, he would have to find another job quickly. He looked for a part-time job in the evening. This time he found a job in a restaurant making hamburgers. He would clean the grill, cook hamburgers, and clean the bathrooms. This time he did not feel ashamed of doing anything. He was mentally prepared to struggle.

His same routine came back. Every morning he would get ready in a pressed suit and tie and put his resume and certificates in a briefcase. He travelled to different boroughs looking for jobs. Queens, Brooklyn, Bronx, and sometimes, Staten Island and Manhattan as well. There were massive layoffs on the West Coast, in the aircraft industry, and a big flux of experienced engineers rushed to the East Coast for work.

Ramesh met many people from India, on trains and at interviews. All were looking for jobs, carrying their resume in their briefcase and dressed in suits. They would relate their experiences at the interviews, and if they knew of any job openings, they would inform him.

In 1972, industries were reinventing and going through re-organization. There were frequent layoffs. Ramesh got another job in an engineering firm, but after couple of weeks he was laid off. It became a routine for him to lose and gain employment. Nobody could say where he was working, or whether he was with or without a job.

Chapter 17
Desi
1973
New York

On weekends, friends would come to Vijay's place regularly, and Rebecca was like their Godmother. The unmarried people could make one or two dishes, except inept Ramesh. His job was to clean the dishes after meals. Afternoon lunch was usually a feast. Later, they played games and sometimes they enjoyed bridge or teen patti, the Hindustani version of poker.

Vijay's children were the center of attention. They were spoiled, and pampered with toys, chocolates, and Indian kurtas. The married men who had not brought their families to America missed their homes and children.

Sometimes in the late afternoon, everyone would go together to watch an Indian movie, at the gym of a local school. There.were no cinema theaters showing Indian movies. When half of the movie was over, there was a break called an interval. At the interval, lots of Indians would walk outside of the gym, to stretch their legs or to eat snacks. They chatted with friends and strangers, and that is how they made new friends. They ate samosas and other treats, made by an Indian lady who earned a little extra cash. In New York City, Indian restaurants were hard to find, and all were expensive. Most Indians, who were immigrants, could not afford to eat out in those days.

Occasionally one of the friends would bring a bottle of scotch to Vijay's place. Back home, everyone was used to Indian whisky or rum. Here they drank only Johnny Walker Red. No one had developed a taste for bourbon or any other local whisky. Scotch would bring up the nostalgia of home. They missed their families, friends, and their comfortable life back in India. Here they had to do every job, including cooking, tidying rooms and cleaning toilets. In India one could hire people to do these chores. It was a period of transition from being dependent on others to becoming fully independent.

Everyone had dreams, of going back home one day, richer and respected. Some were waiting to complete their education, while others desired to make money before returning home. But, no one was ready to go back from an independent society to a restrictive environment where everyone was butting into their personal life.

Everyone had their sweet, romantic memories, favorite movie songs, and poetry that reminded them of home. Vijay was the only one who could sing and play a little tabla. Friends would always request Vijay to sing. With sips of scotch and a wooden table serving as the tabla, the familiar movie songs were sung repeatedly. The friends would join the singing, in their hoarse, out-of-tune voices, and the nostalgia of back home would set in again.

The same stories repeated every weekend, with the same songs, and the same illusion of going back home. Over the years, the trips back to India became few and fewer. They forgot time was the biggest enemy of memories. The memories of home became blurry.

Chapter 18
A Suitable Bride
1975
New York

In India, there is no Thanksgiving Day. With the onset of brutally wintry weather in New York, it was a difficult day for Indian people. The streets were deserted, and all the shops were closed. It became a time to get together, for songs, with dishes from home and holiday turkeys for the uprooted families. Vijay empathized with the loneliness of his bachelor friends. He would invite all of them to his house for Thanksgiving dinner. Vijay's family agreed to cook turkey and a vegetarian meal. Friends gathered at Vijay's place, and everyone was excited for the upcoming Christmas vacations. Many talked about visiting India that winter.

Everyone had jobs except Ramesh, but he was the least worried. He had finally saved enough to go back home. He bought gifts for his family and close friends. His parents had written asking him to come home and to prepare for marriage. His parents had lined up five girls, and Ramesh had to choose one that would become his wife. One girl was an engineer, two girls were doctors, and the other two girls were from wealthy families. His parents had sent him photographs of all the girls, and they all looked pretty in the pictures. He brought the photos to Vijay's home one snowy Saturday afternoon.

"Tell me, Vijay, which, girl I should choose?" Ramesh showed pictures of the girls to Vijay. "These two girls are from wealthy families, and their families have big connections. Their parents are ready to give my parents a very hefty dowry. They already have offered five hundred thousand rupees in cash," Ramesh said to his mentor Vijay.

Vijay looked at him in a disdainful way, "The dowry you will get, are you going to bring it here?"

"No," Ramesh replied quickly.

"Marrying a rich girl, who is used to all luxuries of life, will create more problems for you here. They will expect a chauffeur-driven car and maids to help around the home. Can you provide those luxuries? How about the engineer girl? She belongs to the same caste, and as your mother wrote, she is in the same profession as you."

"She is good looking, but my answer is no. I don't want to marry another engineer, because I don't want any competition."

"OK, how about these two doctors?"

"Those two propositions look good. Both are a little on the heavier side, but they could make a lot of money in this country. I could have a Mercedes, a big house, and a large-screen TV."

"You should marry a prospective doctor. You will be a much richer man. You are an easygoing man. If someone gives you a pension of a thousand dollars a month, you will not step out of the house. Just watch TV."

Vijay thought for some time. He remembered the promise he made to Mona before moving to America.

"If I suggest to you a different girl, would you like to meet her in India?"

"Who is she?"

"She is the daughter of a family friend, and I treat her like a younger sister. I will not tell you her name yet, but she is one in million. She is extremely attractive and tall; she suits your height. A little dark-skinned but she comes from a very decent and well-educated family. Her parents have no money, and they cannot afford a big wedding or any dowry," Vijay said.

"Is she a doctor?"

"No, she is not a doctor, nor is she an engineer. She has master's degree in economics. She has a wonderful job, a managerial position at a top company. She is intelligent and has an intense sense of business."

"Her parents are not rich, she is not a doctor, and her family has no dowry to offer me. You still want me to marry her?"

"You may get what you desire, a beautiful and rich girl from India, but remember beauty is skin deep. If your choice is superficial, then why go back home? Marry here. You are going to settle down here. There are beautiful girls in America who are looking for an engineer."

"That's good to know."

Vijay emphasized, "You need a beautiful wife, who could accept a job, wash dishes, do laundry, take care of your children, and take care of you. The kind of woman who is brainwashed by her parents to treat her husband as God, and her salvation in this world comes through serving her husband. You can only find that kind of woman in India. I just want you to meet her, not necessarily marry her. Perhaps you may like her."

"You are saying she is dark-skinned. Then how could she be beautiful?" Ramesh interrupted.

"You are narrow-minded. You are saying all dark-skinned women are not beautiful? Millions of people who come from India, Africa and many other countries are not beautiful?" Vijay was getting angry.

"No, I don't mean they are not beautiful. I meant they

are dark, and I prefer light skin," replied Ramesh sheepishly.

"Sometimes, you astound me. You have a fetish for white skin. Why go to India? Go to Scandinavian countries, anywhere in Europe, or advertise in papers." Vijay was at his wits' end.

Vijay continued, "I have been progressive all my life. In this modern world, I believe both wife and husband are on the same level. It was a love marriage when Rebecca and I got married. We were young. Our marriage had many difficulties, but we grew together and accepted our marriage. Time has changed. You will be marrying a modern, educated woman. It is better that you choose your own destiny, than letting your parents choose for you. The girl I am recommending, from day one, she will walk beside you," Vijay emphasized. "Equally."

"For your sake, I will definitely meet her," said Ramesh.

"Not for my sake, for your own sake. You will be the luckiest man, if she said yes to someone like you." Vijay tried to be cool.

"Now, tell me who she is?" Ramesh asked.

"My father knows the family. They are also of the same caste. Your parents know her family," Vijay replied.

Ramesh went back to India in December 1975 and agreed to meet Mona in India. He called his mother to put Mona on the list, as one more suitable bride.

Chapter 19
Marriage Proposal
1975
Kanpur

Mona was working as an account manager in Self-Insurance Company for the last three years. She was posted in her hometown, Kanpur. Vijay knew Ramesh was coming to India to get married, so Vijay called his father Rahul to suggest that Ramesh and Mona should meet.

Vijay's family lived in the upstairs apartment, and Krishna's family lived one floor below them. Both families spent time together. One day, late in the evening, Rahul invited Krishna and Usha up to his apartment.

"We saw each other two hours ago, and you are calling us again now. Is everything okay?" Krishna asked.

"Everything is fine. I wanted to talk with both of you on a serious matter, and not in front of your children. Let us go and sit in the living room," Rahul replied.

Rahul and his wife Kirti sat on one sofa. On the other sofa, Krishna and Usha sat together.

"Krishna, do you know Vijay's cousin, Ramesh?" Rahul asked.

"Yes, I remember him. He is the son of your distant cousin, the retired civil surgeon, Dr. Charan and his wife Nishi."

Rahul raised his hand a little to stop Krishna from saying any more. "We all are of the same caste. Ramesh's father called me. His son has come back to India from America, with the intention to get married and bring his bride with him to America. They have shown interest in Mona. Ramesh is an engineer and has a green card, and I know the family very well," Rahul said.

"But?" Krishna said.

"Why don't you ask Mona if she would like to meet him? Vijay called me from America and recommended we set up a time for the two to meet. It could be a good match for Mona, as she always had a dream to live in America," Rahul said.

"I know we all are of the same caste, and your cousin is a retired civil surgeon. But I have heard many things about your cousin Charan. Everyone knows he has an extraordinarily strong temper. He mistreats his wife. I do not know how Mona will adjust in that family," Krishna said.

Rahul said, "He was a tyrant. He mellowed down after his retirement. Most of his time he spends in temple and in his charitable dispensary. Why are you being worried? Mona will not live with them. She will be living with her husband in New York. I know Ramesh from childhood. He is a nice boy, and I am confident he will treat Mona well."

Usha and Krishna looked at each other and then Krishna said, "You must make it clear to them that I cannot afford cash or a big dowry. It needs to be a simple marriage."

"Oh, don't worry. I will make it clear to them," Rahul said.

Parents of both families consented. As the next step, Mona and Ramesh were to meet each other. The meeting was arranged for the following day. Ramesh would pick Mona up from her office and take her out for coffee.

Mona knew Ramesh from childhood. She had seen him several times at local community functions. He never showed interest in her. Mona was told by her friends Ramesh avoided dark-skinned women. She could not understand why he was showing interest in her now. He knew she had dark skin, so Mona wondered whether Ramesh had changed after living in America.

She had a master's degree in economics and a prestigious managerial job. She had a strong command over the English language and spoke in a fluent, soft tone. She earned more than many suitable grooms. However, in her community, men were still considered superior to women. Mona was not ready to compromise to the self-assumed superiority of men, and she never thought she should be considered inferior to any man.

The main reason that prospective grooms rejected her was that her father had no money to pay a dowry. The first demand from a groom's parents was the amount of cash her father could offer. At age twenty-eight, Mona learned to keep her hopes for marriage realistic.

Mona's routine was to get up before sunrise, heat water on the stove, make chai for everyone, and prepare breakfast and lunch for the family. Both of Mona's parents would leave home early in the morning to open the factory.

Mona looked after her sister Binny, who was five years younger. Every morning Mona had to shout ten times to wake her up. "Binny, wake up. It is time to go to work," Mona would call from the kitchen.

"Please, Didi, give me five more minutes. I will be up," Binny would say.

"Hurry. You will be late again," Mona called out to Binny.

Mona prepared a breakfast for her and packed lunch to take to work. Mona was like a mother to Binny. She took on the burden of her younger sister in addition to her job and her chores at home.

Binny was not good looking. She was dark, chubby, and short. After her graduation, with great difficulty, she found a job as a filing clerk at Elgin Cloth Mill. The family loved Binny for her simplicity and good nature. She was an excellent cook.

After work, Mona would help her mother in the kitchen to make dinner and then clean the dishes. When all the chores were done, she would try to relax in bed with her eyes closed and dream of a better life. Her exhaustion would overtake her dreams, and she would be fast asleep in few seconds.

Chapter 20
The Meeting
1975
Kanpur

Mona's office was on Birhana Road, the business hub of Kanpur. Self-Insurance Company had leased two floors in the Kanodia building. The company gave Mona two rooms on one floor, one small and the other, adjacent a long hallway. She had a staff of eleven clerks, including one head clerk, one secretary and a person who ran errands and made tea. The staff and the head clerk were sitting in the spacious room. Each table was two feet apart and three feet behind the other table, like in a school classroom. Mona sat in a small room and the secretary occupied a corner, with the typewriter in front of her.

Ramesh came to her office at noon. He was late by two hours because he had been busy planning a trip to Lucknow City the following day to meet two other prospective brides. He wandered through the hall until he found Mona's office. He tapped on the door and stepped in front of her.

"Hello, I am Ramesh."

Mona was startled for a few seconds. She was reading a report with her head down. She raised her head, *Oh my God, who is this handsome man?* she murmured silently.

Ramesh, she remembered, was a tall, lean person. Seeing him after years, he looked different. He was always good looking, but he had gained weight in last few years and looked more handsome with his long sideburns. He was wearing a red silk shirt and black pants. The top button of his shirt was open showing his hairy chest, and over the shirt he wore a cream raw silk coat. For a moment she thought him to be a movie star.

"I am sorry that I'm late. If you are not busy, can we go for coffee or for lunch?" Ramesh said.

"I don't drink coffee, but we can go out for tea. My name is Mona. Hello." She stretched out her hand.

He was impressed with her reply and the confidence she showed. They both were standing awkwardly. He was in front of her desk, and she faced him. Both were aware that other employees in the office were watching them and waiting for their next move.

Suddenly both said at the same time, "Let us go out."

He walked outside the office and waited for her.

She arranged her sari quickly, opened her purse, took out a small mirror, and dabbed at her face with a small handkerchief. She gently bit her lips and licked them with her tongue to bring moistness and redness. Lipstick was forbidden in her family. Her grandmother's strict rule was, "Unmarried girls are not supposed to put on lipstick." She knew the other employees in the office were looking at her. Shyly she put her face down and walked out.

Outside her office she remembered that in Kanpur, there were no good coffee or tea shops nearby where they could sit and talk without being watched by others. One out-of-the way place was Mambo Restaurant on the Mall Road, which was quite far from her office.

The city was full of people she knew. Passersby looked at Mona with amusement. In one hour, the whole city would know that Krishna's unmarried daughter was roaming the city with a man. That was an invitation for gossip and rumors within her community.

Ramesh was also thinking of the same problem. The city had no taxi service. He had a desire to sit near the banks of the Ganges River and talk with her, but there was not a small café nearby where they could own a shred of privacy.

A cycle rickshaw was their only choice. They found one, and Mona told the rickshaw puller the directions to Mambo Restaurant. The lunch hour was busy with people going to and fro. To avoid the curious looks of passersby, she asked the rickshaw driver to pull down the hood over them. Mona lowered her gaze but managed to catch a glimpse of her handsome companion who was looking at her.

Chapter 21
Mambo Restaurant
1975
Kanpur

Mambo Restaurant was famous for North Indian dishes and had a room for the customers who liked a little privacy. The waiter took them upstairs where tables for two were arranged in small cubicles.

"We are already late. Let us have lunch and tea afterwards. What will you have?" said Ramesh.

She ordered one paratha stuffed with potatoes and yogurt on the side.

"That's all? What about chicken curry?" he asked.

"You forget, I do not take any kind of meat. I am a vegetarian," Mona said.

Mona knew in her heart that she had tasted meat and sipped whiskey with Coca-Cola three years back when she was in Bombay. Nobody knew her secret. After she came back to Kanpur, she remained a vegetarian and had not touched meat or alcohol since Bombay.

"Oh, ho, I didn't know." There was a pause for a second. "Nobody mentioned that to me. But never mind. My mom and dad are vegetarians. Order something else, another dish with no meat," he suggested.

She was not used to taking a big lunch in the afternoon. Her lunch and breakfast together, was one meal before coming to the office. That morning she had two thick pieces of

Indian bread and last night's leftovers, with a glass of milk. She always loved milk. In the afternoon she took another glass of milk with two small, salted biscuits.

He ordered two parathas, one plate of chicken curry and one plate of mutton kabobs. He was not contented and ordered one more paratha. To finish his plate, he ordered one plate of mutton biryani. Mona thought, *If I marry this man, I must cook a big meal every day. Maybe two.*

She was relaxed after lunch. They talked of trivial things, about the city, the transport system, about food and the chilly weather.

"The transport system in Kanpur is lousy. There are no taxi stands," Ramesh said.

"You are right, there are hardly any taxis in the city. Most of the people use the cycle rickshaws or ride on bicycles," Mona said.

"You know how to ride a bicycle?"

"Yes, of course, I know how to ride a bicycle. I come to work every day, riding my bicycle," Mona said.

"Well, I don't know how to ride a bicycle. But in New York City, you do not go to work riding bicycles. You use the subway train," Ramesh said.

He asked her which college she graduated from and about her job.

"Where did you study?" Ramesh said.

"I studied in different cities at different convents, wherever my dad was posted. I did my college studies, undergraduate, and master's at the Christ Church College. For the last three years, I have been working in the Self-Insurance Company, as a manager. What about you?" Mona said.

"I did my intermediate studies at Kanpur, and engineering from Banaras University, and after working for four years in Calcutta, I went to America. For the last three years, I am working as mechanical engineer in a lock manufacturing company," Ramesh said.

"What sorts of locks?" Mona inquired.

"All types of locks. Small locks for travelling, locks for houses and even locks in the banks, where you deposit money or jewelry," Ramesh replied.

Mona could sense that he and his parents had already inquired about her and her family and their poor financial condition. This formal meeting was for him to approve or reject her. He thought she was cute, and she found him handsome, calm, and gentle.

"You know I like you," Ramesh said. Mona gave him a sweet, shy smile.

Mona became a little more interested to inquire about his life in America, about his friends and how he spent his evenings. Some relatives and friends had told her stories of women in America. Mona was interested to know how women cope with everyday life there.

"Do you know any local women there? I mean, do you have a girlfriend?" Mona said.

He was quiet for a second. "Oh, yes, a few of them," Ramesh replied.

"How are they? I hear American women are very friendly, and they work awfully hard."

Ramesh could not fully comprehend the question. "Oh yes, they are friendly. Girlfriend means you are in for fun and everything," Ramesh said.

"I see."

"I had fun with dozens of women. It is not difficult to get friendly with a girl over there. We are men, we have strong urges," he bragged.

"You think only men have all the urges and women don't?" She murmured silently.

Ramesh looked at Mona. She dropped the subject.

"When are you going back?" asked Mona.

He was honest with her, "I am going tomorrow to another town, to interview two prospective brides. I will make my final decision after coming back from there, about which girl I choose to marry. The marriage will take place within two weeks before I return to New York. Within a month, I will send plane tickets for my future bride to fly to New York."

They parted in a very cordial manner. She went back to her office. The next day, Ramesh was off to interview two suitable doctor brides.

Mona's chances of marrying him were bleak. Both other prospective brides were doctors. A doctor wife from India was considered a prized catch and a money-making machine in America.

Over the next few days, Mona waited for Ramesh to take a final decision. She was in great suspense, and the uncertainty was scattered across her face. If he asked, Mona had no choice but to say yes. She was getting old, her parents were worried, and they had her younger sister to arrange a marriage for. Very soon, Mona was going be cast aside in favor of Binny.

Mona thought, *Ramesh has come from America, and I have a great desire to go there, and do my Ph.D., in economics. My plan is to work in America and make a lot of money there to help my parents. I do not want to miss this chance. I will have to marry some man if he was of the same caste. I finally met Ramesh after eight years. I like him; he was pleasant, well educated, and belonged to a well-known family of the community.*

Ramesh's parents had already done the legwork through mutual friends. Inquiries were made, about Mona's family including their wealth, her family connections, her education, and what sort of job she had in the Self-Insurance

Company. However, the most important requirement was that she had to be a virgin. If not, Mona would be rejected as a suitable bride for Ramesh.

Mona thought about the strangeness of the man's world. They want to be first in everything, first in climbing the mountains, first to cross the river, first to sleep with a virgin. Women for ages had been in hopeless situations. They were killed before the ceremony for not being virgin, or being a virgin, they were often sacrificed to God, for a favor.

Chapter 22
Marriage
1975
Kanpur

One of Mona's family friends vouched for her of being pure and untouched. Virginity was highly prized for the groom's family and if the bride is not a virgin, both families could lose their reputation in the community. The word 'virgin' haunted Mona. She would shiver if anybody brought up the topic. Mona had lost her virginity ten years back. But before the marriage through the secret surgery by Dr. Kapur, she would be a suitable bride and a virgin.

Ramesh's hope of marrying a doctor was shattered. Both doctors were from rich families and were leading comfortable lifestyles: a chauffeur -driven car, maids and other servants, and fat shopping allowances. Both women rejected him. His pride was wounded. He had no other girl to interview for marriage, and only fourteen days left before going back to the United States. He had to decide. Either he was going back without a bride, or he was to say yes to marrying Mona.

Mona impressed him. She could be an asset to him back in America. She had the confidence and determination to persevere in a new country. His main objection was her dark complexion. For him, a beautiful woman meant a fair-skinned person. His family members liked Mona. They were surprised at his logic of fair color. No member of his family was ready to agree with his thinking. Time was growing short for his departure, and there were no other girls to interview. In the end, he agreed to marry Mona.

A message was conveyed to Mona's family that Ramesh said 'yes.' He never came to propose to her; no rings were exchanged. The marriage proposal was unexpected, but welcome.

Mona's family was full of joy. They all feared Mona would remain a spinster. She was twenty-eight, and she had been rejected, by many suitors. Behind her back, Mona was called an old lady. Her community was happy and jealous about her marriage to Ramesh. She was going to America. Her relatives said she must have done some virtuous deeds in her previous life. God must be pleased with her that she had found a handsome husband, and he was taking her to America. Everyone knew her biggest desire was to go to America and do her Ph.D. in economics there.

Both families did not let Mona or Ramesh spend any time together. To Mona, it seemed she was marrying a stranger. There was no love, no friendship, and no walking in the park hand in hand.

Sarla Devi said, "Krishna and Usha did not see each other before marriage. You are both from the same caste and raised in the same community. You have your whole life ahead to know each other."

Ramesh and Mona met a few times during the wedding festivities, but not alone. There were always family members around. The whole family was busy in organizing the wedding. Mona approached her mother.

"Mom, I want to have another meeting with Ramesh."

"Why do you want to have another meeting when you are already engaged, and you see each other almost every day at different wedding ceremonies?" Usha replied.

"Mom, I want to know more about Ramesh. Can't I have another meeting with him before the marriage?" Mona asked.

"I will talk with your grandmother. She is the final authority and remember to be gentle when you ask. I don't want her to get angry."

Mona remembered three years back her disastrous meeting with her grandmother when she begged for approval to marry Karan.

Sarla Devi was sitting on the mattress in her room. She was reading the holy book Bhagvad Gita. Usha had already talked with her. She knew what Mona wanted to ask her.

Sarla Devi looked up and arranged her glasses and said, "Why do you need to have another meeting?"

"I want to know more about him, Dadi Ma. Just one meeting, please," Mona replied.

"In a one-hour meeting, what more do you expect to find out? Which side of the bed he sleeps on, or you will tell him that you always sleep on your stomach?" Sarla Devi said.

"Dadi Ma, please," Mona requested.

"Look, Mona Beti, we believe in family. Ramesh comes from a good family, and they are not asking us for any cash or dowry. He belongs to the same caste and community. What more do you want to know? I know Ramesh's mother Nishi. We meet often in the temple, and she is a gem of a woman. You are lucky to have such a good mother-in-law. I also know Ramesh's father well. His abusive tongue and insulting nature are famous in the community. He should be thrown in the River Ganges. Anyway, I will send a message to arrange the meeting," Sarla Devi said.

The message was sent to Ramesh's mother.

Ramesh's mother Nishi liked Mona, and she was not ready to lose an educated and intelligent daughter-in-law. She knew Ramesh's preferences well. Nishi thought, if they meet, the question of skin color may arise, and Ramesh may say something offensive to Mona. Nishi was hesitant and made an excuse.

"We all are busy in wedding preparations, and there is no time left to have another meeting. They can talk during the religious ceremonies," Nishi said.

Ramesh had to depart in ten days. Mona and he met a couple of times for religious ceremonies, but they could never talk alone. They met at city hall for the official registration of their marriage. The marriage certificate was necessary for Mona to get a passport and visa to move to the U.S.

City hall was crowded. They were sitting on benches, waiting for their turn. Their parents were busy with the registrar's clerk. Mona was itching to ask Ramesh a question. She caught his attention by coughing. Whispering, she asked, "I know I am not what you normally find beautiful. How come you agreed to marry me?"

He was taken aback. He did not know how to answer her. He looked straight towards his mother who was talking to the clerk. Nishi judged something was not right. She looked over to where they were sitting.

He replied, "I was looking for the inner qualities in a woman, and you have all of them."

"And what are those inner qualities you found in me?" she asked innocently.

Before he could have been caught in an impasse, he saw his mother standing there. Ramesh's mother interrupted their conversation. "Let us stand in the line. Your turn will come soon."

Mona was now going to devote her body and soul to an unknown person for the rest of her life. In return, she would have the opportunity to move to America.

Vedic ceremonies were performed two days after registering their marriage in the court, when the astrologer had matched their horoscopes. Invitation cards for their wedding could not be printed as there was not enough time. All the relatives and guests were informed by phone, and Mona's family members travelled to different towns to invite relatives personally.

No one was there to help Mona and her parents. Usha's brothers refused to help their sister and did not come to the wedding. They had a long-lasting disdain for Krishna. Amar was posted in America during this time. Krishna had only two priorities, his factory which was defunct, and his religious rituals. He was sad that his first daughter was leaving the country. Instead of being helpful, he was depressed, aloof, and participated minimally.

Mona's mother Usha rose to the occasion. Both mother and daughter together made the arrangements. Relatives and friends joined to help. They made tasty salty snacks and sweets and helped Mona prepare the stage for the ceremonies. The decoration was simple, with garlands of marigolds and light silk cloths hung with small lights, and the party procession was shortened. Mona put all her effort into planning the food; it had to be excellent. The cooking on the wedding day was handled by a popular caterer Ram Saran Halwai, She bargained hard for the best food at the best price.

Mona had some small savings that she spent on wedding gifts and for all the important wedding ceremonies that had to be performed. Every expense was calculated down to each paisa. She supervised and helped everybody during the wedding.

The ceremony was performed in the family temple, with Ramesh leading Mona four times around the fire, and Mona leading Ramesh three times around the fire. They pledged in front of the holy flame to be together despite adversities. Mona was wearing a red sari; her arms were full of red bangles, and artificial sparkling jewelry. She looked gorgeous.

The wedding was successful, under the circumstances.

One thing bothered her until the last day of the wedding. She was not a virgin. After her rape, Dr. Kapur had promised her that she could make Mona a virgin again for her wedding night, and Dr. Kapur followed through on her promise. She could not lay her cards out in front of Ramesh and was unsure of his being open-minded enough to understand what happened to her. She could not count on his empathy to accept her not being a virgin.

Chapter 23
Lights Off - Lights On
1975
Kanpur

Late in the evening, Nishi took Mona to Ramesh's room. The bed was adorned with flowers on the white sheet, the symbol of purity. The sweet fragrance of gardenia surrounded them. Mona knew she was supposed to act like a novice. At night, she insisted on turning off the lights, though he was keen to keep them on.

"Please don't turn the lights on," Mona said, turning the lights off.

"But, darling, I can't see in the darkness, and I want to see you in the light." Ramesh turned the lights on.

"You have your whole life to see me in the light." Mona turned the lights off again.

"But, darling, I want to." Before Ramesh could utter more, she put her finger over his lips and Ramesh became speechless.

He found it difficult to be intimate with her. He tried and made a big cry, and he was done. Later he made a few more attempts, and it was more difficult and painful for him to make a union.

Mona slept longer the next morning but awoke to the noises around her. She sat up immediately; Ramesh was nowhere to be found. Nishi was standing near her bed, surrounded by other ladies who were whispering to each other. Mona's face turned white. She did not know what was happening. Her mother-in-law led her to the bathroom for a change of clothes.

When Mona came out of the bathroom, Nishi and the other ladies were not there. Last night's white bed sheet was gone; a new sheet was in its place. She looked from the window and saw the group of ladies giggling and laughing, as they held last night's bed sheet in their hands. Ramesh's family was rejoicing, pointing to something on the sheet. She looked from the window and could see stains on the sheet.

Mona realized that Ramesh's family was rejoicing at the stains of blood on the sheet. She was wondering where the blood came from.

Chapter 24
Honeymoon
1975
Mussoorie

Mona and Ramesh went to the Mussoorie Hills Station Resort, in the mountains, for their honeymoon. Ramesh's parents tagged along with the honeymooners, and Ramesh was irritated at them for coming. He knew they would not leave the newly married couple alone. A day later, he quietly checked out of the hotel without telling his parents. He took a room in another hotel and escaped with Mona. It took his parents two days to find out where they were.

Mona was having a wonderful time. They went to see waterfalls and had a picnic in the woods. Ramesh would kiss her at every chance, hug her, open her blouse, and play with her breasts. She became bold and encouraged him. Ramesh was hesitant to do anything beyond kissing. She was confused that he was not doing more.

The night before they were to return from the honeymoon, Mona was gentle, and encouraged him to perform. He tried, and it was very painful for him. He was leaving for America in two days. They both went for a walk in the morning.

"Darling, let us sit down on this bench. I have to tell you something," he said.

Mona trembled, and she was frightened. Had he discovered what she was dreading--that she was not a virgin?

She turned her face to the other side and waited for the bomb to drop. She was not sure whether to confess or keep quiet.

"First of all, I don't have a job waiting for me when I go back."

"How will we survive?" Mona said.

"You do not have to worry. I will find something by the time you come. I will have a job." He was looking at her. "You are well-qualified. In America, women find jobs sooner than men," Ramesh said.

"I did not know," Mona said.

"Darling, I am sorry I didn't perform well. You see, I never slept with any woman before. It was my first time, and my foreskin had always been tight. I did not know for a man it could be equally painful during the first time. My skin is torn, and it is painful. I am swollen from that night. After landing in New York, I will go to a doctor," he said.

She looked concerned, "It is fine with me. I can wait. Why don't you see a doctor here? You still have two days before you go back."

"No, no, if anybody comes to know, it will be an insult for the whole family," he replied.

"It could get worse. It can get septic. It is better to see a doctor here," she said.

"No, no, you forget my father is a doctor," he interrupted.

"Alright, if you like to be treated by your father, it is fine with me," she said.

"You do not understand. My father is a doctor, and I watched him dressing wounds of many patients. I know how to take care of myself. The day I reach America, I will go straight to a doctor. Do not worry. No one in the world needs to know," he said.

This confession astonished her. His big talk of going to bed with lots of women in America was false. She came to know later that most men tell exaggerated stories of their jobs and encounters with women.

She grinned whenever she remembered. Poor Ramesh, the stains on the sheet exhibited his blood. She broke a thirty three-year old virgin.

Chapter 25
Ramesh Back In The U.S.A.
1976
New York

There was a heavy snowfall in January of 1976 in New York City. After returning to America, Ramesh went to a hospital for surgery one gray morning and, wet and cold, trudged through the snow to get back home. He got his tight foreskin removed. For years he was shy about his own body and felt inadequate. He was surprised after the surgery that he felt comfortable and relieved. He was regaining strength, and he longed for Mona's warm passion.

He called Mona every day after his return. She was his newfound love. He dreamt every night of her voluptuous body, her smooth skin and how closely he wrapped his legs around her. He was thankful to his cousin Vijay, who was right; Mona was truly one in a million. It was a wise decision to marry her. He praised Mona's intelligence to all his friends.

Soon after his return to America, Ramesh found a job to work in a factory. The company manufactured lingerie for women. The company had two manufacturing plants, one in Long Island and the other in Paterson, New Jersey. He was offered a job in Long Island to supervise the maintenance of the machinery. Though he never liked maintenance work, the salary was good. He had few choices, so he accepted the offer.

Two weeks after getting the job, Ramesh moved out of Vijay's place and rented a one-bedroom apartment in a nearby building.

Ramesh met Teresa one night at the company's annual Winter party at the Regent Club. His boss thought the party would be the best opportunity for Ramesh to meet the owners and the staff of both branch offices. Teresa had worked for two years at the New Jersey factory as a personnel manager. She lived in New Jersey across the Hudson River, near George Washington Bridge.

The Regent Club party was in the evening, at Mutton Town, Long Island. Ramesh had driven his old Dodge Duster, and he was proud to arrive at the party in his own car. In the parking lot, he became apprehensive after seeing expensive Mercedes, BMWs and Jaguars parked at the venue. He circled twice around the block and parked his car far away from the club.

He was standing in the hall with his boss when Teresa walked in with a companion. Ramesh looked at her and thought an angel had come down to earth.

She was a beautiful woman. She was tall, blond-haired, with a supple body, thin waist, rounded hips, round face, and big crystal blue eyes. She was wearing a strappy backless dress, disregarding the nippy Winter chill. His eyes widened. He marveled at her bare back in the dim light. They were introduced by his boss, who quickly stepped aside to meet other guests. Her companion joined another conversation, and both Ramesh and Teresa were alone on the steps. Captivated by her beauty, he could not take his eyes off her.

He was mesmerized, and she felt awkward at his staring.

"Is there something wrong with my dress?" She asked, avoiding his eyes.

He suddenly realized what he was doing. He apologized. "Oh, no, I am sorry. You are a beautiful girl, and I could not take my eyes off you. I thought you were a movie star."

"Thank you, but I am a woman, not a girl," Teresa replied.

"I am sorry," said Ramesh.

They were standing on the steps, facing one another. They were of the same height, but Teresa looked taller with high heels.

"I am Teresa. And you?"

"My name is Ramesh. I am an engineer, who joined the company recently," Ramesh said.

They shook hands.

"Can I get you a drink?" he asked.

She thought for a second. "Chardonnay would be nice."

"Please stay here. I will bring our drinks in a minute," Ramesh said.

He knew a little about scotch but had no knowledge of wine. He insisted on chardonnay and spelled it out for the bartender. When the bartender showed him the label on the bottle, Ramesh was satisfied. By the time he came back to the steps, Teresa was no longer there. He found her among a group of young men and women. He stood near the bar and placed the wine glass on the counter. Ramesh saw her walking towards him.

"Where is my wine? I have been waiting for it," she smiled.

Her smile excited him, and he blushed apologetically. "I am sorry it took me a little time to get your wine. Frankly, I do not have any clue about wine. I did not know whether chardonnay was red or white wine."

She laughed, "I am glad you are honest with me. Do you say, 'I am sorry' every few seconds?"

He thought about how beautiful her teeth were. She could be a model for a toothpaste company. Teresa took him around the party and introduced him to everyone. Ramesh knew a lot about cars and impressed those he met with his knowledge of different makes and models. Ramesh and Teresa remained together until the party was over.

Ramesh was enamored by Teresa's beauty and intoxicated after having a few drinks. He did not remember how he managed to reach home. On Monday, his boss told him that everyone was impressed with his profound sense of humor and exhaustive knowledge of automobiles.

They all liked him, and one of Teresa's friends invited him to another party the following Saturday. Ramesh was thrilled. During the next few days, he dreamt about Teresa.

The party was on Saturday. By Thursday, he was on edge about whether to call Teresa. He was hesitant and worried that she had forgotten him.

The same afternoon he was summoned by his boss. "This call is for you," his boss said.

"For me?" Ramesh asked.

"Pick up the phone. I have a dentist appointment and will be out of the office for two hours." His boss walked out.

"Hello, Ramesh," a smooth, romantic voice said at the other end.

He could not believe his ears. He was longing to hear the sweetest voice on earth.

"Hello Teresa, how are you? I am sorry I didn't say bye to you when I left the party," he said.

She started laughing over the phone, "You don't remember what happened when you left the party?"

"Not much," he said apologetically.

She was laughing. "You said bye to everybody. You shook my hand several times and wouldn't let it go, and everybody was laughing."

"I am sorry," he said in faint voice.

"You don't have to be sorry for everything. We all had an enjoyable time. I called to ask you, if it is OK with you, I can pick you up this Saturday. I will be passing through Queens to go to Long Island," she said.

"Actually, I was thinking of asking you if I could pick you up," he replied.

"It will be inconvenient for you to first drive to New Jersey to pick me up, and later drive me back home. You are on my way to Long Island, so I think it would be better if I pick you up," she said.

"Are you comfortable driving alone at night?" he asked.

"You don't have to worry. My building is in safe area," she replied.

"I understand, but driving alone in the night?"

"Ramesh, this is America, not India," she replied forcefully.

They decided she would pick him up around six-thirty on Saturday evening. They exchanged their telephone numbers, and he gave her his address. He asked her to pick him up at the corner of Franklin and Main Street.

Ramesh had vast knowledge of Indian history, religion, and yoga. In this era, young people in America were curious to learn about India, meditation, ashrams and trekking the Himalayas. Ramesh knew there would be lot of questions about India at the party.

Teresa picked Ramesh up at the corner. The party went very well, and he impressed all her friends. He was invited to a few more parties, and some of Teresa's girlfriends invited him to their places to learn more about Indian culture.

Teresa was very jealous of the invitations her friends gave. She guarded Ramesh closely for the next few parties until they became good friends. Teresa was curious about India, especially food and Transcendental Meditation. Teresa and Ramesh started meeting three to four times a week.

She insisted one evening that Ramesh have coffee at her apartment. When he knocked on the door and came inside, he was astounded to see a spacious living room, but decorated with garish paintings and artifacts that lacked symmetry or order. Some paintings were lying in a corner and a pile of miscellaneous items were scattered on the floor. Her kitchen smelled, the dirty plates were in the sink, and she had not taken out the trash for a few days. It surprised him that such a beautiful and meticulously dressed woman would have a house in shambles.

"I am sorry, my maid has not come this week, and the apartment is a mess. The maid takes care of all the cleaning," Teresa said.

She offered him a cup of coffee and sat on the other sofa. She removed her shoes and put her feet on the edge of the table. He saw her feet in nylon stockings, and they were very tiny in comparison to her height. Her legs were long, and her thighs were round. He never thought it would be so difficult to drink a cup of coffee.

He was nervous and wanted to take her in his arms. He got up and walked across the apartment to see the view of the Hudson River. Her apartment was on the thirtieth floor and the balcony faced New York City. In the evening, the reflection of tall buildings in the river was spectacular. He was engrossed staring at the Manhattan skyline and the surrounding buildings lit up as if by magic.

Teresa joined him on the balcony. She came close to him; her shoulder was rubbing against his. Though the weather was cool, he was sweating. There was a sweet aroma coming from her body that made him want to be even closer to her. His face turned red, and his body was trembling.

"Is everything all right, Ramesh? You are shaking," she asked.

"I am fine. The coffee made me feel hot. What brand it is?"

"Madras coffee," she said with a serious face. After few moments, she smiled.

He looked at her.

"I am just kidding. This is a Colombian brand."

They were silent for a minute.

"I must go now. Tomorrow is a busy day for me," he said.

Her face showed that she did not like the idea of him leaving so soon. But she smiled and walked with him, "Oh, yes, I too have a busy day tomorrow."

They walked to the door together. He turned and looked at her for a moment and pecked her gently on her cheek. She kissed him back. For the first time in his life, a blonde angel pressed her lips to his cheek, slipping her tongue to the corner end of his lips. He felt delirious and reached home dreaming of the kiss.

While he changed into his pajamas, he remembered he was married. Once a week he called Mona, and he always ended the conversation with the words, "I love you." He did not call Mona that night.

His sleep was turbulent. He dreamt of a White Fairy trying to save him from a Dark Creature who was putting her tentacles around him. The next morning, he was fine, and he realized his dream to meet a fair-skinned woman had finally come true. He did not dare to lose the opportunity. He decided not to tell Teresa he was married, and he did not tell Vijay about Teresa. Ramesh did not call Mona that week.

Chapter 26
White Goddess
1976
New Jersey

February of 1976 was very cold. Ramesh and Teresa went to see a movie on a Friday evening. The theater was walking distance from her apartment. The sky was cloudy and dark. By the time they left her apartment, it started drizzling. After the movie, it was pouring; they could not find any taxi nearby. The sidewalk was slippery, and their umbrellas were of no help. They ran holding hands and reached Teresa's apartment totally drenched. Ramesh tried to leave when she opened her apartment door.

"Alright, Teresa, I will call you in the morning." Ramesh stood in front of her ready to bestow a parting kiss.

"I don't want you to go home in this weather. You will catch a cold. Come inside and I will make hot chocolate for you," Teresa said.

Her apartment was warm. They removed their heavy raincoats and she put them in the bathroom to dry. He dropped his wet jacket on the floor and stood near the fireplace rubbing his hands together and trying to keep warm. He was wet from top to bottom. Rainwater was dripping from his hair. She gave him a white towel to dry off and then went to her bedroom to change. Peeling away her wet clothes she wrapped a robe around her body and came out to the living room. He was gently wiping rainwater from his face.

She looked at him. "Why don't you sit down on the chair while you dry your face?"

"I am wet. I will spoil your velvet cushion," he said.

"It does not matter," she said.

He did not move.

She watched him for few more seconds and then said loudly, "Ramesh, sit."

He sat down on the edge of the chair.

She watched Ramesh dry himself in slow motion. Teresa lost her patience, "Let me dry your hair and face." She took the towel from him, putting her legs around his knees. She cleaned his wet face and bent over him to rub the towel over his wet hair.

Ramesh inhaled her strong aroma that pierced his nostrils. Her breasts were revealed from her open gown. He could not bear it any longer. His hands moved to hold her waist, and her arms went around his neck. He stood up and both bodies became intertwined.

The next morning, he woke up to the sound of the telephone ringing. Teresa was calling on the phone.

"Hi. Did I wake you up?" she said.

"It is fine; I have to get up anyway. What time is it?" he asked.

"It's eleven-thirty," she said.

"Oh my God!" By that time, he realized he was sleeping in Teresa's huge bed. He looked around and was surprised his clothes were not there.

"What happened?" she asked.

"Nothing, I just realized it is already eleven-thirty and I am totally naked." He sat down in her bed looking at his body. "I think I should be off."

"Don't leave. I will be back by twelve-thirty. Wait for me, I will bring hamburgers, and we can have lunch together," Teresa said.

"But where are my clothes?" Ramesh looked around.

"I have given all your clothes to the laundry at the corner. I will pick them up on my way back. Go to the next bedroom, open the closet and take out one of the robes," Teresa said.

Ramesh put the phone down, and he reflected on what had happened last night. He did not care if her house was in a mess or her bed was not made.

Teresa's bedroom was huge, and her bed was even larger than a king-sized bed. It looked like a big divan. His eyes moved from one end of the wall to the other. She had large paintings on the walls with nude figures of beautiful women, their faces disguised with veils or masks. The wall over the divan had thick hooks attached to it. One side wall was a full-size closet from one end to the other end. On the ceiling, he saw round mirrors in a hexagonal pattern. Ramesh was intrigued by the setup of the room.

He smelled her pillows and found traces of last night's perfume. The blood rushed in his body. He went to her bathroom, and he could not believe his eyes.

Teresa's bathroom was three-fourths the size of his present apartment. Expensive black marbled tiles covered the floor. On the walls were frescos of women, their faces masked, their beautiful bodies playing with water in a pool. One end of the bathroom held a big Jacuzzi, and on the other end, a full-size mirror. Next to the mirror was a bathtub and a tiled shower,

Ramesh looked at his naked body in the mirror and flexed his muscles. He was a handsome man, athletic and fair with thick hair and a broad forehead. He was lean and exercised to remain trim.

Ramesh put toothpaste on his finger and rubbed it on his teeth and gums to refresh his breath.

He went to the next room. In contrast to her bedroom, it did not have any decorative pieces, but it was organized. He opened the wardrobe, and it was full of men and women's robes in varied sizes. He took out a brown robe and tried to cover his naked body. The robe was large for him, so he tried another that fit him well.

He peeped through the living room window. The rain had stopped. The sky was not dark, and the clouds were thin, though no sun was out. He could see snow on trees, and snow-covered leaves on the ground. It was a beautiful sight.

Ramesh walked back into Teresa's bedroom and took out a book from the corner rack. The book was full of explicit sex acts and positions, and it gave instructions on how to manipulate each other and enhance desire. He looked at another book, and he was wonderstruck. The book was about gadgets and how to use them to enhance the pleasure of sex.

He heard the noise of the elevator stopping on the thirtieth floor. He hurriedly put the books back and walked out of Teresa's bedroom.

Ramesh sat down on the sofa. The nude poses of sex acts brought his thoughts back to Mona. A few months ago, he was the happiest man on earth. Mona had swept him off his feet. Mona was the first woman who gave him assurance and love. She did not laugh that he could not perform. Ramesh could not consummate marriage with Mona then, but he knew she was waiting patiently for him to send her a plane ticket now.

His thoughts went back to Teresa. He had a renewed sense of confidence. He should have waited for one more year before marrying and taken Teresa back home. She was a white, beautiful trophy. Everyone would have asked, *Where did you find this Goddess?*

He did not know which direction to take. Every day, he was growing closer to Teresa. He had forgotten the face of Mona, and whenever he tried to remember her, his mind would replace her with Teresa's face. He was in a dilemma.

He heard a noise at the door and looked up. Teresa was smiling with her bright face. As her blue eyes looked straight towards him, he suddenly forgot Mona and opened his arms.

They both were hungry. She slowly opened his robe, and he undressed her, garment by garment.

"Let's eat, I am starving," she said.

Chapter 27
Indulgence
1976
New Jersey

Soon after Ramesh met Teresa, he learned that the maintenance engineer of the New Jersey plant was retiring. Ramesh applied for that position and with the help of Teresa, he was transferred to the Paterson plant. He lived in Queens and drove forty-five miles each way to work. On the way home after work, he would stop by Teresa's place, and they would spend evenings together.

"Ramesh, why don't you just move to New Jersey? That way we can spend more time together," Teresa said.

"Let us leave it as is for the time being. Most evenings I spend with you already," Ramesh said.

Teresa, the daughter of wealthy parents, was a wild child. She became aware of her body when she was thirteen, and a few of her friends encouraged her to try drugs at an early age. She never learned to be tidy, and she never learned to cook or clean for herself. She lived on junk food, and her meals were often frozen dinners. Even making breakfast was a chore she avoided.

At heart, she was a passionate woman, who rebelled against all the norms of society. She was particular about her body hygiene and appearance. She would go to the gym daily and maintained a perfect figure. She was bright and skilled at her profession. Hopping bars, having casual affairs, and doing drugs were part of her lifestyle. That was what she taught Ramesh.

"Ramesh, do you smoke?" Teresa said.

"I used to in my college days, but I have quit for a long time now," Ramesh said.

"Good, we can have some fun with smoking weed," Teresa said.

"But I have never smoked weed," Ramesh said.

"Don't worry, you will like it," Teresa said. In the same way, she taught him how to snort coke.

Ramesh and Teresa's indulgence started with drinking, but sometimes he would smoke weed or do coke with her too. Their love making fluctuated between gentle to whipping, tying each other up and other new masochism tricks. Teresa was not new to the game. She knew what to expect from him, and she taught him unusual ways to please her. She had sex toys in her closets and many gadgets for enhancing their pleasure. She loved that he was a novice. It was fun to experiment, and she enjoyed introducing him to the intricacies of sadistic pleasure.

"Teresa, what are all these gadgets?" Ramesh wondered.

"This is a whip, these are handcuffs, and these are leather shackles." She described each gadget.

"And what they do?" Ramesh asked.

"These gadgets can enhance your pleasure," Teresa said.

"How?" Ramesh asked.

"Let me show you. Take off your clothes, Ramesh. Come on, hurry up. Lay down in bed, on your stomach. Good boy. Now let me do the work, and do not say a word," Teresa instructed.

Teresa took out hand cuffs from her closet and attached his right hand to one of the hand cuffs on the right-side bed post. In the same way she cuffed his left hand to the left side post.

Ramesh tried to say something.

"Not a word," Teresa said. She took out shackles from the closet and the same way she tied his feet to each of the bed post. She took out a leather whip and hit him hard.

"O, O, O," Ramesh said.

"You like it," Teresa said.

"Oh, no," Ramesh said.

Teresa hit him hard again.

"No, O, O," Ramesh shouted.

"Unless you say, 'Yes, I like it,' I will keep whipping you," Teresa hit him again with the whip.

"Oh, my God. It is very painful," Ramesh said.

"Say, 'Yes, I like it.'" Teresa hit him again.

After a few more whips, Ramesh surrendered.

"Yes, I like it," Ramesh said, feeling the relief from the whip.

Then they made love.

For the next few days, Ramesh could not sit properly and had to rub ointment on his bottom every night. Teresa was an aphrodisiac. After the disastrous wedding night, it was a unique experience to make love freely. His wish was granted to seduce a White Goddess, and he would go to any length to please her.

Teresa controlled his love making. He was her slave, ready to fulfill all her commands. She would tie him to the bed, whip him, and make him do all the tricks. In the process of learning, he forgot to please himself. She would put a dog collar around his neck and roam from one room to another.

Teresa would call out, "Come on, my doggie, come, come, there's my good doggie."

Ramesh did not realize he was sucked into dissipation, and his mind lost reasoning. Drinking and doing drugs became part of his lifestyle. Somewhere in his mind, a voice would tell him he was sinking too deep, but for him to leave Teresa was not possible. She controlled his soul.

Teresa never bothered to ask him about his personal life. He was happy that no one, not even Vijay, not his co-workers, least of all his wife, knew about his White Goddess.

Chapter 28
Duplicity
1976
New York

Three months had passed since Ramesh arrived in America, and he had not sent a ticket for Mona to come to the states. Everyone in his family, especially his mother, wrote to him every week to ask when his bride Mona would join him in America.

At first, Ramesh called Mona every day and would repeat the words 'I love you' to her. Over time, he started calling her only once a week. In the last four weeks, he called her only three times and Mona was growing agitated.

None of his friends knew what was going on, though they had noticed Ramesh had more confidence recently. He talked about sex and women often, and he started describing women only as sex objects.

Vijay's father wrote to his son about why Ramesh had not yet sent the plane tickets for Mona. Vijay was busy starting his own consulting company and did not realize that Ramesh had not sent the ticket. Though they were living one block from each other, Ramesh avoided spending time with Vijay ever since he met Teresa.

Vijay called Ramesh, "Hey, what is going on? I hear you've not sent Mona the plane ticket."

"Ay, big brother, I was thinking to wait for some more time," said Ramesh.

"Three months have passed since you came back to America, and you would like to wait for some more time. What do you mean?" Vijay asked.

"I mean, I am not settled yet," Ramesh replied.

"You are not settled yet? You have held a steady job since you came back from India, and you have rented an apartment. You do not visit us, and when we call you, either you are not there, or you are very tired. We have not seen you for months. What is going on?" Vijay was surprised.

"There is nothing going on, brother. Mona is an excellent girl. The only thing is, she has dark skin," said Ramesh.

"What! How has this returned to your mind?" Vijay said.

Vijay was nervous. He bit his lip. He suspected there was something else going on and before Ramesh could do something stupid, he wanted to know the full story.

"Listen, why don't you come over to my house on Sunday? Rebecca can prepare us a nice Indian meal. Afterwards, we can chat and see an Indian movie at the school," Vijay said.

"No, brother. Don't involve Rebecca in this," Ramesh retorted.

"Fine, I will send Rebecca to see a movie with her friends, and we both can have a talk, alone.," Vijay replied.

"That will be fine," said Ramesh.

On Sunday, Vijay had invited a few other friends to join them for lunch. All the other friends brought home-cooked food. Ramesh, who never learnt to cook, brought a pie from the local bakery.

"Rebecca, you make an excellent chicken curry, and your mutton kababs are very tasty," said Ramesh.

"Thank you, Ramesh. Mona is an excellent vegetarian cook too. We are all waiting to taste her cooking. When is Mona coming from India?" Rebecca said.

Vijay interrupted to ask which movie they were planning to see.

"The movie name is 'Mr. India' and the celebrity Sri Devi is the star," she said.

"Oh boy, she is beautiful," said one of the friends.

"But she is dark," remarked Ramesh.

The group of friends stared at Ramesh. They left soon after lunch to see the movie, while Vijay and Ramesh stayed back.

"We have more than three hours to talk about why you are not calling Mona. Now tell me, frankly, is there anything going on between you and Mona?" Vijay asked.

"No, nothing of the sort," Ramesh replied.

"Then what is the reason?" Vijay asked.

"She is attractive, but she is very dark," Ramesh tried to explain. "I can't stop comparing her to the white girls around us. Their skin shines in darkness, and their nipples are pink."

"Stop, stop. What is going on in your mind? Are you only capable of looking at a woman based on her physical aspects? Don't you see any other quality in a woman?" said Vijay.

"I can't help myself. When I see a fair-skinned woman, my whole body goes through a change. When I touch a white woman's skin, my mind goes berserk," Ramesh said.

Vijay could not comprehend what Ramesh was saying. When Ramesh was in India, he called Vijay often to sing the praises of Mona. How had things taken such a different turn?

Vijay asked, "Now what are you going to do? How long you will delay her coming here, and what benefits will you derive from it?"

"I don't know," Ramesh replied.

They remained silent for a while. Vijay noticed what Ramesh had said about touching a white woman's skin.

Vijay asked finally, "Are you sleeping with another woman?"

Vijay's question caught Ramesh off guard. Vijay's eyes were penetrating Ramesh's own. Ramesh could not bear to lie and confessed the truth about Teresa.

"Vijay brother, I have fallen in love with an American girl. She is the most beautiful woman I have ever seen." Ramesh told Vijay the whole story.

"Oh my God, you are not only crazy, but also stupid. If you were so enamored by white skin, then why did you agree to marry Mona?" asked Vijay.

"When I met Mona, I was extremely impressed. I had slight hesitation at that time, with her appearance. But my parents overruled my objections," he said.

"You are a grown man. You could surely have said no if this bothered you so much. When you came back from India, you were so happy with Mona," Vijay said.

"I still say she is a nice woman. The only problem is -- she is not beautiful in my eyes," Ramesh said.

"Oh, Ramesh, you are impossible. Your fetish for skin color will create havoc in your life. What are you going to do? By postponing her coming to America, you will make the matter worse. You will ruin her life, and it will be a scandal in the community back in Kanpur," Vijay said.

After a few minutes, Vijay asked him another question, "Are you serious about this other woman?"

"Yes, Vijay," Ramesh replied.

"What about her? Is she also serious about you?" asked Vijay.

"I think she is equally serious," replied Ramesh.

"You think, or you're sure?" asked Vijay.

"We spend most evenings together, and I stay at her apartment often," said Ramesh.

"Hmm. Things do seem serious. Did you tell her that you are married?" asked Vijay.

Ramesh hesitated, "I have not. First, I will go to India to tell my parents and annul my marriage to Mona. Once that is taken care of, I will propose to Teresa."

Vijay told Ramesh thoughtfully, "In matters of love, it is better to lay the cards out from the beginning. You should have been honest with Teresa when you met her. Why don't you tell her now and see her reaction? You see, eventually, there will be a time to confess. And at that time, you risk losing everything because the girl you love may reject you, and Mona may not take you back. You will lose both women you care for," said Vijay.

"Vijay, I agree and will talk with Teresa. Please promise me you will not tell Rebecca any of this, until I go back to India and talk with my parents."

Ramesh went home in a dejected mood. He knew that if he did not send the ticket to Mona, the community will abandon his family. His father, known for mistreating his wife, had rebuilt a respectable reputation after many years. That reputation would once again be ruined if Ramesh broke off the marriage to Mona. Ramesh was afraid of his father and was protective of the place his family held in the community. On the other hand, he was determined never to lose Teresa. She was his life. He could not decide what to do.

The next day, he reluctantly bought a one-way plane ticket for Mona, and did not mention his marriage to Teresa.

Chapter 29
The Ticket
1976
Kanpur

Mona looked at the plane ticket again. How happy she was, excited and full of dreams about her new life in America. After Ramesh had left for America, some of her friends had planted doubts in her mind. 'Ramesh will never call you. His American girlfriend will not allow you to come to America. Every year, he will fly back to India to impregnate you. In the next six years, you will bear six children. You will remain stuck in India for the rest of your life.'

Those frightening stories never bothered Mona. She believed Ramesh was a considerate and loving gentleman. Mona was deeply religious; she did pujas to please the Gods and to ward off the ill omens. She had slight anxiety about going to America, so she called a priest to perform a puja for her safe journey, for Ramesh's welfare, and for any forthcoming calamities.

Her personal wardrobe was limited to a few saris. She had never worn jeans or slacks, and she knew that no one would offer her a job wearing a sari in New York. She had to change into American clothes and decided that she would buy them there.

Mona faced the reality of leaving Kanpur. The smells of delicious street food and the familiar scent of early morning coal dust from the powerhouse brought tears to her eyes. Her parents and friends were full of emotions as well. With any small reminder that Mona was leaving, Mona's loved ones would shed many tears. The only person excited for her was her sister Binny, who was determined to go with Mona to America.

Rebecca wrote to Mona informing her not to bring any spices to America. They were not allowed in the airport, and if discovered by customs, all her spices would be dumped in the garbage. However, Rebecca did not mention anything about Vijay or Ramesh. Mona knew Vijay helped to arrange the marriage and was thankful to Vijay for fulfilling his promise to bring her to America.

Chapter 30
Departure
1976
Kanpur

The day arrived to leave Kanpur. All of Mona's relatives and friends poured into her home to say farewell and give her gifts to take abroad with her. Everyone had some advice to give Mona on what to do and what not to do in America, as if they had lived there for years.

"Be careful, New York is a dangerous city. Do not venture from your house after dark! They will kidnap you," someone said.

"Who will kidnap me?" Mona said looking up at everyone.

"They," someone said louder.

Mona was to travel by train from Kanpur to Delhi. From Delhi, she would fly to New York. Before she left for the train station, Mona had a private conversation with her mother.

Usha said, "Listen, you are my precious child who has suffered to get to where you are now. You are a strong girl, and I want you to keep your head high to move forward in this world with dignity. God will always be with you."

Her mother-in-law told her a small story from Ramayana, about the ideal couple, God Rama and Goddess Sita, who never quarreled or never snapped at each other.

"Listen, Beti, you should follow in Sita's footsteps. Always obey your husband," her mother-in-law said.

They reached the railway station on time. Everyone who had already said farewell in the morning, were there again on the platform. Her friends were buying food, sweets, magazines, and books to entertain Mona on the journey.

The train reached the platform in slow motion, and the tears and farewells continued. One of Mona's aunts rushed in with marigold garlands, and others in Mona's family looked around for that same vendor. Soon, Mona had her neck buried in garlands and could not take them off.

The train departed. Mona's relatives and friends walked beside the moving train until the train finally whistled out of sight.

At the airport, she found a gathering of relatives from Delhi, saying their farewells and giving her additional garlands. She thought she was unique but, looking around, there were lots of Indians who were going abroad for the first time, and all were covered in flowers.

When it was time to board the plane, Mona found herself in tears. She remembered her mother, father, Binny, her grandmother and new found in-laws. As she wept, she heard the announcement for boarding the plane. She did not want to leave her family. She wanted to stay back in smog-filled Kanpur City, the only home she had ever known.

Mona reached the United State in late March of 1976. She was twenty-eight.

Chapter 31
America, Here I Come
1976
New York

The plane landed in the late evening. The weather was cold, and the people around her were in warm overcoats. Mona was full of excitement yet exhausted by the long journey. Mona did not anticipate the month of March to be so cold. She had only her old, tattered shawl wrapped around her.

Mona was tired and nervous, keen to see familiar faces. Rebecca and Ramesh were at the airport to greet her. Vijay was out of town.

Mona saw Rebecca and quickly ran to embrace her. "My God, it is very cold here!" Mona rubbed her hands.

"My sweet Mona," Ramesh pretended he was excited to see Mona. He cleverly surrounded Mona in his arms and went on kissing her face. For an Indian woman, kissing in public felt like a big embarrassment. She was perplexed and felt great discomfort being kissed in front of other people. She pushed Ramesh and stiffened, but Ramesh would not stop.

"Welcome to New York," said Rebecca. "Obviously, your husband is happy to see you."

Both ladies helped Ramesh load luggage in Rebecca's car. Ramesh's car was in the repair shop.

"Oh boy, these suitcases are heavy," Ramesh said.

"So, this is New York! I have heard a lot about it. Ramesh, you told me the city is full of tall buildings, but I don't see any!" Mona said after sitting in the car.

Ramesh and Rebecca both replied at the same time, "The tall buildings are in Manhattan, and this is not Manhattan."

Ramesh explained, "Manhattan is twenty miles away from the airport. We live in Queens, eight miles away from the Kennedy Airport."

"Let us take the circuitous route via Manhattan. The sky is clear. Mona will see the beauty of the city," Rebecca said.

"From Manhattan, how far is your place?" Mona asked.

"Another twenty-miles," Ramesh said.

"So, we would need to travel forty miles, that's like going from Kanpur City to Lucknow City. It will take four hours. I will see Manhattan some other time," Mona said.

"No, darling, this is not India. Now you are in America. Here there are freeways. Forty miles by freeway means forty minutes. We will reach our place in one hour," Ramesh said.

They were in the car, and Rebecca said, "We are getting the smell of the spices."

Mona felt a little embarrassed and said in faint voice, "Ramesh's mother sent a big bag of spices for him. The custom officer threw the bag in the garbage, but the suitcase still smells of spices."

"Oh my gosh, all the spices were thrown in the garbage can," Ramesh said.

"Look who is lamenting! Ramesh, you of all people! First learn how to cook and then you can worry about spices," Rebecca said.

There was little traffic on this Sunday evening. Rebecca droves fast on the expressway. Ramesh and Rebecca were full of questions about the relatives in India.

"How are my dad and mom?" Ramesh said.

"Your mom is fine, and your dad had a little cough. Otherwise, everyone in your family is fine," Mona said.

"What about your family? How is the factory running?" Ramesh said.

"The factory is in bad shape. My dad had to sell one machine to pay the wages of the workers. They were not paid for the last two months," Mona said sadly. "But grandmother Sarla Devi remains in good health. Binny will always be Binny."

With silence, they continued the drive until tall buildings were visible. On her left Mona could see the lights on the Statue of Liberty. Behind her, she saw the Verrazano Bridge and in front of her, she saw some of the tallest buildings in the world. Blocks full of lights towered one over another.

Mona held her breath for a second. It was spectacular. Her big eyes opened wider.

They reached home later than expected because there was an accident near the Brooklyn Queens Bridge.

Rebecca dropped Ramesh and Mona off in front of their building.

"Oh, Ramesh you live here. How far does Rebecca live from here?" Mona said.

"We live in a house at the turn of that corner, not far, about a quarter of a mile. Once you are settled, you can see me anytime," Rebecca said.

It was nine in the evening when they were alone inside the apartment. Mona was surprised the apartment was almost barren. All it contained was a few mismatched chairs, a small dining table, and a threadbare sofa. The bedroom was as sparse as the living room, with one steel bed and a lumpy mattress. Mona thought, *'Back home our maid lives better than how Ramesh is living now.* Ramesh had furnished his apartment with items he found on the curb, discarded by others in the neighborhood.

"Darling, after reaching New York, I went to a doctor and now I am free from the problem I had before. Let me try now. You will see, I won't have any pain," Ramesh said.

"Let us wait, Ramesh, let me freshen myself first."

"Darling, you are as fresh as a rose. Let me show you." Ramesh was in a hurry to show Mona that he was fit after the surgery. He pushed her on the edge of the bed. She was tired and keen on taking a shower, but he was eager to show his sexual prowess. He had learned many tricks from Teresa. Making love was quick and painful for Mona. His timing had improved, and it was clear that he felt fine.

"Did you see, darling, I felt no pain. Now I can perform well," Ramesh said.

She was tired and needed a bath. She took clean clothes and went to the bathroom. After a bath, she felt renewed.

Mona was wearing the nightgown she had chosen in India, anticipating the occasion of seeing Ramesh again. Mildly transparent and low cut, it revealed her breasts.

Mona remembered when she bought the nightgown in India. The first thing Binny asked Mona, "Didi, when you will wear this?"

Mona smiled.

"You will wear it at the airport before you meet

Jeejaji?" Binny asked.

Mona looked at Binny with her big eyes.

"No. You will wear it before opening your luggage at the customs. The custom officer, after seeing you in this satin gown, will let you go with all the spices in your suitcases," Binny said, acting childish.

"Behave yourself, otherwise I will not invite you to come to America," Mona said.

The revealing night gown remained a common joke between Mona and Binny.

Mona walked into the bedroom wearing her sexy nightgown. Ramesh was already sleeping. She could not sleep. The time difference meant that it was morning in India. Her mental clock was not yet tuned to New York time.

Her eyes were closed, but her mind was moving from one thought to another, remembering her parents, and the old life she left behind. She thought ahead to her new life bonded to a man whom she had only spent ten days with.

She went into the living room and turned on the black-and-white TV. Mona was surprised at that late hour to see some shows were still on the TV. In India, there were only four channels and those ran for a few hours. She turned the knob from one channel to another and sat down on the sofa. The room was warm and cozy. She dozed off watching TV. Early the next morning, Ramesh got up suddenly when he reached for Mona and found was not in bed. He rushed to the other room and there she was, fast asleep, curled up on the sofa. Her gown was open; he bent down and kissed her. She woke up. He picked her up in his arms and headed back to the bedroom.

"Hi," Ramesh said.

"Hi," Mona smiled.

"I panicked when I did not see you in the bed," Ramesh

said.

He pulled down her satin gown. Ramesh thought, he still had plenty of time to tell Mona about Teresa. In the meantime, why not have fun? They were husband and wife.

Chapter 32
Settling In America
1976
New York

Teresa's parents retired and had decided to settle down in Florida. Teresa left New York for three weeks with her parents to help them move into their new home.

The next day after Mona arrived, Ramesh took Mona to a Woolworth department store. She was awed to see the selection of household and clothing items available under one roof. She was interested in buying everything, and he did not stop her. When they were in the check-out line, she asked, "How much will the bill be?"

He looked at the items and said, "My estimate is about three hundred dollars."

"Three hundred dollars! How much is that in rupees?" "Considering one dollar is equivalent to ten rupees, the bill is approximately three thousand rupees," Ramesh said.

"Oh my God, such a lot of money! Do you have that much cash?" Mona asked.

"No, but I have a credit card. It has a credit limit of five hundred dollars, so we can buy things now and pay for them later," he said.

"What do you mean, 'pay for them later?' "

"Credit cards loan money to you when you need to buy things," Ramesh said.

"What, buy things on loan? No, I do not want any of these items. I will buy things only when I have cash." She left her shopping cart behind and walked out of the store. Ramesh tried to explain, but she would not listen.

"No, I will never take a loan. Look at what happened to my family. They are buried with debts and cannot pay even one rupee back on the principal. I won't take any loans," Mona said adamantly. She walked fast.

After reaching home, Ramesh made her sit on the broken dining chair he had found on the street and explained how the financial system works in America.

"First of all, never show your tantrums in public. People will think we have come from some uncivilized country."

Mona's face turned white, "I am sorry. I remembered my parents' situation and I panicked."

Ramesh pulled out the credit card from his wallet. "Now let me explain, this is not an ordinary piece of plastic. This card is given by the bank, which thoroughly investigates your financial background and gives you a limit on the amount you can spend. That limit is called a credit limit. In India, generally how much money do you keep in your wallet?" Ramesh asked.

"Around twenty rupees," Mona replied.

"Here, if you must buy a refrigerator or a piece of furniture, you may have to carry more than a thousand rupees. Won't you feel it is a lot of money to carry? Would you feel comfortable carrying that amount in your wallet?" Ramesh asked.

"No, it is too much. I have never carried that amount in my life," Mona said.

"If you have a credit card with a limit of two thousand rupees, then you don't have to carry that much cash with you. The card lets you spend the money. And if you pay the bank the money you spent before the due date, then the bank will not charge you any fees or interest," Ramesh said.

"Is that how it works?" Mona said.

Ramesh emphasized, "The American economy runs on buying often and discarding items quickly. Credit cards help in the buying spree. Banks and merchants invented the idea of credit to buy items, use them, discard them, and start the cycle of buying again. The world economy runs on buying by Americans. It is not like in India where you buy something and keep the item for your whole life. Here, the whole economy runs on credit cards, "Ramesh said.

Mona looked at him with wonder.

"So, I do not have to carry that much money. I just need to pay the bill on time." Ramesh put his arm around her shoulders. "Mona, you have a master's degree in Economics, but I have grasped how the American financial system works."

Mona was astounded. Looking at Ramesh with her big eyes, she said in a whispered voice, "Sorry."

The next day Mona went back to the Woolworth store with Ramesh and with the credit card, bought the items which she had left behind, plus a few more.

In the evening, he took her by subway to show her the Empire State Building. Mona was fascinated by everything –the subway lines, the grocery stores, the department stores, and the tall buildings. When she looked up, she could not see the top of any building.

Mona was awed by the subway and bus systems. She saw the intensity of people, everybody in a hurry to get somewhere. Most people ignored their surroundings, and she noticed many non-smiling faces. Even her fluttering eyes and beautiful smile did not get any response from the bustling crowd.

Ramesh took Mona to the Macy's department store in downtown Manhattan. As Ramesh opened the door for Mona to enter the store, they encountered two Indian ladies dressed warmly for the chilly weather. They walked out of the store as Ramesh and Mona entered. Both looked at Ramesh, who was dressed in a well-cut winter coat with a woolen scarf wrapped around his neck, and then turned to look at Mona who was shivering in her old, tattered shawl.

One of the ladies whispered to Ramesh, "Brother, you brought your wife from India. She is shivering. At least buy her a winter coat." Giving Ramesh a cold look, both ladies walked out.

Ramesh was embarrassed and his face turned red.

Mona asked Ramesh, "What happened? What did that lady say to make you angry?"

"Forget it. Just a silly remark."

Mona was amazed to see a nine-story building covering one full block. Each floor was full of items offered for sale, and every item was displayed elegantly, especially the women's makeup, clothes, and perfumes. She wanted to buy everything, but the prices seemed beyond her reach. She felt a little sad looking at what she could not afford.

Roaming around the store, they found the denim department. There, Mona found Gloria Vanderbilt jeans, the rage of the time. Mona's face lit up with excitement. She always had dreamed of wearing jeans. She remembered looking through American magazines with pictures of actresses modeling jeans. How beautiful those women looked, sleek and confident, in Gloria Vanderbilt jeans. She picked up a pair. When she looked at the price tag, she put them back immediately.

"Darling, go to the fitting room and try it on," Ramesh said.

"No, this is expensive. The tag says a hundred dollars for just this pair."

"Just see how it fits you. You do not have to buy it. Trying is free. Go inside, just try it on," Ramesh insisted.

She put the jeans on and came out of the fitting room. The jeans fitted Mona perfectly. She could have modeled for any fashion magazine. She reluctantly took off the jeans.

"Why don't you browse the makeup department and see if you want any lipstick? I must go to the restroom. I will be back in a few minutes," said Ramesh.

He returned to her side after twenty minutes, and she was worried. He had a package in his hand.

"What took you so long? I was all alone waiting for you," said Mona. "In another few minutes, I would have started crying. You know I am new here and do not know what train to catch. What is that in your hand?"

"Just a package. I bought a shirt in the basement department. There you get most of things at discount prices."

"Let me see."

"Don't open it here. See it at home," Ramesh said.

It was too late to visit the Empire State Building, so they postponed the visit and headed back to their apartment instead. Ramesh was quiet on the way home.

At the apartment, Ramesh gave her the Macy's bag. When Mona opened the package, she found the Gloria Vanderbilt jeans that she had tried at Macy's. Tears came to her eyes, "How could you? It is so expensive," Mona said softly.

"Welcome to America," Ramesh said.

"How did you pay for this? Did you have cash?"

They both laughed.

"Mona, go to the bathroom and try it on again. I want to see you wear them," Ramesh said.

As soon as Mona went into the bathroom, Ramesh took the elevator down to the underground garage in their building. He hurriedly opened the trunk of his car. There he had stored a big box, wrapped in beautiful colored paper, showing a sketch of a man a woman with their lips joined. Hearts were pasted on the box, with a card and bow on top. Ramesh picked up the package, closed the trunk, and ran back towards the elevator.

In front of the elevator, he noticed that the box had a card and red bow. He hurriedly pulled off the card and the bow, put the card in his pocket, and then put the bow back on the package.

The elevator stopped at the third floor, and he quickly dashed to the apartment. Mona was standing at the door in her new jeans.

"Ramesh, where did you go? I came out of the bathroom, and you were not there. Please do not play hide and seek with me. I get frightened. Why are you panting?" Mona asked.

Ramesh put the package on the bed and came closer to Mona. He gently kissed her and said, "Welcome to America. This is for you."

Mona looked at him with surprise and tore the paper off. She opened the box and found a fine winter coat.

Mona could not say anything. She put her arms around Ramesh with tears flowing from her eyes.

Last week, Ramesh had bought the finest and most expensive coat as a birthday gift for Teresa, and it had cost him two weeks' salary.

Mona got up early in the morning and made a hearty breakfast for Ramesh. She was growing to like him. Ramesh was whistling. He was looking forward to seeing Teresa upon her return from Florida. But he was worried and conflicted about how to break the news to Mona. He was now concerned about hurting Mona's feelings. Ramesh knew Mona was very smart and calculated that he would have to play the game very carefully.

The next few days were exciting. Mona was adjusting to the new culture. She was excited with so much to learn and explore in the city, meeting people from diverse backgrounds, tasting new kinds of food, and seeing an abundance of every gadget, makeup, clothing, books, magazines, and furniture. Her fear of living in a new place was gone.

They enjoyed local restaurants and snack shops. The first time when Ramesh ordered a cheese pizza with pepperoni, she was fascinated with the small, round pieces on the top of pizza.

"What are those round pieces?"Mona asked innocently.

"Those are the thin slices of spiced bananas. Try them; they are tasty," he replied.

Mona acted like a novice and tried one piece, then another, and she ate four pieces. She knew it was meat. She had tried pepperoni pizza in Bombay with Amar Uncle.

After reaching home, Mona asked Ramesh, "Ramesh, the round pieces on the pizza did not taste like banana. They were soft and banana slices are crunchy. What were they?"

Ramesh confessed, "That was meat, Mona. If you live with me, then you will have to eat meat and cook it for me."

"Fine, I will try to cook meat, but I don't know how to prepare meat dishes."

"Simple, you can learn from Rebecca. She is a connoisseur on how to prepare chicken and meat dishes, and you are an excellent cook of vegetarian dishes. You can teach each other."

Pepperoni pizza quickly became Mona's favorite dish. She got hooked on it. She thought pizza was the best food she had ever tasted. Later, she became an ardent fan of Big Macs. They had little money, so their outings were restricted to pizza or hamburger shops. Ramesh introduced Mona to beer, and later gave her scotch mixed with a little cola. Hamburgers were tastier with beer and mixed cola. Her struggle with guilt and traditional values ended back when she stayed with Amar Uncle in Bombay.

Her newly found romance with her husband gave her a fresh beginning and solace. She would shed her clothes and stand in front of a mirror, looking at her skin. It had started glowing more in the last few days.

Chapter 33
Wolf In New York
1976
New York

Ramesh was at work, and Mona was alone in the apartment. The telephone rang in the morning. She answered.

"Hello," Mona said.

"Hello, Mona, this is Vijay. Welcome to New York!"

"Oh, Vijay Bhai, when did you come from your business trip?" Mona said.

"I came last night. Can I see you, in the next half-hour?"

"Sure, Vijay Bhai," Mona said.

Mona was excited. Vijay had promised her when he had left India to bring her to the U.S., and he fulfilled his promise. After a while, the doorbell rang. Mona rushed to open the door before she could ask who was there or look through the peephole.

"Hello, Vijay Bhai," she opened the door.

Mona was surprised. "Oh, it is you! What are you doing here?"

"Hello, Mona, I thought I will spend a few moments with you alone," Amar said.

She was stunned and remained quiet.

"Won't you ask me to come in?" Amar asked.

Mona with reluctance opened the door.

"Vijay and I both were coming to see you. He got a call,

and he will be here very soon," Amar said.

She closed the door behind her. They looked at each other. Suddenly he tried to hug her. She pushed him back with fear and anger.

"We are together again. Far from India. Now nobody can separate us," Amar said gently.

She was fearful. He may push her on floor and rape her again.

She was standing far from him, but Amar came closer. "So, what have you been doing for the last four years?"

"Amar, I am a married woman." Mona stepped away from him. "That is all you need to know."

"Do you need anything? Are you comfortable here?" he asked.

He walked towards her, and she evaded him.

"You don't know how happy I am to see you here. I flew from Chicago just to see you," he said.

He came closer to her. She moved to the other side of the old dining room table.

"Is something bothering you? You know I love you."

"Please don't start this again."

"Mona, we had best time of our life in Bombay. It was short but sweet. It was worth the risk."

Her heart was thumping fast with fear.

"Listen. You are my Uncle, and you raped me. For you, it was worth the risk. For me, it was not, and I hate you. Let me make it clear, I love my husband. He trusts me, and I will never betray him. If you ever try to do anything to disrupt our marriage, I am sure that I will kill you."

He moved towards her again. "Just listen to me."

"Out of my apartment! Get out!" She erupted in anger, "Get out."

She opened the door.

Amar walked out and she locked the door from the inside. She sighed with relief and held back angry tears. Vijay and Rebecca both came to see her soon after.

Chapter 34
Adjustment
1976
New York

On Saturday morning, the sky was covered with partial clouds. Rays of sun shone through the clouds, with warm winds blowing lightly. Mona was lying in bed. She did not want to get up early. Ramesh had left already, with the ready-made excuse of working on Saturdays. They were invited to Vijay's place for dinner that evening. She was going to meet their friends for the first time.

Ramesh came home early and found Mona in the bedroom sleeping on her stomach. Sunlight poured in from the curtains, over part of her back. He saw his wife sprawled in the sun, partly clad in her satin pajamas. He thought about how lucky he was to find Teresa and Mona, both young, attractive, and full of life. He was having a blast, and all his friends would envy him if they came to know he had two beautiful catches.

He shed his clothes and tried to creep into the bed. His clumsy haste woke her up.

"When did you come? What's the time?" she said.

"Darling, it is two in the afternoon," he said.

"Oh my God, is it that late? I slept for such a long time." She sat up and realized his clothes were on the floor, and he was naked.

"What are you doing with your clothes off?" she asked.

"I thought I could take a little nap with you," he said in muffled voice, rubbing his hands gently over her stomach. Mona climbed over Ramesh, and they made love. They woke up when the sun was already down.

That evening, they started preparing for the dinner at Vijay's house. Mona was getting ready, putting on the last touches of makeup. Ramesh came out of the bathroom, with a towel around his waist. He came behind Mona and put his arms around her waist.

"You look beautiful," said Ramesh.

"My sari will get wrinkled, and we will be late for the party," she whispered.

"Yes, I know," he replied.

Her sari did get wrinkled, and she had to change into another outfit. She took out the Gloria Vanderbilt jeans and a short muslin Lucknowi top to wear.

Chapter 35
Party
1976
New York

They were late for the party. Mona's flamboyant entrance at Vijay and Rebecca's silenced every guest for few seconds. She was wearing Gloria Vanderbilt jeans with high heels and a white muslin V-neck, button-less top. The see-through top displayed her black brassier and showed a little cleavage. Her long hair, smooth flawless skin, and curved figure stunned everybody. All eyes were on her.

Vijay moved forward from the corner of the room. "Hello, friends, meet Ramesh and his wife Mona. Welcome to America," he said, gently holding her arm.

She was introduced to each of the friends individually and struck up conversation. They talked about India's politics to American politics, from the labor market to the discrimination of immigrants. The second bottle of Johnny Walker Red was opened; they drank and drank, except Mona. She was surprised that Indian ladies were drinking scotch mixed with Coca-Cola.

Mona was feeling thirsty. She looked at Ramesh. He was waiting for a hint. Quietly he handed Mona a glass of cola mixed with a little scotch.

Mona smelled scotch, but she was thirsty, she gulped down the cola quickly. The taste was harsh and smooth at the same time. In a few minutes, she felt relaxed and started talking with everybody, as if she knew them very well.

Ramesh had learned many tricks with Teresa and was waiting patiently to experiment with Mona later, when they were home. He brought Mona another glass of cola. This time Ramesh put a full peg of whiskey in it. He thought this was the best way to tame the dark tempter to do his tricks, making her drunk.

"Here, Mona, drink some more cola," said Ramesh.

Mona took a sip and discovered it was mixed with a lot of scotch. She was not happy.

She looked at Ramesh with stern eyes. She turned towards Vijay, "Vijay Bhai, can you add a little more ice and, if possible, more cola to my drink?" Mona handed the glass to Vijay.

Mona and Ramesh were the guests of honor. Vijay's home was not the appropriate place to pick a fight with Ramesh. Sitting next to Mona, he got up quickly. "It's all right, Vijay. Let me pour more ice and cola," he said.

Ramesh brought back the glass and she took a sip again. The mixture still had a strong taste of scotch. Ramesh put his finger under her chin and whispered to her, "Take a big sip. It is bad manners to take a small sip. When someone says 'cheers,' the custom is that you have to clink your glasses together and say 'cheers.' You then look into the other person's eyes and gulp down a big sip."

"Cheers," Ramesh said.

"Ramesh, you are getting me drunk. I won't be able to stand," Mona whispered.

Ramesh whispered back, "Darling, don't worry, I am with you. I will hold your hand."

Ramesh said 'cheers' several times, and Mona obeyed by swallowing down the scotch each time. He forced her to finish her drink within a few minutes. Suddenly she burped loudly. Everyone turned towards her and smiled. Mona, with her eyes roaming, smiled back. Ramesh put his right hand over her shoulders, and she held his left hand in hers, for support. Vijay saw all of this from the corner of his eyes and once more had second thoughts about his suggesting the marriage between Mona and a crazy man like Ramesh.

Ramesh and Mona stayed at the party late, and he forced her to have one more drink before they left. When they reached home, Mona was drunk. Ramesh was happy to see Mona drinking, and his scheming mind was working on the evening's dissipation. He knew that if he got her drunk, he could manipulate her the way he wanted. Whatever tricks he learned from Teresa, he wanted to experiment on Mona. An Indian wife would accept her duty and do anything for her husband. All his fantasies could be fulfilled if he could get her drunk.

Chapter 36
Entrapment
1976
New York

Teresa returned from her trip to Florida, and after work Ramesh would continue to spend time with her. He would take one or two drinks with Teresa, play a masochistic game, and then go home. At home, he would take another drink of scotch and coax Mona to join him.

"Come on, take a sip, I will pour very little and mix it with Coca Cola."

"No, Ramesh, you made a very stiff drink at the party, and I was drunk with two sips. I don't like the taste of it," Mona would say. "I can hardly remember that night because of the drink."

"Don't worry. I will make it a light drink. At least take two sips. Nothing will happen, and I am here. I will take care of you. Give me your company. I don't feel like drinking alone."

At first, she refused blatantly but slowly at his persistence, she started joining him in drinking an evening cocktail. He made it a ritual and forced Mona to have a drink before dinner. At night, he would not let her take rest. In the beginning, it was sweet caresses and gentle pats on her behind. Now, the gentle patting became spanking on her derriere.

"Ramesh, please, Ramesh, you are hitting me hard. Stop it!" Mona cried.

"Quiet, woman. Let me do what I want," Ramesh said, half drunk.

"Ramesh, it is very painful. I don't like this," Mona said.

Ramesh slapped her across the face, "I am your husband, so you belong to me. Your body is mine. Do what I say as a dutiful wife."

Mona was shocked, but she remained quiet. She grew compliant because he was her husband but in a corner of her mind, she came to question the strange practices of her marriage bed.

He bought toys from a sex shop–handcuffs, blindfolds, and leather whips. Sometimes he would use his leather belt or a leather whip to hit her hard on her buttocks. He would tie her hands and legs to the bed and force her into his weird experiments. Every morning, her whole body ached badly. She was bruised and scratched. Mona accepted his sex deviations as a dutiful wife. Ramesh wanted to control Mona's mind and body the same way that Teresa controlled his soul.

Ramesh was gentle and enthusiastic with Teresa, but he was rough with Mona and could not control himself. He wondered why he was in a hurry with Mona. He started drinking more, and his nervousness around Mona was killing him. In a brief time, Ramesh developed a fear of inadequacy towards Mona. To overcome his fears and control her, he started insulting and cursing her.

"You stupid woman, why didn't you iron my light grey shirt? Don't you remember I have to go for lunch with my office colleagues? I don't know who gave you a master's degree," Ramesh said. "You're a dark woman; I don't like your face."

Mona, an educated and self-respecting woman, was reduced to a low-level servant. She was demeaned and verbally abused daily. The few days she had spent with him after marriage in India were wonderful, but after coming to America, he was a changed man. It was as if he had a hidden demon inside of him. Making her drunk, he would become a monster and curse her.

Ramesh would say "You are an ugly woman, a dark bitch! How could anyone come close to you?" Mona's face would turn red with shame and sadness.

In bed Mona would turn her back towards Ramesh, and soon after he would take her in his arms and start kissing her. "My Mona, I love you."

Mona was confused. She could not comprehend this love and hate situation. What was going on in Ramesh's mind?

From his pillow Mona would often smell the scent of a different perfume that she had never used, but she could not pinpoint where it came from.

Ramesh did not tell Mona about his intention of leaving her. For him, it became fun to sleep with two women, one like milk and the other like brown chocolate. Every morning, Mona gave him his tiffin lunch, and he would ask her to put in double portions. She never asked him why he needed the extra food. She did not know the lunch was shared by him and Teresa. After a romantic time with Teresa in the evening, he would come home drunk and have his salacious pleasure with Mona at night.

Mona forgot what love was. From morning until night, her thoughts were focused on how to keep Ramesh pleased, and in good humor, to avoid being slapped and cursed. She never dreamed that marriage could be torture. She was already abused enough by her Uncle. Now she found herself continuously insulted and abused by her husband.

I am a dedicated wife. This is my upbringing -- to fulfill all my husband's wishes. It is a passing phase. Ramesh will change. She kept these hopeful thoughts in front of her every day.

Chapter 37
Looking For A Job
1976
New York

Ramesh would leave for work early in the morning, and Mona was free for the entire day. She roamed from one store to another and looked at the abundance of items to buy that she did not need. Mona was bored after a month of wandering in subways, trains, and department stores. She always remembered her ambition of doing a Ph.D. at Columbia University.

One evening at Vijay's home, Mona started a conversation. "Vijay Bhai, I get bored sitting at home or mindless shopping. I think I should look for a job."

Vijay liked Mona's idea and told her to look up accounting jobs in the Sunday *New York Times*.

Ramesh objected. "Why does she have to look for a job? She can stay at home, to cook and clean the house!"

Vijay looked at Ramesh sternly. "Times have changed, Ramesh. Nowadays, women do not like to stay at home doing nothing. Mona is a highly educated woman. Why wastes her talents? If she prefers to work, let her work. By working, she will add to your income."

Mona was happy to hear this from brother Vijay, but Ramesh had a frown on his face.

Mona started buying every Sunday morning newspaper at the nearby liquor store. The Sunday edition of the *New York Times* was full of advertisements and jobs. One Sunday at the liquor store, she met three men from India. All of them were well-qualified and looking for a job. One was an engineer and the other two were doctors, but none had found a job in their own professional field. They were working in restaurants as servers for one dollar and eighty-five cents an hour. They were disheartened and lonely. The men were all married and missed their families and children living back in India. Mona was sad to hear their stories. *Welcome to America,* she thought.

Mona found plenty of job openings in accounting, and she sent applications to large companies. She got many replies thanking her for applying, but they were all rejection letters. She was invited to a few interviews, where she spoke only to the receptionists and rarely by higher management.

One weekend after a dinner gathering at Vijay's house, she brought up the topic of her job search among her friends.

"I am well educated, and the advertised jobs exactly suit my skill set. I prepare for my interviews thoroughly." Mona paused. "But I still get rejection letters."

Her friends were sympathetic but had no solution.

"Maybe it is discrimination. You are from India," one friend said.

"I think it is because you are a woman," the other friend said.

Vijay understood the situation. "Mona, if you want to survive in this country, you have to chew the high education pride and start at the bottom. Lower level accounting; then work up to the management position."

He encouraged her to update her resume and take a few accounting courses at Queens Community College to establish her credibility.

She changed her resume and aimed for a clerk position to start. Mona was determined to find a job and was willing to sacrifice her qualifications to put her foot in the job market. Two weeks later, Mona got a job in a brokerage firm, Becker's Securities, which dealt in stocks and bonds. The company's office was on Wall Street near the New York Stock Exchange. She had to take train number seven from Flushing to Grand Central Station. From there, she took the D train to downtown, and walked two blocks to reach her office near Ferry Terminal.

Mona did not mind changing trains and walking two blocks to reach her place of work. She enjoyed the feeling of independence. Though Ramesh still bothered her at night, she was getting her confidence back. She would get up early in the morning to cook, clean, and polish Ramesh's shoes. Mona started going to Queen's College to do some additional courses. She was focused on achieving her objective of someday getting a Ph. D. and finding a suitable job. In the meantime, she learned the world of work in America.

Mona's job at Becker's Securities was easy. She simply had to put the codes on the securities bought and sold. The salary was meager, five thousand dollars a year, but she was happy. She had a job and made a few friends in the office. To her, some people at her office seemed odd and their lifestyle was quite different than hers.

Mona's boss, Billy, was an unkempt man, with a day's growth of whiskers and stained shirt collars. In the office, he seemed to be half asleep. He sipped coffee and smoked all day. It was difficult to sit next to him. Though he seemed disorganized, he was good at his job and an expert coder. A few days later, she came to learn that Billy had married three times and had children from all the three wives. To pay alimony to his first two wives, Billy had to take a second job as a taxi driver in the evening, which explained why he was tired and sipped coffee all day in the office.

Billy was a smooth talker and a big flirt. Mona could never comprehend how all the girls in the office clamored to go for lunch or spend an evening with him. The very first week on the job, he invited her for lunch.

"Hey, little Chocolate Bar, how about if I take you out for lunch?" Billy said. But looking at Mona's stern face, he changed his mind and dropped the invitation.

Mona's colleague Rosie taught her how to code securities. Rosie was good looking, young, and intelligent. Mona and Rosie became good friends.

"Mona, it is a simple job. Do not worry; you will pick it up in two days. You can always ask me if you have any questions," Rosie said.

After work, Rosie would go to a bar to have a couple of drinks. There she would become friendly with a new person at the bar and end up with him in bed.

In the office the following morning, she would relate the previous night's encounter in detail to Mona. Most of the time, the people Rosie met would never call her back, but she was unaffected. For her it was just fun. Mona could not comprehend Rosie's lifestyle.

"Rosie, don't you feel afraid of spending a night with someone you don't know? I mean, having sex with a stranger. Isn't it dangerous?" Mona said.

"No, I judge the man. Is he a one-night stand person, or is he someone who seeks a relationship? Before having sex, I take the necessary precautions. If he does not have a condom, I keep a few handy in my purse," Rosie said.

"What about your feelings?" Mona said.

"Listen, kiddo, I do have feelings. If I like the man, I continue the relationship. In the last ten years, I had five or six serious relationships. In the end, they all failed. I am still looking for a good man, but in the meantime, I am having fun," Rosie said.

In every step on the job, Rosie was helpful. Rosie was a kind friend who saved Mona a couple of times when Mona coded the securities incorrectly. Rosie took all the blame. She guided Mona closely, and in a brief time Mona became an expert at coding.

Rosie was skilled with makeup. No blemish could ever be seen on her face. Mona knew virtually nothing about makeup, and what little she had learned was through looking at magazines. Rosie taught Mona the art of makeup and changed Mona's outlook on modern fashion.

From that point onward, Mona's clothes and makeup were impeccable when she attended parties. She transformed from being meek to becoming a fashionable queen of the party. Ramesh became jealous of her popularity and bothered her more perversely at home. Mona's makeup skills allowed her to cover up the bruises Ramesh left on her face.

Chapter 38
Friends
1976
New York

Soon after Mona's arrival in the States, Rebecca and Mona bonded and became inseparable. They would see each other a couple of times in a week. Rebecca had noticed bruises on Mona's arm and neck, and sometimes a black mark appeared near her eye, though Mona tried to hide the bruises with careful makeup.

"Mona, what is that mark on your neck?" Rebecca asked.

"Oh, nothing. I was frying fish in the wok, and I accidentally dropped it, so the oil sparks jumped and hit my neck. The marks will go away soon," Mona replied. Mona touched her neck and vowed she would be more thorough in her makeup.

"The marks look big for an oil burn," Rebecca said.

"It will go away, in a few days." Mona was a little fidgety.

One day after work, Rebecca saw Mona touching her eye. "Mona, what happened? Your eye looks black, and your face is swollen, like you were hit. Did you go to see a doctor?"

"No, do not worry, I will be fine. Let us talk about this coming weekend party." Mona looked worried. She was in denial and accepted Ramesh's torture as her fate.

Their friend group would go to picnics and outings in Central Park often and attend performances of Indian actors touring the United States. Mona could have never dreamed of seeing those shows in India. Rebecca was a huge fan of Indian actor Amitabh Bachchan, and she loved to see his performances on the stage. Vijay, Rebecca, and Mona all attended his shows in New York. Ramesh was never around. He always had an excuse to avoid getting together with the group.

Sensing Ramesh's absences, Vijay called him. They went out for coffee.

"Ramesh, in the last few months you have gained weight. Looks like Mona is feeding you well. Whenever we meet, you show a lot of affection to her. Your craze of the White Fairy is gone?" Vijay said.

"Vijay, she is the breath of my life. I can't survive without her."

"What do you mean? You still in contact with her?"

"Vijay, I love her. We work together, and I go to her place after factory hours to spend time together," Ramesh said.

"And what about Mona?" Vijay asked.

"After spending the evening with Teresa, I go home and I sleep with Mona," Ramesh said.

Vijay was quiet for few minutes, "Ramesh you are playing with fire. It is a dangerous game."

"Look, brother, I cannot live a moment without Teresa, and we have decided to get married. It is a matter of time; I will tell Mona soon. In the meantime, why not enjoy both," Ramesh said.

Vijay's temper shot up and he wanted to scream at Ramesh, but the matter was too delicate. "Ramesh, I can only suggest, it is better to be honest with Mona. The longer you hide it from her, the more painful it will be."

A few days later, Vijay bought an Impala Station Wagon that had eight seats. Every weekend, the group of friends went out for picnics, or to the mountains or visited Niagara Falls. Most of the time, Ramesh was absent. He would make an excuse about work at the last moment, and let Mona go with Vijay and Rebecca. Vijay detected that Ramesh had not yet told Mona his intention to leave her or about his relations with Teresa.

Mona left the brokerage firm after five months. She was offered a job in Estate Planning at the company Friedman LLP. The job at Friedman was at an entry level, but it was in her field of expertise. Ramesh was jealous of Mona getting a well-paying job at a reputable company, and he started punishing Mona more.

Chapter 39
Teresa's Place
1976
New Jersey

Teresa was insistent that Ramesh move to New Jersey and live with her.

"Ramesh, we have already decided to marry. Why don't you move in with me? You are paying rent and traveling an extra forty miles to your job every day. What is the use?"

"Sweetheart, you are right. But I do not want to break my apartment lease. It will cost me a fortune."

"Fine, then I will move in with you, and we can live in New York together. And I have still not met any of your friends. Why don't you take me to New York and introduce me?"

"My apartment is not in good area. Patience, my dear sweetheart. None of my friends know about you or my intention of marrying you. Neither my parents know of our plan. If I introduce you to my friends, the news will travel to India, faster than a blink, and my parents will not be happy. I need to go to India in December and break the news to them first."

"Ramesh, then take me with you. I want to see India."

"Let me break the news first. Then, you can visit India with me any time you want to."

Teresa was not happy with Ramesh's reasoning, but it was October, and she was willing to wait for another two months.

Mona's job at Friedman LLP would start the first week of December, and Mona getting a new job gave Ramesh an idea to send her away. He needed space to think clearly, though he had made up his mind already to divorce Mona.

To make Teresa happy, he wanted to stay a few days with her. He coaxed Mona to make a short trip to India. "Mona, this is the best opportunity! You got a job in your own field. Once you join the company, you will not be able to go home for the next few years."

Mona was reluctant. She came in March and going back to India in November for only fifteen days made no financial sense. Mona did not want to waste the money for such a short visit home but decided to go after Ramesh's unending pressure. She hurriedly did all the shopping and bought gifts for both families. She wanted to honor her family and show them her newfound success.

She thought it would be a good break to be away from Ramesh for a brief time. She was tired of his behavior. Financially, they were still not secure. Mona was sending money to her parents who were in bad shape, and Ramesh was sending money his father who insisted on getting a monthly money order from his son even though he did not need the extra funds.

Chapter 40
Back Home
1976
Kanpur

Mona's journey was long and tiring. She boarded the Air India flight from Kennedy International Airport in the evening and reached Heathrow Airport in London the following morning. She spent the entire day at Heathrow Airport. Her flight took off that evening and reached New Delhi Airport the next morning. From there, she took the train and reached Kanpur in the evening. Mona was excited to see India again.

She was received at Kanpur like a princess, and everyone was keen to hear about her life in America. She shared the gifts she brought with her family and friends. Everybody thanked her for thinking of them.

India had not stood still waiting for her to come back. Her father and mother went to the factory, and Binny went to her job. Her grandmother had become ill. She was sick, all the time, listless and complaining of vague pain. All she could do was sit in her armchair. In the evening grandmother called Mona into her room. Mona's family joined, all sat on the floor near Sarla Devi's feet.

"Beti, how is America?"Sarla Devi asked.

"Dadi Ma, it is a great country. Tall buildings, abundance of food, and clean," Mona said.

"Cleaner and bigger than Bombay?" Binny wondered.

"Yes, Bombay does not have tall buildings like New York skyscrapers," Mona said.

"Are you happy there?" Dadi Ma said.

"Can I say one thing?" Mona said.

Mona made a face, and everyone looked at her. "America is different. I don't want to lie to you, so please ask me no more questions"

Mona made obligatory visits to Ramesh's parents. Her strict father-in-law was unhappy that she was not pregnant and warned her that the firstborn baby had to be a son.

"Your first duty to the family is to have a son. I am fed up with my elder son for having daughters," growled Charan, her father-in-law.

Mona's mother-in-law, Nishi, understood her problems in America. "Don't depend on Ramesh. He is spoiled. He has inherited all the unpleasant habits of his father," Nishi said, "It is up to you, to make a better future. Do not ever think of coming back. America is your home now."

Mona looked at her mother-in-law affectionately.

People came to see her, both known and unknown. Some came for financial help thinking Mona was rich in the United States; others wanted to know how to come there.

Her parents were financially worse than when she left. Binny had changed her job and was now working as a file clerk in a small firm. Mona did not know what to do, except promise her mother that she would send more money each month. Her parents were also worried about getting Binny married.

"Don't worry, mom. From next month onwards, I will send you more money. If you find a nice groom for Binny, let me know. I will help out even more," Mona said.

"Binny, when I become a citizen, I will sponsor all of you to come to the U.S.A. You are taking diligent care of mom and dad now," Mona said. "And we can all be together then."

Ramesh stayed at Teresa's place for ten days when Mona was in India. His excuses with Teresa were getting complicated. He was nervous. He could not sleep at night. He was not sure how much more he could lie but began to feel comfortable with the arrangement with two women. With the White Goddess and Dark Temptress, he was living a double life and wanted to leave the situation as it was.

Chapter 41
Back To U.S.A.
1976
New York

When Mona returned from India, she was surprised to hear that Ramesh was going to India at Christmas time.

"Why did you not tell me of your intention of going to India? We could have gone together," Mona said.

"Well…," Ramesh said. His thoughts started to churn.

"Ramesh, why are you going to India? I just saw your parents, and they are in good health."

"Mona, you don't understand. My dad called me to come to India," said Ramesh.

"Your dad did not mention that to me. When did he call you?" asked Mona.

"My dad called me after you left. He said it is urgent. It is about his bungalow, a property matter. He wants to write his will, and he needs to consult me."

"Your dad wants to write his will, and he needs to consult you?" Mona repeated thoughtfully.

"Shut up, Mona. You are asking too many questions," Ramesh said. Mona could not accept his lame excuses, but she kept silent and did not challenge her husband.

Chapter 42
Unexpected Turn
1976
New York

Ramesh's flight was to leave in the evening from Kennedy International Airport. Ramesh had promised Teresa he would see her before leaving the country. That morning brought the worst snowstorm on the east coast. Some freeways were closed, and Mona's office was shut down due to the weather. Ramesh made an excuse to Mona that he needed to drive to his factory in New Jersey for an urgent work matter. Mona pleaded with her husband, "Why you are going to work? The weather is awful, and your plane departs in the evening. Please don't go."

"You don't understand, Mona. It is the Christmas season. All orders need to be completed in time for sale," Ramesh replied.

"You mean to say, without you they cannot run the factory? Look outside. It is snowing heavily. You cannot see more than four feet away. How will you drive the car?" Mona said.

"Quiet, woman! Do not bother me. I will be back soon. And do not bother to take me to the airport. I have asked Vijay to drop me off at the airport. He will be here around three-thirty," Ramesh said.

"Please do me a favor. As soon you reach work and when you leave, please call me," Mona insisted. Ramesh ignored her.

After Ramesh left, Mona was restless. It was difficult for her to pass the time. Every few minutes she would pick up the receiver as if she heard the phone. Four hours passed, and Ramesh did not call. It was already noon, and he had to be at the airport by six in the evening.

Life took a strange turn. Mona called his factory. "Hello, I am calling to speak to Mr. Ramesh. I am his wife. The weather is bad, so I wanted to make sure that Mr. Ramesh reached the factory safely."

"Madam, the factory is closed today. Yesterday, management anticipated harsh weather and told all workers to stay home," the lady at the other end replied.

"If the factory is closed today, then how are you answering the phone?" Mona asked.

"Madam, this is an answering service. We will convey the message that you enquired about Mr. Ramesh," the lady replied.

Ramesh came back in a foul mood, around four in the afternoon. Vijay was waiting to take him to Kennedy International Airport.

"Hello, Vijay. I am sorry, Mona, the completion of orders took a long time. As soon they put the goods in the truck, I left the factory." Vijay and Mona both stared at Ramesh. Before she could say a word, he picked up his luggage. "Let us go, Vijay. Mona, you don't have to see me off at the airport," Ramesh said.

"No, I want to see you off," Mona said.

"Let Mona come with us," Vijay said.

Ramesh was not happy.

Ramesh put his luggage in the car, and they left for the airport. She had many questions, but in front of Vijay, Mona remained silent.

It was snowing, so Vijay was driving slow and carefully. The traffic was bumper to bumper.

At the airport Ramesh embraced her tightly, as if they were not going to meet again. With her head resting on his shoulder, she sniffed the same perfume which she smelled from his pillow.

After dropping Ramesh off, Vijay and Mona rode home. They each said little.

Vijay was sad when he reached home that night.

Rebecca saw him unusually subdued. "What's the matter with you? What happened?" Rebecca asked.

Vijay could not hold the secret. He told Rebecca about Ramesh falling in love with someone else and his plan to divorce Mona.

Chapter 43
They Meet
1976
New York

The next morning, Mona had a headache. She was not feeling well, and a strange fear was taking root. She took the day off from work. She was still in bed when the telephone rang.

"Hello," Mona picked up the phone.

"Hello?"

"Yes, who is this?" Mona said.

"I am Teresa White, the personnel manager at Ginger Lingerie Manufacturing Company. With whom am I talking? Is Ramesh at home?"

"I am his wife, Mona. He left for India yesterday evening," Mona said.

"Are you sure you are the wife of Ramesh who works at Ginger Lingerie?" Teresa said.

"Of course, I am his wife. Why are you asking?" Mona said.

"Well, the answering service sent your message to my department. Yesterday you called our factory to enquire about your husband. Our company likes to keep a close relationship between our managers and their families, so I thought as the personnel manager of the company, I would like to meet you," Teresa said.

"That is very nice of you," Mona replied.

"I have come to our New York office on company business. Do you mind if I stop by to visit you?" Teresa asked.

"Why don't you come after Ramesh returns from India?" Mona hesitantly replied.

"Well, we already know Ramesh so it's not necessary for him to be there. I could be at your place by noon. I won't spend more than a few minutes if it is OK with you?" Teresa said.

Mona gave her the address and quickly cleaned the house. She took a shower, dressed in a nice sari, and put on a little bit of makeup. She was ready to receive Teresa.

At noon sharp, Teresa rang the bell. Mona opened the door and in front of her stood a beautiful lady. Mona noticed her blond hair, blue eyes, smooth white skin, immaculate dress, and matching jewelry.

"I am Teresa, and you are the wife of Ramesh," Teresa said.

"Yes, I am Mona. Please come in," Mona replied.

Teresa was equally surprised to see a beautiful woman standing in front of her. She noticed Mona's height, curves, flawless skin, and shining black hair.

"Oh my, your apartment is beautiful. How nicely you have decorated it! It gives a feeling of a cheerful home," Teresa said.

"Thank you. Would you care for a cup of tea or coffee?" Mona had the unsettled feeling that Teresa was judging her.

"Sure, I will have a cup of tea. Do you mind if I take a few pictures of your apartment? I would like to put them in our company's monthly newsletter. Everyone would be happy to see how our workers live at home." She glanced around.

Mona brought tea and salted cookies from the kitchen. "Please take some biscuits with your tea," Mona said.

"No, thank you. Can I use your bathroom?" Teresa said.

Teresa came out of bathroom.

"On second thought, can I have another cup of tea?"

"Sure." Mona went into kitchen to make more tea.

"Thank you. I am getting the delicious smell of cooked chilies," Teresa said.

"Oh yes, I make *rajma*. It is an Indian dish made with red kidney beans with spices. Would you like a taste?" offered Mona.

"In India, you make chili but in this vegetarian style. Can I try a little portion?" Teresa said.

Mona gave her a small cup.

"It is delicious," Teresa said.

"You seem to like Indian food," Mona said.

"Yes, Ramesh and I share his tiffin daily. I thought he was a good cook, but now I know he has a wife who cooks for him," Teresa said, and Mona glanced at her.

"We all share our food," Teresa said.

They sat down and chatted for some time. Teresa wanted to know more about Mona's life and about her wedding. In return, Mona asked Teresa what job she was doing at the company and how she became friendly with Ramesh. Teresa patiently dodged Mona's questions.

After a few minutes, Teresa said, "I think I should leave now."

Mona followed Teresa to the door. Teresa said goodbye. Standing beside Teresa, Mona was getting the familiar scent of her perfume.

Teresa never expected to meet a smart and beautiful young woman. She was stunned to think that she trusted Ramesh and had no inkling of the game he was playing. He was married. How could he be so cunning?

Teresa could not comprehend why he never told her. Teresa thought, *If he could leave his beautiful wife, then he could tire of me and leave me too.*

Mona remained in a thoughtful mood for the rest of the day. At night, she tossed and turned in bed. She could still smell the strong scent of Teresa's perfume. She woke up with a jolt as she recognized the smell. The smell on Ramesh's pillow was the same perfume Teresa was using!

Mona wailed and cried. *Ramesh was having an affair with Teresa this whole time!* Many thoughts came to her mind, and she felt helpless. Only nine months had passed since she came to America. What had happened? She never thought Ramesh could hurt her like this.

In the morning, Mona was getting ready to go to her job when Teresa called her to ask if they could meet for lunch at some place. Mona agreed to meet Teresa in a restaurant nearby her place of work. Both were hurt badly by the realization of Ramesh's infidelity. When they saw each other, both women had eyes full of tears and rage.

"Tell me, Mona, how did you not detect Ramesh was playing both of us?" Teresa said.

"How could I? He married me. He was my husband! We had friends and a rich social life. At night, he was sleeping with me. It never occurred to me that he was having an affair. I want to ask you the same question. , Why did you not have any clue?" Mona said.

"Every evening he would come to my apartment after work and spend a few hours with me. He always had an excuse to go back to New York to sleep there. When you were in India, he stayed at my place for fifteen days and gave me full assurance of marrying me. I trusted him," Teresa said.

Mona asked Teresa how they met and what lies Ramesh told her. To her surprise, Teresa had never asked

Ramesh about his family, his friends, or his living situation. Teresa had trusted him and assumed too much. Similarly, Mona never probed about his job, why he was coming back late, or why he would come home drunk daily. Both ladies poured their heart out, and they had no tears left. They were angry and full of spite.

They remained silent for a while; both were victims of Ramesh's duplicity. They could not imagine Ramesh could be such a heartless person.

"What are you going to do?"Teresa asked.

"I don't know. I am new to this country, and he is my husband," Mona said and looked over at Teresa. "What are you going to do?"

"I am going to burn his ass so badly that he will remember it all his life."

Teresa was ready to do something, but Mona did not know what she could do. Mona was still in shock. They parted and talked over the phone occasionally, promising to remain friends. They never saw each other again.

Chapter 44
Disappointment
1977
New York

Ramesh's trip to Kanpur City was not successful. No one agreed with him on his plan to divorce Mona. His parents advised him to be mature, as he was a married man who had asked for Mona's hand. His family told him to forget Teresa.

Ramesh's whole family was sitting in the living room, his dad Charan, his mom Nishi, his brother Sundar, and his wife Umi.

"Why do you want to marry an American girl and divorce Mona?" Charan said.

"Dad, she is exceptionally beautiful. She is very fair, blond hair, blue eyes," Ramesh said showing her picture.

"Hum, she is beautiful. What do her father and mother do and where do they live?" Charan said.

"Her mother and father both inherited lot of money from their parents. They never worked and their philosophy was always, to make love not war. They are retired and living in Florida in a colony, with people who share the same kind of thinking," Ramesh said.

His father looked at Ramesh's mother Nishi and said, "Look at your son. You sent your son to achieve something in America, and what he has achieved? He met a white woman, and now he wants to marry her and live with a hippie family who has never worked a day in their lives."

Looking at Ramesh, his father continued. "If something happens to that white girl, and she turns dark, then what will you do? You will divorce her and marry another fair skin woman. I will not accept this kind of behavior!"

Ramesh's parents lectured him about there being more to marriage and life than fair skin. He should consider Mona's other qualities, and if he divorced her, the whole community would isolate Ramesh's family.

His father said, "It is a question of honor, respect and tradition. Mona is our daughter-in-law, and your white girlfriend will never be our daughter-in-law."

Ramesh was not happy. His parents would never accept Teresa. Not one member of his family took his side. But Ramesh was determined to separate from Mona. He returned New York after three weeks.

His return flight landed in New York in the morning. It was cold and snow blanketed the runway. Planes were hovering, waiting to land.

Ramesh thought many times about what he would say to Mona. Mona had taken the day off, but she was not in the mood to go the airport. Vijay volunteered to pick up Ramesh. Vijay was keen to know what Ramesh had decided about the divorce.

The flight was only an hour late. It took time for Ramesh to come out of customs. Vijay waved to him. "Hello, Ramesh! How was your trip to India and how is your family?"

"India is fine, and everyone in Kanpur is fine. I don't see Mona!" Ramesh moved his head from side to side.

"She has taken the day off, and she is waiting for you at home," Vijay said.

"Good, I wanted to talk with you before I see her," Ramesh said.

Vijay looked at Ramesh. "Let us put the luggage in the car first."

On the way home from the airport, Ramesh told Vijay, "No one in my family agrees with me. My family has left it up to me to decide, but they made it clear that if I divorce Mona, I will not be welcomed home with Teresa. They do not want the wrath of whole community. Tell me, what I should do?"

"Don't ask me what you should do. You created this ruckus, and you should resolve it."

"I cannot leave Teresa, and I feel guilty about sending Mona back home. Mona keeps the house spotlessly clean, she cooks the tastiest food, and she even polishes my shoes. On the other hand, Teresa does not have any of those qualities. I have to do everything for her."

"You feel guilty!" Vijay was not happy to learn Mona polishes his shoes.

"You don't know Teresa. In bed she is like a tigress. Is it possible that I continue to keep both women?" Ramesh said.

Vijay looked at him in wonder. "How the hell you are getting such stupid thoughts! Sex has eaten your brain. You do not deserve Mona. If you had such a low opinion of Mona before marriage, why did you choose to marry her?"

"At that time, I had a high opinion of Mona. When I met Teresa, everything changed," Ramesh said.

Vijay was frustrated. "Look, choose what you wish, but I will not let you spoil Mona's life. If you want to get a divorce and send her back to India, you will make an enemy of me. If you let her stay here, you will have to wait to file for divorce until she becomes a citizen."

"But citizenship will take a few years!"

"Well, if you and Teresa are serious, then you can wait."

Ramesh reached home. Vijay let Ramesh take out the luggage from the car.

"Won't you come inside?" Ramesh asked.

"No, I have to go back to my office," said Vijay.

"Come in for a few minutes and say hello to Mona," Ramesh said.

"OK, only for a minute," Vijay said.

Ramesh lugged his suitcases up to the apartment. Mona was waiting for him at the door. The aroma of Indian food spread through the corridor. Mona was looking radiant, wearing an orange sari and a matching blouse. Ramesh approached Mona and embraced her tightly.

"Hi Mona, I've missed you so much," he kissed her.

Mona was waiting for Ramesh sternly, and she was ready to confront him. His tight embrace and kiss made her anger toward him melt a little.

"Hi, Mona," Vijay said. He was stiff.

"Hi, Vijay Bhai," Mona said. Seeing Vijay made her feel nervous about confronting Ramesh.

"Alright, Ramesh, I need to leave now. Bye, Mona." Vijay walked towards the apartment entrance.

"Wait, Vijay Bhai. I have set the table for three. Have lunch with us and then go," Mona said.

"Lunch cooked by you is very tempting. But thank you, Mona. I must go to my office; I have a meeting. I will see you in the next few days, after Ramesh settles down from his trip," Vijay said, and he walked out. He did not like to face Mona during such a heated situation.

"How is everybody in India?" Mona inquired.

Mona was angry, but she softened after Ramesh expressed that he missed her while he was in India. Seeing him in a good mood, she decided to wait before confronting Ramesh about his affair.

"Everybody is fine there," Ramesh said and went to the bathroom to wash his face. As Mona started setting the food on the table for lunch, Ramesh came out of the bathroom and sat down on the sofa. Mona went back into the kitchen to make tea for Ramesh.

Ramesh thought, before he breaks the news, why not enjoy Mona one last time? "Mona, come sit next to me," Ramesh said. Mona came from the kitchen slowly and sat on the sofa. He put his arms around her. He started kissing her passionately.

"You don't know how much I've missed you." He put his hand under her blouse.

"Ramesh, not now. Wait," Mona said.

"Come on, Mona, I have been waiting for a month to take you in my arms."

She protested again, "Take it easy, Ramesh. Lunch will get cold. Eat something and rest for a while."

He pushed her on the sofa and tried to remove her sari.

"Ramesh, please, why don't you wait?"

"Do what I say, or else I will divorce you and send you back India. Do not resist me again!" Ramesh shouted.

Mona was astonished at his attitude. She was expecting him to take her in his arms, cajole and kiss her, and apologize for his affair with Teresa. Instead, he was pressuring her to undress instantly, under the threat of divorce. Her body was not ready, and she spurned his advances.

She resisted, and he forcefully pulled her sari down.

"You bitch, you will never change," Ramesh said.

Mona was stunned and could not speak or think.

After his fill, Ramesh took a shower. While getting dressed, he said to Mona, "I think we should file for divorce. There is no use of us going on like this. I don't like your behavior."

Mona felt a growing anger at Ramesh for repeatedly talking about divorce. "Why are you bringing this up?"

Ramesh ignored her and picked up the phone to call the factory.

"Damn it. No one is picking up the phone. I am going to the factory. I will be back late this evening."

Mona was shaking with anger and humiliation. She picked up her sari from the floor. She was furious about the way he threatened her with divorce. *He was still chasing after Teresa But, she was his wife.*

Chapter 45
Rejection
1977
New York

Ramesh drove to the factory only to find his and Teresa's offices locked. No one could tell him where Teresa was. The factory manager Robert Holt saw Ramesh at the locked doors and brought Ramesh into his office.

Robert handed him an envelope. "Business is slow. We are cutting down on people. I am sorry your services will not be required anymore. Here is your two weeks' notice and salary," Robert said.

Ramesh was stunned. He remained silent.

"And if you ever need references for a job, you can give my name."

"I don't understand. I thought business was booming, and I was doing an excellent job," Ramesh pleaded.

"I like you, and you are a good engineer, but Christmas was slow. This is management's decision. I can't help it."

Ramesh asked, "I was wondering, is Teresa here today?"

"Teresa left the company two days after you flew to India," his boss said.

"But why?" Ramesh was surprised.

"She got married and moved. Florida, I believe," his boss replied.

"What, she got married!" It took more than a minute to sink into Ramesh's mind that Teresa married and disappeared from his life.

Ramesh left the office. He lost his job and he lost Teresa all at once. He was jilted, abandoned by the White Goddess who was his life. His senses deserted him. He wandered around the factory and checked with other colleagues. Bit by bit, from those willing to tell him the truth, Ramesh found out the real reason he was fired: Teresa found out about Ramesh's lies and made a big uproar in the factory. Gossip reached up to management

Ramesh did not remember where he parked his car, so he wandered in a daze until he finally found it. He sat for a moment, considering his options to reach Teresa. He was in shock. He could not comprehend why Teresa had left him. *Married? To another?* He did not know what to do. All his hopes disappeared with Teresa.

He went to a bar near his apartment building and spent the rest of day drinking. All day he sat there, looking at the people around him. Young couples, old couples, and beautiful women sat at the bar for a drink or two. His mind was blank, and he kept gazing at people.

Chapter 46
Subdued
1977
New York

Ramesh returned home drunk that night. It was cold and snowing lightly. Mona was waiting for him. She warmed up dinner. Ramesh sat on the sofa and opened a bottle of scotch. He poured liquor into two glasses and handed her one glass.

"Finish your drink and stand in front of me," Ramesh demanded.

Mona took a few sips of scotch and stared at him. She was pent-up with anger; she wanted to wring his neck.

"Take off your clothes," Ramesh said.

"You see me naked every day. What do you get by seeing me naked when you are drunk?"

He was angry and wanted to kick someone, and Mona was there. He got up, putting his finger under her chin, and put his other hand on her breasts.

"You had your fill in the morning. Why do you want me to take off my clothes again? First you want a divorce, but now you want my body." Mona pulled away from him. " You are tired and drunk. Go to bed,"

"I said, take off your clothes!"

Ramesh twisted Mona's arm; she was in pain. He waited for few moments, "You know why, because I want to compare you with someone." He loosened his grip.

"Teresa is gone. Now you should start respecting me," Mona said boldly.

He looked at her with stern eyes and slapped Mona. He slapped her again. Mona tried to confront Ramesh, but he pushed her against the dining table. He removed his belt and struck her.

"This is the way you should be managed." His desperation turned to violence. Ramesh hit her hard. She turned away to protect her face. Then he stopped, sat down on the sofa, drunk and tired, head down. Soon, he fell asleep.

Mona leaned on the dining room table. Blood seeped through her sari. *What did I do to deserve a beating like this? It was Ramesh who was being unfaithful, and it was he who wanted to opt out of the marriage. Why am I married to such a cruel man?*

Her life had changed in last few months; she knew she could not continue to stay in this apartment.

While Ramesh was sleeping on the sofa, Mona quietly called Rebecca. Mona needed someone to guide and counsel her. "Rebecca, I am not feeling well. Can I come and stay with you?"

"Are you alright?"

"No, I am not. Ramesh slapped me, then hit me with his fists and belt. I do not know what he will do next. I am having pain all over my body." Mona began to sob.

"Oh my God, how dare he hurt you?" Rebecca had noticed Mona's bruises over the past few months and suspected Ramesh's violent nature. "Pick up some clothes and come immediately to my place. You are always welcome here," Rebecca said.

Mona quietly packed the necessary items in a suitcase and took a taxi to Rebecca's house. Seeing Mona in such a vulnerable condition shocked Rebecca, and tears came into her eyes.

Rebecca embraced Mona, and Mona burst into sobs that she could not control. "I never knew he was having an affair this whole time. Instead of apologizing, he lashed out at me."

Chapter 47
Mona Leaves
1977
New York

Ramesh woke up late in the evening with a headache. He looked out from the window to see the dark sky. No lights were on in the apartment. He stumbled from the sofa.

"Mona, get me a glass of water. What is the matter, Mona? Why are the lights not on?" Ramesh called out.

Ramesh waited and realized Mona was not responding to him. He roamed the whole apartment. She was not there. He thought, *It does not matter. Where else could she go in this big city? She will be back.* He walked into the bedroom and went to sleep.

When Ramesh woke up the next morning, he was hungry. He was sure Mona would be back by now. After not seeing her in the apartment, he was confident that she would be waiting outside the door, with folded hands to apologize for her behavior. He opened the door, but she was not outside. He was concerned and waited for another half an hour. He thought of calling her work or the police, but on second thought, he called Rebecca instead.

Rebecca picked up the phone. Ramesh sounded panicked. "Hello, Rebecca, Ramesh speaking. Is Mona there?" Ramesh said.

"Why, what happened? Why would she be in our house?"Rebecca pretended.

"You see, I came back yesterday, and I saw her for a short while. Then I had to go to work. When I returned, she was not at home, and I have not seen her since," Ramesh said.

"Yes, she is at our place, but she does not want to see you. Please, do not call or come to our place," Rebecca said.

"I am her husband. Tell her to come to the phone and talk to me!"

Rebecca looked at Mona, and Mona shook her head.

"Ramesh, she does not want to talk with you, "Rebecca said.

"Tell her, I am her husband and I demand that she come to the phone!"

Mona took the phone from Rebecca, "Hello, Ramesh."

"Mona, what sort of nonsense is this! Come back home now. Otherwise, you know what I will do," Ramesh threatened.

Mona put the phone down.

"Listen, Mona, Mona," Ramesh shouted into the receiver. He said to himself, *If she does not want to come back, let her stay there. Good riddance.* But his rage and anger rose up.

Ramesh was furious. He dialed Vijay. "Hello, Vijay, what is happening? Mona is at your place, and you have no courtesy to call me. Tell her she should come back home immediately, or I will send her back to India!"

Vijay cut the conversation. "Ramesh, I am in a meeting. I will call you later. Wait for my call."

"Alright." Ramesh hung up.

Vijay did not call Ramesh back that day, and Mona stayed with Rebecca.

News travelled fast among their friends. Everyone came to know what was going on with Mona and Ramesh, and no one was happy.

Ramesh tried to call his friends. No one would pick up the phone.

I do not give a damn if my friends do not want to talk with me, Ramesh thought.

Ramesh considered sending Mona back to India. He would find out where Teresa was living, and he could beg her to come back.

Ramesh tried to cook and made a mess in the kitchen, so he heated up a ready-made TV dinner from the grocery store. Every part of his life had failed. He had no job. Mona and Rebecca did not want to talk with him, and Vijay was angry with him. His friends shunned him. Teresa had left him.

He hoped Mona would come crawling back to ask for forgiveness. She had not even bothered to ask how he was doing. The smell of unwashed dishes was awful. The house was dirty, and being spoiled and chauvinistic, he had never learned to recognize his faults and never to say 'sorry' in his life.

Chapter 48
Marriage Commitments
1977
New York

Mona had been living at Vijay's place for the past nine days. One day while drinking tea, Rebecca said, "Mona, you married Ramesh after meeting him only once. You took a chance on him, and it was a disaster. Why do you want to remain married to this man who has hurt you?"

Mona said, "In India, marriage emphasizes the family more than the groom and the bride. If the family is well-respected, they can put pressure on the couple. The control that our elders have over the family is strong. Whatever decision the family elders decide for the young couple, the couple must abide and follow. It's different here in America, where people are independent and make their own choices."

Rebecca stared at Mona, "You are giving me the solution to your own problem. You are not in India, and here you are not under the spell of a controlled society. Here you are as free as a bird. You can pursue what you desire, with no restrictions or prejudices. Why do you want to remain chained to the yoke of archaic religious customs? You pray every day for Ramesh's long life and good health, just so he can kick you, insult you and abuse you?" Rebecca took a sip of tea.

Mona said, "You were not born in India. Being a girl in India is different. From the day you come into this world, daughters are told that they are inferior to man. Even your training and education revolves around marriage and producing children. The goal of your whole life is to please your husband and accept however he treats you. Your husband is your lord, and he is your salvation in this life and in coming births. You cannot change the cultural and religious thinking. Even after Independence and new laws."

Rebecca got up and paced around, "Wake up, Mona, this is the twentieth century. You are a woman, and you need to take charge of your life. Take a stand, value your worth, and put yourself first. You can reach the stars! That is why this country is called the land of opportunities. If you work hard, you can achieve your ambition in this country."

Mona remained in turmoil. Ramesh was not treating her well, and their marriage was on the rocks. She came to America with ambitions and dreams that were not yet fulfilled.

Chapter 49
Never Said Sorry
1977
New York

As the last resort, Ramesh picked up the phone and called Vijay. "Hello, Vijay, how are you?"

"I am fine. How are the things at your end?" Vijay said.

"Can we meet?" Ramesh said.

"Of course, any time." Vijay said.

Ramesh and Vijay met later that day at a coffee shop. Vijay knew Ramesh had lost his job, and Vijay shook his head in disappointment after seeing Ramesh. He felt sorry to see Ramesh in a pitiable condition, with an unshaven face, uncombed hair, and unclean body. Ramesh smelled as though he had not taken a shower for days.

The waitress brought them coffee and Vijay pushed aside his cup. Looking at Ramesh squarely, he asked, "So, how are you doing, Ramesh?"

"I am fine, and how is Mona doing?" Ramesh said.

"She is fine. I heard that you lost your job. I thought you were doing well in that company."

"I was, but it was my mistake. When Teresa came to learn that I was married, she overreacted and created an uproar at the factory. Teresa immediately left the company, and then I was fired as a result."

"Do you think Teresa overreacted? You lied and cheated on her, and you cheated on Mona. In India, you would have been thrown out of the family," said Vijay. He slammed his hand down on the table.

"Bhai, she is gone. My White Goddess left me. She married someone else." Ramesh still could hardly say the words.

"You got what you deserved," said Vijay. "You are a stubborn man who cannot overcome his ego. You must apologize to Mona."

"Why should I apologize? Mona left the apartment on her own. If she wanted to come back, it is her choice."

"We all know how you mistreated and abused Mona. You have ruined her life. Remember when you called me from India, thanking me for introducing you to her and saying that you love her. What happened to you? Don't you feel ashamed for your thinking?"

"Well, I was blinded by love for Teresa. Mona does have a few good qualities," Ramesh mumbled.

Vijay interrupted sarcastically, "She has a few good qualities! You do not have even one decent quality. We can take care of Mona, and unless you realize and repent, there will be no further use of talking with each other." Vijay stormed out of the coffee shop with anger and said to himself, "Jerk."

Ramesh face was etched with disappointment.

Chapter 50
Two Weeks Later
1977
New York

More time passed, and reality hit Ramesh hard. Teresa was gone. Married to another. He needed Mona. She had a stable job, and he needed money for drinks to be with his friends at bars. More importantly, he needed a woman to take care of him.

He became desperate and called Vijay to request permission to visit Mona. Ramesh was still not ready to admit his mistakes.

Vijay agreed and arranged a meeting at his home. Vijay, Mona, Rebecca, and Ramesh were all there. Mona was sitting on one sofa with her sari covering her face, and Ramesh was sitting on the other sofa. Vijay and Rebecca were standing behind Mona supportively.

Ramesh got down from the sofa and kneeled on the ground facing Mona. "I am sorry, Mona, I was blinded by Teresa. I behaved very inconsiderately. I apologize. Please forgive me and come back home. I promise, I will fully respect you and never raise my hand to hurt you." He folded his hands, "Please, Mona."Mona got up and moved away from Ramesh.

Rebecca went inside her bedroom and brought the Holy Gita. She told Ramesh to put his hand over the Gita and repeat the words he had promised to Mona. He did as he was told.

Mona remained silent. There were only two alternatives for her. She could annul the marriage, go back to India, and forget her ambitions. Her other choice was to stay with Ramesh and give her marriage one final chance.

Mona decided to give one more chance to Ramesh and their marriage.

"Ramesh, I have a few conditions that you have to promise me. Number one, you need to join Alcoholics Anonymous. Secondly, you will have to control your temper. You cannot insult me, curse me, or beat me. You will treat me respectfully as your wife and not your servant. And thirdly, you will throw all your crazy sex toys in the garbage."

The words 'sex toys' raised Rebecca and Vijay's eyes, but they remained silent.

"I will agree with all your conditions. Please, Mona, come home."

Mona came home later that day. Ramesh found a new job in an engineering firm. Though Mona got rid of all his sex toys, she was not ready to sleep with him in the same bed. She slept in the bedroom while Ramesh slept in the living room. Mona saw that Ramesh fulfilled his promises, and after sometime, she allowed him to sleep in the bedroom with her. Slowly, life returned to normal.

Chapter 51
Surprise
1977
New York

Two months passed since Mona and Ramesh reconciled. Mona was busy setting up the apartment again, but for the last few days, she was experiencing back pain and nausea. She went to see Joyce, her doctor.

"Hi, Mona, how are you? You are not due for your annual checkup. Are you ill?" the doctor asked.

"Doc, I am feeling nauseous every morning and often have headaches. I thought I should get checked out to be safe," Mona said.

"Hmm, let me examine you," Joyce said.

Joyce examined Mona thoroughly and asked Mona questions about her health and lifestyle. At the end of the exam, Joyce said, "Mona you are in great health."

"What do you mean? I am having nausea every morning. How can I be in fine health?" she asked.

"I thought you knew," the doctor replied.

"If I had known the problem, then why would I come to see you?" Mona countered.

"Mona, you are pregnant," the doctor said.

"What!" Mona caught her breath. "Doctor, this is not possible. How could I be pregnant?"

"Why is it not possible?" the doctor asked.

"My husband I have taken all the precautions," she said hesitantly.

"Sometimes, precautions don't work. You are a healthy person you have no health problems. Come back next month for a prenatal checkup," the doctor said.

Mona reached home devastated. *Why am I pregnant now, when I am not sure if we will be together for the rest of our lives?*

Ramesh still drank daily, and at the slightest whim, he was ready to jump into bed with Mona. She sat on her bed and tried to analyze how it was possible to get pregnant. Ramesh never bothered to take any safety measures. Mona, on the other hand, was punctual in taking her birth control pills. She had stopped using the pill only when Ramesh left for India. For three weeks, she thought there was no need to spend money on birth control. The day Ramesh came back from India, he forced himself on her. *One moment, one time, unprotected,* she concluded. *I am to be a mother.*

Now, all her ambitions had to be put on hold.

Mona was on the verge of a new career and focused on getting her Ph. D. She thought the best option was to get an abortion. She could have a baby years later when their relationship was stronger. She could ask her doctor for the address of an abortion clinic, travel there, and avoid telling Ramesh. She found out quickly that she could not make the decision on her own. New York law required the consent of both mother and father for the abortion.

Mona decided she had to tell Ramesh. She would wait for the best moment to convince him that an abortion was their best choice. She made a vow never to have unprotected sex again.

When Ramesh came home from work that evening, Mona served him dinner with his favorite dishes. Mona could not hold her thoughts and blurted out she was pregnant.

"When you came from India, you wanted to have sex. You should have given me time to take precautions because now I am pregnant," she said. "We are going to have a baby!"

The only words he heard were, they were 'going to have baby.' He jumped up from the chair and started dancing with her, "We will have a son. My father's wish will be granted! A son, a son!" he exclaimed.

He immediately picked up the phone and called India. Mona tried to stop him, but he pushed her back. The message was conveyed to his family that Mona was expecting. The phone was given immediately to Mona.

"Here, take the phone and talk to my mom. Put the sound up, so I can hear also," Ramesh said.

"Hello Mummyji." Before Mona could say anything, her mother-in-law said, "Congratulations, Beti, we were waiting for this good news for many months. God has granted our wish. Eat well and take care of your health."

"Yes, Mummyji, I will," Mona said.

The phone was given to her father-in-law, "Congratulation, Beti, it is wonderful news and remember my words. The firstborn child must be a son. I want a grandson to continue our heritage. We all need to pray to God for a son."

The telephone was given to Ramesh's sister-in-law, Umi. "Deveraniji, congratulations. We will go to the temple every day to pray for the health of your son."

Mona had to talk with each of Ramesh's relatives and listened patiently to their blessings. She was told about the challenges of pregnant women, what food she should eat and avoid, and what pujas she should perform to have a son.

Mona could not sleep at night. She should have gone to a clinic to get the baby aborted. She was miserable and felt trapped. The next day at dinner, Mona decided to discuss the idea of an abortion with Ramesh.

"Ramesh, you know our marriage is still not on steady footing. We are not stable financially. It's a difficult environment to bring a child into." Mona held her voice steady. "We can get an abortion."

Ramesh was not convinced. "Mona, my whole family is waiting for an heir to the family. They are convinced our first born will be a boy, and even the family astrologer has confirmed this. Why should we abort this baby?"

"But I have a new job. Who will stay home during the day to take care of the baby?" Mona asked.

"I will. I will find a job where I can work the night shift. Remember, it is a sin to have an abortion," Ramesh said.

He was adamant to have the baby. Mona believed she had no choice but to continue the pregnancy, though she was unhappy. Mona accepted the decision to keep the baby, thinking, As *a mother, I will nurture and shape the future. I am a strong woman.*

Mona called her parents the next day to tell them she was pregnant. She called Rebecca and told her the good news as well.

"Oh my God, you are going to have a baby. How wonderful. Mona, you must have a daughter! You don't know how much I have dreamed of having a daughter," Rebecca said.

Chapter 52
Sandy
1977
New York

Time passed quickly. During the last few months of her pregnancy, Mona became more religious. Praying in the morning and in the evening, she begged God for a son. For her, either a boy or girl were equally welcome, but she remembered the warning words of her father-in-law. *Your sole duty is to bear children, and the first-born has to be a son. Otherwise, you will fail as a wife.*One early morning, Mona went into labor suddenly and was in a lot of pain. After waiting for hours for her to deliver naturally, the doctors decided to do a caesarian section. Her daughter, Sandy, was born with the loudest cry.

The ob-gyn doctor soon told Mona her fate. "There are dangerous complications from the birth. Mona, do not ever think of having a second child. You could have a painful miscarriage, and you and the child both could die."

The news was disturbing, and Mona was crying at the hospital. It was a big blow to Ramesh's family, as they were sure that the child would be a boy. The blame was directed towards Mona, who did not bear a son.

Ramesh was consoling, "Mona, it is all right. It is God's will. We should accept his gift with thanks and blessing." Mona was surprised to hear his openness.

But Sandy's birth brought out Ramesh's practiced cruelty in other ways. Sandy resembled Vijay and had similar fair skin. Ramesh taunted Mona sarcastically, that Sandy must be Vijay's daughter.

Chapter 53
Acceptance
1977
New York

After Sandy was born, Mona took a leave for a few months. Then Mona went back to her job. She and Ramesh moved into a two-bedroom apartment. Ramesh had an unsteady job history. With most jobs, he either got fired or he resigned, as he could not manage the pressure of meeting deadlines. Ramesh's ego was still high. He could not control his drinking habit, and he was becoming an alcoholic.

Ramesh never helped Mona in the household chores. He was lazy. Mona was the bread winner, the maid, the cook, and the caretaker of their baby. But she tried with hope to make their life better.

"Ramesh, why don't you control your drinking habit? You drink in the morning, and your drinking continues until late in the evening," Mona said.

"Mona, I am trying," Ramesh said.

He returned to his old habits. After drinking, he would abuse her verbally and taunt her for having Vijay's baby. Mona vehemently denied this. Ramesh knew Sandy was his offspring, but intentionally aimed at Mona in his anger.

"Where is Vijay's daughter? Is she sleeping?" Ramesh said.

"Ramesh, Vijay is like my brother. Do not ever call her Vijay's daughter. She is your daughter, and only yours," Mona said sternly.

Ramesh remained demanding. Mona was his property. Sometimes, he could not control his temper and slapped her. Whenever Mona spurned his demands, he would become violent. He had forgotten his promises of good behavior when he had placed his hand on the holy Gita.

"Ramesh, you promised me that you will not raise your hand to hit me. What happened to your promises?" Mona said. Whenever she saw Ramesh was angry, Mona would take Sandy to her bedroom and lock the door.

Mona had accepted the abuse as part of her life. She became immune to his curses, his slaps, and his idiosyncrasies. Ramesh never showed tenderness, love, or romance. She felt that her soul had died.

Vijay and Rebecca knew what was going on. They were concerned about Mona after realizing that Ramesh had deteriorated. To keep peace and normalcy, they tried not to interfere but kept watch. At one point, they suggested that Ramesh seek counseling, and he refused their advice by claiming that there was nothing wrong with him.

Rebecca stayed closed to Mona. "Mona, it is sad to see you live this miserable life." Rebecca said.

"Rebecca, it is my fate. I have to go through this torture."

Chapter 54
Longing
1977
New York

Though Mona's heart was broken, she never lost her passion for high achievement. She continued to take pre-requisite courses in college to start on her Ph.D. program in economics. She was determined to do her Ph.D. and help her parents back in India.

Vijay and Rebecca were always there to support and encourage her. Mona, Sandy, Vijay, Rebecca and their children, Anand and Sugund, would go to picnics and parties together. Ramesh avoided the gatherings, rarely accompanying them.

The traditional Indians were still singing the blues and longing to go back to the motherland, but nobody went back for long. Those who went back home returned to the U.S. with disappointment. Mona asked about their experience.

One of her friends said, "Too much family interference."

Another friend said, "Children could not adjust to the school system."

Someone else said, "Could not adjust to their lifestyle."

They were not happy in India for their own reasons, and the idea of going back home diminished as time rolled on. Mona's friends worked hard and started achieving their goals in the United States. The wives supported their husbands and worked equally hard. The wives had jobs, took care of children, and kept their houses clean.

The first generation of families from India was thrifty. They saved money for their children's education and to buy a home. They studied to become American citizens. The time had come for Indians to move out of old and dirty apartment buildings in the five boroughs, and they started buying nicer homes on Long Island and in New Jersey.

There were a few families who did not have any money or spent more money than what they earned. Ramesh was one of those who did not have money and seldom had a job. He could not think of buying a place of his own. He was happy if he had liquor to drink. Mona was sad to see what Ramesh was becoming.

Chapter 55
Babysitter
1979
New York

Whenever Ramesh was out of a job, he took care of Sandy at home. Although he loved his daughter, he would become bored with playing with her and impatient with the demands of a two-year-old. He soon would take a drink and watch TV. He told Mona, "I am at home. We will save some money on the babysitter."

In a brief time, Mona observed her daughter was neglected at home. Ramesh would not clean her, and Sandy would get uncomfortable rashes. Mona found a family one floor up in the building. They were willing to baby-sit Sandy.

"Ramesh, I understand it's difficult to care for a baby. If you can help me, then please take her to the babysitter on the floor above us and bring her back in the evening before I reach home," Mona said.

"Mona, do you think I cannot take care of Sandy?" Ramesh said in defiance.

"No, don't misunderstand me. She is a baby, and babies need to be changed whenever they are dirty," Mona said sternly.

Mona was trying to make her marriage work. With Teresa forgotten, Mona was trying to be the ideal wife for Ramesh. With Sandy in the picture, her responsibilities increased. There were childcare expenses, money to send home and Mona was working hard to keep the peace with Ramesh. Most of the time, Ramesh was out of the house pretending to look for a job. He would go out, sit at a bar, and return home drunk.

Mona's friends loved her and appreciated her intelligence. She was respected in the community, and that would make Ramesh feel jealous and angry. He would spend more time in the bar. He had no control on spending money and always borrowed money from her. If Mona did not agree to his demands, he would try to hurt her physically. Mona hoped he would turn around one day.

One year passed as peacefully as Mona could make it. The babysitter's family had a twenty-year-old daughter, Susan, in college. A sweet and pretty girl, she was fond of Sandy. Mona would let her play with Sandy often. One evening Mona came home early from work. She opened the apartment door, and she was shocked to see Sandy sleeping unattended on the sofa. Susan was lying on the dining table, and Ramesh was all over her.

"Oh my gosh! What is going on!" Mona shouted.

Susan quickly pulled her pants up and ran out of the apartment. Mona's face was red with rage. She looked at Ramesh angrily and picked up Sandy. She walked into her bedroom and closed the door. Ramesh knocked on the bedroom door.

"I am sorry, darling. I do not know what came over me. Please, I am sorry. I promise this will not happen again," Ramesh said.

Mona did not open the bedroom door. "Go to hell. I don't care."

Ramesh slept in Sandy's room that night. The next day as she got ready, he apologized and pleaded with her repeatedly. Mona ignored him and took Sandy to a daycare center near her work.

Mona decided that it was better to leave Ramesh permanently and go back India. In the evening, she sat down with Ramesh and told him.

"I know I am not a citizen, and I also know you can make me go back to India. Your threats have lost their meaning. If I must go back to India, it is fine. At least, I will have peace and start my life afresh, without your threats," Mona said. "The time has come for me to make a decision. I cannot live a life of torture with your abusive behavior. Your promises have no meaning. Every time you promise to change, you go back to the same unpleasant habits. If you want another chance, you will have to change, and I need to see results. No drinking, get a job, no women, and become organized."

"Mona, my darling, I promise I will do what you say. Please give me time to change," Ramesh said.

Ramesh agreed to turn his life around. He would sleep in the living room. Mona was angry, and she had not forgotten the sight of Susan's legs up in the air. After the incident, Susan's family moved to a faraway building.

The next few years were peaceful. Mona forced Ramesh to see a psychiatrist, which helped him to change. He got a job in an auto parts manufacturing company. Their relationship improved, and he joined Alcoholic Anonymous again.

"Mona, darling, give me some time, I can't live without whisky. Let me have a few drinks."

His drinking habits continued, and his demands remained the same. To keep peace in the household, Mona let him sleep with her.

Whenever Ramesh was sober, he would be nice to Mona and Sandy. "My sweet Mona, I love you. You both are my angels. I cannot live without you." Ramesh repeated these same words over and over.

In his drunken mood, however, he was a monster. Often, he slapped Mona in front of Sandy, and Sandy would start crying. Mona would pick Sandy up and go to her bedroom.

Mona was patient in thinking about her future. She had already filed the application to become a citizen and expected a call for her interview any day.

Chapter 56
Wrong Step
1981
New York

Mona became a United States citizen in 1981. She could not make up her mind to leave Ramesh, and he could not restrain his drinking. She learned to live an abusive life with the cycle of his violence and later, his apologetic behavior.

Many of Mona's friends were pressing her to leave him, but her relatives in India were putting pressure on her to make the marriage work. They said, 'One day, he will get better.' She had to wait for that day.

Nishi, her mother-in-law, called Mona, "Beti, Ramesh will be fine. Every morning you pray to God. He will turn around."

Mona prayed and waited for the day Ramesh would turn his life around.

Vijay left his job and planned to start his own consulting business to create chemical plants. To celebrate Mona's citizenship and Vijay starting his own business in Los Angeles, both families agreed to take one last vacation together. They decided to go to Virginia Beach for a weekend enjoying the ocean. At the beach, they rented a two-bedroom suite with a small kitchen. Each couple had one bedroom, and they shared the kitchen.

Each morning, Mona and Rebecca made tea and sat with the family at the balcony to see the rising sun. The view from the balcony was stunning. At the far end of the horizon, the breathtaking sun shined over the ocean, as if it were going to take a dip. At night, the full moon reflected on the sea, and the roaring waves stirred the flame of desire. Ramesh would not let Mona sleep.

They would spend all day on the beach, and in the evening, they would go to a fine restaurant for a candlelit dinner. Ramesh would start drinking at breakfast, and by lunch time he would lay on the beach, drunk, and gaze at the women around him. High waves and beautiful women in bikinis made him restless.

Mona was watching Ramesh. He was overfriendly with Rebecca. He tried to hold Rebecca's hand or put his arm around her. Rebecca shrugged him off gently each time. Mona subtly hinted to Ramesh to behave. That did not deter his actions, and he continued to bother Rebecca to the annoyance of Vijay.

On the last day at the beach, they all decided to have an ice cream sundae at the soda fountain shop. The shop was at the far end of the beach.

"Let me get some extra cash, in case the children want to buy something else," Rebecca said. She got up from the sand and went back to the hotel room.

A short while later, Mona noticed that Ramesh was missing. Mona put Sandy in Vijay's care and told him, "Vijay Bhai, you walk ahead with the children, and we will join you at the ice cream shop."

Mona rushed to the hotel room. She heard noises coming from Rebecca's room as if she were fighting with someone. Mona pushed open the door and saw Ramesh had pinned Rebecca down on the bed and was trying to pull her swimsuit down. Rebecca was struggling to escape from his grip.

"Ramesh, what are you doing!" Mona shouted.

His attention was diverted by the sound of Mona's voice, and picking that moment, Rebecca kicked hard at his groin. Ramesh crumpled on the ground.

Mona started kicking Ramesh while Rebecca pulled up her swimsuit.

"You wanted to rape me! Take this!" Rebecca kicked Ramesh hard.

"And you have always tortured me!" Mona said. She grabbed Rebecca's sandals and hit him hard everywhere.

They threw Ramesh out of the room.

"Let me tell my husband Ramesh tried to rape me. Vijay will beat the hell out of him," Rebecca said.

"Please, do not tell any of this to Vijay. He will kill Ramesh," Mona said.

Rebecca was furious. She did not want to stay another minute in the hotel and insisted on leaving for New York immediately. Vijay returned to the hotel with the children.

"What happened? I waited for one hour. Why did you not come? Where is Ramesh? Why this sudden packing? I thought we were going to leave in the evening. And here are your melted sundaes," Vijay said.

Mona responded, "Vijay Bhai, the sky is cloudy, and the weather could get worse. We all have to go to work tomorrow, so it is better to reach home early."

Everything was packed up quickly and the luggage was loaded in Vijay's Impala Station Wagon. The only person missing was Ramesh. Nobody knew where he was, so they decided to wait.

"Where the hell is Ramesh?" Vijay wondered.

Two hours later, Ramesh turned up drunk, with his face and arms bruised in many places. He could not describe what happened, and there was no time for an explanation.

Vijay pushed Ramesh in the back seat, and they drove to New York. Ramesh snored while Mona tried to keep a polite conversation going. Rebecca was fuming with anger.

Chapter 57
Facing Reality
1981
New York

Mona could not sleep that night and kept thinking about Ramesh's behavior at Virginia Beach.

The next day at work, Rebecca called Mona at her office. They agreed to go out for lunch together. At lunch, Mona apologized for Ramesh's behavior.

"Mona, do you remember when Ramesh hit you and you stayed in our house? You forgave him thinking he would change, but yesterday, you saw how he continued to act abhorrently," said Rebecca.

Mona put her head down in shame.

"If you believe in your old traditions, you can live with him, and he will go on treating you this way. I love India, too. I lived in India for thirteen years and visited several times after marrying Vijay. It is a beautiful country that I respect sincerely," Rebecca said.

"He is frustrated. He has no job," Mona said with tears in her eyes.

"Mona, do not try to make excuses for him. The year is 1981. One of the reasons you married him and came to America was to fulfill your dreams. Mona, some time back, you told us that Columbia University sent you a letter to complete the prerequisites to get admission to do your Ph.D. This is the perfect chance to do that. Do not forget your parents' financial situation. They depend on you, and you send money home to them every month. Decide whether you prefer to support your hardworking parents or support a useless, unemployed loser," Rebecca said. "And there is Sandy. She cannot be brought up seeing Ramesh behave as he does."

"Rebecca, I am sorry Ramesh made an advance towards you," Mona was in tears. "I am sorry for everything…"

"Mona, he should be put in jail. He is a sex maniac," said Rebecca. After a pause, she continued. "Mona, no marriage is perfect. You will have to choose your own path. If you think life will one day get better and Ramesh will change, you are deluded. Think carefully, Mona. You can create your own destiny if you make a change now. It is your life and no one in this world oversees your happiness except you alone."

Rebecca continued, "What you do is nobody else's business. Remember, Mona, do not be a martyr. Every day there is a dead martyred woman somewhere in the world. Do you want your life to exist only as a memory?"

Mona had nothing to say. She hung her head down with a grim expression. More silent tears dripped down her cheeks. She was confused and could not decide what to do.

Chapter 58
The Last Straw
1981
New York

Mona returned to her office after lunch but could not concentrate. The whole afternoon she was thinking about what Rebecca said. She picked up Sandy at daycare and was on automatic pilot as her daughter chattered the whole journey home. At the apartment after work, she felt tired and dejected. Ramesh was not at home, and the whole apartment stank of vomit.

Mona immediately called Rebecca. "Rebecca, sorry to bother you. Can I bring Sandy to your place, and can you please take care of her tonight? The apartment is stinking with vomit, and I will have to clean the place because I don't want Sandy to get sick."

Rebecca knew Ramesh must have been drunk the day before. She asked Mona, "Why don't you let him clean up after himself?"

"He is not at home."

"Alright, bring Sandy, and bring an extra set of clothes. I will drop her off at the daycare center in the morning. You can pick her up in the evening," Rebecca said.

After delivering Sandy, it took Mona a couple of hours to clean the whole house. She was exhausted, so she took a shower and locked her bedroom door before going to sleep.

Ramesh came home late that night. He was drunk again. Mona was sleeping, and he had knocked at her bedroom door several times. When he threatened to break the door, Mona opened the door slightly. Ramesh pushed himself in and threw Mona on the bed.

"I am your husband. You should obey me and do what I say at my command."

His hand was at her throat.

"Please stop," Mona said.

"I will kill you if you say stop." He put his hand on her throat, then slapped her. "Do what I say, bitch. Stand in front of me!" He shouted.

She stood up and pretended to remove her night suit. She ran towards the door. He caught her, and they both fought. She continued to hit him with her fists and legs. He caught her by her hair and pushed her face on the bed.

"How dare you kick me at the beach? And here you are trying to hit me again. Now I will show you how I can hurt you!" he shouted.

He hit her face with his fists. He used her hairbrush to hit her shoulders and her back. Ramesh was in a rage. He tore her clothes as she was trying to cover her face. Ramesh held her hair and dragged her into the living room.

"I will teach you a lesson you will never forget, ugly bitch."

She was on her knees, half naked and shivering. He thrashed her again.

Ramesh pushed her onto the floor, and with her hairbrush, hit her hard on her buttocks. He stood up and kicked her a few times before walking out of the apartment. She could not bear the pain and passed out.

Mona opened her eyes after a while. Her whole body was trembling with fear and pain. With great difficulty she tried to stand but lost her balance. After a while, she got up again and walked slowly to the bathroom.

She looked in the mirror. She was disheveled, her face swollen and scratched. Her lower lip had a cut, and her breasts and stomach had bruises from the hairbrush. She touched her hips. They were bleeding, with the big splotches of blood on her thighs. Her swollen body ached.

That was the worst beating she had ever had. Her mind was blank, and she could not comprehend what was going on.

She was used to insults and verbal abuses every day, and a slap. This crossed the line. She wept for a long time sitting in the shower. She did not remember how she came back to her bedroom and collapsed with exhaustion. When she awoke, Ramesh was not in the apartment, and a piece of paper was lying on the dining table.

I am sorry for last night. I apologize for drinking and raising my hand on you. I love you. Please forgive me, Ramesh.

Chapter 59
Divorce
1981
New York

Mona called Rebecca. "Hi, Rebecca, how is Sandy?"

"She is such a sweet doll. You can give her to me permanently. Vijay took her to the daycare center already. Have you taken another day off?" Rebecca asked.

"I need to talk with you. Can I come over to your place?" Mona started sobbing loudly.

"Mona, what happened? Why are you crying?"

Mona could not stop crying.

"I will come to your place. Please, do not cry," said Rebecca.

Rebecca arrived in twenty minutes. She could not believe her eyes looking at Mona's bloody and swollen face.

"Oh my God, what happened?" Rebecca asked.

Mona put her arms tightly around Rebecca and could not stop her tears.

"Rebecca, please do not leave me alone." Mona was trembling.

"What did he do to you?" Rebecca asked.

It took Mona time to relate what happened the previous night.

Rebecca was enraged.

Rebecca got up and looked for Mona's suitcase. "Let us go. You cannot remain here, stuck as the ideal Indian woman that Ramesh can abuse. Curse this man. This is getting dangerous. Mona, come, let us go, now," said Rebecca angrily.

Tears were flowing from Mona's eyes.

"I don't want to be burden on your family," Mona said.

"What burden? This is what friends are for. You are part of our family. You stay with us if you need to. Get out of this harmful atmosphere and reorganize your life. We will support you," Rebecca replied. "That bastard could have killed you."

Mona refused to go to the police station. Nothing was reported to the police. Vijay knew many doctors, and they all helped nurse Mona back to health. Mona remained in bed for more than a week. She stayed at Rebecca's home. Her friends all rallied behind her.

Almost five years old, Sandy was sad and baffled, "What happened to my mom? Where is my dad?" No one was ready to tell the child a horrible story.

Mona's dream of a happy family had vanished. She reckoned with reality: Ramesh would never change. Enough was enough. She could not bear any more humiliation or threats to her life. Two weeks later, Vijay called Ramesh to tell him that Mona wanted a divorce.

After filing for divorce, Mona stayed with Rebecca and Vijay for a month, until Ramesh vacated the apartment fully.

Divorce was not easy. The whole family and community from India got involved. Mona had to deal with not only her personal emotions, but also the pressure from both families and far-flung relatives. Most of Mona's friends sided with her. They all knew for the last five years what was happening between her and Ramesh.

The families in India, however, had a distinct perspective. Ramesh cleverly told his family false stories of Mona. He complained to his family, and everyone was under the impression that Mona treated him badly. Mona's parents could do nothing but remain silent. In India, the community sides with the man's family.

Mona's in-laws put pressure on her for reconciliation. When her mother-in-law Nishi called, Mona said, "Mom, he beats me, and I almost died from it. How can I reconcile?"

Her father-in-law Charan took the phone from Nishi and declared to Mona, "So, what if he slapped you? He must straighten you up. Remember, he is your husband. First you mistreat him, and then you file for a divorce. We cannot show our face in the community! Reconcile and go back to Ramesh. To divorce is against your duty and will be a great insult to our family."

She never considered how tedious it would be to file for divorce. She was sad and emotional. The continuous telephone calls from India were disturbing. Relatives did not want to hear the real story. All they wanted was that she reconcile with Ramesh.

Vijay and Rebecca supported her decision for divorce. When they moved to California and Vijay established his consulting business in Los Angeles, the second and third floor of the house they owned in Flushing was rented. They kept the first floor vacant, as Vijay often visited New York for business and called on Mona regularly. In the middle of her divorce, Mona realized that her best friends had moved to Los Angeles. Mona knew she would be alone in New York and needed to fight her own battles now.

Ramesh was giving Mona trouble at every step. In the beginning, Ramesh refused to agree on the divorce. He filed a petition for reconciliation. The judge granted them a reconciling period of three months. Mona was horrified when Ramesh moved back into the apartment. It was suffocating to live with him under the same roof. In front of Sandy, he would act like a loving father, and when Sandy was not there, he would act like a monster.

"You want a divorce? Just you watch, I will make your life hell. You have tarnished my family's name in the community. Just wait and see, I will tell everyone what a bad person you are. I am warning you, you better come back walking on your knees, otherwise...," Ramesh threatened.

Mona with tears in her eyes looked at him and walked into her bedroom. The waiting period for reconciliation was a nightmare. She marked the calendar date when Ramesh would move out. When he vacated, she took the whole weekend to scrub the house clean of his odor.

To add to Mona's miseries, her sister Binny had a serious cycling accident. Her left leg was broken at three places and the medical treatment was expensive. To help her sister get well, Mona sent her parents all the savings she had. She took out money from her credit cards, and sold her gold jewelry and bangles, the last family heirloom from her grandmother.

Ramesh asked for full custody of Sandy. He filed frivolous legal motions changing dates for the court. He claimed, "Mona is a bad mother and neglects her daughter. She brings men home, and the whole night there are parties going on. She has stolen my family heirlooms and money."

Ramesh's parents sent him money to fight the case and take custody of Sandy. He hired a famous lawyer. Mona's lawyer was young and smart, but a novice. Her lawyer did her best, but on many occasions, Ramesh's powerful and influential counsel overshadowed her.

Until the final custody of Sandy was decided, the judge ordered Sandy to stay fifteen days with Mona and fifteen days with Ramesh. It was Mona's responsibility to take Sandy to visit her father and bring her back. Ramesh moved to Buffalo, four hundred miles away, to harass Mona. She had to take Sandy to meet him in bad winter weather, and if for any reason Mona was late by a few hours, Ramesh would call his lawyer to complain.

Ramesh taught Sandy how to insult and kick Mona. Sandy in her tantrums was starting to learn violence. It was hell for Mona to teach Sandy to unlearn those inappropriate words and insults.

Mona's salary was not enough to meet all the expenses. Lawyer's fees, daycare center fees, and the money taken out from charge cards put Mona in heavy debt. One day, she thought of an idea. A new Indian grocery store had opened on their street. The shop had items imported from India; the only thing lacking was fresh Indian sweets and snacks. Mona could make excellent sweets and equally good snacks. She made a sampling of Indian sweets and took those to the owner of the shop. The owner of the grocery store tasted them and liked them.

"These sweets are good. Can you make them in large quantity?"

"Yes, I can make them. I can make samosas and other savory snacks too," Mona said.

He asked Mona to make sweets and snacks fresh for his shop. She started earning some extra cash on the side.

That phase did not last long. The whole apartment was full of spices and ingredients, and the apartment smelled more strongly than a restaurant. Vijay Bhai was fed up with her enterprise. On one of Vijay's visits from Los Angeles, he reprimanded her.

"Mona, stop this snack business. You are wasting your precious time for little money. Did you move to this country to make snacks or to do your Ph.D.? Not only does this apartment smell, but the whole building smells of spices."

Mona stopped making snacks and decided not to indulge in any other side business.

Her Uncle Amar frequently came from Chicago to New York on government business, and whenever Vijay was in New York, they both would visit her together. Amar never came alone to visit her. To her surprise, he would remain quiet and behaved like a gentleman. He always brought toys for Sandy. After filing for divorce and living alone in New York, Mona became independent and gained back her confidence. She could manage any situation, but still the presence of Amar made her uncomfortable.

Chapter 60
Pitiable Situation
1981
New York

Mona could not afford a two-bedroom apartment and planned to move to Jamaica, a lower income neighborhood of Flushing. Her lease was over in two months.

Whenever Vijay and Rebecca were in New York, they made it a point to see Mona. They both were concerned about her. One evening, Vijay and Rebecca gathered for dinner at Mona's place, and the discussion veered towards how they could help Mona.

"Mona, we know you are a brave woman, and your salary is not much. You send money home to your parents, and Sandy goes to school and after school to a daycare center. How long will you live like this?" Vijay said.

"I can manage," she replied, as her eyes were holding back tears. Rebecca was also tearing up, looking at Mona.

Vijay cleared his throat and began, "Listen, we do not want to disturb your way of life, but you should think about your daughter's wellbeing. The salary you are making will not take you far."

"Tell me, Vijay Bhai, what I should do? I am doing my best under the circumstances. That wretched Ramesh is not leaving me in peace. More than six months has passed, but the divorce is still pending in the court. A while back, he sent a petition to the judge that I stole his family jewelry from the apartment. Recently, he sent another petition to the judge that I emptied out his charge cards worth thirty thousand dollars, and that I hit him when I dropped Sandy off at his place," Mona said. "All lies."

Mona continued, "I don't know why the judge listens to him. He sends a petition, and the judge postpones the hearing for a month. You know my sister Binny had an accident, and I had to send all the money I had to my parents to cover the doctor and hospital fees. I am behind on paying my rent, and I am getting desperate."

Vijay and Rebecca both were quiet and sad. They did not know how to help Mona.

Mona said, "I have requested the full custody of Sandy. Whenever she is back after staying with him, she suffers from cough and cold and I had to rush her to an emergency room. Ramesh teaches Sandy to hate me, that I am a bad mother. He tells Sandy to be violent with me and throw tantrums. Last time she was with me, she slapped me. I have never seen Sandy do that before. She is only five, and she has learned to be a baby tyrant."

Chapter 61
Proposition
1981-1982
New York

Vijay and Rebecca went back to Los Angeles, but every day they thought about how to help Mona.

"Vijay, we must do something," insisted Rebecca.

"I agree with you. Let us think it over."

"Why don't you tell Mona to move to Los Angles? There are many good schools. I am sure Sandy would love it, and Mona can do her Ph.D. in any of the universities," Rebecca said.

"No, Mona can't come here until the custody battle and the divorce are settled. Ramesh would not let her leave New York State."

"Then let her come with Sandy, without Ramesh's permission."

"Rebecca, don't you ever suggest this to Mona. Once she comes without permission, under the law she will become a fugitive. From that point, it will be difficult for her to get legal custody of Sandy," Vijay advised.

A month later, Mona gave them good news over the phone. She was granted the divorce and full custody of Sandy.

"Congratulation, Mona. How did this happen so suddenly?" Rebecca said.

"One incident happened, which hastened the divorce proceeding," she said. "Ramesh had come to New York City for Sandy's custody hearing. At night, he went to a bar and had a fight with another customer. The police came and put Ramesh in jail. The judge, hearing the incident, granted me the divorce and full custody of Sandy."

Finally, Mona could focus on her own goals. She completed the prerequisites for doing her Ph. D. program in economics, and she applied to Columbia University. Looking at her academic record and glowing recommendations from her employer, Mona was accepted for the Ph.D. program. Mona could work under the guidance of Professor J. Martin, an authority on suburban town development.

Mona had proposed her thesis on the idea of suburban city planning and on the economically independent development of the suburban towns. She selected for her case study the city of Jamaica in Queens. The city was once a prosperous town but went under during an economic slowdown. Half of the shops had closed, and businesses were moving to other places. To bring Jamaica back to life was a heroic task. Her thesis was about how a struggling suburban town could be redeveloped, sustained, and prosper again on its own.

Columbia University gave Mona a grant of three hundred dollars a month. The university reduced her tuition fees and gave her a scholarship of five thousand dollars a year. The tuition at Columbia University was high, and she still needed another forty-thousand dollars that she could not afford.

Vijay and Rebecca gave serious thought to Mona's situation, and after three weeks, they gathered at Mona's apartment in New York. Vijay said, "Mona, we have a proposition, and we hope you will consider it. We want you to finish your Ph.D. in economics as soon as possible. You can take a heavier course load and finish it in the next five years.

That will keep you busy and keep your mind distracted from the negative experiences you faced."

Mona interrupted, "Vijay Bhai, how can I finish my Ph.D. in five years when I am buried with all kinds of debts and must work? I am unable to get a student loan as my debts are too high. That is one of the reasons I am moving to a cheaper apartment. I am thinking of postponing my studies until I am in less debt. Columbia University, looking at my financial situation, has given me a scholarship to reduce my fees. Still, it is impossible for me to pay the rest of the tuition. It's forty thousand dollars, Bhai."

Vijay stopped her, "Mona, I know you are struggling and that's where we come into the picture. Rebecca and I have decided to pay for your education and pay for Sandy's daycare. We know you will not accept this offer outright, but please think of it as a loan rather than a gift. You can pay us back when you start earning again. This is what friends are for, and I hope you don't refuse this offer."

Vijay continued, "We want you to consider not moving into that rundown apartment building in Jamaica. Our house is only three blocks away from where you live now. The second and third floors of our house are rented, but the first floor and basement are vacant. We left the first floor vacant intentionally so that whenever we come to New York, we will have a place to stay. Since we will be in L.A. a lot of the time, we would like you to move into our first-floor apartment while you go to school."

"How could I take over your apartment? I can't afford the rent!" replied Mona.

"Listen, we don't want the rent," Rebecca said.

"Let me explain," said Vijay. "There are four bedrooms. You can use two bedrooms and keep the other two locked. We come to New York regularly, so we will be using those other two bedrooms. In a way, you will be helping us by becoming a caretaker of our house. We are friends. If we are not able to help you when you are in need, then what is the use of friendship?"

"I think it is a fair proposition," Rebecca said.

"You are going to pay for my education, which is around two hundred thousand dollars, free accommodation, and the daycare for Sandy. Is it I am dreaming, or it is a miracle? Rebecca, I cannot live at your home for free. I must contribute something," Mona said.

Vijay thought for a minute and said, "Alright, you pay for the usage of electricity, the gas and water; we will take care of all the other expenses."

Mona looked at Rebecca with a nod of thanks.

"Let's go and see the place," said Vijay.

They all went to see the house. Mona remembered many times there, sharing parties with friends or hiding away from Ramesh.

"Wow, I never thought I would live here!" said Mona. She began to sob with joy. "Thank you, thank you."

Before leaving for Los Angles, Vijay and Rebecca had the house repainted, and all the three floors renovated. The creaking floors and noisy stairs were replaced with new wood.

Mona asked, "Vijay Bhai, do you think Friedman LLP will let me work and take time off if I needed?"

"Maybe. I know this much: that these big companies often have an educational program for the enhancement of their employees, and sometimes they reimburse the education fee," Vijay said. "Let's look into their policies."

"I can see the future now, Vijay Bhai. Thank you," said Mona. "Again and again."

After a few weeks, Mona moved into Vijay's and Rebecca's home. It was in a safe neighborhood and near the daycare center for Sandy. Mona was grateful to Vijay and Rebecca; she was determined to succeed in her program.

Chapter 62
Hard Work
1981-1986
New York

Mona put her full effort into her Ph.D. She would leave home early in the morning, taking Sandy to the daycare center that was three houses down. Mona would take the 'D' train to go to Columbia University. Some days she would travel to the suburban cities she was studying and talk with city officials, residents, and merchants to gather the data for her dissertation. On other days, she would spend all her time in the library, analyzing data and reading reports. Mona handled it all. Her job accommodated her studies and Sandy thrived in a gifted program at a local school.

Mona finished her Ph.D. in the next five years. Her thesis was finally complete and Columbia University was pleased with her work. A few chapters of her thesis were published in a prestigious economic journal. As a result, many reputed consulting firms offered Mona a job, but out of loyalty she remained at Friedman with a promotion. Her thesis was accepted by the City of Jamaica for an action plan, and Mona's recommendations became the blueprint of a successful transformation of the city. After leaving Columbia, the university reimbursed more of the tuition fee, and Friedman paid the rest. She was indebted to Rebecca and Vijay for helping her.

Chapter 63
Remembrance
1986
New York

Dr. Karan Swarup was sitting in his office on Third Avenue, near the United Nations Building. As he flipped through the *Economic Times* magazine, he was surprised to come across the article from Mona's thesis. He saw Mona's picture at the top of her article in the July 1986 issue. He was thrilled that Mona had made it to America and had achieved her Ph.D., just as she always said she would. She looked the same–beautiful and smiling. He remembered how they sat together under the banyan tree, unaware of the cruel world around them. He recalled how she walked into his house like a princess with her shy smile. Fourteen years had gone by since their engagement was broken by their society.

After their engagement ended, Karan went to France where he joined the World Bank as a Senior Vice President. He was considered one of the topmost economists in the world and was now affiliated with the United Nations in New York.

Karan tried to forget about the happy days with Mona and buried his love deep in his heart. Seeing Mona's picture in the *Economic Times* made him remember his old feelings, and he knew he wanted to reconnect with Mona. What was she doing in New York?

Karan called his secretary into his office. He gave her a

copy of the *Economic Times*. Showing her Mona's picture, he asked, "Miss Thelma, could you please find out this lady's phone number?"

Karan was leaving soon to travel to France for a vacation with his wife and son. Before he left for France, he made up his mind to call Mona.

Karan's secretary found Mona's number quickly, and he picked up the phone to call her. Karan was excited.

After eating an early dinner of tomato soup, Mona was reclining on the sofa debating about whether to have yogurt or an ice cream. Her telephone rang. She picked it up.

"Hello. Who is this?" Mona said.

"Mona, this is Karan," the voice on the phone said.

"Who? Karan?" The receiver fell out of her hand. She never thought that she would ever hear his voice again.

"Hello, Karan. I am sorry. I thought…" she was interrupted by him.

"I know. Congratulations on getting your Ph.D."

"Thank you, Karan. How did you find out?"

"Mona, you are famous. I read your article in the *Economic Times*. When did you come to New York?"

"It is a long story. I have been living in New York for the past seven years. I got married when I arrived, but we have gotten a divorce. What about you?"

"I am married to a French woman, and we have a son. I left Kanpur and went to France to join the World Bank. My head office is in France, but I am working with the United Nations. I have been living in New York for the last nine years. How have you been? It has been long time. How nice to hear your voice." Karan was excited.

"I am fine," Mona said with tears in her eyes.

"Listen, Mona, I have to go. My family and I must catch a flight tonight to France. We will be back after one month. I will call you. You must meet my wife and son. You do not know, Mona, how happy I am to hear your voice! Bye," Karan said.

"Bye," Mona said. This was big news for Mona. Her mind flashed back, and the past came in front of her. Mona waited for a month and then another and another to hear from him, but Karan did not call her.

In the meantime, as these things happen, Karan had a serious accident in France. While navigating a steep mountain road, another car crossed in front of him and the collision was fatal. His wife and son both died in the accident. Karan remained in the hospital for six months. Mona did not hear about the accident for a long time, and when she came to know, Karan was still recovering in France.

She did not have the strength to call Karan.

Chapter 64
Lonely
1986
New York

Vijay's consulting business thrived. He and Rebecca were settled in Los Angeles, but they came to New York to see Mona walk the stage at Columbia and graduate with honors with a Ph.D. They stayed for three days and celebrated each evening. After her graduation, Mona's was promoted in her a job, but she knew that her life would never be the same.

Mona was feeling lonely. Despite her success at Columbia with her thesis, her past haunted her. Memories of Ramesh's cruelty, his savage beatings, and his disregard for her or Sandy's happiness never left. She could not sleep at night. To distract herself, she started reading literature on abused women, and she often visited women's shelters in New York. She learned she was not the only one who experienced abuse. Many women suffered.

To combat the loneliness, Mona went out to parties often. Mona was young, attractive, and therefore popular. Her group of friends often tried to bring over Indian customs. Each Spring, they would replicate the Holi Celebration, having a loud, happy party, complete with throwing colored flour at each other and drinking their fill of scotch in place of bhang. Mona never attended. For her, Holi was a sad day. She could not forget her rape on the day of the festival, and remembering it gave her shudders. At other events, men, with desire in their eyes, looked at her. Wives were jealous and not happy, seeing their husbands talking and laughing with her. Mona often heard remarks, "She is young and beautiful. Why does not she find a man and leave our husbands alone?"

Being alone and single in the big city, a few successful men would invite her to go out with them. Those men thought she was casual fun. Mona, knowing their intentions, and with great tact, would avoid these situations.

She discovered some men did not understand the meaning of the word 'no.' One of her Freidman colleagues was very persistent. One day he pinned her against her desk and tried to kiss her. Mona slapped him hard on the face. The company fired him the same day, and as long she worked in the company, the men did not dare to come near her.

She was tired of being pursued by men. She was disgusted. She wanted to get out of this rut and move to a new place.

Chapter 65
Living Together
1986
New York

Amar occasionally called Mona to ask how she and Sandy were doing. Mona would not pick up the phone or would hang up quickly, but Amar was very persistent. She was relieved that he was in Chicago and far from New York.

In the month of August, it was hot and sultry. Mona decided to take Sandy to the Coney Island Amusement Park on a weekday when the rush of tourists had passed.

She took the day off from work, and by chance the weather had changed abruptly. It was raining heavily and the temperature dropped. The weather was unpleasant, so she cancelled their trip. She was relaxed and reading a book at home while Sandy was playing in her room. Her doorbell rang. She wondered who would be visiting her at this time. The bell rang again. She looked through the peep hole and was surprised to see Amar. Mona opened the door. "What are you doing here? You live in Chicago!"

"Hello, Mona. I came to New York for meetings. Yesterday it was hot, but today it is very cold. I got stuck outside, shivering, and feeling cold. I realized the only person who could care for me is you. Therefore, I came straight to your apartment." Amar was shaking and he started to cough.

"What makes you think I will take care of you? And how did you know I was at home?" Mona said.

"I called your office, and they told me you took the day off," Amar said.

"Go to a hospital. How can I take care of you?" Mona said.

"Please, Mona, let me stay here until the evening. As soon as I feel better, I will go back to my hotel," Amar said.

Sandy was playing in her room. Hearing Amar's voice, she came to the living room.

"Hi, Sandy. My sweet little daughter. How are you? Do not come near me. Your Uncle is not feeling well," Amar said.

Sandy looked at her mother in an inquisitive way. Mona did not like to create a scene in front of Sandy, and knew she was stuck with Amar. Mona took his temperature and saw that it was high.

"Take two tablets of Advil and take rest on this sofa. And do not dare come near me." She went to her bedroom with Sandy. By the evening, the rain was gone, and Amar was feeling better. He left her apartment, much to Mona's relief.

In the evening three days later, her doorbell rang, and she saw Amar standing there. Mona opened the door. "You are still in New York?"

"Hi, Mona. I just came to thank you for taking care of me. Can I play with Sandy?" He brought in a bouquet of flowers, a box of chocolates, and a doll for Sandy.

Two days later, Amar was again at her door with a box of chocolates, flowers, and another new toy for Sandy.

"Now what?" Mona said.

"Mona, I am leaving for Chicago tomorrow. I wanted to see Sandy before I go," Amar said. "May I come in?"

"No. Say goodbye. That's why you came."

"One minute of your time then."

This time, Mona put her foot down. "Be honest. In one week, you have brought all these gifts and you have delayed going back to Chicago. What do you want from me?" Mona said.

"Nothing, I just like to play with Sandy," he replied.

"No, there is something more. Come on, out with it. What do you want?" she asked him again.

"It is nothing," he replied.

"Fine, then leave." She was not the same Mona, who could be pushed around. She was strong and determined.

He looked at her and said in a whisper, "Mona, please listen. Do you know why my wife left me? Because I cannot have children. And after Sandy's birth, you also cannot have children. If we live together, Sandy will have a grandfather, you will have me, and no one would suspect anything other than us being a family living together."

"You are disgusting. After what you did to me, do you think I would ever come near you?"

"Think over it carefully. It could be a clever idea for both of us. I am leaving now, but I will call you tomorrow." He left.

Mona slammed the door and paced the floor in her living room. Sandy watched her mother, "Mom, what happened? Why did you slam the door so hard?"

"Nothing, my sweetheart." Mona said.

Despite Mona refusing him, Amar was persistent, leaving phone messages and dropping flowers on her doorstep. She was tired of his arguments. She did not know what to do. In her culture and upbringing, the concept of sharing her life with her father's brother was totally forbidden.

Still upset with Amar, Mona came to know through mutual friends that Ramesh was in the hospital for the third time in two months. Too much drinking had ruined his liver. His elder brother had come to take him back to India. Ramesh did not contact Mona before leaving. Numbed by Amar, she could only pray to forget Ramesh and reconstruct her life to her own design.

Chapter 66
New Horizon
1986
New York

Amar was calling and pestering Mona often. She was tired of his phone calls. "Mona, please think it over. We are far from India. Nobody will come to know," Amar pleaded.

"Listen, this is impossible. Please stop thinking about it. It is against our culture and unethical. It will happen over my dead body," Mona said.

Mona wanted peace and considered a move away from a hectic New York lifestyle. She wanted to go to a place where no one knew her, to start a new beginning. The west coast was booming with jobs, and dynamic cities were blossoming quickly around Los Angeles.

Companies in Los Angeles were recruiting aggressively, and Mona heard they would even pay for her moving expenses. Some firms also gave huge signing bonuses to join them. Rebecca was trying to convince Mona to move to Los Angeles.

Rebecca was in New York. During lunch one day, Rebecca pointed out the advantages of moving. "Mona, Vijay says there are plenty of jobs available in your field and new homes are being developed in the suburbs. Mona, think it over, seriously. The weather here is better than Kanpur."

"Rebecca, I will think about it. I am also tired of the freezing weather," Mona said.

The nation's leading consulting firm, McCreighton & Company, advertised for a Senior Associate in their Los Angeles office to help develop suburban cities in Los Angeles County. Mona saw that McCreighton was a world-wide company with a global outlook that served leading businesses and governments, and the job description was a good match for her talents. She applied, and to her surprise, they called her for an interview. She impressed the vice president of the company, and later that same day, they offered her a job with double her present salary and a generous benefits package. They agreed to pay for her remaining education costs and all her moving expenses to Los Angeles. The only catch was that Mona could not leave McCreighton for at least three years.

Amar was on a long-term assignment in Germany, so Mona decided this was the best opportunity to leave New York. She was nostalgic leaving the city. Her married life started in New York and ended there. She wanted to begin a new life, in a new town, with new opportunities and did not want to leave any trace of herself in New York.

Mona went back to the Macy's department store in downtown Manhattan one last time. Its nine stories were still full of items from around the world. She remembered the first time she visited the store, shivering in her tattered shawl while Ramesh was padded with his warm winter coat. He had bought her Gloria Vanderbilt jeans and wrapped a new cashmere winter coat around her. She thought of how she fought with Ramesh about buying items on credit.

The last few weeks in New York were hectic. Friends invited her for farewell dinners and went with her to the airport to see her off. She remembered how she felt when she left India with her community surrounding her with good wishes and goodbyes. She knew she would never see some of these friends again.

Chapter 67
Los Angeles
1987
Los Angeles

Mona left New York in 1987 on a gloomy winter day. When she reached Los Angeles, it was a bright and sunny day. She felt a renewed hope and confidence. She was forty, with a ten-year-old daughter, a divorce, an amazing job, and a Ph.D.

McCreighton & Company hired a moving contractor to pick up Mona's belongings in New York and ship them to Los Angeles. The company also paid for Mona's travel expenses, and gave her a per diem allowance of 150 dollars per day until Mona settled down in Los Angeles. Within a short time, Mona's apartment was empty, and her obligations settled. With airline tickets in her hand, she and Sandy took a cab to JFK International Airport.

In the aircraft, Mona and Sandy occupied the first two seats in the row while an elegant woman occupied the window seat. Sandy was difficult to control on the plane. She wanted to sit near the window.

"You want to sit near the window?" the lady asked Sandy.

Sandy nodded and gave her a cute smile.

"Come, I will sit next to your mom, and you can take my seat," the lady said.

After getting full custody of Sandy, Mona put a lot of

effort to change the bad attitudes that Sandy had learned from Ramesh. Now at the age of ten, Sandy was a well-behaved child and had a shy but charming manner. "Thank you, Aunty," Sandy said.

"Good, you can see mountains and rivers and towns below and I can talk to your mother." the lady said.

Mona and the lady started chatting with each other.

"Thank you, Mrs. ...," Mona said.

"Mrs. Harris, Dora Harris. You can call me Dora. And you?"

"You can call me Mona," Mona said.

They talked about different subjects during the six-hour flight. Mona was curious about Los Angeles. Mona came to know that Dora had powerful connections in the city of Ocean Beach. Her son Dan Harris was the mayor of Ocean Beach.

"Mona, which company do you work for?"

"I work for McCreighton & Company. It is a consulting firm, and I work in suburban development."

"I know the firm. They did some work for Ocean Beach when my husband was the mayor of the city."

Mona was surprised, "What a coincidence."

"Where will you be working?"

"I will be working in their head office in downtown Los Angeles," Mona said. "How is Los Angeles? This is my first trip."

"You will love Los Angeles. The county has more than eighty cities. Most of the cities are open, and very few have multistory buildings. Only the downtown area is crowded, with tall buildings. People work hard there, but it is a more relaxed atmosphere. Not like in New York, where people are always in a hurry, tense, and impatient. The city is full of diverse cultures, and you can visit a variety of restaurants, the mountains, the beaches and many museums."

"I am looking forward to seeing all of these places," Mona said.

"You speak good English with no Indian accent."

"Most of my education was in Catholic schools and colleges."

They did not know how the six hours on the plane passed. Mona fascinated Dora with her knowledge of economic conditions of women around the world. Dora inquired about how women managed their lives, both in poor countries and in rich countries. They were about to discuss the status of abused women in emerging economies, when the captain announced that they were scheduled to land. Dora gave Mona her phone number. "After you settle down in Los Angeles, give me a call. We should meet and have lunch together," Dora suggested.

Mona was equally impressed by Dora.

At the airport terminal gate, Mona and Sandy were received by Vijay and Rebecca. They embraced repeatedly, as if they were seeing each other after years.

Rebecca said, "My little Sandy. She is taller than the last time I saw her."

Vijay said, "Welcome to sunny California. The climate is like Delhi, but milder. Not too cold and not too hot. You will love it."

On the drive from the airport, Mona knew Dora was right; there were not many high-rise buildings. The city sprawled for miles with suburban communities of one or two-story houses covering the hills and valleys.

Mona's office was in downtown Los Angeles, and her job took her to outlying suburban cities. Mona's job as a consultant was to travel to and revitalize the economies of troubled cities with recommendations for planning and economic development.

Mona stayed with Rebecca and Vijay for two weeks, because her employer had given her that time off to settle down in Los Angeles before beginning her job. She spent most of the time looking for an apartment.

Rebecca's children had grown up. They had started to work full-time, one as a surgeon, and the other as an engineer. With her children settled, Rebecca was successful as a real estate agent and was learning stock market investing. Every morning when Mona got up, she saw Rebecca calling her stockbroker with the *Wall Street Journal* spread out in front of her.

"What are you doing early morning on the phone?" Mona asked.

"I am buying some stocks and putting options on other good stocks," Rebecca said.

"What is a stock option?" Mona asked.

"It gives you the right to purchase or sell a stock at a specific price," Rebecca said.

"Ah, that sounds like a waste of time and money. Have you ever made any money?" Mona said.

"I usually make at least my personal pocket expenses each month. It is not a waste of money if you play it safe. Have you ever tried the stock market?" Rebecca asked.

"No, I did not, and I don't want to. I don't gamble."

"It is a part of life: to learn to gamble. To learn how to win and how to lose."

"I've gambled in life, and so far, I have been a loser," Mona said.

"I know. You learned a lot in your married life. Now it is all in the past."

"You are right," Mona said.

"Come on, give me five hundred dollars. Do not worry if you lose, I will reimburse you. I want to teach you how to grow your savings by leveraging the stock market," Rebecca said.

Mona looked at Rebecca and gave her a five-hundred-dollar check. Rebecca opened Mona's account at Merrill Lynch and introduced Mona to the basics of the stock market. Mona was a quick and digested Rebecca's teachings very well in a fleeting time. Mona knew to buy low and sell high, and she doubled her money over the next four days.

"Mona, you are a very sharp learner. Try to read business magazines and the business section of the newspaper every day. Look at the economic trends in the country. With your Ph.D. in economics, you will understand this quickly. Calculate risks and place your bets like a poker player. With luck, you could be a winner, and you could make tons of money," said Rebecca.

To Rebecca's surprise, Mona played the stocks expertly. She outdid Rebecca in buying and selling stocks and placing bets on options.

Meanwhile, Mona's household goods had still not come from New York. She knew she wanted to move to a place close to Rebecca. She finally found an apartment nearby, in Lakewood, two miles from Rebecca's home. The apartment was spacious with two bedrooms and two baths. The school was within walking distance, and the grocery stores were not far. After Mona's furnishings arrived two weeks later, Mona and Sandy settled comfortably into their new apartment.

She liked her job, and as a consultant to different cities, she came to know many local politicians and council members.

Mona had built up her confidence. She bought a new Buick for driving across Los Angeles and dressed smartly in business suits and elegant high heels. She was independent, and she was thriving.

Chapter 68
Dora
1987
Los Angeles

Two months later, Mona called Dora to thank her for the help on the plane. Dora was happy to receive a call from Mona, and she invited Mona for lunch. One Saturday afternoon, Mona met Dora at an outdoor restaurant filled with tanned, well-dressed people. She was with her son Dan, a six-foot tall, good-looking man. Dan had a broad chest, blue eyes, and blond hair.

"Hi Mona, you look pretty in your black suit. Very professional," Dora said. She greeted Mona with a light hug, and Dan stood up.

"Our company emphasizes a formal dress code. We always must look professional in the office, and sometimes it carries over into the weekends. Dora, you look equally pretty in your pink paisley dress.". Mona sat down and looked at the menu. With lowered lashes, she glanced over at the handsome blond man sitting next to Dora.

Dora smiled and signaled to the waiter they were ready for the order. "Oh, where is my head! Meet my son, Dan Harris. I believe I mentioned him to you on the plane. He is the mayor of the City of Ocean Beach."

"Please to meet you, Mr. Harris." Mona put her hand forward.

"Please to meet you, Miss…" Dan looked at his mother.

"Mona," Dora said quickly.

After the introduction, Dan said, "Got to go. Community meeting." He nodded and left.

"He is always busy. I schedule coffee or lunch when I can," said Dora, "but he can get a phone call and there he goes." She looked very proud.

"I must thank you, Dora, for being so kind on the flight," Mona said.

"My pleasure. Your daughter is cute."

Dora was in her late sixties, and she had lost her husband a few years back from a sudden heart attack. Dan was her only son. The Harris family was well-established in Ocean Beach and was known for their wealth and depth of political connections. Her family could claim many relatives as senators or governors in states across the country.

The family was involved in every aspect of the Ocean Beach community. They helped charities, served on hospital boards, participated in town planning commissions, volunteered in parks programs, and pushed for senior housing projects. The city gentry were always eager to receive an invitation to exclusive Harris parties.

Dora was a politically ambitious woman. Her first step was to get Dan elected as a city council member. The next step was to become the mayor of Ocean Beach and after that, run for the position of state senator. Later, he could aim for the U.S. senate. She dreamed that one day her son would be President of the United States. She had mapped out her son's career step by step. For Dora, things were working out as she planned.

Dan was already the mayor of Ocean Beach, a prosperous coastal city with a population of over two hundred thousand. Dan had all the qualifications to move ahead. He was a respected lawyer, with a juris doctorate from

Harvard.

At lunch, Dora talked with Mona and subtly asked her many personal questions about her life and continued the discussion of abused women, focusing on big cities, Los Angeles, Chicago, and New York City. Mona admitted to Dora that she had recently been divorced. Dora listened to some parts of Mona's disastrous marriage.

"You know, Dora, he would insult me, and sometimes he would beat me with his belt. It was horrible."

Dora felt deeply sorry for Mona.

"Mona, divorce in India does not sound common. How does marriage work in India, compared to the United States?" Dora asked.

"When you marry, it is almost a community event. Whatever you do, you must act knowing that your family's honor and future will depend on how you handle your marriage." Mona paused and took a breath. "Families in India don't encourage divorce. In a conservative society, it is exceedingly difficult to get a divorce,"

"What about here, in the United States, if an Indian man divorces an Indian woman? What do families say?" said Dora.

"Here, even in an open society with less tradition, women are treated equally poorly. Families still exert much pressure in spite of thousands of miles between. During my divorce, I read many articles and met lot of abused women from both India and America. They each had their own sad story to tell."

"Oh, that is terrible. Whether it is India or here," Dora said. She found Mona an intelligent, well-informed person who could be potentially useful in the future. She wanted to stay in touch with Mona. Dora had an ulterior motive.

A few days later, Mona received a call from Dora, "Hi,

Mona, how about lunch next Saturday? I want you to meet someone."

"Who?" Mona said.

"She is Dan's girlfriend," Dora said.

They met for lunch at the Katella Deli. Mona found Aviva beautiful and strong. She was striking with dark hair, pale skin, and blue eyes. Aviva was in her early thirties. A staunch believer in equal rights, she had definite ideas about gender roles and relationships. She was the daughter of a senator in Washington, D.C.

Aviva had her own opinions on mistreated women. "In Los Angeles County, there are many shelters. But, I think we don't need another shelter in Ocean Beach. People here are wealthy. Therefore, that kind of abuse just doesn't happen."

Mona offered her perspective. "It is not the question of rich or poor. Rich women are equally abused in our society."

Dora commented, "There are not many shelters in Ocean Beach. Mona is right. Women are abused despite their socioeconomic status. In Ocean Beach, we have seen many abused women, and children who endure beatings and poverty." Dora looked at Mona and Aviva. "You both should visit a shelter and see for yourself."

Dora was inclined to help women with lesser means. The idea to create a shelter struck her, and she decided to explore it. She thought a large, new shelter for women with services, training and support could be a good opportunity for Dan to enhance his reputation and his political career. Dan could become one of the first champions of abused women in Ocean Beach. Being first was politically important.

Mona and Aviva visited one of the shelters together, and Aviva was appalled after listening to the women's stories.

"Oh my God, I never knew how much women go through in our city!"

Mona and Dora met several more times over lunch. They had many discussions on destitute women, sexual assault, abuse, and the ill treatment of women. Mona shared statistics on the economic devastation to the community when women were abused.

Over the next few months, Dora was ready to open a shelter for abused women. Dora persuaded Dan, as the mayor of the town, to allocate land and secure temporary office space for the facility. With his ever-growing influence with city council and the development division, he accomplished what he set out to do. There was help from the wide world of their family's connections, too.

The construction for the women's shelter started in 1988. On Saturdays and Sundays, Mona would help Dora in designing the operating model for the shelter. Mona felt she had accomplished an important goal.

Chapter 69
Aviva
1987
Los Angeles

Aviva was the daughter of a wealthy and influential senator in Washington D.C. He was the chairperson of two important committees, defense, and budget. Aviva was his only daughter. Her mother died when she was ten. Most of her childhood was spent at a private convent girls' school, and her college education was at an elite women's university. Aviva was a good athlete and black belt holder in karate. In college, she was known for being conservative with her relationships and allowed no hanky-panky.

Aviva's father and Dan's father were in the same committees. Aviva met Dan when they were doing summer internships under their fathers. Dan and Aviva quickly fell in love. Aviva was jealous of any other woman near Dan. They often fought with each other.

"Dan, I told you, not to be so close to Wendy."

"Easy, Aviva, easy. She just gave me a friendly kiss. Don't be jealous."

"I do not care. I don't want you to look at other girls."

Their love did not last long. Dan's flirtatious habits and Aviva's jealousy created constant tension and conflict. Unable to compromise, they both walked away from the relationship.

Aviva took a job in a non-governmental organization as a data analyst in Los Angeles, and Dan went into politics. .

When Dan became a council member and later mayor of Ocean Beach, Dora looked at the bigger picture of Dan's future. She thought it was good politics to connect Dan back with Aviva and her family, and she pushed them to revive their love for each other.

Chapter 70
Ramesh and the Pujari
1987
Kanpur

Ramesh left the United States in 1987. He was sick when he reached India, and doctors were concerned at the prognosis. His family put him in a hospital. A few months later, looking at his failing health, the doctors sent him home.

Next to Ramesh's house was the family's local temple. When Ramesh was eight years old, he would go with his mother and listen to the discourse on Gita by the Pujari. Ramesh and Mona got married in that temple. The Pujari, or priest, who married them, had retired from the regular duties of the temple, and now the temple was run by his son.

The old Pujari was living with his son behind the temple. Every day before sunrise, the old Pujari would take his cane and go to the park to teach yoga to the community. After teaching yoga in the park, he would come back to the temple and bathe. After the bath, he participated in morning prayers. For the rest of the day, he sat in one corner and recited Gita or took his afternoon nap. In the evening, the Pujari gave lectures on the Gita to the temple attendees. That was his routine seven days a week.

Ramesh could see who was coming in or going out of the temple from his room's window. One day he saw the old Pujari looking towards him. Ramesh turned his face to the other side and tried not look back. The same afternoon, the

Pujari made a surprise visit to Ramesh and his family. The Pujari sat on a mat, a distance away from Ramesh in the Sid Asana Yoga position.

"Son, I have come to see you, as I heard you are not feeling well," the Pujari said.

Before Ramesh could reply in his frail voice, his father whispered to the Pujari, "His condition is serious. His liver is almost gone, and he is weak. The doctors have no hope." Dr. Charan said sadly. "We have brought him back from the hospital. They say nothing can be done anymore, and I am a helpless father who does not know how to save my son. Only a miracle could save him now."

The Pujari looked sternly at Dr. Charan and then looked straight into Ramesh's eyes and asked, "How you are feeling, my son?"

"Miserable," Ramesh feebly replied.

"You want to live?" asked the Pujari.

"Of course, I want to live! What a question!" Ramesh replied.

"You will have to do penance."

"I will, I will, if I can get well," Ramesh replied in his faint voice.

They looked at each other with intensity. The Pujari's bright, shining eyes penetrated Ramesh's body. Ramesh trembled.

"I will come again," The Pujari left the house abruptly.

Over the next couple of days, Ramesh did not see the Pujari sitting on the mat. No one had heard from him. A few days later, the Pujari was at the door of Ramesh's house once again.

He had one bag full of small packets. He asked Ramesh's mother to boil milk. The Pujari opened one packet and took out some Ayurvedic pills.

"Take them with boiled milk, four times a day. At night, rub this oil on your body. In the morning take a sponge bath with lukewarm water. Before sunrise and sunset, sit in Sid Asana, and breathe deeply ten times. Slowly increase your deep breathing until you can do this for half an hour. Never forget your breathing exercise. It is important to detox your mind and body. I will see you every morning to check on you," said the Pujari.

Ramesh's father, who was a conventional doctor trained in western medicine, did not believe in ancient treatments. He regarded alternative treatments as bogus.

When the Pujari came out of the room, Ramesh's father asked, "You gave him Ayurvedic medicines? Don't you know I am against these medicines?"

"I have known Ramesh from the day he was born when you brought him into the temple for God's blessing. Last week when I saw Ramesh, he was in a pitiable condition. You told me that modern medicines were not improving his condition. If you reject my treatment, in a way, it means you want him to die," the Pujari said.

"No, don't say that!" Ramesh's father replied.

"His mind is contaminated, and his body is contaminated. He needed to be detoxed. I want him to live. You can go on giving him your medicines and let me try mine. With the grace of God, he may live."

His father took the bag, and the Pujari left.

Ramesh felt better by the end of the week. Everyone was surprised as Ramesh's health started improving. He could walk slowly, and he could eat his mother's cooking. Color came back into his face. The Pujari would come every morning and sit in the Sid Asana position on the ground, eyes closed, and chant mantras quietly. To Ramesh's family, it was a miracle, and the Pujari was God's messenger.

Chapter 71
Houses
1990
Willow Grove

Mona was determined to show the world she was a high achiever. In her job, she was considered industrious and dependable. Her challenging work was rewarded well, with hefty bonuses. Mona sent money home to her family in India. She paid off all her loans with her bonuses and started to save for rainy days. Mona continued to invest in the stock market and made astute moves.

In the late eighties, the Los Angeles housing market was booming. The price of homes increased by a couple of thousand dollars each month. Mona, after living for three years in an apartment, planned to buy her own place. She asked Rebecca, who was now a seasoned real estate agent, for help to buy a house. Mona was doing well in her job, and she could easily pay the monthly mortgage. Rebecca suggested that Mona start with a small place that would be adequate for her and Sandy.

Mona had a large wish list. The house needed to have a big back yard for Sandy to play and at least three bedrooms. She did not want an older house. She knew she could not afford to live in the area where Vijay and Rebecca were living, in Willow Grove, where even the older homes were expensive. A new housing complex of a hundred homes was being built in Eucalyptus Springs, a neighboring city. Mona wanted to live near Rebecca, and the new housing tract was close to Willow Grove.

Rebecca found Mona her dream home. The housing complex was called Katella Park. It was a newly constructed house with three big bedrooms, spacious family room, big kitchen, and a backyard for Sandy.

During a tour of the house, Rebecca pointed out more features to Mona. "My, my, this is a beautiful house. The amenities are great, it has a dishwasher, automatic garage, and sprinklers. They are ready to upgrade the carpet if you pay a little more," Rebecca said. "It is an excellent value for this area. The property will only appreciate."

Mona had enough money saved in the bank for a down payment. A contract was drawn up and within 90 days, the house belonged to Mona. As the weeks passed, Mona came to know a lot of people who lived nearby. They invited her to their homes, and Mona hosted parties and gatherings. She made new friends and acquaintances.

Mona's life was on a smooth track: she loved work with McCreighton, and her social life kept her weekends busy. She continued to enjoy her strong friendship with Rebecca and Vijay. Rebecca introduced Mona to other neighborhood families, and she became part of a regular group. Despite this, Mona was lonely. Rebecca suggested Mona meet eligible bachelors.

"Mona, I know a few bachelors and a few divorcees as well. I will introduce you. Let us see how it works out," Rebecca said.

"I think, Rebecca, I am not ready yet," Mona said. "Just lonely."

"I know, Mona, you had an unhappy marriage. That does not mean all men are bad. You will find a good man," Rebecca said.

Mona's friends were concerned about her happiness. They believed she should get married again, and they all were searching for a suitable man.

Mona was forty-three years old. Age had given her more poise, confidence, and beauty. She was blossoming, and men would clamor to talk with her.

Mona knew it was not easy to find a suitable match. Who could accept her and the responsibility of caring for her thirteen-year-old daughter? She went out with a few unmarried men.. Some were interesting, but they were not ready for commitment. Things never worked out, and she could not find the right chemistry with anyone. After experiencing her fair share of setbacks, Mona stopped thinking of marriage and going out. Instead, she concentrated on her career.

Mona's eyes and ears were always open, and she watched how other people were buying investment properties. Her analytical mind helped her to make shrewd bets, and in the debacle of the stock market in 1988, she made a fortune. One day Vijay, Rebecca and Mona were out for dinner.

"Let us toast to my beautiful wife, Rebecca, for closing a deal of two million dollars. She will get a hefty commission," Vijay said.

"Oh really?" Mona said.

"What about Mona, who made tons of money in the stock market," Rebecca said.

"Truly. I am proud of two beautiful ladies, my wife, and my little sister. Both talented and enterprising. I toast to both of you!" Vijay said.

"So, what are you going to do with this fortune?" Rebecca asked Mona.

"That was what I was going to ask you. I would like to

invest some of the money in real estate. Can you help me?"

"That is smart thinking. Let me see. I will let you know if I come across a good bargain."

With the help of Rebecca, Mona bought two rental properties.

Chapter 72
Women's Shelter
1990
Ocean Beach

The shelter for abused women was called the Harris Shelter. It opened in 1990 with big fanfare, and it was well received in the community. It helped women in counseling, job training, food, clothing, and temporary housing. It was subsidized by the city of Ocean Beach and by private contributions from local citizens and non-profit organizations. Inside the shelter, there was a main room, three counseling rooms, and ten rooms with double beds for women to stay. The shelter also had a library and a fully stocked community kitchen, where subsidized food was served to the residents for a small payment. Dora had big plans for expansion. She envisioned training women in different skills and helping them find jobs within the community.

The Harris Shelter inauguration was held outside the building with ribbons and streamers flowing in the breeze. Members of the press and TV stations CBS, NBC, and ABC were all there with their cameras. Dan and Dora got recognition from every attendee. Even the governor sent commendations to both.

Dora was thankful to Mona for her expertise and advice. She had asked Mona to give a speech at the inaugural of the shelter.

Mona stood up. She was nervous. She wanted to keep

her personal emotions under control and keep the speech optimistic. She started slowly and had the audience's full attention.

"In every stratum of society, we see heinous crimes committed against women. The humiliation of being beaten, insulted, and assaulted never leaves you. The trauma a woman suffers will remain for the rest of her life. The women of Ocean Beach have suffered long enough. They are asking for justice and for the opportunity to participate in what many of us take for granted. Feeling helpless is a fate even graver than injustice. Under the eyes of God, men and women are equal. This shelter is dedicated to all those people who are ready to stand up and protect women."

The audience clapped and stood up to honor her speech. Dora was to be the director of the center, and Mona was persuaded to become an honorary director and advisor.

At the inauguration, Aviva and Dan were standing together. Dan threw glances at Mona when Aviva was not looking. Once, Mona caught Dan looking at her, and she stared back at him. Aviva was burning inside as she watched them both from a side glance.

Chapter 73
The City Of Ocean Beach
1990
Ocean Beach

Dan was elected for a second term as the mayor of Ocean Beach in 1990. After the election, scandal erupted in the city. The Chief Financial Officer had duped the mayor and council members with false reports. Millions of dollars were missing. Dan was furious for trusting him. He had been a reliable and respected CFO many years before Dan became the mayor. No one knew that the CFO had a compulsive habit of gambling. He lost millions of dollars over the years and borrowed extensively from loan sharks. To pay back the loan sharks, he wired money from city accounts and covered up the transactions with false invoices. A new auditor discovered his theft, and he was immediately fired.

Dan and the council members tried to take credit for discovering the CFO's fraud and put out press releases praising Dan's diligence in the audit. The city was in technical bankruptcy, and they controlled the damage inflicted upon the city and their own careers. Now to demonstrate strong civic medicine, Dan was desperately looking for a trustworthy replacement that could clean up the mess. He interviewed several candidates, but no one was qualified for the job to his satisfaction. He wanted to make a bold move to enhance his leadership as mayor.

Dora liked Mona and found her professional reputation

at McCreighton to be top flight. She was excellent in administration, shrewd in finance, and efficient in managing people. Dora thought this was the best opportunity to show Mona appreciation for her help. She also realized that Mona had a great presence: smart, beautiful, and untainted by political scandals of any kind. Dan had been impressed by Mona's ideas during the construction of the women's shelter.

"Dan, why don't you ask Mona to interview for the role? She is smart, capable and a new face for the city," Dora said.

Dan burst out laughing. "Are you kidding? A woman CFO of Ocean Beach! Though, she looked beautiful in her wrap-around at the inauguration the other day. What do you call that?"

"It is called a sari. It is the way Indian women dress, and it looks elegant, timeless and beautiful," Dora replied.

"A sari ...." He remembered their glances towards each other that day at the ceremony. He had never seen a woman looking so beautiful. He had not been able to take his eyes off her.

Dan snapped back to the present. "First, a woman and second, an immigrant from India to be the controller of accounts for Ocean Beach?" He thought it was a joke. He refused to interview her. "No, mom, no way." Dan was blunt.

Dora was shocked. "What is wrong with you? Why are you so disdainful of a woman CFO? She holds a good position at McCreighton. She has a Ph.D. Is it because she is darker than you and from a different country?"

"No, mom that is not the reason. It's just too...well, it's too much change."

Before Dan could say another word, Dora stated, "What harm is there if you ask Mona to interview? If she does not meet your expectation, you can reject her for the job. Dan,

I want you to call her."

Dan knew fighting against his mother was futile. He agreed to interview Mona.

Mona met Dan at his office, three years after their first meeting at Katella Deli.

Dan had kept Mona waiting for an hour before he called her into his office. She entered his office for the interview with confidence and poise. She was in stark business attire, wearing a black jacket, a well tailored white blouse, dress pants, high heels, and conservative jewelry. Her hair was thick, glossy, and tied back in a conservative bun. Her makeup emphasized her large, glowing eyes. Dan's notions of male supremacy and disdain for a woman's intellect were the main barriers preventing him from selecting a woman. He had read her resume a couple of times and letters of recommendations from other companies where she had worked. He was impressed. She met all the requirements of a CFO, and he was now intrigued. Here she was, an astonishingly beautiful woman standing tall in front of him, impeccably dressed and groomed, educated, and more than qualified to run the city's financial department.

"Alright, what I should call you, Miss or Mrs.?" Dan said looking at her.

"Please, call me by my first name, Mona," she said.

"Fine, now tell me, what makes you think that you can solve a budget with millions in deficits and still keep Ocean Beach's bond ratings high? Ocean Beach is in bankruptcy. We've got a million-dollar problem to deal with."

"Mr. Mayor….," Mona said.

"I've got another meeting in ten minutes," Dan interrupted her. "Tell me, how you can solve the problems of Ocean Beach?" "Mr. Mayor, my main job at McCreighton & Company is to go from city to city and study the root causes of city problems. Why is the city in a deficit? I work out the solution, balance the budget, and put the city on a better path forward. Here are a few cities I saved, which were previously bankrupt and under financial depression. Now they are thriving with healthy reserve funds for emergencies." Mona pulled out a lengthy list of cities. "You can ask the mayor of Jamaica City, New York. There is no problem I have not encountered. I am confident I can solve the problems of Ocean Beach."

He was surprised that a soft-spoken woman from India had such an excellent command over the financial issues of small American cities. Mona had a strong understanding of the financial woes of Ocean Beach. He asked her for specific recommendations in the interview questions and she had the right answers to all of them. He had once thought to dismiss her instantly and tell his mother that Mona was not the right fit for the job.

Dan's plan failed miserably.

Mona enchanted Dan's mind, and he could not think of any more questions to ask her. "I will send my recommendations to the council board, and if they agree, we will call you soon for a second interview," he told Mona.

He recommended a second interview to the board. Though he had originally thought of sending her out the door in a few minutes, he did not realize he had spent two hours talking to her. He was impressed. He could not focus on work, and in the evening, he praised Mona to his mother.

Mona was interested in the job. It offered excellent pay, many benefits, and a prestigious title with the opportunity to help the city. The job would be very demanding, and she knew that the late evenings would turn into late nights. Nevertheless, she was ambitious, and this was the opportunity of her dreams. She could finally prove to everyone, especially those back home, that she was a high achiever. She would command respect as the person who saved a city.

When Mona told Vijay, he looked at her.

"Mona, why do you want to accept this job? The city is in bad shape. You will have to toil for many extra hours, and you may not be able to save the city from bankruptcy. Presently, you get a lot of time for Sandy, and you can concentrate on your hobby, the stock market, where you are making extra money to enjoy some luxuries."

"Vijay Bhai, you know me, and you also know how badly our community has treated my family. I have confidence I will not fail, and I am ready to take a chance. I can bring Ocean Beach back to its glory. Once the city is back on track, the whole community will pay full respect to my father for what his daughter has achieved," Mona said.

Mona was called for a second interview and a third, final interview by city council board members. The third interview was the most important for getting the job. After the interview, the whole board unanimously agreed to hire her. She was chosen as the Chief Financial Officer of the City of Ocean Beach with an impressive salary and promised she would get a hefty bonus if she solved the City's financial problems in a year.

Chapter 74
Trip To India
1990
Kanpur

Mona decided to make a trip back to Kanpur before starting her job for the City of Ocean Beach. She was keen to show her parents that their daughter had accomplished an impressive milestone. She was an achiever, a woman who succeeded against all odds.

It had been ten years since she had visited last. It was monsoon season when she got there, and the clouds had no mercy on the city. The Ganges was overflowing and at some low-elevation neighborhoods, the rainwater flooded the streets.

Sandy was fourteen and growing into a charming young girl. Her family was happy to see Sandy for the first time. All of Mona's relatives talked and praised Mona for the way she raised Sandy. There was a small celebration within the family to celebrate Mona's visit. Binny, an excellent cook, had made lots of sweets and snacks for the family and especially for Sandy.

Mona's father Krishna was suffering with acute arthritis, and he had developed glaucoma which diminished his eyesight. Krishna had sold his factory, but the court cases against him were continuing. Their lawyer's opinion was that her father may go to jail if he did not repay his debts. Her mother's wealthy relatives were not ready to bail the family out in spite of the shame.

Mona looked over her family situation much as she would look at a bankrupt city. She was sad, but realistic. "I know that no rich relative is going to help to pay off these lenders. Don't worry, I will pay off the rest of your debts," Mona said.

"But Beti, you are already sending money," Krishna said. "With your help we were able to get Binny married. We tried our best. Why take on more burdens?" He looked far into the distance. "I wish I had a son, A son to take responsibility for these problems."

"Dad, the times have changed; my gender does not matter," Mona said.

Krishna stayed quiet and went into the other room.

Binny was a simple person, short and a little heavy. She was plain to look at, and after her accident, Binny could not walk straight. She had to put pressure on one leg to walk without pain, and her walk became a limp over time.

Mona' parents had tried to get Binny married. It was challenging to find someone willing to marry an awkward woman. After a big search, her parents found a groom for Binny, and paying a big dowry in cash, they married Binny off to that man. One month after the marriage, Binny was sent back to her parent's home for no plausible reason. With a failed marriage, Binny's reputation was tarnished and getting her married again was out of the question.

In 1981, when Mona had become a U.S. citizen in New York, she had sponsored her family to migrate to America. Mona's parents were reluctant to move, and Binny could not leave her aging parents alone in India.

Mona tried again from California to bring her family to the United States. "Mom and dad, your sponsorship is already approved. Why don't you come to America? Other people are eager for the opportunity to settle in America, but you refuse to budge."

Mona's dad took some time to reply. "No Beti, at the age of seventy-nine years, every breath of my body is filled with Indian soil. It is impossible to leave this place and die in some foreign country. Let me peacefully die here,"

"You will be with family. We will take care of you both," Mona said.

"Take Binny with you. She is an excellent vegetarian cook and she can open a restaurant," her mom said.

Binny mimicked her mom and said in her mother's tone, "Take Binny with you. If I go, who will take care of you? No, I am not going if you both do not go."

Every day, they had the same discussion about moving to the United States, but no decision was made. Mona paid off all her father's debts. She wanted nothing more than for her parents to live peacefully.

During Mona's visit to India, family and friends came to call. Ramesh's brother Sundar and his wife Umi came to the house to meet Mona. That day the weather was cloudy and hot. They had tea and snacks made by Binny. Umi was curious to know why the divorce happened, and why Mona did not take care of Ramesh when he was sick in America. It was very awkward for Mona to explain the situation to them.

"Life in America is different than India. I did take care of him, but it was difficult," said Mona. "Why don't you ask Ramesh about why I divorced him? Please drop this matter, and we can talk of something else."

Mona was not ready to tell them her side of the story. It was of no use; it was part of a painful past. Ramesh was gone out of her life. Why open old wounds? She was firm, assertive and courteous but essentially told everyone to mind their own business.

"This is a personal matter. Many years have gone by. Please do not bring up this topic again," Mona told everybody.

A cousin let it be known that Ramesh was in Kanpur living with his parents and that he was still sick.

Krishna suggested, "Beti, why don't you visit your in-law's house? It may be nice to let Sandy see her father and meet her grandparents."

"Never, never, as long as I have a breath in my body!" Mona became terribly angry on hearing Ramesh's name. She lashed out at her father. Later she felt ashamed for her behavior and apologized to him for being rude. She told her father and mother the full story.

"Dad, let me tell you why I divorced Ramesh. You do not know how badly he treated me. He used to beat, curse and abuse me," Mona said. She opened the back side of her blouse and showed them her dried wounds and marks.

Her parents were stunned. After hearing the full story, her father got up and came closer to his daughter and embraced her. He said softly, "I am sorry, my child. I did not know how badly he hurt you."

A few days later, she had a surprise visit from Ramesh's parents, Dr. Charan and Nishi. Ramesh's parents were frail and sick. They came to see Sandy.

Mona touched her in-laws' feet, as a sign of respect. She called Sandy, who was hiding shyly.

"Sandy, they are your grandparents. Go and touch their feet to get their blessing. Go, go," Mona said.

The grandparents were happy to see their granddaughter. They played with Sandy. "See, we brought many gifts for you. This mini sari, this Punjabi suit and these silver anklets for your feet," Nishi said. They avoided any mention of Ramesh.

The weeks passed with visits from friends, and Mona had plenty of time to arrange her parents' affairs. Soon, Mona's stay in Kanpur was ending. It was time to go back to the States. The day before leaving, Mona and her parents went to the temple for the blessing. Ramesh's house was next to the temple. She felt emotional as she walked up the steps towards the temple. Mona remembered her wedding day that took place in the same temple. She could not control herself and looked up at the window across the road. There she saw Ramesh's shadow. She immediately covered her face.

Chapter 75
Ramesh: A Bitter Life
1990
Kanpur

Mona left India, and Kanpur had a respite from the monsoons. No rains fell, but the sky was cloudy, and by August the city was burning.

Ramesh was sitting in his room. He was bitter when Mona filed for a divorce. According to him, the meaning of marriage was that she was obligated to stand by him despite the adversities. He was not ready to admit what harm he had done to Mona. He believed he had full rights over his wife, and she had to obey his wishes.

He had recouped his health. Yoga helped him to get strong, and under the Pujari's guidance, he learned to control his outbursts and rage. He never told the Pujari about Mona because it was too private to him. Despite the improvement in his health, Ramesh was not at peace. His soul was agitated, and he did not know why. He could not sleep at night.

He listened to the Pujari's discourse in the temple every evening, and it mellowed him a little but the hot well of anger in his mind persisted. Three years had passed since he had moved back in with his parents and when Mona came to India for a visit.

When he came to know his parents went to see Mona, he was not happy. He longed to see Sandy, but his ego took over.

"Why can't Mona bring Sandy here?" was his only thought. He refused to meet Sandy at Mona's parent's place. He believed that would be an insult.

His parents were full of praises about Mona and impressed by how well Mona had raised Sandy.

"Why did you go to Mona's parent house? Have you lost all your pride? It is a big insult for our family," Ramesh said.

His father said, "Listen son, we know you and Mona are separated, but Sandy is not at fault here. We wanted to meet our granddaughter and therefore we went. If you are keen to see your daughter, we support you visiting her. No one is going to stop you."

One day, Ramesh was sitting on his bed watching people from the window when he had the feeling someone was looking at him. There she was. Mona entered the temple, and her face was covered. He saw his daughter holding her mother's hand. He could not bear it anymore. He looked at them again from the window. They were gone. Suddenly, he did not know what came over him. Tears started flowing from his eyes. He cried. It was no use to continue like this, and he made the decision to end his life.

Next day he went to see the Pujari at the temple.

"I am miserable. I want to end my life," said Ramesh.

"In this world everyone is miserable for reasons of their own. Should everyone end their lives?"

"Then what should I do?" asked Ramesh.

"Upanishads say self-annihilation is a sin; a man given to fear cannot achieve anything. Fear does not make a man a hero; one cannot achieve anything in this world with fear. The strength of mind comes to him who learns to control his fear and therefore his life."

"How can I learn to control my life? I am burning

inside!"

"Control cannot be achieved when one is bitter. From bitterness, anger crops up, and from there, delusion. If you abuse your senses, they get worn down. But when they are properly cherished, they become useful and bring you knowledge and efficiency. Discipline is essential in all the activities of the mind and senses."

Ramesh let his mind go back to his childhood. From his earliest days, he realized that he had wrongful notions embedded in his mind by society and fortified by his own early experience with his father, Dr. Charan. There were rumors and gossip buzzing in the community about the family's terrible experiences with his tyrant of a father. Ramesh remembered, with one look from his father, his mother would shiver. Charan beat his mother, Ramesh's elder brother and him. On many occasions at the dining table, his mother was slapped or kicked by his father, and Ramesh would pee in his pants from fear.

Ramesh was told that men were superior to women. But how could Mona be more intelligent and successful than him? His anger and remorse did not fade. He could not comprehend that men and woman were equal; that they were two wheels of the cart and complement each other.

The Pujari encouraged Ramesh to go to an Ashram. "Son, go to the mountains. My friend runs a hermitage. There at the banks of River Ganges near the city of Haridwar, you may find peace and understand the true meaning of life."

One week later, Ramesh left for the Ashram near Haridwar.

Chapter 76
Painful News
1990
Ocean Beach

Mona returned from India and was busy starting her new job. Each day that Mona, Dan, and the council members had meetings, challenging decisions needed to be made to help the city. Dan and the council members were surprised by Mona's analytical mind and her grasp of the city's financial situation. In the beginning, it was hard for Mona to convince Dan to accept her recommendations. His ego could not accept a woman from India telling him where to make cuts to the budget or to reverse certain policies. It took him a month to understand that Mona was capable of comprehending problems quickly and making sound decisions.

Two months after she arrived from India, Mona was sitting up late reading the Wall Street Journal in her living room. She had said goodnight to Sandy. The telephone rang. It was a call from India, and her sister Binny was on the line. The connection was scratchy. It was hard for Mona to hear her sister clearly.

"Hello Binny, how are you, and how are mom and papa?"

Mona could tell Binny was distraught. "Mom was doing puja. Suddenly she rushed to the bathroom. She vomited blood in the sink and collapsed. The doctor said it was a massive heart attack."

"What, what are you saying, Binny? Mom had a heart attack. And is she still alive?" Mona asked.

Binny was sobbing. "No, she has passed away."

"How could this happen? When I left, mom seemed so healthy…." Mona said. She felt dizzy.

"We don't know. It is God's will," Binny said.

"Oh my God, oh my God…. " Mona's great sobs prevented her from saying anymore.

Sandy awoke and came out of the bedroom. "Mama, what happened? Why are you crying?"

Mona took her daughter in her arms, "My little baby, your grandmother is no more. You remember how she was hugging and kissing you, as if she knew she wouldn't see you again."

Mona sobbed in front of her daughter. Sandy tried to console her mother by putting her thin arms around Mona and holding her mother's hands in her palms. Mona sometimes cried silently and sometimes howled loudly. But nothing could bring her mother back.

The time comes when one prefers to be near family for comfort and solace to each other. Mona longed to be with her father and sister to grieve with them. Her father was devastated, and Binny was numb with shock. Her friends Vijay and Rebecca were on vacation with their families in Europe. There was no one here to share her sorrow. She was in a fit of despair. She wanted to fly to India to be with her family, but reaching there would take her a couple of days. Her father forbade her to come.

"Papa, I want to come and be with you," Mona said on the phone.

"Beti, it is of no use. Usha was a very pious woman. Your mother is in heaven, sitting at the feet of God," Krishna said.

"Papa, I want to come," Mona said.

"It doesn't make sense; you just came to India. Travelling with a child is very tedious, disruptive to her life. You have joined your new job. Don't come," Krishna advised.

She did not contact her family for the next few days to allow them time to organize the religious ceremonies for Usha's departed soul. Mona's father and Binny were left alone at home after the funeral services. Mona was keen to know the details and called Binny. To Mona's surprise, her mother's brothers who had turned their back on her, paid for all the pujas and religious ceremonies.

Mona felt isolated and angry. To Binny she demanded, "Why did you let mom's brothers come to the funeral? When she was alive, nobody cared for her. Where were they when she was having a rough time, and creditors were knocking down her door? Dad was on the verge of going to jail. At that time, none of her wealthy brothers bothered. What was the use of their visiting and spending lot of money on a dead soul, just to show their relatives they cared and to keep a false pretense among the community?"

To Mona, it was very painful think about never seeing her mother again. Mona remembered the last time when the train from Kanpur departed for Delhi. She had waved from the train window and saw her mother's smiling face, and she never thought it would be the last time.

It was a revelation for Mona. She was going to live alone and die alone.

Chapter 77
Struggle
1990
Ocean Beach

Mona's new job in a near-bankrupt Ocean Beach was not easy. Mona had to negotiate with lawyers, keep the press releases positive, and work with uncooperative staff. The city council gave Mona one month to submit a plan to bring city expenditures under control. After one month, Mona submitted the report, and the council approved of her plan. The council chairperson said, "The city council agrees with your recommendations, and we authorize you to do what's needed to implement the plan." Mona had proven her worth.

Working with Dan was an enigma. In front of the office staff, he was cordial, but whenever they were alone, his comments to her were precise and short, to the point of rudeness. Mona found Dan very sharp and savvy. He would comprehend and take charge of tricky situations very quickly. Though he exhibited a cold professionalism toward Mona, in the community he was known as a man with a good heart and helpful nature. He was dedicated to his city and had ideas to improve it. An organized administrator, everyone loved him in the city.

Mona was new to the city and was having difficulty earning her employees' respect. Her subordinates were holdovers from the previous CFO's staff. They would not listen to her, and other colleagues would ignore her, thinking she was an outsider who got the job only through Dan's help. She had two choices, either quit or fight it out. She was a fighter, and she was ready, but she needed a friend in the office to help her understand the system.

Janet Tracy had been the staff secretary ever since Dan's father was the mayor 30 years ago. Her work experience and knowledge of how the city operated made her invaluable to many mayors. In the office, there was a joke: mayors may come and go, but Janet would always be there.

She was sixty years old, married once and divorced, but still beautiful. She was thin and blond, with light blue eyes, and she had an impeccable taste for clothes. Nothing escaped her. She knew the secrets of many city officials and collected gossip on both in and outside the office.

Mona knew Janet's birthday was coming soon, and she did not miss the opportunity to get close to such a powerful resource. Mona made a dark chocolate cake and, along with it, gave Janet a beautiful bouquet of flowers. Mona's thoughtfulness caught Janet by surprise but did touch her heart.

For her morning coffee break, Janet sat down with Mona. She was interested in Mona's background. "I heard you were working for McCreighton & Company. It is an impressive consulting firm. Once they hire you, they don't let you go."

"My contract with them was for three years, and just at that time, the Ocean Beach offer came. McCreighton could not match the offer, and I wanted to take on the next challenge, so here I am," Mona said.

They started taking coffee breaks and lunches together regularly. From Janet, Mona learned how the system worked in city hall. Interested businesspeople brought gifts to make deals. Her predecessor had made many false promises and negotiated the wrong deals with the wrong businesspeople.

"If you look at your predecessor's records, you will find lot of false deals," Janet said. "The city is still suffering because of his tricks."

-"I never imagined politics were so full of corrupt men and women," said Mona.

"Most are dedicated people. It is the greed and temptation of a few that is difficult to control."

"Is Dan like that?"

"No, he is not corrupt. He is sincere and resolute. But remember, he is a Don Juan of the town and a lady killer. Women succumb to his smooth charm. And he has the Harris family ambition."

"I did not know he was a flirt. I have met his girlfriend."

"You mean Aviva? She was and then wasn't. Aviva broke it off six months ago. Dan's mom, Dora, loves Aviva. She was not happy when Aviva broke up with Dan."

"She is beautiful, and Dan is so handsome, intelligent and he always says the right thing. What was the reason she broke up with him?"

"I agree he is handsome and intelligent. He wants to be a senator and one day the president of the United States. It made sense for Dan and Aviva to date because Aviva's father is one of the wealthiest senators in the country. But Aviva is a one-man person. She was not ready to share Dan with other women. When a woman smiles at Dan, Aviva's temperature would start rising. Do not ever cross Aviva. She is a black belt in Karate. I am sure they both like each other, but Dan cannot stop sleeping with other women. So, they mutually broke it off."

"So, you say, Dan can't be trusted regarding women."

"History is history," smiled Janet.

Chapter 78
Curiosity
1990
Ocean Beach

One day, Janet and Mona were having lunch at a coffee shop. Mona had read in the newspaper about the love affair of a married senator in D.C. Mona asked Janet, "Tell me, Janet, why does a successful politician act like this?"

Janet laughed. "When a powerful man thinks he is untouchable, he commits mistakes, and that can be his downfall. Some of them go down a slippery slope and come out still a winner, but some go from the slope down to the gutter."

"But how could a decent man behave like that?" Mona asked. "There are no secrets nowadays."

Janet knew Mona was hinting at Dan. "Everyone has a weakness. Dan is a highly intelligent man and full-blooded American. If he plays his cards right, he could be a senator, and he could be the president of the country. He is a capable man, but his weakness is beautiful women," Janet replied shrewdly.

"Why should Aviva tolerate his infidelities? I never thought Dan would be such a person."

"Let me get to the point. His mother has one obsession: that one day her son will be president of the United States. She has accepted his flings as minor irritations. But any serious obstruction of her ambitions must be removed. On the other hand, Aviva was fed up. She could not tolerate his escapades. Therefore, she left him," Janet said.

"Aviva is a nice girl, and Dan is handsome and intelligent. They seem ideal for each other. Both come from powerful families. Then why not form an alliance?" Mona said.

Janet interrupted, "Hey, careful, lady. You are repeatedly saying he is handsome and smart. He is a womanizer. Do not succumb to his charm. Do not let that cunning man ever kiss you. He is a Scorpio, and his lips are full of venom. Once you kiss him, you will never be the same." Janet pretended to be serious.

Lunch was over. Janet and Mona went back to their work. Janet knew it would just be a matter of time before Dan would taste the Indian delight.

Mona thought Janet was weird. Why did she warn Mona about Dan being a womanizer? *I would never let Dan kiss me. I would not let him come near me. That is why I always sit three chairs away from him in the meetings.*

Mona came to know a few more details about Janet. She had started her career under Dan's father. Dan's father grew close to Janet, but he was married with a child, and they broke off the affair before the newspapers got any hint. Janet knew a lot about Dan Harris' family and Dora's role as wife.

Chapter 79
Wolf In Kanpur
1991
Kanpur

Time passed fast. Many things happened in one year. Mona's father became blind. He could not take a step without the help of Binny. Mona called her dad in India several times during that year to persuade him to migrate to the States, and his answer was the same.

"Mona Beti, I told you, I want to die in India, where your mother died. Don't ask me repeatedly the same question." Her Dad was a stubborn person, and Binny refused to leave her dad alone in India.

One year had passed since her mother died. Mona decided to go to India to attend the pujas and religious rites for her mother's departed soul to give closure to her own grief. She was going for ten days. Taking Sandy out of school to go to India was not easy.

Rebecca offered her help. "Why do you want to take Sandy with you? You are going for only a brief period. Leave Sandy with me. I will take care of her."

"Thank you, Rebecca, but I don't want you to be burdened with her," Mona said.

"What burden? She is like my daughter. You go and give closure to your grief," Rebecca said.

"Thank you, Rebecca. It is so nice of you," Mona said.

Mona made arrangements for the trip and shopped for

gifts for the family. Leaving Los Angeles on a bright, cold day, Mona's plane reached Delhi the following morning, and the same afternoon she took the train to Kanpur. She was very emotional and tried to hold back her tears. The train was on time and reached Kanpur late in the evening. She was astonished to see her Uncle Amar waiting to receive her at the railway station. They boarded a cycle rickshaw.

"What are you doing here? I thought you were in Chicago?" Mona asked with a frown on her face.

"Nobody informed you. I was posted back in India, a year after you left New York," Amar said.

"But why have you come to pick me up? Where is my sister, Binny?" she said irritably.

"Mona, calm down, I will explain." He put her luggage in the rickshaw.

They sat down in a rickshaw, and Mona tried to keep her distance from him. "Now tell me!" Mona said.

"Last year I came to attend your mom's funeral. After all your relatives were gone, your father forced me to stay for one more week. Your father's eyesight was gone, and he was helpless. He insisted that I take care of him. I realized my blind brother needed me. I took an early retirement and settled down with my brother."

"So, you seized the opportunity to exploit my sister." Mona gave him a look of disdain.

"Don't say that. I am serving my brother and helping my niece. Listen, Mona, you are here only for eight days. Don't disrupt the peace of the house," he said in a deep voice.

Mona and he remained silent for some time.

"What is your true motive to leave a lucrative job and stay here to take care of my dad?" she asked.

"Mona, let me say it again. When I attended your mother's funeral, your father was devastated. He repeatedly said to me, 'I cannot survive without your mother.' At that time, I promised your father that I will take care of him. Once the funeral was over, he reminded me of my promise. I took my retirement, and here I am, living with him," he explained.

Mona remained silent, and a few minutes later, another thought came in her mind. "Are you sleeping with my sister?"

He turned his face away and kept quiet. Mona repeated the question. After a while he said, "What a question! No," Amar said.

Mona looked at him. His face betrayed the lie he was telling. She was in a silent rage. Now he was exploiting Binny.

They reached home. When she saw her father and sister, Mona wailed and cried. The tears would not stop. She was lost. She almost expected that her mother would come out to greet her. No, it was impossible. She was gone.

The next four days were spent in completing the religious rites. On the fifth day, Mona sat down and looked around at what was going on in her family. Amar had moved his belongings into Mona's room and occupied her bathroom. During her visit, he was sleeping outside, in front of her father's room. Her father had become frail and irritable. He would shout at Binny, and she would shout back. The only person who could keep peace between them was Amar. He was the head of the household.

Mona thought the only way to get out of this mess was to bring her father to the States. Mona pleaded again to her father, "Dad come to USA. I will take you to the best eye doctors in Los Angeles."

"Mona Beti, you have asked me to come many times, and this is the last time. I am saying no. I will die here," said her father.

Mona turned to her sister to discuss kicking Amar out of the house. Binny said, "I know you don't like Uncle, but if he is gone, who will take care of our father? At this stage of his life, Uncle tries to fulfill all his needs and whims. We are alone, and we need help in the house."

"Why don't you hire a woman to help you?" Mona asked.

"Our father is too proud to let a woman give him a bath or change him when he wets himself in bed."

"Why can't you hire a man?" Mona asked.

"A male servant in the house? You know our community is very conservative. In which way a male servant will be more devoted than Uncle? He meets all of dad's needs. You know very well I cannot get a job. No company is ready to hire a disabled woman. The doctor's fee, his medicines and other expenses are adding up. Where will we get the money?" Binny said.

"I will send more money," Mona replied.

"I am thankful to you for regularly sending money home. It is not fair for you to keep sending more. And you know very well, you cannot be the solution," Binny continued.

"Then what is the solution?" Mona asked.

"Leave us as we are. You cannot solve our problems sitting ten thousand miles away. You can't jump on the plane any time we need your help," Binny replied.

"I am your elder sister, and you don't know what type of wolf Amar Uncle is!" Mona said angrily.

Binny looked at her sister and replied, "After mother's death, I was alone with Dad. All men in the neighborhood looked at me with their greedy eyes. No one cared that I am plain, or that I walk crookedly. The only reason they showed interest is because I am a young woman living in a posh neighborhood and own a large apartment. Since Uncle arrived, other men do not look at me with those eyes."

Mona remained quiet for few moments and then asked,

"Do you, ...I mean, ... does he sleep with you?"

Binny was quiet at the question. She hesitated then replied, "Uncle is security. A wolf can be an insurance against other wolves." Binny did not meet Mona's penetrating eyes.

Mona found it difficult to accept what was going on. It was painful to see the triumph of evil over good in this world. Mona was sad. The distance between her and India was getting farther. She was an American citizen, and America was her home now. She left India with a heavy heart.

Chapter 80
Venom
1991
Ocean Beach

Mona came back to Los Angeles unhappily. It was impossible to tolerate how human exploitation worked. Every morning when she prayed, she asked God, "How do you let good and evil live side by side?" To avoid bad thoughts coming to her mind, she started concentrating more on her work and on the stock market. Mona was doing well in her job. The council members were impressed, and all her suggestions were implemented.

The mayors of other cities came to know how efficient Mona was, and she received a few more offers of employment. For her, it was too early to think of changing jobs. Her office staff and council members started respecting her. She and Dan were now working together well after a rocky beginning. Dan would ask her opinion on any city problem, and she would waltz into his office any time.

She was still restless. There was a fire burning in her body, but she did not know why. She could not stop thinking about Dan's affairs with many women. At night, she dreamt of a vague, tall figure.

Mona established good working relationships with other colleagues except Carter, the Director of Parks. He was ill-mannered and spoke rudely to everyone.

Carter started meddling in her work, and he would not

follow the city's rules. His budget reports were late, and sometimes he would not submit them. He was spending money on items not approved by the budget committee. He ignored her in front of other members. Many of the council members were afraid of his insulting attitude. No one was willing to tell him to back off.

"Carter, why did you spend so much money on new golf carts when the city bought two dozen golf carts last year?" Mona asked.

"Ah, don't worry about it," Carter replied as he walked away.

One day at the staff meeting, Carter was talking with a group of colleagues about the football game from the previous weekend.

"Mr. Carter, may we please have your attention on agenda item number 13 (a)? The football talk can wait until after the meeting," Mona said.

Carter did not acknowledge Mona and continued to talk about the game. Mona was irritated.

"Carter, if you'd like to continue talking, please leave the room. But please do not disturb the meeting," Mona said.

Carter got up and looked at her as though he were going to strangle her. He left the room, whispering, "Fuck you."

Mona and other staff members heard those words. She adjourned the meeting and went to her office. She closed her office door, stood alone in front of her desk, and started shouting.

"Carter, you never listen to me. Take this!" She moved her right fist in front of her as if she was boxing.

"And take this," moving her left fist. "Because I am a woman, you don't listen to me? I will not allocate any budget for your department," Mona said. "Because I can!"

Mona was so pent up with anger that she did not realize Dan had entered her office and quietly closed the door. He sat on a chair behind her and watched. Mona turned around. Her face was red with anger.

Dan saw her eyes were wet. He stood up and came close to her. He gently looked at her and calmly took her face in his strong hands. He lifted her face, Mona closed her eyes, and with his thumbs he wiped the tears from her face and softly brushed his lips against her cheek. Then he kissed her succulent lips. Her closed eyes opened wide and closed again for few moments. She was still clinging to him when Dan moved back.

"My little Cobra, don't worry. I will take care of everything. Now will you please go back to work?" he said.

Mona lowered her face and walked to her seat. She was bewildered at what happened. Her face was flushed and hot. A shiver passed through her body that rendered her insensible. For the rest of the day, she could not help but think of the kiss of the scorpion. What would he do next? Would he kiss her again? She ran tongue over her lips. Her lips still had the taste of his Panama cigar. She licked the venom.

More thoughts came flooding into her mind. *Not again, never again, one mistake was enough.*

But the smell of his cigar was still in her nostrils. Dan awoke her longing. Her tongue moved over her lips repeatedly for the taste of the bittersweet kiss. She could not concentrate on her work and went home early.

The following day, Mona arrived at the office to find that Carter was not there. A day later she learned that he was given another assignment away from the head office.

In her romantic life, nothing changed. Dan treated her as if that day had never happened. Mona's mind was saying *'A kiss is just a kiss,'* and she could not comprehend why she was fretting so much about it. The kiss was beyond her intuitive reasoning.

Dan would say, "Good morning, Mona, how are you today?" "Hi, Mona, how was your day?"; "That was a good meeting, and you did a good job."

Dan was unaware of the effect he was having on her. He would talk, make jokes, and walk away from her as if that kiss meant nothing.

She found herself waiting for Dan, and with some pretext, she would try to make conversation. If he were out of town or late, an uneasy feeling would envelope her.

Chapter 81
Sunday
1991
Ocean Beach

Mona felt restless and bored with the same invitations to Indian parties in Eucalyptus Springs. Most of those weekend parties were filled with gossip and superficial talk ranging from what jewelry was purchased to what saris one brought from India to who did not go to India that year. It was all too familiar for Mona.

Men would sit in one corner and discuss the problems with their bosses, how many new contracts their company got, how much progress their company made and how high their company's stock prices were.

"My boss is going through a divorce, and he is very short-tempered. For any small mistake, he jumps on the whole department," one of the guests said.

"Our company is doing very well. They are getting a lot of new contracts, and the company's stock is going up," the other said.

Among the women, no one would talk with Mona about her struggles, or about her job. Some people would mention her divorce and comment on how her husband treated her. Mona did not like the topic to be brought up. That was old news, well in the past.

Women who had high profile jobs like hers or who earned high salaries as doctors had their noses up in the air.

The first question they would ask is, "When you are going to India? Why have you not brought your family to U.S. yet? My husband and I go to India every year." Or "Gold is cheap. Have you bought any for your daughter's future dowry? Start collecting now!"

Another person would ask, "Your daughter is still in a public school? Both my children are in private school. In public schools, the quality of teaching is much worse. The public schools are full of crimes and drugs."

Mona would sneak away, without getting into any heated conflict or discussions. Vijay and Rebecca and their children, Anand and Sugund, had planned a three-month tour of India. Vijay's parents had passed away, so he had no intention of visiting Kanpur. Sandy had summer vacation for three months, and she wanted to go with Vijay's family on the trip. Mona was reluctant to send Sandy with them.

"Why don't you let Sandy go with us? She is part of the family," Rebecca said.

"Rebecca, Sandy is still young. She will bother you all the time," Mona said.

"Oh, come on. She is a doll. She is my sunshine," Rebecca said. "And she is almost a young lady. She will be fun."

Sandy jumped in, "Mummy, I am not young. I am fourteen years old. Please let me go, please."

"You promise you won't bother Aunty?" Mona said.

"I promise, I cross my heart," Sandy said.

Summer approached, and Sandy left with Vijay's family to visit India. For the first few days, Mona was busy analyzing her stock portfolio. She had made a small fortune due to the 1988 meltdown of the stock market. After organizing her paperwork, to keep herself busy, Mona started going to the office for a few hours on Sundays. She would prepare for her Monday morning meetings.

Mona had keys to the main door. Some people worked in the office on Saturdays, but no one came to work on Sundays, including Dan. Working on Sundays gave her undisturbed time to do her job.

One Saturday evening, Mona attended an Indian party. The women were to come dressed as a typical village girl from India. Mona decided to dress like a Rajasthani girl. She wore a colorful Rajasthani skirt and matched it with a colorful blouse. The skirt was made with nine yards of cloth, with intricate colorful designs and glass work on it. The blouse was skimpy, with a high midriff and bare back. She wore no brassiere underneath but tied the blouse at the back with thin strings.

The party went past midnight. Mona came home late and crashed on her bed, lacking the energy to change her clothes. After awakening late on Sunday morning, she looked at her dress and thought, *Oh my God! It is already eleven o'clock.* She thought of changing into jeans but had second thoughts. *Why do I need to change? No one will be in the office on Sunday.*

She dashed water on her face, brushed her teeth, grabbed a few office papers and her keys, and rushed out the door. Dressed in the same costume she wore at last night's party, Mona drove to the office, ready to prepare important reports.

After finishing her report in the office, Mona put her pen down. She was yawning. She pushed her office chair back, turned the wastepaper basket upside down and stretched her legs onto it. Mona put her hands behind her head, closed her eyes, and relaxed for a second. Mona did not know when she dozed off.

Dan entered her office and saw her sleeping, a beautiful damsel. Her round breasts heaved under her blouse. Part of her skirt had fallen to the ground.

Dan's eyes glued to her serpentine curves and her bent knees on the wastepaper basket, revealing her smooth bare legs. Dan thought if he would have been an artist, he would have painted her in this same stretched pose. Her chest moved up and down, and Mona was a perfect picture of one unconcerned about the world around her. His eyes turned to her beautiful legs again. He had never seen such well-shaped legs, and he could not resist looking at them

Dan stood there for a long time, as he did not wish to wake her up. Suddenly Mona heard a noise. She was startled to see Dan standing in front of her. She did not know how long he had been there watching her. She jumped onto her feet and froze at his unexpected presence, embarrassed by her unconventional clothing and by being found sleeping.

"Hi, Dan…I was working on the agenda for Monday … I don't know… when I dozed off….," Mona stammered.

He came closer to her and put his index finger under her chin and raised her face. She was timid and could not look at him. She closed her eyes, her breathing was fast, and she was waiting for his next move. He bent down and kissed her gently.

"You look beautiful," Dan said. He kissed her again. It was a long kiss. Her arms trembled and went around his neck this time. Her lips kissed him back.

He picked her up in his arms and pushed the papers away from her desk, placing her gently on top. It was unexpected, wild sex. The union of a hot white stallion and a willing dark mare.

Chapter 82
Awakening
1991
Ocean Beach

Mona reached home late that afternoon, feeling as though she was floating in the air. She did not try to find the logic in what happened and felt no regret. She was intoxicated with the feeling of pleasure. She thought of his embrace, the tightening of her legs around him, his kisses, and how he fumbled with her nine yards of skirt.

A small flame in her body rekindled. She was dormant for a long time. Someone had put energetic reawakening back into her. She liked Dan from the beginning, or she fell in love with him at some point along the way. Her mind could not decide. But she did know that she was not ready to give up on herself. Today was the ultimate reawakening that showed her she deserved love.

On Monday morning, she woke up feeling rejuvenated. She discovered contentment and no longer felt alone, isolated, or unloved. She yearned for a man's touch, and she finally found fulfillment after many years. She was humming in the shower. *What is happening to me?* She did not understand how there was no guilt or shame. Her mind and body were in harmony.

She reached her office a few minutes early and noticed Dan was already in his office. The window blinds of his office were open. He saw her, and looking around to ensure no one was around, he sent her a flying kiss. Her heart thumped fast. She gave him a charming smile and turned to her work.

The next three months passed quickly. It was easy for them to meet at her house, as Sandy was in India for the summer. Mona had no neighbors, because the houses on either side of her were for sale and empty. With no one around to see him, Dan parked his car inside the garage.

She told him her story, how she was tortured by her husband, divorced, and had started a new life in California. She did not mention the rape.

"You know, I fell in love with my economics professor. That was my first love, and we even got engaged. But our caste system did not allow us to marry," Mona said.

"What do you mean your caste system? How old were you at that time?"

"I was twenty-four, but still, we are obligated to marry in our own caste and with the consent of our family."

"It sounds weird."

"What do you mean?"

"Because, if two adults love each other, and they want to marry, why would you need anyone else's approval? You will be the one living with the person you choose."

"To comprehend, you will have to understand Indian culture," Mona said.

"What happened when your family found a husband for you, and he tortured you?"

"That was different. But tell me more about your life."

"In my school and college days, I was a football player. Not what you call football, which is called soccer here. The game is to try to snatch the ball from the other team and score as many touchdowns as possible," Dan looked at Mona. "And not only we kept the score of the game, but also…,"

"I am listening," Mona said.

"All of the boys had a black book. The player who scored the most girls in a week would be an MVP, or most valuable player." Dan chuckled quietly.

Mona looked at Dan.

"You kept a black book?"

"Sort of, but later in college, I became more selective. I only chose the most beautiful girls."

Dan's stories were full of escapades. He had slept with so many women, famous actresses, socialites, and political figures. His mother and Aviva knew about many of them, though not all. Mona put aside her questions. Dan had enveloped her mind, body, and soul.

Mona would go home after work, and Dan would join her. Sometimes she would cook lunch or dinner for him. He loved her cooking, but the spicy food would bring tears to his eyes and drops of sweat on his forehead.

"Oh my, it's too spicy! I need water!" Dan said.

"The masala I used had some chilies. Next time I will choose a milder blend. Here, have, some more water," Mona said.

"Oh my, I need ice cream," Dan said. Mona would repeatedly wipe his forehead with a napkin.

She had never seen a rough, hairy man like him close to her hairless, smooth skin. She would call him Hairy Bear and he would call her Dark Mare. He was an insatiable lover who put his full effort into giving her pleasure. She struggled to keep up.

For Dan, women were God's greatest creation, to be cajoled and romanced. He knew the words for each part of the human body in French and in Latin. He knew many poems to glorify and admire those parts.

"My little Dark Cobra, wrap your legs around my body and devour me," Dan would say.

His lips were ready to kiss her trembling body, to give and seek pleasure. Vibrating between ecstasy and trance, she had no choice but to surrender. "My Hairy Bear hold me tight. Let me melt in your arms." Mona loved everything about their relationship.

Chapter 83
Feelings
1991
Ocean Beach

In one month, life changed for both. They were intoxicated and dreamt of each other through the entire day. They could not wait to meet in the evening and quench their passion.

Beyond the physical connection, they shared common interests. They both enjoyed reading and were very fond of American history. They loved to discuss the influence of Jefferson and Lincoln on American history and current politics. They had a similar taste in music and their favorites were Joan Baez and Michael Jackson. One of their differences was that she could not comprehend opera, while he did not understand Indian classical singing.

"Why do you like Lincoln and Jefferson?" Dan asked one day.

"Because they both fought for equality and justice for the people. And how come you like Joan Baez and Michael Jackson?"

"Because Baez inspires me for political justice and Michael Jackson is one of the best entertainers in history. Why don't you like opera?"

"Because I do not like when someone talks to me through song. Why don't you appreciate Indian classical music?" Mona asked.

"Indian classical musical is sung in small notes, and I can't understand what they're singing about."

They were keen to travel. He had toured different countries, and she had dreams of exploring the world beyond the U.S. They promised each other to travel together. They took a trip to Sacramento under the pretext of attending an economic development conference. She stayed in a hotel, and he stayed in the state guest house. At night, he would sneak into her room.

They enjoyed taking showers together. They loved to rub and scrub each other's back. She would playfully tease his body, with soap slipping from one hand to the other, sliding and exploring the fragrant surface of the other's skin. They would laugh and joke.

One day after a bath, she looked at herself in her bedroom mirror.

"How do I look?" she wondered aloud.

"You look beautiful," he replied drying his body with a towel.

"What do you mean I look beautiful? You did not even look at me," she said.

He jumped out of the shower, the towel around his waist.

She faced him, letting the towel hang loosely over her curvaceous body. Seeing her long neck with long tresses, her supple shoulders, her slender waist, her flat stomach, her curved voluptuous hips meeting her round thighs, he could not resist walking towards her.

"I could devour you."

"Stay there," she instructed.

He stammered, "You are God's creation. You are mythical, my Dark Cobra." He took another step towards her.

"Hairy Bear, I told you to stop. Do not come near me,"

she said smilingly.

"The only thing I'd change is that you need a little trim down there," he said with a devilish smile.

"A little what?" she looked at him.

"I can do it, my Dark Cobra." He mimicked scissors with his fingers. Smiling, he walked towards her.

"What, you are shameless! Do not dare to come near me, Hairy Bear! I said, do not dare!" she ran to one corner of her bedroom.

He followed her and she ran into the other room. He ran after her and she ran again, and the chase went from one room to another. They laughed and pulled each other's towels, until they got exhausted from running.

She was in love and could see nothing beyond her feelings. He was her love, her God, and her salvation was through their intimacy.

Outside of Mona's house, they never interfered in each other's lives. As time passed, slowly their lives became inseparable. Being near each other, at work or at conferences reminded Mona of the California brush waiting patiently to be ignited, and once on fire, uncontrollable.

Late August, Sandy came back after her summer trip to India. Sandy's return meant that their rendezvous at Mona's house was no longer possible. They had no other place to meet except to drive miles away from the city, and that was an impractical solution. The idea of making love in the car was very romantic and adventurous to her, based on what she had heard and seen in movies. But it was tedious, to move around in a small car with a giant.

Mona asked Dan one day, "I don't understand, why do we need a secret place to meet? You can come to my place any time, even if my daughter is there. You can meet her. Don't you love me?"

"Yes, I do love you. But Mona, you should understand that declaring our love and being together openly is complicated."

"Why is it complicated?"

"Aviva and I attend many social gatherings and political functions together. My mother still wants me and Aviva to get back together. I have to pretend. Aviva's father just arrived from Washington, D.C., and I had to take him out for dinner. He has clearly hinted that my political future is attached to my relationship with Aviva. I need Aviva to leave me on her own terms, and then it will be easy for me to persuade my mother. About you."

"That means our love depends on whether Aviva leaves you. If she does not leave you, then you can't love me."

"Please, Mona, do not say that. I love you. If you say so, I will leave my political career behind."

Chapter 84
Deal
1991
Ocean Beach

Janet's desk was outside of Dan's office. A veteran fox, her ears and her sharp eyes knew every movement and heard all the gossip. Janet was inquisitive about why Mona suddenly declined any lunches with her. She took long breaks for lunch and returned late, often rushing into a meeting at the last moment. For the last three months, Mona's face was radiant like a new bride. She seemed happy.

Janet would glance questionably at Mona, and Mona would thwart Janet with her charming smile or mention something about a medical appointment or meeting a repairman for a home project. Janet loved inside information but heard no rumors yet about Mona's life. She suspected that there was a man in Mona's life and wondered who the lover could be. Janet came to a logical conclusion. Mona had a lover, and the person could not be from city hall, because she saw no cozy interplay and unusual visits at her office. Mona's affair took her from the building. Janet concluded it was not important for her to know who the lover could be if it did not involve office people. The fox knew her territory.

Janet was more curious to know what was happening in Dan's life. He was eating lunch, but not in the cafeteria, nor had he been seen with his typical beautiful lunch dates at local, trendy restaurants he frequented. She was keen to know where he was going to lunch and with whom. Aviva was still in Dan's life, and Janet watched all the moves quietly. *Did Aviva finally tame Dan?* she wondered. *That would fit in with Dora's plan.*

When Mona's daughter returned from India, Mona's radiance was gone. Mona was quiet. Janet was surprised. Janet racked her brain to figure out what was going on with Mona.

"Mona, is something bothering you? Are you all, right?" Janet asked.

"I am fine, Janet. Just a little tired," Mona said.

"How was your daughter's trip to India? Did she enjoy herself?"

"Sandy said she loved it." Mona did not reciprocate the smile.

Ocean Beach city hall was a hundred years old. A two-story building, it had two wings angled into one another in a V-shape. At the start of the wing on the second floor was Mona's office, and the start of the other wing was Dan's. They could see from their windows into the other's office.

Janet kept a keen eye on Dan, but still had no firm fact about what was going on. One day, she tip-toed into Mona's office unannounced and saw Mona standing near the window. Janet's eyes followed Mona's gaze across to Dan's office, where she saw Dan sending flying kisses to Mona.

Before anyone could notice her, she quietly walked out of the room. *Mystery solved,* thought Janet. She now saw how their absences made sense. Janet reasoned that knowing Dan, it was only a matter of time, with Mona and Dan working so closely together. The major surprise was how she missed seeing it coming. She concluded it would be a passing phase for Dan—another score to add to his black book.

A few more days passed, and Janet noticed Dan

growing irritated for minor things. Janet wanted to get Dan to admit his affair with Mona. It was better to catch the bull by the horns.

Mona was away from the office for a seminar. Seeing the opportunity, Janet walked into Dan's office and closed the door.

"Hey, Dan, how are things?" Janet said.

He was surprised to see Janet closing the door. "Good. Why did you close the door? Is it something important?"

"Oh, it's nothing. I just wanted to have a private chat with you. As I see it, since Mona has joined this office, you have been busy," she said.

He lowered his glasses and looked at her. Janet's gaze penetrated straight into his eyes. He did not know where to look; he put his glasses back on and pretended to read a report.

"What did you want to talk about?" he said.

"You were young when your dad and I were together," Janet started, "and…."

"I know everything. You don't have to tell it again, but why you are bringing up this topic now?" he interrupted.

"Please, let me finish. Your dad and I would sit in his car. It was usually dark around us, but we lived in fear if discovered by someone. His whole political career would have been over. We looked around in our area for a hideout, and we finally found one. I had the money. With the help of your dad and connections, we found a secluded house behind a grove of trees, in Lakewood. I still own that house. No one bothered us for years to come until your mother discovered our relationship. Dora wanted me to be fired. But your dad knew I could create a scandal, and that would have ended your father's political career," she said.

Dan narrowed his eyes. He knew what Janet was

hinting at.

"I am not afraid of anybody. Nobody in this world could stop me from loving Mona," Dan stated.

"Yes, somebody can stop you—Aviva's father, the most powerful senior senator. He could stop your political hopes and destroy all of Dora's ambitions for you. I am trying to be honest to help you succeed. It is up to you to accept my help." Janet got up and walked towards the door.

He called her back. "Sit down. What are you offering? And what is the catch?"

"I have been working for the city for the last forty years, and many mayors of this city have progressed to be governors, senators and congressmen. All those men had intelligence, charisma, and political ambition. I chiseled and refined those men. I helped shape their identity, and I skillfully buried their messes. Throughout it all, I was shortchanged, even by your father whom I really loved. This time, I want more. I want to taste political power." Janet paused for few seconds.

"What do you want to do in politics?" Dan said.

"I know you are going to run for state senator. The election is next year. I want to be part of the campaign team. I want to move along with you in your career. As you progress, I will progress. I am intelligent, and I have enough experience. I could work on the strategy, collecting funds, or identifying allies. Over the years, I have learned the secrets of a lot of senators, which could also help you. I will let you use my house and keep your secret, in exchange for power," Janet said.

"I never knew you were such a cunning fox," Dan said.

"My offer needs to remain a secret from Dora and Aviva. You will not regret this move. I will be an asset to your career," she said looking straight in his eyes. "And a facilitator of your affair with Mona."

He rarely smoked a cigar in his office, but today, he opened his desk and took one out from his drawer. He lit the cigar and puffed out smoke into ringlets. Dan remained silent for a minute, and then said, "Janet, you are a remarkable woman. I accept your proposal."

That afternoon, Dan came to Mona's office and quietly closed the door. "Look, I have found a place; it is two miles from city hall. It is away from the road, secluded and isolated, a house surrounded by trees. Nobody knows the house is there. It is safe. Let us go tomorrow at lunch."

"I am scared about anybody finding out. I don't want to sacrifice my job. Or your future in politics," she said timidly.

"Don't worry. Trust me," he said.

She looked at him and grew quiet. There was no turning back from here.

Chapter 85
Hideout
1991
Ocean Beach

Mona followed Dan's car the next day during lunch and felt nervous. Reaching Janet's house, she thought, *Dan was right. Few people would notice that there is a house here. It's deep within a small forest.*

The house was meticulously clean. Window blinds shut out the sun and any view from the street. They quickly made love, without removing their clothes.

At the office, nothing changed, and no one missed them. To thwart the watchful eyes and gossip, they went to Janet's house in their own cars, and they never came back into the office together. Mona worked diligently, and Dan continued to escort Aviva to political dinners.

But Mona still had many questions. She asked Dan who owned the house.

The only answer Dan gave Mona was, "My sweet Mona, I took care of everything, trust me."

The next day at lunch, they went again to Janet's place.

"Dan, tell me, who lives in this house? I can sense a woman's touch. Why won't you tell me?"

"Mona, my sweet Mona, trust me, this is the safest place. It doesn't matter who owns it," Dan said.

They went to the house again on Saturday. Sandy was surprised to see her mom busy with work or meetings for so many hours. It became a routine for Mona to make an excuse of working on Saturdays. On one of those Saturdays, Mona and Dan went to their hideout. They peeled off their clothes, jumped into bed, and quickly enveloped their bodies. After a heated encounter, exhaustion caught up with them. They drifted off to sleep.

Mona awoke from her sleep and felt as if someone was moving in the room. Looking around, she saw Dan sleeping like a contented bear. Nothing appeared to be disturbed. She picked up her clothes and tiptoed into the bathroom. Mona dressed and wanted to put on makeup quickly. She opened the medicine cabinet to see if she could find lotion for refreshing her face. The cabinet was empty, but there was a small, heart-shaped locket, tucked away in one corner.

Mona was curious. She picked up the locket and opened it. There she found a faded picture of a man and a woman. Her eyes remained fixed for more than a minute. The woman was young, blond, and very pretty. The man was much older but handsome and distinguished.

Mona quickly put the locket back in the medicine cabinet and came out of the bathroom. Dan was awake and getting dressed. Mona picked up her purse and took out her makeup.

"Let us leave. It is getting late. Sandy will be waiting for me," she said while putting on her lipstick.

Before she got into her car to drive home, Mona could not control her curiosity and asked him again. "Dan, why do you want to keep our affair secret?"

"It is better to wait. When it is the right time, I will tell my mother."

"Tell me, when will be the proper time?" Mona asked patiently.

Mona opened her car door and looked back at him. "I

saw a picture of a man and a woman in the medicine cabinet. The woman was very pretty. Standing next to her was a handsome man. He looked much older than her. Do you know who they are?" Mona said.

Dan knew it must have been a picture of Janet with his father. He was irritated that Janet had not removed the picture from the medicine cabinet. He remained in deep thought.

After remaining quiet for a minute, he said, "The picture you saw was of Janet forty years ago. The man standing next to her was my father. Once my father and Janet were close. My mother came to know about their affair, and my father had to make the choice between Janet and the prospects of becoming senator. It was a hard choice. I was only a few years old. He made the hard choice and left Janet. He became a senator, while Janet never left the city and her job. Janet kept it all a secret."

"I understand," Mona said.

Dan told Mona the rest of story and of the promise he made to bring Janet onto his political team.

"So, Janet knows our secret," Mona said.

"I had to. You see, Mona, with Aviva around constantly, I became desperate to see you. I wanted to find any place where you and I could be alone. It was too risky to be at your place."

Mona was beginning to understand the quid pro quo and the game he had to play.

"Janet is trustworthy. I am used to these scandals, and my mother would ignore our relationship as a minor affair. But my supporters would make you the villain. I do not want to lose or hurt you. By bringing Janet into politics, I am killing two birds with one stone. Our relationship will stay a secret, and Janet will never harm you," Dan said.

"So, we continue this game of hide and seek ...," Mona

was disappointed and closed the door of her car. She felt sad. For the next few days, Mona remained aloof and avoided Janet.

Chapter 86
Saved By The Bell
1991
Ocean Beach

A month later, the California governor invited Dan and his staff to an event honoring the five most financially efficient cities in the state. Ocean Beach was chosen as one of the top five cities. Dan and his staff, along with a few political supporters, including Mona, Dora, and Janet, were part of the team attending the celebration. Dan intentionally did not invite Aviva. The event was at the Sheraton Hotel in Sacramento. Everyone on their team was given accommodations at the hotel, hosted by the State of California. Dan's room was on the ninth floor and Mona's was on the fifth.

Dan was honored with a plaque for managing the finances of Ocean Beach. At the award ceremony, Dan was looking at Mona. His face expressed his gratitude to Mona for turning the city around. In the evening, there was a party at the Sheraton ballroom. Mona arrived wearing a maroon gown, showing her shining bare back. She was stunning, and all eyes were on her. Dan was drinking champagne, and he was in high spirits. Janet was watching them. Dora was busy networking with other politicians.

Dan approached Mona and asked her for a dance. While dancing, Dan pulled Mona towards the elevator. "Let's go up to my room," Dan said.

"What, are you crazy? Everyone is watching us, and your mother is here. Do you want us to get into trouble?" Mona said.

"I don't care. I will go first. You follow me in the other elevator. My room number is 915. I will wait for you at the door."

"No, I won't come. Go by yourself!"

"Mona, please, I love you," Dan pleaded. He turned from her and walked towards the elevator.

After returning to her table, Mona said, "Excuse me. I have to go to the restroom," and quietly walked over to the elevators.

Dan was waiting for Mona at his door. As soon as she crossed the threshold, he picked Mona up and laid her on the bed.

"Dan, Dan, my dress will get wrinkled," Mona said.

"OK, remove your dress," Dan said.

Downstairs, the guests were enjoying eating, dancing, and drinking. No one noticed where Dan and Mona went except the watchful eyes of Janet. Ten minutes after Mona and Dan left, Dora returned to the table.

"Where is Dan? I wanted to introduce him to one of the senior state politicians who can help him in the upcoming election. Janet, can you look for him?" Dora said.

Someone sitting at the same table said, "I last saw Dan dancing with Mona."

Another person said, "No, I saw Dan taking the elevator. Maybe he went to his room."

Janet saw Dora heading towards the elevator. She quickly ran towards the reception desk, picked up the phone and called room 915.

Dan, after letting the phone ring several times, finally picked up the phone. "Hey, Dan, your mother is on the way to your room," Janet said.

"What, my mother!" Dan slammed down the phone.

"What happened?" Mona asked.

"My mother is coming up here. Hurry up, put on your clothes, and go to your room. Do not take the elevator. Walk down the back stairs. I will see you down in the banquet hall. Hurry!"

Mona quickly put her dress on. Dan gave Mona her purse and opened the door. Seeing nobody outside, he pushed Mona out, pointing to the stairs.

"Oh, my shoes," Mona said.

"Forget about your shoes. I will hide them. Run!"

Mona never walked downstairs in bare feet that fast in her life. She quickly opened the door to her room, on the fifth floor. She was out of breath and fell back onto her bed. After her breathing became normal, she got up. Her dress was wrinkled and stained. She changed into another gown and found some other shoes and returned to the banquet hall. Dora was not there. She looked at Janet.

"Thank you, Janet," Mona said and picked up her half-filled coffee cup. The coffee was cold.

Dora reached the ninth floor and rang Dan's doorbell. Dan opened the door. "Oh, hello, Mom. What's up?" He was smoothing his wrinkled bed and picked up his jacket.

"What are you doing in your room? Everyone is celebrating downstairs. I wanted to introduce you to John Davis, a senior advisor to the governor." She was observing Dan and looking around the room. Her eyes stopped for few seconds. She saw a pair of women's shoes with the heels jutting out from under the bed.

Dan saw what his mother was looking at. "Mom, I was not feeling well. I drank too much, too fast. Now I am feeling a little better. You go downstairs. I will join you soon," Dan said.

Dora was curious to know who owned those shoes. She turned around and started walking towards the door, her eyes alert. Meanwhile, Dan kicked Mona's shoes under the bed.

"Let me go the bathroom for a second." Dora went into the bathroom.

She looked around and found nothing in the bathroom. After a minute, Dora came out. "Alright, son, see you downstairs soon," Dora said.

In the banquet hall, Dora saw Mona was sitting at the table, and noticed that Mona was wearing a green dress and matching green shoes.

"What happened? You changed your dress," Dora said.

"Coffee spilled on my dress. I went up to my room to change."

"Well, I like your green shoes. Enjoy the party," Dora said.

Janet was very protective of Dan and Mona. If Dan's mother was a little suspicious, Janet always had an alibi ready and had saved them many times. Dora remained curious to know whose shoes were under Dan's bed. Meanwhile, back in Ocean Beach, Aviva had no clue what was going on.

Chapter 87
Penance
1991
Haridwar

Ramesh left Kanpur and trekked the entire day along the banks of the Ganges to reach the Ashram. The next day, he saw glimpses of a white building surrounded by trees. Behind the building, he saw snow-clad mountains on three sides. The fourth side was the River Ganges.

The Ashram looked like a star shining resplendent among the mountains. At the foot of the hills was the River Ganges, winding, gushing, flowing with full force towards the plains of India. Ramesh wondered whether this place would bring him inner peace.

The Ashram was surrounded with five feet of brick wall, and at the entrance there was a tall gate. To arrive at the main temple, Ramesh passed through the gate and climbed a steep flight of stairs. Marble tiles surrounded the temple. Behind the main temple, there was a community kitchen, and on the other side, there were small huts for resident devotees and guests.

After reaching the main temple, he set off to find the chief Guru of the Ashram. He asked one old Pujari who was cleaning the temple, "I have come from Kanpur. Pujari Rajnath has sent me to see Guru Harinath. Where can I find Guru Harinath?" Ramesh said.

"Guru Harinath is not here in the Ashram. He has gone

on a pilgrimage to visit a few holy places," the Pujari said.

"When will he come back?" Ramesh wondered.

"I don't know. After six months, or it could be longer," the Pujari replied.

"Oh, then who is taking care of the Ashram?" Ramesh asked.

"Guru Ma, Sita Devi. We all affectionately call her Guru Ma," the Pujari said.

"The head of the Ashram is a woman? How is that possible?" Ramesh was stunned.

"Brother, I am surprised at your question. In the eyes of God, we are all the same. Why can't a woman be the head of an Ashram? This Ashram is God's place, and God does not discriminate between man and woman," the Pujari said.

Ramesh was starting to understand his mistake. "I am sorry. Where can I find Guru Ma?"Ramesh replied.

"Guru Ma takes rest at noon. You must also be tired. Go and eat food in the kitchen and then take rest. I will let Guru Ma know Pujari Rajnathji has sent you from Kanpur. She will let you know when to meet her," the Pujari said.

Guru Ma was in her early eighties with dark skin, long shining silver hair, and thick silver eyebrows. A soft-spoken, enigmatic and charismatic person, she came to the Ashram looking for peace fifty years ago. She had stayed there ever since. Ramesh met many people in the Ashram from different countries who were tired of possessions and conflicts, and were looking for inner peace.

Ramesh went to see Guru Ma that evening. She was circled by Pujaris from the Ashram.

"Son, you have been sent by Pujari Rajnath. He told us a little about you, but we would like to hear from you. What do you think this Ashram can do for you?" Guru Ma said.

"I have no peace in my mind. I can't control my ego,

my desires and my hatred," Ramesh said.

"Son, the life and discipline in the Ashram is rigid. All of us work together to run the Ashram, and it is arduous work. To achieve what you want, you will have to change yourself. Do you think you can live a rigorous life of the Ashram?" said Guru Ma.

"Yes, I will put my full effort if it brings me peace," Ramesh said.

For three days, Ramesh roamed around the Ashram. He was amazed to see the cooperation among the devotees. Each one was doing their assigned chore with love and a cheerful outlook. Guru Ma woke up devotees every morning by chanting hymns and playing on her guitar. Her melodious voice helped the devotees feel God's presence everywhere, and they were spellbound. Ramesh would sit behind her with his eyes closed in a trance, to forget his prejudices and hatred.

He was given the assignment of cleaning the toilets and bathrooms. For Ramesh, it was tedious to do that kind of work. To his surprise, other devotees were ready to help him with a smile. He would get up at four in the morning to sweep the temple area before devotees would start their various chores. Later he would clean the toilets and bathrooms. In the evening, he would read and listen to the discourses of Guru Ma. He discarded his shirt and pant, and instead, he started wearing a white kurta and white dhoti.

As the time passed, Ramesh became a friendly figure in the Ashram. Guru Ma and other Pujaris liked him. Being an engineer, he was helpful in plumbing repairs. He was called upon for all minor problems. He was good at speaking English; he became an interpreter between the visitors and Ashram Pujaris.

One day Ramesh asked Guru Ma, "What actions should I take to get rid of my ego?"

"Be humble, my son," Guru Ma said.

"I am trying, Guru Ma, but I still have fire burning in my heart."

"It is not the action but the attitude that liberates a person. Color, caste, and creed are fabricated by selfish people. God created a pure human, and the human corrupted himself with evil thoughts," Guru Ma said.

"I will try to change my attitude," Ramesh said humbly.

Chapter 88
Karan
1992
New York

Vijay's consulting business flourished, and he had to travel frequently. He had clients all over the world. Rebecca's real estate business was prospering. Rather than selling high-potential homes to others, Rebecca bought good bargain properties for herself and Vijay to rent out as an additional source of income. They were rich and had a powerful reputation. Vijay was well-known in the Indian community. He was the president of the Indian American Association of Los Angeles and Orange County for the last two years.

One day, while on a business trip in New York, Vijay was invited to a friend's party in Manhattan. There he met an internationally renowned economist, Dr. Karan Swarup, and they struck up a conversation.

"You are from Los Angeles. I heard it has a nice climate like Delhi. Surprisingly, I am in the U.S. for the last twelve years, but have never been to Los Angeles," Karan said.

"I am not from Delhi, so I cannot compare the climate of Delhi and Los Angeles. I am from Kanpur," Vijay said.

"You are from Kanpur! I lived in Kanpur fifteen years back. Rather, I started my career in Kanpur," Karan said.

"You started your career in Kanpur? What were you doing there?"

"I was an economics professor in Christ Church

College," Karan said.

Vijay became more attentive. Mona also studied at the same college, around the same time. He remembered the fiasco of her engagement. He looked closely at Karan. *Could it be?*

"That is wonderful, you lived in Kanpur, and I was born there," said Vijay. "We have a lot to talk about. We should meet again. I have a meeting with my client, early in the morning. Are you free for lunch tomorrow, at noon?" Vijay said.

"I also have a meeting in the morning. Can we meet for lunch around one? This lunch will be on me. And my secretary will call you to set up a place to meet," Karan said.

"Great," Vijay said. They exchanged their telephone numbers.

The following day at lunch, Vijay asked Karan, "Do you remember Mona? She was doing her master's in economics at the same college," Vijay asked.

"You know, Mona and I … we were engaged, but the circumstances did not let us marry," Karan said.

Vijay told Karan what happened after Karan left town.

"Karan, after you left Kanpur, Mona took a job in an insurance company as an account officer. One of my distant cousins, who was an engineer, married Mona, and she came to United States. She suffered a troubled marriage where my cousin treated Mona awfully. He used to beat her and abused her mentally and physically."

"Oh my God. I am sorry to hear that about her life. Why didn't she file for divorce?" Karan said.

"She thought my cousin would change one day. She realized after a time that he would never change. Many years later, she finally asked for the divorce. My cousin harassed Mona a lot until the time she finalized the divorce and received full custody of her daughter Sandy."

"Very sorry to know how her husband treated her." Karan felt sad at this news. "Mona was a remarkable woman then. And now?"

"Mona's lifelong dream was to do her Ph. D. in economics. My wife Rebecca and I encouraged and supported her to do her Ph. D. in economics with a focus on urban development. You know, she is very bright, and she did her thesis with excellence. The City of Jamaica, New York, implemented all of the recommendations from her thesis," Vijay said.

"Yes, I know."

"How do you know?"

"I read about her, in the *Economic Times*. They published a few pages of her thesis."

"After reading her piece, did you contact her?" Vijay asked.

"I did, and we talked over the phone for a while. It was right before I was leaving for Paris. There, I had a serious accident, and I lost my wife and my son. I was in the hospital for months. I was mourning the loss of my beloved family. After my return, I was too depressed to contact her, so I never followed up."

"I am sorry to hear about your family. Now, you can call Mona and catch up for old times' sake," Vijay suggested.

Karan smiled but did not respond.

Chapter 89
Invitation
1992
Ocean Beach

After a week, Vijay returned to Los Angeles. When he saw Mona, he told her about Karan and his accident in Paris.

"Mona, you should talk with Karan. He lost his wife and son, and he was always kind to you. He is one of the most respected economists in the world," Vijay said.

"I didn't know Karan was back in the United States. I thought he was still in Paris," Mona said.

"At least contact him. You have lot of memories together. Ask him how he's doing," Vijay suggested.

"Vijay Bhai, why rekindle an old fire again?" Mona said. She was content with Dan but could not talk to Vijay about her secret romance.

The months rolled on and days were filled with work meetings, social events, and family gatherings. Mona put her thoughts into her life with Dan.

Every year, on January twenty-sixth, the Indian Association of Los Angeles celebrated Indian Republic Day. They would invite a distinguished Indian from the United States to be the chief guest. As president of the Indian Association, Vijay persuaded the association members to invite Dr. Karan as this year's chief guest. Dr. Karan was to make a speech on the economy of India.

Vijay was insistent that Mona should attend the

function.

"Mona, you must see Karan. I am getting you a front row seat to listen to his lecture. And after dinner, please approach him and talk with him," Vijay said.

"Vijay Bhai. How can I see him? Our story ended when my family destroyed our love," Mona said.

"Let the bygones be bygones. You can start your story where you left it many years ago," Vijay said.

Mona was curious to see and hear Karan's speech at the Indian Association meeting. On the other hand, she told herself she was at peace about their broken love after a long time of sadness. She was not ready to face these old, painful memories. She kept telling herself that her romance with Dan fulfilled her need for love. In the end, her curiosity won out over hesitance. She went to the function and exchanged her front seat with another seat to the far back.

Karan looked as handsome as ever. His face had a few wrinkles, and his salt and pepper hair was still thick, which gave him an aura of dignity. Walking with a cane slowly to the podium, he searched for Mona's face, but could not find her in the crowd.

His speech was excellent.

"You are doing well, and many of you have amassed a fortune in U.S. dollars. Do not think of going back to India. Instead, send money to your family back home. Get them out of poverty. Let them live in comfort as you are living here. To improve their standard of living there, encourage them to invest your dollars in local businesses, shops, and factories. That will be your biggest contribution to India," Karan said.

Mona agreed that money sent back to India should be used to improve India's economy, rather than for buying luxury goods. She and Karan were on the same page regarding economic development, much like her research on bankrupt cities.

After dinner, when the time came to mingle, Mona was not there. Mona left the meeting without eating dinner, knowing she could not face Karan. Karan was disappointed and caught an early flight back to New York the next morning.

Vijay was not happy.

"Mona, you let me down. Why have you avoided Karan? You know he was keen to see you," Vijay said.

"Vijay Bhai, you know I can't face Karan. The past is done. In his speech, he said, 'Don't think of going back.' "

Chapter 90
Warning
1992
Ocean Beach

One day, with investors at a posh Ocean Beach restaurant, Vijay discovered Mona and Dan holding hands as they came through the door. That evening, he invited Mona to his house and had a heart-to-heart talk with her. Rebecca, Vijay, and Mona sat in the den with the door closed.

"Mona, try to understand, Dan and you are miles apart. His way of thinking and your way of thinking are different," said Vijay. "For him you are a novelty, a person from a different background. Anything you do fascinates him. He has a reputation of being unfaithful to women."

"Vijay Bhai, he is intelligent and ambitious. You want to say that he fancies me because of how I look, and he does not love me as a person?" Mona said.

"Maybe, maybe not. At this moment, you both are mad with passion. But love? You have to think of your long-term future," Rebecca said.

"Six months from now, after the state senate election is over, we will announce our engagement," Mona said.

"Why not now?" Rebecca said.

"Because, according to him, the time is not right yet. The voters may not like to see us together. I mean, a foreign person from another country standing beside him at the podium...," Mona said.

"Mona, I agree with Vijay that you are being illogical here," Rebecca weighed in.

"You think I am a fool, and I can't make my decisions. All my life, I have had to obey others. I can make my own decisions now. I do not need any of your opinions or lectures. Please, do not interfere in my life anymore." Mona walked out.

Vijay and Rebecca were stunned and looked at each other. That was the first time Mona had ever spoken rudely to them.

Mona was rich and secure now. Her success went to her head, and she was not ready to listen to any advice or suggestions from her oldest friends. Her sharp mind was dulled by the fairy tale romance, and she could not think rationally.

Vijay continued to call Mona and persuade her to understand Dan's character as an opportunist and as a politician. He tried to talk some sense into her, as an elder brother would do for a sister, but his efforts were in vain. Her obstinacy created stiffness in the friendship with Vijay and Rebecca.

Chapter 91
Dreams
1992
Ocean Beach

Ocean Beach City Council was pleased with Mona's performance. She was respected, and her opinion was valued by city council. Her secret affair with Dan was still going strong, but they kept a low profile. Janet's house remained their rendezvous.

Meanwhile, Dora was trying to find out who was in the hotel room with Dan on the night of the Sheraton banquet. She pursued every angle. Whenever she mentioned the topic of Mona, Dan brushed her off by saying, "Who, Mona? She did an excellent job in getting me and Ocean Beach the award. And, she is doing an excellent job as controller, but that's it"

Dora was pushing Dan to revive his relationship with Aviva. "Dan, why don't you think of returning to Aviva? It is beneficial! Think of your future!"

"Mother, Aviva and I do attend these political events, for my future, as you say. But, she is jealous, bossy, and squanders her father's money. We have nothing in common."

Dora could not forget the night at the Sheraton. Dora remembered when Mona had entered the banquet hall, she was wearing a maroon dress and matching shoes. And when Dora saw her after meeting Dan in his room, Mona was wearing a green dress and green shoes. She could see only the soles of the shoes under the bed. The story of Mona spilling coffee over herself sounded false. The thoughts of Mona linking herself with Dan did not pass away, but Dan revealed none of his feelings.

Nevertheless, Dora wanted Mona around. Dora believed Mona was an asset in her city position, but politically, she was a nonentity. She was useful to Dan for upholding Ocean Beach's economy and improving the city's image. Mona was smart to predict financial trends and prevent fallout from any economic slump. Ocean Beach had won awards and was considered an ideal city for newcomers and for local and international investments. Despite Mona's positive reputation, however, Dora could not imagine Mona – dark, foreign, different - as a daughter-in-law or as the mother of her future grandchildren.

Mona watched closely as Dan accelerated his political moves for the upcoming election cycle. Dan escorted Aviva to functions as a practical matter. They continued to meet at Janet's house but Mona felt she was receiving scraps of Dan's limited attention.

Mona was aware that if Dan went back to Aviva, Mona would be labeled his mistress. She was not ready to accept that situation. She knew that her affair with Dan could not last forever. She wanted the commitment from Dan to be his wife.

All the while, Dan and Mona's passion grew into longing. If they did not see each other for a day, neither could bear the pain. They called it love.

One Saturday afternoon, at Janet's house, Mona got up from the bed and moved into the living room. Dan called out to her but she did not respond. He found her on the sofa, curled into the pillows with a blanket around her.

"Mona, baby, come back to me, in bed."

"We need to talk, Dan."

"Now? Here?"

Mona sat up and pointed to the space beside her. He sat.

"Dan, your mother will never approve of our relationship. Dora would never accept a daughter-in-law who is dark-skinned and has no political influence. Your mother likes Aviva, and she wants Aviva and you to make amends. How will you explain our relationship to Dora?"

"I've told you before, I don't love Aviva, and I will convince my mother to accept you. I have money of my own. We can start fresh and build a life together, somewhere away from this political jungle. At a beach city or in the mountains," he replied.

"Or in the Falkland Islands," Mona said with a smile.

Dan gave Mona a quizzical look.

She faced him, "I was joking. Dan, it will be a scandal if we run away together. I have a young daughter, putting down her roots. And this could ruin my career and your career. You can't tell me that you would walk away from your life, from your ambitions."

"Look, Mona, it has been more than a year. I do not want to be caught in this cat-and-mouse game. Why don't you move in with me? All secrets eventually come out. We love each other. How long will we hide the truth from our families and from the world?"

"Your mother and Aviva will kill you," Mona said.

"I feel hopeless, and I cannot live without you. This situation is not fair. Do you have any other solution?"

"No," she replied sadly.

"The only other choice is that someone finds out about us by mistake, and I acknowledge to the public that I am in love with you," Dan said.

Dan had not said the word, 'marriage.' She had no response. She was equally desperate and knew life without him was impossible.

"I don't care," Dan continued. "I cannot wait." Dan covered his face with his hands.

Mona was quiet, "I suppose we must wait, until the election is over…."

Dan decided he would announce the end of his political career at an opportune time. Months passed, and he repeatedly assured her of the plan. Mona was starting to realize that the ideal time to be together would never come.

The campaign for state senator had started. Dan was busy, preparing to run for the next higher office and fielding meetings with donors. Dora was always by his side, and she took Aviva along with her.

One exhausting day Dan seemed nervous and tense. Mona and Dan had finished reviewing a development proposal. He got up and slammed the door shut. At his desk, finally, he blurted out, "It's everything. The campaign, travel…. My mother is pressuring me to marry Aviva. If I get married to Aviva, will you still be my girlfriend? I love you!"

"Dan, what are you saying?" The smile on Mona's face vanished.

"Would you love me and still be with me?" Dan asked desperately.

"Dan, I love you, but how could I be with you if you got married to someone else?" Mona grew angry.

Mona got up from her chair. "Dan, you promised me that you would marry me. I want to be your wife. I will never be your…*mistress*." Mona said this with determination and walked out of the office.

Dan turned his face down. He got up and paced the floor, then followed her. Her office door was locked and the lights had been turned off.

Mona was certain that once Dan began his campaign,

there was no turning back. Their romance would eclipse quickly, like a fading sunset. The one thing that was clear to Mona was that she would never accept being a mistress to Dan or anyone else. She knew this would only bring her pain and anguish. It would affect her career, and herself-esteem. She was not willing to pay the price.

In the coming weeks, sometimes three days would pass before Dan had the time to meet her. He would be jubilant and full of energy talking about the state senate campaign. She was sad and did not know how to express her pain. Mona missed her mother and her guidance.

Dan had awakened her soul and brought back desire. She was worried about losing him. Reason had vanished because her mind refused to accept life without Dan. Her face showed no joy.

Dan kept trying to re-assure Mona, "Don't be afraid! I can see the bright future coming. You will be standing beside me,"

She would look at him.

"Mona, Mona, are you listening to me?" He would hold her in his arms and kiss her as she cried softly to herself. They both were living in a beautiful illusion.

Chapter 92
Blunder
1992
Ocean Beach

Janet was concerned. The election was less than a year away, and Dan and Mona were on their secret honeymoon. Janet was curious about Dan, who usually fancied a woman for a brief period and discarded her once he grew bored. This time, the romance had lasted much longer, and he was getting deeper into it. Their attachment was dangerous for a politically ambitious person because Mona could wreck their careful, strategic plans.

Time passed and the election fever started. Dan became busy with different politicians and donors visiting him. Every day, there were meetings with parades of consultants, pollsters, and speechwriters streaming in and out of his office, along with his mother Dora. Sometimes Aviva made an appearance.

As the election drew nearer, an idea sprouted in Dan's mind. One of the committees formed to manage campaign operations was to oversee campaign funds. The committee received public contributions and documented how the funds were disbursed. Dan thought that since Mona was already comptroller of Ocean Beach, she could take charge of the committee that governed contributions for the election campaign. He thought this position would make it easier for Mona to meet other politicians and gradually get acclimated to his world. He was excited and presented the idea to Mona.

"Mona, I want a person to run the campaign funds committee, some honest person who will take care of the money, with no risk of squandering it or disbursing it inappropriately. Remember what we had to go through with city funds when you first came to Ocean Beach?"

"Why don't you put Janet in charge of the campaign funds?" Mona said.

"She doesn't have as much experience with finance as you do." Dan said. "And I don't want to give her that much power."

"OK, what about your mother?"

"My mother prefers to stay in the background. Why don't you take charge of the money?"

Mona had trouble gathering her thoughts. "Dan, you know I am not politically savvy. Besides, I find that I hate politics and everything that goes with it."

"Don't worry, I will teach you what you need to know. This is the best opportunity to gain experience, by my side. It is settled! You will take charge of the committee and manage the campaign funds."

Dan had thrust the responsibility on Mona while Mona stood in his office bewildered. He walked out of his office, chatting to someone who had called for his attention. Mona was honest; she was a good economist and a faithful accountant. She was uncertain about her new role because she did not know the complications of handling political funds.

Many aspirants who were expecting to get the position of campaign funds manager were unhappy. Janet was one of those aspirants. She thought it was time for Dan to fulfill their agreement by making her that manager, not Mona.

Janet met Dan for drinks one evening. She seemed tense.

"Dan, you promised me that I would be part of the inner circle! We had a bargain."

"Of course, you are part of the inner circle. What made you think you are not?"

"I thought you would let me control the campaign funds."

Dan thought for a minute. "I wanted to keep you free, so that I may utilize you for a special project."

"What special project?" Janet asked.

"You are good at convincing people. I will send you to areas where people are still undecided voters. I think your title could be Deputy Campaign Manager."

Janet was not convinced. Her legs were trembling under the table. Dan's decision hurt her. She had waited a long time for an opportunity to get the respect she thought she deserved from Dan.

Dora and Aviva both were surprised at Mona's position in the campaign. They did not care who controlled the money, but they did not expect Mona to be involved in Dan's election. They thought she was an outsider who did not know anything about politics. She was considered an efficient and hardworking person, but she did not belong in Dan's ascent to power.

Over an early morning breakfast before work, Dora asked Dan, "Why did you appoint Mona to the campaign budget manager position?"

"Mother, there are many people on the committee who could manipulate or steal the election funds. I wanted an honest person to oversee the money, and you know very well that Mona is an honest person."

"But she is not a politician," Dora said.

"Better that she is not. It is all right. She can learn, and, mother, we should have an ethnic touch in the election," Dan said. "That serves our purpose to promote diversity."

"I don't think diversity belongs in politics," Dora said. "Let's stick with the tried-and-true ways of winning in politics."

A day later, Aviva asked Dora, "What is going on? How did Mona become the campaign budget manger?" Aviva said.

"I don't know the whole story. I was wondering the same thing," Dora said.

Dora invited Janet to lunch, hoping to find the underlying cause of the mystery. Janet could shed some light on how and why Mona got such a powerful position.

Janet guessed why Dora had invited her to lunch, and Janet was nervous about blurting out the truth. One wrong word could shatter Janet's dreams of rising to the role of Deputy Campaign Manager, and she could lose the opportunity to make something of her career. Janet was dressed in her best suit for her lunch with Dora.

They met at Franks, a local steakhouse. They ordered iced tea and salads. After a few greetings and social niceties, Janet responded to Dora's question about Mona. "Frankly speaking, Dora, I too am wondering why Dan brought Mona into the picture. I have collaborated with her. She has no knowledge of how elections are run," Janet said.

Janet's expressionless face made Dora trust her. After Dan's father's death, Dora had always hated Janet. Dora set the past aside, recognizing that this was a crucial time. They joined forces, and their common enemy became Mona.

"Keep an eye on them, Janet, and let me know what is truly going on," Dora requested.

"We will not tolerate losing," Janet said. "Deal?"

Dora nodded and sipped her tea.

Dora had no proof, but her gut feeling was telling her

that Dan was having an affair with Mona. If that was correct, then it was a red signal: a dark woman of a different background and no political experience standing with Dan. That could change the balance. Dora knew how Mona would be perceived by the voting public. And the perception would hurt Dan, not help him.

To play it safe, Janet told Dan about the meeting she had with Dora and cautioned him.

"Dan, yesterday I spoke with your mom. She was wondering how Mona became the campaign fund manager," Janet said.

"We are in this together!" said Dan. "I do not care about anybody, as long as Mona and I stay together. I love her, and I will continue to meet her at your house. Unless you have an objection?" His voice raw, he seemed tired and bitter.

"No," Janet timidly replied. "We made a deal."

"Then please don't tell my mother anything. Janet, you're central to my team," Dan said.

Janet agreed that it was better to keep quiet, as she was complicit in the affair by volunteering her house to them. She knew Dan and Mona felt comfortable in her house and thought they were safe.

Chapter 93
Nomination Party
1992
Ocean Beach

Dan worked extremely hard 24/7 in hopes of winning the nomination of his party to state senator. His schedule was packed with meetings, rallies, dinners, and fundraising speeches. The money poured in, and election day finally arrived. Dan was elated to learn that he had won the nomination. The plan of becoming state senator was moving along.

In honor of the good news, Dan hosted a dinner party for his staff and some senior politicians. The party was at the Hyatt, Ocean Beach, with fifty sponsors, donors, and politicians. Aviva was also invited. Dan preferred not to have any interactions between Aviva and Mona, knowing Aviva's jealous nature. He assigned Janet to be Mona's escort, as he would need to remain aloof from her.

Dan's main idea was to introduce Mona to the powerful politicians in his network, hoping that the senior politicians would accept her as one of their own. Janet started to introduce Mona to the veteran politicians. That night, Mona was wearing a creamy satin dress. Her hair was full and lush, with thick curls cascading down her back. Her delicate gold earrings caught the light, and her posture made her look like a queen. She looked stunning.

"Mona, meet Mr. Robert Taylor, our party leader, "

Janet said. "He's Dan's advisor and Dora's family friend,"

"It is nice to meet you, Mona. You did a wonderful job of bringing this city out of the hole," said Mr. Taylor. He started eating the pasta appetizers.

"Thank you, Mr. Taylor. Your advice regarding Dan's speeches was an immense help," Mona said.

"Mona, meet Mr. John King. His area, Senate District 35, is a staunch supporter of our party," Janet said.

"Ah, Mona. So, you oversee the budget. This is our first meeting, but I hope to see you again soon. You look very pretty."

John King pulled Janet aside, and whispered, "I thought I would see Aviva with Dan, but they are sitting at different corners." He turned his back to Mona, "Anyway, best of luck." He wandered off to the bar.

Dan was observing from afar and became irritated. He saw Janet trying to introduce Mona to politicians who were courteous, but cold-shouldered to Mona. Dora watched the scene, observing Dan's irritation and the role Janet was playing to introduce Mona around. She glanced at Aviva and caught Aviva's steely gaze at Mona and her grim face when Mona made eye contact with Dan. Now it all came together. Dora knew that Dan and Mona were having an affair. Dora was angry at Mona for having the audacity to compromise her son's bright political career.

The next day after the party, Aviva called Dora.

"Dora what's going on? Dan did not talk with me at the election-night party," Aviva said.

"Aviva, this was all a political show. Dan had many people to thank that evening. Patience, my dear. Everything will be fine."

Dora was wondering how to confirm Dan's affair with Mona. She looked through her phone book to find a common link between Mona and Dan. The only logical person was Janet. Dora invited Janet for lunch at Panda Inn, a small hotel downtown. Its restaurant had more privacy.

"Listen, Janet, let us get to the point. I know you have sharp eyes. I am sure that Mona and Dan are having an affair. I want the truth," Dora said.

"Dora, this is news to me." Janet acted innocent. "They are having an affair? No, it can't be possible."

Janet was a smart woman, but Dora was one step ahead. "Once, you tried to spoil my husband's career and now you want to ruin my son's career too. Before I get you fired, come on, out with it. I am serious," Dora said.

Janet was afraid of what wreckage Dora would create and confessed the truth. "Dan and Mona's affair started a year ago," Janet admitted.

"A year ago? And you did not tell me!"

"I thought the affair would last for a few weeks, like Dan's usual flings. But it has been going on for a long time. I am sorry, Dora," Janet said.

"Oh, Janet, you are so naive." Dora remained silent for few minutes. "If you want to keep your job, you must not say a word to anyone, especially to Aviva. Watch Dan and Mona like a hawk. And inform me of every move they make," Dora said. "I want a daily report on Mona. She is dreaming of becoming a senator's wife. I do not trust her one bit," Dora said.

"Oh yes, Dora. I will let you know if I suspect anything," Janet said.

Janet always felt small in front of Dora. After her affair with Dora's husband, Janet had begged Dora not to fire her, and Janet was lucky enough to keep her job. For years, she kept quiet and kept alert. She watched how power grew and for whom. This time, Janet decided to be more careful and align herself with Dora, rather than with Dan. She had told Dora about the affair, but she hoped that keeping the hideout a secret would allow her to preserve her eventual move as Dan's Deputy Campaign Manager

Chapter 94
Desperate
1992
Ocean Beach

As a city comptroller now in charge of election funds, Mona's work kept her in the office late every evening. Dan was busy with the state senate election campaign, as he was roaming the whole county to meet people. Mona and Dan had not been alone for weeks, and they were desperate to meet.

They say politics makes strange bedfellows. Dora and Janet made a verbal pact to keep an eye on their common enemy, Mona. Dora's sharp eyes watched Mona's every movement. She had been bitten in her younger days when Janet tried to snatch her husband. After her husband's death, Dora tolerated Janet because Janet kept her secrets and served Dan's purpose well. Now, the stakes were higher because Dan's political future burned brighter than ever. Dora was uneasy knowing that her son could be snared by Mona and risk upsetting their plan. Janet phoned Dora everyday whether she had information or not.

Five weeks remained until election day. Mona saw Dan every day at work, but there were always people around them. Mona was depressed and down. Rebecca and Vijay had not called her in many weeks. Sandy was in New York for a national spelling bee competition. Mona could not concentrate on her work, and she decided to go home early.

Mona gathered her purse and headed out toward the

hall. She was surprised to see Dan in the elevator. It was crowded. One had to squeeze in to get standing space, and her back pushed into Dan's chest.

"Hi, Dan, how are things? You are busy." She felt cozy with her back pushed into Dan.

"Yes, you are right. I hardly get time to breathe nowadays." Dan lowered his voice. "Where are you going?" he asked.

"I am going home. My daughter has gone to New York, so I am alone and feeling a little low. I thought I would cook a nice dinner for myself. For me, cooking is therapeutic," Mona said.

"Well, feel better," Dan murmured, "I will try …." There was a crowd around them, causing Dan to stop and look sadly at her.

As Mona was going home, Dan thought he could try to meet Mona, at her place. He could taste the Indian food she would cook and imagine wonderfully wild sex in her bed. The only problem was that he was supposed to attend an election meeting.

"I've got to go to this damn meeting," Dan said. When the elevator doors opened, he watched Mona exit city hall.

Dan went back up to his office and called Janet inside. "Hey, Janet, I have an election meeting to attend. Can you cover for me at the meeting?"

"Yes, I know the agenda." Janet gathered her briefcase and asked casually, "Where are you going?"

He shook his head and came near her, "I am going to meet Mona at her house," he whispered.

Chapter 95
Betrayal
1992
Ocean Beach

After Dan left, Janet called Dora.

Dora was enjoying a luncheon at her home with two of her friends. She picked up the phone in the other room.

"Hi, Dora, Janet here. Let me give you a tip that I just learned. Dan has gone to meet Mona at her house."

"Fine, I will go to Mona's home and confront them."

"No, not you. You should send Aviva and let her be the one to confront Mona and Dan," Janet suggested.

"Brilliant."

Dora called Aviva just as Aviva was making lunch.

"Hi Aviva, how are you?" Dora said.

"I'm good. I made a turkey sandwich, and I was going to take a bite of it. Would like to join me for lunch? I can make another one," Aviva said.

"No, thanks. I was thinking of joining Dan for lunch," Dora said tactfully. "But other things have come up."

"Dora, how is Dan doing? I have not seen him for the last two months. He is terribly busy!" Aviva said.

"Apparently he is spending a lot of campaign time with Mona. You know, she manages the funding. Mona has taken the afternoon off today and gone home. She was not feeling well. And Dan left to meet Mona at her place," Dora said.

Aviva's face turned red when she heard where Dan

was going.

"Why is Dan going to Mona's place? What the hell is going on?" Aviva said angrily.

"I don't know. Could be campaign finance work. Why don't you find out?" Dora suggested.

Chapter 96
Missing Each Other
1993
Ocean Beach

Mona heard a knock at her door. The day was unseasonably hot for late September. She had just come out of the shower, her hair wet and loose. She peeped outside from the side window and was surprised to see Dan waiting outside. She let Dan inside and they immediately embraced one another.

"Dan! What about that meeting?"

"Forget meetings. Meeting with you is more important," Dan said.

Slowly his senses were aroused by her perfumed skin. Dan could not resist.

"Mona, you smell so good," Dan said.

He picked her up in his arms and laid her on the sofa. He opened her gown, lowered his pants, and their bodies clung together.

Dan tried and tried, but nothing happened. All his efforts were futile. He sat down next to Mona on the sofa.

"I am sorry. I don't know what has happened to me," he said apologetically.

"That is all right, Dan. It happens. Maybe it is the stress of election," she replied.

"Or the stress of not seeing you. It feels as though all our plans, our dreams of a life together, are falling apart."

"Why do you feel that way?"

"Because my mother thinks you are a barrier to my political career."

"A barrier?" Mona was confused.

Dan took her face in her hands, "Mona, I love you."

"I was desperate to see you too, but, Dan, you did not answer. Why am I a barrier?" she faced him.

"Because you don't like politics. Your background is different. You are not one of us. You are dark-skinned, and peoples' beliefs are hard to change, even my mother's."

Mona said emotionally, "Dan, I have a Ph.D. I have worked hard my whole life, and I am a fighter. If you love me, you cannot let these trivial matters bother you."

"I think I should call the campaign off. I will tell the entire world of our love and forget about the election."

She gently put her hand over his cheek and lovingly said, "Dan, you keep saying that. Politics is in your blood, and it is your life. Don't you ever think of dropping out from the election. You will regret that always. "

"Then tell me what I should do. Do you want me to forget you, leave you behind? You are my life! Without you I will not survive. Don't you love me? Do you?"

"Yes, I do love you. Let us do this." Mona looked at Dan and then directed her gaze out the front window. "The election is only six weeks away. The moment the election is over, we will get married." They embraced. Dan was quiet and Mona said nothing further. They remained intertwined for some time.

He left at sunset, breaking both of their hearts.

Chapter 97
Confrontation
1993
Ocean Beach

After getting the call from Dora, Aviva drove straight to Mona's house. She was thinking, *I could kill Mona. How could a nobody like her try to snatch Dan from me?*

Aviva reached Mona's house and saw Dan's car parked in front. She parked her car a block away from Mona's house and stepped out of her car. She walked towards Mona's front door in a foul mood. At Mona's house, Aviva peeped through the window and saw Dan and Mona entwined in each other's arms. She fumed with anger.

She wanted to burst through the door, and she walked towards the entrance to do exactly that but stopped herself halfway. Aviva knew all about Dan's promiscuous habits. It was not the first time she saw him with another woman. She had always ignored those escapades as trivialities and strategized for a successful, long-term political future with Dan. While she still felt very jealous and threatened seeing Mona with Dan, she reasoned that Dora was on her side. Her family's power was on her side.

Aviva moved her car to the far end of the street and sat alone. Her anger grew. She wanted to be calm and find a smarter way to handle Mona. She waited patiently for Dan to leave.

Right when she saw Dan leave, Aviva walked to

Mona's house and knocked on the door. Mona thought Dan had returned, and she opened the door quickly. She was not at all expecting Aviva to be on the other side of her door.

"Hi, Aviva," Mona said. Mona was a little disheveled and in her robe.

"Won't you invite me to come in?" Aviva asked.

Mona let her into the house.

Aviva sat down.

"Let me put on something better. I just came from the shower." Mona pulled her robe close to her body. "Would you like to have some coffee or tea?"

"No, "Aviva replied. "I'll wait in the living room while you get dressed."

Mona returned after changing and sat across from Aviva.

Aviva asked directly, "What was Dan doing here?"

Mona stared at Aviva and said nothing.

"I trusted you, and I thought you were honorable," said Aviva. Her voice reached a higher pitch and she stood up. "I could never imagine you could go so low as to prey on my Dan. Tell me, how long has this been going on?"

Mona shot back, "He is not your Dan. Aviva, you were his girlfriend once, but you broke up more than a year ago. How can you still call him, 'My Dan?' He and I are in love, and he was going to tell everyone about our relationship earlier. The election delayed our announcement. I am sorry that you found out this way," Mona said.

"You don't know, but Dora has assured me that before the election, Dan and I will be married," stated Aviva.

"Please don't insult our love. Dan and I are genuinely in love with each other. We are planning to get married after the election is over," Mona said.

"What a sorry story. Don't you have any shame? You

were going to steal him from me for your personal gain and prestige! You slept with him so that you could be the mistress of a senator." Aviva paced the floor.

"That is untrue. Dan and I will marry!" shouted Mona.

"My God, Mona, I did not know you were so foolish. I am not sure Dan loves me. But Dan and I have a common goal, his political career. We are both born into politics. It is our destiny. Did you really think you and Dan would end up together? You foolish woman. My father has powerful connections; we could destroy you and expose your reputation to your colleagues in city hall. We could ruin you to the point where even your daughter would hate you. Your life would be in shambles."

"Please, do not bring my daughter into this. Dan will accept Sandy as his daughter. He even offered to leave politics," Mona said. She got up and stood in front of Aviva.

"Dan would never leave politics," Aviva said. If he said that, he is a liar. He can't help himself, and he loves only himself and power. You are blinded - by his passion and by yours. Besides, Dora would never let Dan marry you,"

"You're the liar!" yelled Mona. "Get out!"

Aviva came closer to Mona, put her hands on Mona's throat and pushed Mona against the wall.

"You know, I am a black belt in Karate," she hissed into Mona's ear.

Mona was struggling to breathe. She did not know where she got the strength, but somehow, she pushed Aviva away. Aviva fell over the sofa.

"Don't you ever touch me again! Get out of my house!" shouted Mona.

Aviva was furious. "If you ever come near my Dan, I will tear you apart, bitch!" She pushed Mona and slammed the door as she walked out of the house.

Aviva did not notice that Mona fell and hit her head against the sharp corner of a living room table and crashed to the floor. Mona tried to get up but had no strength. After a while, Mona staggered to her feet and struggled to lie on the sofa, groaning with pain in her chest. She was dizzy and the bruise on her head was bleeding. Her back hurt, and she had a terrible pain in her ribs. She closed her eyes. The last thought that drifted into her mind was that she knew Dan belonged to her, and Aviva could not pull Dan away.

Mona's mind was made up.

Chapter 98
Janet Could Manage
1993
Ocean Beach

While driving home, Aviva's mind was racing. She never imagined that Mona and Dan were having an affair behind her back for the last year. Aviva considered her reaction, wondering if she had gone too far in pushing Mona.

The first thing Aviva did after reaching home was to call Dora.

Dora was in her living room sipping wine when the phone rang, Dora saw it was Aviva.

"Hello." She had a smile on her face. *This is working so well,* she thought.

"Dora, you won't believe this. When I reached Mona's house, they were making love on the sofa, and I could not control myself. I waited for Dan to leave, and then I went in to see Mona. There, I lashed out at her, told her the facts. She will remember it for the rest of her life," Aviva said triumphantly.

"I hope you did not show your Karate skills."

"I pushed her, pushed her hard. Then I left," Aviva said proudly.

"What! Was she hurt?" Dora asked.

"Maybe. I don't know. I was angry and I pushed her," Aviva said.

"What? Aviva, you need to calm down Do you realize that if Mona was hurt, Dan's career would be over if the press got a hint of this squabble? It could become a scandal!" said Dora.

"I am sorry. The situation got out of hand," Aviva apologized.

"I need some time to think," Dora said, and she hung up.

Dora roamed around her living room, and then she sat down on the sofa. She picked up the phone and called Janet. "Hi, we need to talk." She relayed to Janet what happened between Aviva and Mona.

"I think you should go to Mona's home and control the damage," Dora said.

Janet said, "I know what to do."

Janet headed straight to Mona's place. The main door was unlocked and she went in. She saw Mona lying on the sofa, with a bloody bruise on her head.

"Mona, Mona! Wake up!" Janet touched Mona's shoulders and lifted her arms. There was a small groan coming from Mona.

"Mona, let's go," Janet whispered. "Let's get you some help." An expert in handling tricky situations, Janet carried Mona to her car and propped her up. Janet drove to a small private clinic in a nearby city, Garden City. Janet knew the staff in the clinic and trusted them.

The clinic was on the side street off Carson Boulevard. It was a single-story building. On one side a small yellow light was flickering, and on the other side, a Red Cross sign was hanging. On entering the building, the strong smell of disinfectants greeted them. All the lights inside and out were dim, giving the clinic a creepy look.

Janet knew the doctor on the duty. She had a bundle of cash enclosed in an envelope, tucked away in her purse.

"Doctor Robert, please let me know how serious her

injuries are. I will wait outside," Janet said.

After checking Mona for forty minutes, the doctor talked with Janet. "She has bruises, and her lower right rib is broken. Slight concussion. There is no other severe injury. But her trauma is serious. I have given her an injection for sedation, and she will go to sleep in an hour. Do you want me to admit her?"

"I would prefer that you don't admit her. Can I take her home?" Janet said.

"Sure, but she needs to be on bed rest for the next week. Monitor her closely. Let me write down a prescription for her," Doctor Robert said.

"Good, she can rest at my place. I will take care of her," Janet said.

"Great. If she develops a fever, please bring her back. Now, how do you want me to manage the situation? Should I write a report for the police?" the doctor asked.

"No, the matter is confidential. No report is to be written. If the police ask any questions, call me. I know the police captain, Jack Miller," Janet said. She handed Doctor Robert the envelope of cash. Janet left the clinic and discreetly brought Mona to her home.

Mona slept the next entire day. Early that evening, a groggy Mona sat up and called out, "Janet, I want to go back to my home. Please take me back. Or call Dan to come. And Sandy will be back from New York in four days."

"Mona, you are in bad shape and cannot stay at home alone. I will take care of you. Rest for the next three days. I will take you home when you are feeling better."

"But, Dan, Sandy."

"Look, Mona. Do you want to ruin Dan's chances of winning the election? There's only six weeks remaining, and he is a sure shot to win. If you go back to your home, and the press comes to know about your injuries, there could be a problem and speculation. You know how they are. Look at your condition! I will take care of you, and before your daughter is back from New York, you will be back in your home. I promise," Janet said.

Before collapsing into a heavy sleep, Mona mumbled, "Sandy, Dan. Sandy.... Dan...."

Late that night, Janet called Dora to update her, "I have controlled the damage. Mona had some injuries, which are now taken care of. She will stay at my place. I have taken her purse away as a precaution. She will be under sedation. After she feels better, I will take her back home," Janet said.

"Thank you, Janet, you did an excellent job handling this so quickly. I owe you one," Dora said.

Janet was happy when she hung up the phone. Her entry to the inner circle was going to be smooth.

Chapter 99
Confused
1993
Ocean Beach

After talking with Dora, Aviva went to her bedroom. She looked at her reflection and noticed that there was not much damage to her apart from her hair ruffled and her makeup being smudged.

Aviva took a shower, changed into a sexy dress, and drove to Dan's place. He was lying on the sofa, gazing at the ceiling, and he suddenly became aware of Aviva's presence in his home. Aviva stood behind him and made him a drink.

He gulped down the drink as if he were very thirsty and gave the empty glass to Aviva. She poured another drink for him. She gently put her hands on his shoulders and rubbed his back. It looked odd to her; a grown man who was thought to be so politically powerful in a sad, vulnerable state.

He was lamenting like a child. "I don't know what is happening. Aviva, please tell me what's wrong with me?" Dan said. "I am caught. I am so confused. My mother wants me to do what I don't want to do. I love Mona."

He was feeling hopeless and dejected. She sat down next to him, gently pressing her breasts against his shoulder. She knew from what Mona mentioned that Dan was considering walking away from his successful political career, and she was determined to change his mind. Aviva was a very persistent and persuasive woman. She knew she had to snap him out of his depressed mood and keep him away from that dark Indian woman.

Her sensual nature guided her in what to do next. She got up and made him his third drink. She sat close to him on the edge of his sofa and put her arms around his neck. She squeezed his head into her perfumed breasts and gently kissed his forehead.

"I know, Dan, we live in a cruel world! I understand your confusion," Aviva said.

"Should I leave politics?" Dan wondered aloud.

"Dan, the chance to become a state senator is within your reach. This is a fantastic opportunity for you. It means that one day, you could be the president of the United States. Do you think you can live the rest of your life with a boring job that you hate? If you leave politics, you will shatter your mother's dream and disappoint millions of supporters. The public may even turn against you and despise you. Wherever you will go, the media will follow you and haunt you," Aviva said, gently grazing her fingers on his chest.

He tried to reply. She put a finger over his mouth and slowly brushed her finger across his lips. "A decision in haste is of no use. There is plenty of time to think, later. Tomorrow. After the election," Aviva said and stroked his head in her breasts.

Aviva hoped this was the best way to rekindle their romance. Her breasts almost bursting from her low-cut dress, the enticing perfume, and her titillating fingers moving across his chest were just the beginning.

He was surprised. Two hours ago, at Mona's place, his desire could not wake his body. Here, Aviva's fingers were doing wonders, turning his body hot. Blood was rushing everywhere. Dan's mind turned blank. It did not take much for his body to take control. They made love and he fell asleep quickly, with a sense of calm washing over him.

Aviva watched as Dan fell asleep. She was still in disbelief that he was willing to lose everything in his life for the sake of a woman, a novelty. She thought of the saying, 'A man's brain lies between his two legs' and smiled to herself.

The next morning, Aviva called Dora from Dan's home. "Good morning, Dora, how is the situation with Mona?"

"Don't worry, it is under control. Why are you speaking in a faint voice?" Dora asked.

"Oh, I am at Dan's house. I spent the night at his place. He is still sleeping upstairs," Aviva said.

"Good, I will meet him at his office because I am going with him to the conference in Washington, D.C." Dora said.

"Yes, I remember," Aviva replied.

When he awoke, Dan was in a happy mood. Aviva was waiting for him at the table.

"Good morning, Aviva," Dan said cheerfully. He kissed her and ate a hearty breakfast. He dropped Aviva at her place on the way to his office.

Chapter 100
New Plan
1993
Ocean Beach

While driving to the office, Dan wondered how he landed in this situation with Aviva. Dan had not slept with Aviva for more than a year. He had no intention to go back to her and considered the evening as a one-night fluke. He could never think of leaving Mona. He believed he still was madly in love with her. His main worry was Mona finding out that he slept with Aviva. She would be furious.

In the morning, Janet went early to the office and arranged a leave of absence for Mona from work. Because matters of leave were private, nobody would come to know what happened to Mona.

Janet and Dora had been waiting for Dan to arrive at the office. They had chalked out a plan. Dan was to fly to the Annual Mayors Conference in Washington, D.C., that afternoon. Dora planned to accompany him on the trip, though Dan did not like that his mother was going with him.

At the last minute, Janet had an idea. "Dora, instead of you going with him, let Aviva accompany him," Janet suggested.

"He won't agree," Dora said.

"Convince him," Janet said.

After reaching the office, Dan saw his mother and Janet waiting for him.

"Dan, what brings you to the office late?" Dora asked inquisitively.

"Hi, mother, I had an errand, that's all. Janet, please send Mona to my office with the latest election budget report," said Dan looking at Janet.

"Mona will not be coming into the office today," Janet said.

"Why not?" Dan said.

"Her daughter got sick and is in a hospital in New York. Mona had to take the first flight to New York." Janet lied with a serious face. "She's on medical leave for her daughter."

"Did she leave any message for me? I need the report on campaign finances. I wanted to take that report and read it on my flight." Dan said with disappointment.

"Don't worry, Dan. Janet will fetch the report from her desk," Dora said.

Dan went to his office and Dora followed him, closing the door to his office.

"You know, son, I don't feel like going to Washington with you today. You should take someone else with you," Dora said.

Dan interrupted, "I understand. I wish Mona would have been here. I could have taken her with me."

"As Mona is not here, why don't you take Aviva with you?" Dora suggested gently.

Dan was astonished at Dora's suggestion. "What! But why? You know I have nothing to do with her," Dan replied. "She is campaign candy, for outward appearances."

"You were madly in love with her last year, and you were thinking of proposing. The media had pictures of you in every newspaper," Dora said.

"I agree with you, mother. She is a wonderful girl,

though pushy, and very jealous of other women. I liked her, and it was not me who dumped her. She dumped me," replied Dan.

"You knew the reason. No respectable woman would tolerate your behavior, chasing mistresses behind her back," Dora scolded.

Dan sheepishly looked down.

"Look, I am your mother. I am proud of my country, and I want to be proud of my son. I want you to be a senator and, if we play your cards right, one day president. I like Aviva. She is as ambitious as I am. Her father is a senator, and you know he is rich and well connected. To succeed in politics, you need those connections and wealth. Her family has both. She rejected you, but it was only because she did not like to waste her time with a womanizer."

"Mother, I need to tell you that I am in love with Mona," Dan protested.

"I know, though you never told me. I have never interfered with your private life. Today it is Mona, last year it was Aviva, and the year before it was Ruth. I can go on counting the women you were in love with. When will you mature? History has many examples of people who married for love and ruined their political careers. Mona is not a politician," Dora said. "She can't be an asset."

"I can teach her about politics," replied Dan.

"You tried to bring her into the political arena, at the nomination party. The politicians and sponsors did not accept Mona. You know very well that it was a disaster. I know she is an intelligent person, who remade your failing city into one of the most prosperous towns in America. And you got all the credit. She is a fantastic economist, and I also know she hates politics. She is not a politician at heart," Dora said. "She belongs behind the scenes."

"But she is the one! The one I love," Dan said with a stronger tone and passion.

"Dan, I nurtured you, and I know you have the potential to go all the way to the top. Do not commit a mistake that would make the public lose your trust. Let them not doubt your integrity, and do not push Mona to become what she hates most, which is a political appendage. She will not help you in the eyes of those who have power."

"Then what do you think I should do?" Dan asked desperately.

"You know that I like Aviva. She is beautiful and has all the qualities that a politician needs in a wife. She is the daughter of a U.S. senator and ten times richer than you. Aviva's father is one of the most influential senators and could enhance your political career."

Dan's voice grew quiet. "You want me to dump Mona."

"That you have to decide. We do not have time. You must catch the plane, and I suggest that you concentrate on your political career for now and think about Mona later. I am going for coffee, and you have to decide soon whether or not to take Aviva along with you," Dora said.

Dora picked up the phone in Janet's office. "Aviva don't ask me any questions. Pack your luggage and be ready for my call. Instead of me going to Washington, you may be going with Dan. Be ready." Dora put the phone down.

After a few minutes, Dan agreed to take Aviva to the conference.

Before leaving to the airport, Dan wanted to talk with Mona. He instructed Janet to find out where Mona's daughter was hospitalized. Dan was perturbed. How could Mona go to New York without leaving any message for him?

"Dan, I tried to contact Mona's friends, and no one has any clue where Mona is staying in New York," Janet said looking at Dora. She had no choice except weaving more lies.

"Dan, you cannot trust Mona. She abruptly left for New York, and she didn't leave any note or contact number behind," Dora said.

"No, Mona is very responsible. It is not like her. I am sure she must have left a note or message," Dan said. "If a critical election situation would arise while I am away, who would be in Ocean Beach to cover for me?"

Dora suggested, "Let Janet manage the election budget until Mona returns. Janet knows what is going on."

Dan said nothing. He looked trapped.

"Dan, this is the peak of election season. I think Mona has proven she cannot handle all the additional responsibilities. Let Janet manage the campaign funds. She is capable and has experience," Dora said.

Dora and Janet eventually convinced Dan that it was better to let dependable Janet manage the campaign funds for the time being. Once Mona officially stepped down from the election committee, the coast was clear for Janet to be second in command. Being Deputy Campaign Manager felt good to her.

Chapter 101
Separation
1993
Ocean Beach

Mona returned home after her stay at Janet's place. She wondered why Dan had not come to visit her at Janet's place before leaving for D.C. and why he did not call her from Washington. Mona was disappointed and stunned. The attack by Aviva frightened her but the silence from Dan hollowed out her heart.

Sandy was coming back from New York the following day, but Mona was still in pain and bedridden. It was not possible for her to pick Sandy up from the Ocean Beach Airport. Mona understood that press leaks about her injuries would not be favorable so close to Dan's election. Mona realized she needed to call Rebecca.

"Hi, Rebecca, how are you?" Mona said.

"Hello, Mona. So, you remember us. I thought you had crossed us off your list," Rebecca said.

"I am sorry. I have been terribly busy, stressed, and I apologize for any unkind words. You know, Dan is running for the state senate, and I am managing the election funds, and I still have duties of the city as well. I hardly get time to relax.""

"I guess we did not understand. As friends, perhaps we went too far," said Rebecca.

."Let us forgive and forget," said Mona.

"How are the things otherwise? And how is my little lollipop?"

"That's why I called you. Your little lollipop has gone to a national spelling bee in New York," Mona said.

"Oh, how wonderful! She is so smart! When is she coming home?" Rebecca said.

"I need a favor. I have taken a few days off to rest. Tomorrow, can you pick Sandy up from the Ocean Beach Airport in the afternoon?" Mona said.

"Of course, I will pick her up. Are you all, right?"

"I am fine, only tired. I will give you the details of her flight, so you won't have any issues picking her up."

"Sure thing. See you tomorrow then," said Rebecca.

Mona was worried about Rebecca and Sandy's reaction when they saw her in bandages. The moment Mona opened the door, Sandy and Rebecca were shocked.

Looking at Mona, Rebecca gasped, "Oh, my gosh, what happened?"

Standing behind Rebecca, Sandy panicked. "Mom, are you okay?"

"Three days ago, after work, I was walking towards my car when two men approached me. They tried to snatch my purse. I fought with them, and they beat me up and ran away," Mona said.

"Did you report this to the police? And who took you to the hospital?" Rebecca said.

"Luckily, Dan's secretary Janet came to the parking lot. She took me to a doctor," Mona said. "And I cannot face, right now, any police complaint."

When Rebecca saw Mona, she remembered Ramesh and the horror of those beatings.

"Mona, you can't stay alone here. You need someone to take care of you," Rebecca said.

Rebecca called Vijay, and they agreed to take Mona and Sandy to their home.

"Mona, you can't work in this condition. You are not going to the office, and you are not going to make any calls. I will call Janet and tell her you are not to be disturbed," Vijay said.

"But listen, Vijay Bhai, the election is in a few weeks, and Dan needs my help." But Mona's plea was cut short.

"I don't want to listen, and tomorrow I will go to the police station to lodge this complaint," said Vijay.

"No, Vijay Bhai, I don't want the police involved," Mona said.

"Why not?"

"Please, don't ask me again. I will not report to the police! It was my mistake that I fought with those two men," Mona said.

Vijay tried to probe more. "Mona, which doctor treated you?"

"I don't know. I was delirious. Janet took me to a clinic, and later she took me to her house. I was staying in her house for three days," Mona said.

Vijay and Rebecca looked at each other unhappily after seeing Mona's condition. They were at a loss about why Mona did not want to file a police report and speculated that Mona was hiding something about the incident. Mona remained adamant not to report the incident and said nothing more.

Though she had not heard from him, Mona was confident that Dan would never leave her. She was afraid that a police report would complicate the matter.

Vijay called Mona's office and said, "Hello, Janet, this is Vijay, Mona's older brother."

"Hi Vijay, how is Mona doing?" Janet inquired.

"She is doing better. I brought her over to our house.

As you know, there is no one to take care of her," Vijay said.

"Good to know that her family is there. We will not disturb her for the next couple of weeks. She is on leave, and her status is confidential," Janet said.

Chapter 102
Team Play
1993
Ocean Beach

Dan was in Washington at the conference, and Aviva was beside him to show full support. Though they were technically registered in separate rooms, Aviva and Dan shared one room. Dan tried many times to call Mona when Aviva was not around, but there was no answer. He did not know if she was in New York with Sandy or if she had come home. Calls to the office landed at a voice recording that said Mona was on leave of absence and to call Janet.

Dora, Aviva, and Janet kept Dan busy after he returned from Capitol Hill. The three women would not leave him alone or let him step into Mona's office. Dan and Aviva were together on the election tours. Dan gave daily speeches in different cities throughout his district, and the news coverage showed Dan and Aviva as a team.

One day, Dora suggested Aviva move in with Dan. Dan protested, "Why should Aviva stay at my place?"

"Dan, this is a very crucial time, and the election is in five weeks. You need someone to take care of you. And it shows a good image to the press of you two together." Dora said. Dan kept quiet.

Aviva worked hard to make Dan happy when she moved into his home. Every evening, Aviva made his favorite dinner and poured his favorite wine for him at the table. She wore his favorite enticing perfume. She would murmur seductive words about his body and his prowess. They would make love on his sofa, and it was more tantalizing and passionate than he could remember. Her soft moans blew his mind.

Aviva's fake climaxes, complete with shrieks and panting, exhausted Dan. She made sure that he had no energy left, not even to look at Mona's picture. Aviva remembered what her mother said, 'Keep your man's stomach full, and below the stomach well fed, and your man will follow you around like a puppy.'

Dan had not received any updates about Mona and was still under the impression that Mona was on leave due to her daughter's illness. After his return to California, Dan thought about flying to New York to see her but had no idea of the address or if she was still there. The three women around Dan did not offer any information about where Mona was. All of Dan's calls to Mona's home were unanswered, and her house appeared empty. With savvy use of answering services, Janet and Aviva ensured that no message could reach Mona and no call from Mona could reach Dan in the office or at his home. His communication with Mona was taken away, and he had no control.

Three weeks passed and Dan was spending all his time on the election and with Aviva. The election was only fifteen days away now.

Janet called Dora to ensure she did not lose her place in the campaign. "Dora, Mona could be back to work any day. Why don't you talk with Dan to give me control of the election budget permanently? I oversaw it successfully for the last three weeks."

"Janet, don't panic. I will speak with Dan."

Dan's ambition was rekindled, and his romance with

Mona seemed to be over. Meanwhile, Dora was pleased with Janet. With Janet's help, Mona's presence was removed from the office.

Dora placed a call to Dan. "Look here, Dan, even if Mona comes back, she won't be able to manage two jobs after her leave. She has been gone too long and has too much to catch up on. It would be better to give Janet full control of the election budget as Deputy Campaign Manager. She has handled everything well over the last few weeks."

Dan gave Janet his official approval to handle the election funds and announced her position as Deputy Campaign Manager. Janet was officially accepted into the inner circle, and Mona was cast out. Dan started concentrating more on the election and had no time to think about Mona, except occasionally in his dreams. Everywhere he went, people cheered for him, and Aviva stood dutifully behind him.

Because Dan was busy with the election campaign, he gave his mayoral responsibilities to the vice mayor, and Mona was to report to the vice mayor when she returned to her job. Mona's office was shifted three rooms away, next to the vice mayor's office.

Mona, still recovering at Vijay and Rebecca's home, saw Dan and Aviva together on TV. She listened to the rumors of Dan and Aviva getting married before the election. Mona ignored the rumors, confident that Dan was still hers.

When she came back to work after three weeks. Mona was shocked to see so many changes in the office. Janet had now moved into the room next to Dan's office, and she had taken all the paperwork regarding election contributions from Mona's office. Janet watched who was going in and out of his office from her new location and could prevent anybody from seeing Dan.

Mona tried to walk into Dan's office, but Janet stopped her right away.

"Mona, please don't disturb Dan. He is on the phone," Janet said.

The next time she tried to see Dan, it was, "Dan is preparing a special election report for the senior party members. He does not want to be distracted."

With a long catalog of excuses, Mona was constantly prevented from seeing Dan. When Mona asked Janet for the paperwork of the election finances, Janet tried to break the news gently.

"Dan says that he does not want you involved at this time. As a comptroller, you have a lot on your plate to catch up on for city matters. To lighten your work, he gave me the responsibility to manage the election budget."

Hearing that she had been replaced was a big shock for Mona. She trusted Janet, but Janet had betrayed her. Mona tried to call Dan on the phone, and Janet answered his phone. When Mona tried to call Dan's house, it was picked up by Aviva. Dora never returned her calls.

All three women blocked Mona from talking with Dan altogether. Dan was not happy, as he was still utterly confused about what happened during Mona's leave of absence and why she was too busy with comptroller responsibilities now to see him. Janet and Aviva worked in tandem to keep them separate.,

As the days passed Dan and Mona saw each other a few times in the office to chat about city problems. Janet and Dora were always present, and they never gave Dan and Mona space or time to talk alone. Mona could never tell him what happened. Dan was pushed to concentrate more on the election. He was out of the office most of the time, and he fully entrusted his responsibilities to the vice mayor and to Janet.

Mona had been squeezed out of decision making and tossed out of whatever power she once had.

The election was a mere eight days away, and the office buzzed with rumors that Dan and Aviva were to be married before the election.

Mona could not imagine being so isolated from Dan. The inevitable was in front of her now. It did not matter about their love and promises to each other.

Fate and power had torn them apart.

Chapter 103
Jolt
1993
Ocean Beach

On Wednesday, six days before the election, Dan's staff was busy. Dora had invited her friends to a luncheon at a restaurant. Aviva was helping Dora at the lunch, and Janet was with them to collect checks for the election fund.

Meanwhile, Dan was alone in his office. Mona knew of the ladies' luncheon. Finding an opportunity to be alone with Dan, she walked into his office. He was sitting on his chair, writing something.

"Hi Dan, how are you?" she asked feebly.

Dan raised his head, "Oh, Mona, so good to see you." He did not get up from his chair.

They looked at each other, and their look burned with the memory of past promises made. He put his pen aside and spoke first.

"I know we had great plans to leave power and a public life behind to start fresh someplace else. It was a dream, not a reality. I cannot leave politics. It is in my blood, and I see the future in my grasp," Dan said.

"I know and I agree. You should not leave politics," Mona said.

After a pause, Mona said, "The rumor in the office is that you are getting married to Aviva tomorrow."

"Mona, the marriage between Aviva and me is an

arrangement. You understand, right, an arrangement, much like in India. There is going to be another election after two years for a California senate seat in D.C. Aviva's dad could help me reach my goal," he replied.

"What about our promises? You forgot them all."

"No, I have not forgotten. They were sweet dreams, but impractical."

Mona bowed her head and Dan saw the tears in her eyes.

Mona wept.

"Please, don't make me feel guilty. We had a wonderful time together, and we should leave it there. You are a strong woman, and you are a survivor. I am sure you will get over it."

Mona turned her face towards the window.

Dan stood up and walked behind her, putting his hands on her shoulder. She shuddered with his touch. He whispered, "I still love you, Mona. We can still be together."

"How?" she asked without turning.

"Simple. When I get married to Aviva, we can continue our relationship. I will find another place for us to be alone."

"And when your people find out?" Mona asked.

"My people? They know I have power and whatever I tell them, they'll accept. It's no secret; Lots of politicians in Europe have mistresses," Dan said, "My father made it work…"

"Dan, we have discussed this before. I love you and I want to be your wife. But I will never be your mistress," Mona said.

"Mona, we can make it work. You are special. Oh boy, you are a tigress in bed." His face twisted with a roguish smile, and his lips nibbled the back of her neck.

Her tears dried up, and her eyebrows furrowed into a

frown. She turned to face him.

"Dan, I thought you were honorable. You want me to be your mistress, a sexual object for your pleasure. You are disgusting, and you have no respect for women. You would dump the woman you love to boost your political career," she accused.

He went on talking, oblivious to her pain. She had feared this outcome for a long time. He could leave all the things in the world, but he would never leave politics.

Mona walked out of his office.

They met a few times before the election, but there was always a crowd around them. He always gave her a beautiful smile and she reciprocated with a defeated look. He married Aviva four days before the election.

Over the next few weeks, her mind was troubled. She was unable to think clearly. She never thought she would lose Dan, and she was dreading a future without him. Living without him was impossible. He was with her in every moment of her life, by her side as they talked, slept, and dreamt.

In the last few weeks, her life had totally changed. Despite the pain, Mona knew she was a survivor. She had endured Ramesh's insults and beatings, Amar's rape, and her devastating breakup from Karan. She could fight the entire world, but the pain of losing Dan was unbearable. She sat thinking for hours.

Dan won the election with a huge majority. Mona heard he had gone back to his old habits, though he was married. There were a few affairs and scandals. Some were reported in newspapers, and some were hushed. They never saw each other again, and he never called.

Mona left her job in Ocean Beach and rejoined McCreighton & Company, her old employer, as a vice president.

For Dan, Mona was like a photograph which, with time, faded away. Mona became a painful memory that Dan could hide under the bustle of romances, scandals, meetings, and rallies.

Chapter 104
Ramesh In Ashram
1994
Haridwar

After three years, Ramesh still lived in the Ashram, thirty miles from Haridwar, near the mountains. To control his ego, he put his full effort into meditation. It was a challenge for him to resist and discipline his desires. He went to different holy places in the mountains on pilgrimages, but he found no peace.

He did not know how to express himself and went to see Guru Ma.

"My mind is not at peace," Ramesh complained.

Guru Ma replied, "Son, continue to meditate, contemplate and be humble."

For three years he had meditated, but his troubled soul could not give him peace. He was still arrogant in his perceived superiority over women and felt overwhelming anger towards Mona for divorcing him. He was bitter with Mona because he was not ready to admit what harm he had done to her. In his mind, she was his wife, and his wife had to obey his wishes.

Ramesh asked Guru Ma how to control his bitterness.

Guru Ma replied, "You have to control your senses. Control cannot be achieved when one is bitter. From bitterness, anger crops up and from there, delusion. If your senses are abused, they get worn out. But when they are properly cherished, they become useful and bring knowledge and efficiency."

"And how can I control my ego?" Ramesh asked.

"Ego brings anger. No one can get rid of their ego entirely. If one can, then the person becomes Mahatma. I think one should put in arduous work to bring his ego down to the level that it harms no one," said Guru Ma.

Ramesh meditated for another year, but peace remained elusive. He decided to leave the Ashram after four years.

"Guru Ma, I am still not at peace. What is my future?"

"Son, your past is the road map. Look at your past; that is your future," Guru Ma said.

"I had a dark past. Do you mean that my future will remain bad?" Ramesh wondered.

"It depends. If you do not want to change, then you will repeat the mistakes of your past. And if you want to reflect on your past and alter the course, you can still have a bright future," she advised.

That was the first time Ramesh understood. He would never get his inner peace and obliterate his sins unless he asked Mona for forgiveness.

Chapter 105
Old Remembrance
1994
New York

One Sunday afternoon, Mona was sitting in her bedroom thinking of the days gone by. She was remembering her college days, all the hopes she carried in reaching each of her goals. She thought of what her life might have been with Karan by her side.

Her telephone rang. She picked it up.

"Hello, Mona, how are you?" Karan said.

"Karan…?" Mona snapped out of her daydreams.

"Are you surprised to hear from me?"

"Well, I was just thinking of my old college days." Mona's voice trailed off. "What could have been."

"How wonderful those days were," he began. "I was thinking about you, so I thought, let me call and see how you are. How nice I was thinking about you, and you were thinking about me." They laughed together on the phone.

"I am sorry, Mona. After we last spoke a few years ago, I had a serious accident."

Mona said, "I know. I am so sorry for the loss of your family. I did not have the courage to call you because I was not sure what to say."

"I understand. I was keen to see you, last year, when I came to California."

"I heard your talk, but I left early that evening. …"

"I know, Vijay told me. You know that Vijay and I have become good friends. Whenever he comes to New York, he stays with me. We often talk about you," Karan said.

They went on talking, remembering sweet memories of happier days.

"Mona, do you remember how we used to sit under the banyan tree on the banks of the Ganges River? I rested my head on your lap and felt truly at peace," Karan said.

"I remember. Do you remember that you always welcomed me into your home by saying, 'Welcome, my Princess, to my humble abode,' and I always replied, 'Thank you, Prince, this royal mansion is very impressive. !'"

"Yes, I remember your exact words."

"Mona, you need some time away. Vijay has mentioned that you are feeling down, so I invite you to come to visit New York, for a vacation. I will arrange everything."

"Thank you, Karan, but no. I don't feel ready to visit New York."

"Or, if you prefer, I can come and see you in Los Angeles," Karan suggested.

"It would be painful to see you and have my old feelings pop up again. Seeing you would remind me of our painful breakup and how we could not marry because of the old ways."

"India is changing fast. Unfortunately, the caste system is still prevalent. Lower castes and Dalits are treated horribly. But some progress is there and embracing change. Mona, we both are mature now. It is your life, and I want you to find happiness. My invitation remains open."

"Thank you, Karan. I know I can rely on you. One day I will accept your invitation," Mona hung up.

Sandy was standing at the door, listening to the conversation.

"Oh, when did you sneak in?" Mona asked playfully.

"Mom, who were you talking to?" Sandy had a grown-up look on her face.

"An old friend," Mona said.

"What is his name? Do I know him?" Sandy pressed.

"His name is Karan. I knew him, long before you were born," Mona answered.

"Oh, Karan Uncle. I know him," Sandy said.

Mona was surprised, "How do you know of him?"

"Through Vijay Uncle. I talked with Karan Uncle over the phone, several times at Vijay Uncle's home. Vijay Uncle told me everything about you and Karan Uncle," Sandy said.

Mona was surprised and angry to learn that Vijay had shared all this information with Sandy. "He did what?"

"Mom, when I became thirteen, you said that we are not only mother and daughter, but also friends. We should not hide anything from each other." Mona smiled at how wise Sandy was becoming.

Sandy continued, "Mom, now I am almost seventeen. I love you. I can't see you sad all the time." Sandy put her arms around Mona.

Chapter 106
Redemption
1994
Ocean Beach

The year passed uneventfully, and Mona was recovering from the breakup with Dan. The hurt became distant but returned sharply whenever she saw Senator Dan Harris in the newspaper or on television. Her work at McCreighton & Co. was challenging and rewarding to her, as she was at the policy-making level. Mona became the most highly paid person at McCreighton. The hours were long and unforgiving, but she grew to love the pace. The demands of her job blocked out everything else in her life that she did not want to think about.

One evening after work, she picked up groceries. As she was walking out toward the parking lot, she was sure that she was seeing a ghost. She shivered and could not believe her eyes. Ramesh was standing outside the store, waiting for her.

She could not run or backtrack, as he was standing right in front of her.

"Hello, Mona. I was waiting for you," said Ramesh.

"Ramesh! What are you doing here?" Mona was shocked and a slew of questions came to her mind, "When did you come to America? Why are you here? And what do you want?"

"You have asked so many questions in one breath. I came to the U.S. two months ago. I was in Florida. I came to

Los Angeles a few days ago because I wanted to talk with you. Please do not say no," Ramesh answered.

"We have been divorced for many years. What is there to talk about?" Mona replied.

"I have been watching you and Sandy every day since coming to LA, and I must congratulate you for raising Sandy into an amazing young woman."

Mona's face turned red. She stepped back and tried to move away from Ramesh.

"Don't misunderstand me. I am not the same Ramesh."

Mona looked suspiciously at him.

"I plucked the courage today to face you. I promise that I am not going to harm you or Sandy. But I must talk with you, and after that, you will not see me again. Please." He was persistent, "Can we have a cup of coffee together? I can come to your place."

"No, not at my place. I will meet you in a coffee shop." Mona was no longer the person who would let Ramesh take advantage of her. She would face him on her own terms.

"Thank you, Mona. There is a café called New Paris near your house Please bring Sandy with you too," Ramesh said.

"Listen, Ramesh, I don't want you to meet Sandy. It would be difficult for me to explain all of this to her. I will be at the coffee shop tomorrow at four," Mona retorted confidently. She turned away from him and marched to her car.

Mona was not sure why he was in Los Angeles and what he wanted to talk about. She thought of calling Vijay and Rebecca but changed her mind. She wanted to face Ramesh alone.

Ramesh arrived at the coffee shop on time, smiling, carrying a bouquet of flowers and a large box.

He began, "I could not resist bringing these flowers for you and this doll for Sandy." He looked around sadly. "This place looks nice. It reminds me of the first time we met, and I took you to the Mambo Restaurant in India."

She glanced over at the flowers and the doll. "I told you I don't want any problems. Sandy is now in her teens and would have no use for your doll. Please take it back."

"Keep it for my sake. Give it to someone else. Though I am dying to see her, my main purpose is elsewhere. Let me order coffee first. What will you have?" Ramesh said.

"Just coffee," Mona said curtly. "Now tell me, what do you want to talk with me about?"

The waitress brought two coffees. He sipped his coffee. "This coffee is excellent." Ramesh paused. "When I divorced you ...,"

She glared at him.

"I mean, when you divorced me, I was very bitter and sick. I went back to India. By the grace of God, now I am in good health, and I have not touched alcohol for the last fourteen years."

He continued. "The last time you came to India, I was very keen to see Sandy. I wanted you to visit me. My parents went to see Sandy, and I was annoyed that they saw you. My bitterness grew. When you were in the temple near my house for a blessing, I saw you and Sandy both. At that moment, I could not control my bitterness. I howled and I cried."

Mona looked down.

"I went to a hermitage and stayed in an Ashram for seven years. But my mind was not at peace. Many temptations and prejudices burned inside me. I have learned to control some of them."

He remained silent for few moments.

"My mind was tormented with the memory of the

cruelties I inflicted upon you. I realized my soul will not have peace unless I ask for forgiveness for my actions. From my childhood, I have never said sorry to anybody because I never repented my actions. The Ashram made me realize the real meaning of repentance. I returned after seven years, and I have come to see you. I hope you can find it in your heart to pardon me for the cruelties I committed. I promise I will not bother you or come near Sandy. I will leave this place, but I am simply asking you for your forgiveness to live my life peacefully." He stood up with tears in his eyes and folded his hands in front of Mona.

Mona was astonished. She expected that he had returned to harass her and make her life miserable again. She had never seen tears in his eyes. He was standing with his hands folded, and she was not sure whether it was an honest apology or another trick. She took a deep breath.

"Ramesh, please sit down. I am happy your health is back. We divorced and our lives progressed in different directions. I moved to Los Angeles. Things happened in my life, both good and bad. I am not a saint, and my exoneration of you does not hold any value. I left my past behind in New York, and I do not want to bring it back to the present. I have no hate left. But, if you want forgiveness, ask God, and not any human." She looked at him. "One thing I would like to request. Please stay away from Sandy. When she is an adult, I will let her decide if she would like to see you. It will be up to you to tell her what you feel," Mona said.

"Now let us talk about other things. What are your plans? Are you going to stay in America or go back to India?" she asked.

"My parents passed away. I am not sure what exactly I want to do in my life. My friend in Florida has a small manufacturing plant. He wants me to help him to run that company. The last few years of ascetic life brought forth many changes in me and provided me with a lot of discipline."

They started talking about their families back home but realized there was not much to say because most of their elder relatives had passed away. They sat together in quiet sadness.

He paid the bill and they both stood up to say goodbye. Ramesh walked out of the coffee shop and did not look back. Mona stayed at the coffee shop for a while. Memories of her marriage flooded back to her—when she landed in New York, gave birth to Sandy, studied hard for her degree, and worked hard at her jobs. She was stung by the pain of what can happen to two people stuck in a marriage.

She stood up and walked out of the coffee shop, leaving behind the flowers and the doll at the table. Today was the end of her turbulence in her life, she vowed.

Chapter 107
Reflection
1995
Ocean Beach

Another year passed. Her heart still ached to remember when Dan left her humiliated and broken. He betrayed her to the passion of politics and power, and sometimes she would feel sad and lonely. At the height of her affair, she spurned the advice of her closest friends. Her attitude alienated many, and it took her a long time and earnest effort to win her friends back.

Her biggest source of strength was her daughter, who was now a young lady of eighteen. Sandy tried to sympathize with her mother's pain. She remained close to her mother and did not let Mona feel sorry for herself.

"Mom, I did not know Dan was such a bad man. He cheated you, and I hate him for it," Sandy said.

"My baby, understand. Love is good only if it's based on truth and trust," Mona responded.

"One day, luck will be on your side. You will meet someone who really loves you."

Mona smiled, "Maybe. It is hard to find a truly compatible soul."

Chapter 108
Knock On The Door
1995
Ocean Beach

Mona was now forty-eight. She was beloved by her clients and respected at her work. She was beautiful and took care of her health by exercising regularly at the gym. She was fit and slim. Everyone complimented her for her radiance and youthful appearance. She spent her spare time helping at the women's shelter.

Mona kept positive and reasoned that every memory has an expiration date. She knew she had to move on, leaving behind her painful memories.

Every year, Mona hosted Thanksgiving dinner. For Mona, this Thanksgiving dinner was a special occasion because Sandy had invited a friend to join them.

Mona had asked Sandy several times who she had invited. "Who? Is it a boy from your chemistry class?"

"Mom, you will meet the person very soon," Sandy said.

"Is it a he or she?" Rebecca said.

"From your school soccer club?" Vijay asked.

"All of you are so nosy. I am eighteen now!" Sandy said, giggling. "Maybe I'm a woman with secrets!"

They were busy talking and laying the dinner plates. Mona was putting the last touches on the food. Sandy quietly slipped out of the house from the back door. A few minutes later, the doorbell rang.

"Sandy, your friend is here. Go and open the door, and we'll find out your secret!" Mona said.

Everybody looked around. The doorbell rang again.

"Where is Sandy?" Mona asked. "Sandy, your friend has arrived."

"Mona, forget Sandy. You open the door," Vijay advised as he was chopping the salad.

Mona walked to the door and opened it. Her mouth was open in surprise because an elegant and handsome man was standing at her doorstep. She recognized Karan's face immediately. Sandy stood next to him with one of her arms linked in Karan's arm. He was carrying a basket of food, a flower bouquet, and a bottle of wine. He leaned on a stick with a silver handle to keep his balance.

"Hello, Princess, how are you doing? Won't you let me in?" he asked after a while.

Mona looked at Sandy, and Sandy smiled in approval.

"Yes, my Prince. Welcome to my little abode," whispered Mona.

"This not a little abode, my Princess, it is a mansion," Karan said, as he entered her house.

They both laughed and embraced each other.

The End

Epilogue

A couple of years later, Dan won a second term as a California senator and went to work in Washington, D.C. He was a rising star on Capitol Hill. The Harris family settled in an expensive Washington suburb. Often Dora's pictures were in Harper's Bazaar magazine, attending a party or fundraiser. Aviva had gained a lot of weight after having three children. Dan was still playing his old tricks. Janet transitioned into a powerful political figure in Sacramento. She still knew all the secrets.

The Harris family had forgotten about the Ocean Beach shelter for abused women. It was neglected and grant money dried up. Mona and Rebecca took over the project of running the shelter and expanded its funding and programs to help women throughout Los Angeles County.

Vijay's engineer son, Sugund, joined Vijay's business and they were doing well. Rebecca was enthusiastic about her job in social work. Meanwhile, Ramesh settled down in Tampa, Florida. Mona never heard from him again.

Karan had left his job at the World Bank to head the economics department at the University of Southern California. He still had a house in Paris, where he and Mona would visit often for vacation.

Sandy was studying law at Howard. She had a boyfriend, Jimmy, and they were living together.

Reflecting upon her life, Mona realized how much she had achieved as an immigrant living in a country where women were free to assert themselves. Sandy continued the battle against discrimination in her mother's footsteps and was in the forefront of conversations on women's rights.

Sandy always reminded her mother, "I know you came from India. But watch my life unfold. I am the proud daughter of an immigrant woman from India who worked hard, raised me as a single parent, and achieved much in her career. Because of your arduous work, I can live a free and happy life. One day I can be the President of the United States."

Glossary

Bhai– Brother
Babu– Respectful word for father or Gentleman
Beti– Daughter
Bhabhi– Elder brother's wife
Bhajan– Hymns
Bhang– Cannabis.Sativa plant, to form a paste that is added to food and drink. A mild intoxicant.
Bhangi/ Bhangan– Lowest caste sweeper Man/Woman
Brahmin– Highest caste Hindu
Chamar– lowest caste Hindu
Choli– an Indian Blouse
Chowkidar – Watchman
Dadi– grand-mother
Daverani– Sister-in-law
Dalit–lowest caste/untouchable
Didi– Elder sister
Dhobi – Laundry man
Elphanta Caves– Rock cut fifth century caves of Shiva, near Bombay.
Frungee–Foreigner
Gopis– Female friends and lovers of Lord Krishna
Gora – White (Slang for Englishman-During British Raj in India)
Gora Sahib – White Boss or English Boss
Holi– Festival of colors (The colors used to be made of turmeric, moon paste, flower extract and leaf extract.
Jeejaji– Sister's husband

Jeeji–Elder Sister
Ji– Added at the end of name as Sir or Madam.
Jinn– Devil
Kahjuraho Temples– The ancient temples famous for carvings of Kama Sutra on the walls of the temples, a big tourist attraction in India
Kaisth/ Punjabi/ Madrasi– People of different region or caste in India
Khansama– Chief cook
Kurta– A type of shirt
Lehenga– printed or embroidered with design an exceptionally large skirt.
Lingam– Male penis
Lord Krishna– A Hindu God – a major deity in Hinduism
Masala Chai– Herbal Tea
Maya– Circle of life
Memsahib – Lady (slang for an English woman, presently used for modern woman)
Paan– Betel leaf with areca nuts
Pankhi– Small hand fan
Pooja–Prayer
Popi– Kiss
Ram & Sita– Legendary God, a perfect married couple
Rotis–Indian Cooked Bread
Sahib – Sir, boss
Sari– Typical Indian Lady's dress
Sarkar– Sir, Boss
Satyagraha – Peaceful Protest
Sepoy– Soldier
Tabla– Pair of Indian drums, played by hand, to support other Indian musical instruments.
Tandoori– Food made in a charcoal clay oven.
Yatra–Journeys

Popular Indian Foods

Achar
BhelPuri
Biryani
Cashew Nut Barfi
Chaat
Chicken Tandoori
Chicken Tikka
Chicken Tikka Masala
Chocolate Barfi
Dal
Dhai Bhalla
Dosa
Garlic Naan
Guchhi Pallove
Idli
Jaleebi
Kababs
Kala Jamun
Kalakand
Kesari Cham Cham
Kheema Palak
KheemaMuttar
Kuchoomar
Ladoos
Lassi
Maki Ki Roti
Malai Kulfi
Medhu Vada

Mushroom Curry
Mutton Curry
Mutton Kababs
Mutton Pallove
Naan
Pakoras
Panni Puri
Papd
Pista barfi
Pork Vindaloo
Prathas
Ras Malai
Rasgoola
Roomali Roti
Roti
Sag Paneer
Samosa
Sarson Ka Sag
Shahi Paneer
Shammi Kababs
Tandoori Aloo Paratha
Uthappa
Vegetable Pallove

ABOUT THE AUTHOR

Pushpinder Sadana came to the United States in 1972 from Delhi, India, and worked in the aerospace industry until his retirement. His debut novel, *Longing*, tells the story of Mona and her journey from caste-bound tradition and social pressure in India to triumph and equality in the U.S. Despite heartbreak, she overcomes cruel challenges and achieves her dreams of success – and love. Sadana lives in Southern California with his family and is a member of two writing groups.

www.ingramcontent.com/pod-product-compliance
Lightning Source LLC
LaVergne TN
LVHW100504110826
845146LV00002B/507